RUSSIAN ROULETTE

*Elizabeth Darrell titles available from
Severn House Large Print*

Unsung Heroes
Shadows over the Sun

RUSSIAN ROULETTE

Elizabeth Darrell

Severn House Large Print
London & New York

This first large print edition published in Great Britain 2007 by
SEVERN HOUSE LARGE PRINT BOOKS LTD of
9-15 High Street, Sutton, Surrey, England.
First world regular print edition published 2005 by
Severn House Publishers, London and New York.
This first large print edition published in the USA 2007 by
SEVERN HOUSE PUBLISHERS INC., of
595 Madison Avenue, New York, NY 10022.

British Library Cataloguing in Publication Data

Darrell, Elizabeth
    Russian roulette. - Large print ed.
    1. Great Britain. Army - Military police - Fiction
    2. Military bases, British - Germany - Fiction 3. Murder -
    Investigation - Germany - Fiction 4. Detective and mystery
    stories 5. Large type books
    I. Title
    823.9'14[F]

    ISBN-13: 978-0-7278-7584-6

Printed and bound in Great Britain by
MPG Books Ltd, Bodmin, Cornwall.

My warm thanks to Lieutenant Colonel (retd) John W. Lanham OBE, Special Investigation Branch, Royal Military Police, for his professional advice and guidance on military criminal procedures.

If I have wandered from the straight and narrow the blame is all mine.

One

The evening was degenerating satisfactorily. The top brass had departed, leaving the younger element to indulge in traditional mess antics. Flushed with alcohol they were throwing themselves into the horseplay, growing ever wilder. The girls were as reckless as the men, holding their long skirts high for freedom of movement as they 'tightroped' along the backs of settees, or leaped from one 'safe house' to another represented by rugs scattered like islands on the sea of polished parquet.

He was in his element. He had surely earned professional kudos during today's high-powered conference. He was now enjoying the type of evening he revelled in: walls hung with heroic battle scenes, table set with regimental silver, white-coated stewards, stimulating conversation, deference to rank, handsome uniforms, the loyal toast. Then, hectic letting-off of steam!

Well on the road to getting agreeably tight, he had his eye on a luscious lieutenant who had responded to his verbal foreplay during pre-dinner drinks and was now exhibiting long tanned legs as she wobbled precariously along a chintz-covered perch. He stepped forward, grinning, and kneed the settee. As she fell to the seat cushions he had a gratifying view of black lace panties. He would have those off her before the night was over. The glance she flashed him while scrambling unsteadily to her feet told him he would meet with little resistance.

A carrot-haired subaltern soon instigated a game of rugby. The large toy pig used as a ball had clearly suffered the indignity before. It was no longer pink and bore a number of stains on its stuffed body. The men entered into the scrum with enthusiasm. It offered them leeway to handle the girls, and to head-butt the balls of anyone needing a score settled.

Stripping to his shirtsleeves for the fray, he caught Mark studying him with dark intent. He had heard Reena giving Mark hell in the adjoining bedroom as they had dressed for dinner. She had a sharp tongue; needed firm handling. He knew! He grinned across at Mark and shook his head. He needed his balls in good order for what he planned with the sexy lieutenant.

She seemed to think they were prime specimens when she studied them a couple of hours later in the dim gymnasium. They made hectic love on one of the soft-landing mattresses, confident they wouldn't be inter-rupted at that hour. High on alcohol and sex, he then embarked on naked gymnastics.

She soon joined him, scrambling along parallel bars, vaulting the horse and swinging monkey-wise on ropes. Their attempts on the trampoline failed dismally. They collapsed in a giggling heap.

He then discovered he had another erection and moved to cover her again. 'Feel that? Shame to waste it.'

She slowly grew passive beneath him. He began to suspect she had fallen asleep, but he was in no mood to forgo an orgasm. Afterwards he lay back gazing muzzily at the rafters and listening to the girl's heavy breathing. Pity he was leaving in the morning. She was hot stuff!

He soon began to shiver. Time for bed. Rolling from the trampoline he shook the girl several times with no result. He left her and, following the trail of his discarded uniform, he struggled to dress.

'Whoa,' he muttered drunkenly, almost losing his balance as he pulled on trousers over underpants that were back to front.

Seriously cold by now, he longed to fall into a soft, warm bed. Trouble was he had to walk halfway around the perimeter road to reach the junior officers' married quarters. He hoped he would remember which was Mark's, and that the bastard had left the door on the latch.

He returned to the trampoline, where the girl was dead to the world, breathing heavily. He shook her more roughly several times. Still no response. He tried pulling her into a sitting position but she was as limp as a rag doll.

'C'mon, 's all over. Time for beddy-byes. Teddy bear-byes,' he slurred, half giggling. 'C'mon, can't stop there.' He shook her several times more, but she was in a world of her own. Clasping her sagging body against his jacket, his fuddled brain was unable to sort out the problem. It had been a very taxing day, one way and another.

Gentle slaps on her cheek had no better effect. Desire for a bed was growing greater by the moment, so he eventually loosened his grip and she collapsed heavily to the canvas again. Muttering Russian imprecations he collected her clothes from the floor and tucked them carefully around her nakedness before heading for the door.

As the crow flew the distance wasn't great, but as the crab walked it took him some time before the outline of the rows of houses loomed. After pressing his nose against several identical entrances he managed to find the number he sought. The door would not yield when he pushed it, so he yelled Mark's name as he rang the bell and thumped the knocker. He then slammed his fists on the wood until they hurt. Not a sound from within; no light coming on. They appeared at upstairs windows in nearby houses: curtains were parted. He yelled Russian insults at the peeping Toms and kicked Mark's door in frustration. It got him nowhere. The lights went out again one by one.

He would have to return to the mess and lay claim to a sofa for what remained of the night. There were no available bedrooms, which was why Mark's arm had been determinedly twisted to offer overnight accommodation.

Reasoning that if he continued along the perimeter road he was bound to return to where he had started, he resumed his unsteady progress vowing to get back at Mark for this before he flew out.

The road ran for a short stretch between scattered trees. Badly in need of a pee, he turned to face one and unzipped his fly. While fumbling in his back-to-front underpants he was suddenly enveloped by rough, foul-smelling cloth that covered him from head to waist.

'Wha' the...' he spluttered against the sacking, unable to get his mind around what was happening. Some joker still playing mess games? Irritation turned to alarm as he felt his arms being pinioned to his sides. Fear surged through the alcoholic haze to bring clear thought. Christ, the IRA hooded their victims before kneecapping them! Urine ran freely down his legs, soaking into the tight, strapped trousers as he was forcibly marched over uneven ground by his silent captor.

The girl surfaced to discover she was naked, ice-cold and nauseous. Her head thudded unbearably. Recollection returned. God, she had succumbed to a well-built charmer with

11

a sexy smile and dark eyes that promised excitement beyond her wildest dreams. She had been hooked from the first sight of him.

The sex had been uninhibited, liberating! When he had started performing gymnastics she had joined him eagerly. For that brief time she had known unrivalled ecstasy; total freedom of spirit. It had been heady. It now seemed humiliatingly sordid.

He must have seen her as an easy lay, and she bloody had been. Just this once. The other guys had tried their luck and failed. Tonight had been a blind, heedless impulse. How *could* she have cavorted with him on the exercise equipment? Then on this trampoline; clasping each other face to face as they jumped and tumbled.

Her heartbeat accelerated as she recalled how easily she had allowed him to take her a second time, and then a *third*. No, she had tried to push him away, told him to get off. The bastard had gone ahead anyway.

She struggled to sit up. Her head felt as if it would split open. She was never as ill as this after a party. Had he put something in her drinks? Doubling over, she wept tears of rage. With herself. If details of this got out her career would take a plunge. Jack Keegan was a chauvinist; he barely tolerated women officers. What she had done tonight would fuel his righteous attitude.

Rage turned to guilt. What if Peter got to hear about this? She loved him; wanted that wedding in June. Although he was quite

12

probably having it off with dusky beauties in Brunei, he would act the betrayed lover if he discovered *she* had been playing around. Different rules for the female of the species!

Lowering herself gingerly from the trampoline, she painfully began to dress. She was shaking with cold, her teeth chattering. Her hair was a mess; her long uniform skirt was crushed. The large clock on the wall showed three forty-five. Good. Hardly likely to be anyone around to see her return to her room.

The chill hit her as she quit the gymnasium and locked the door. Every step drew a groan. She felt terrible; wondered if she could make it as far as the mess. Knew she had to. She was due to give a lecture after breakfast. A hot shower and several hours' sleep wrapped in blankets should do the trick, and Jack Keegan would be none the wiser.

There was no sign of anyone on the road, where thin mist hung in patches. She would make it without being seen, and *he* was due to fly back to England after an early breakfast. Everything would be fine. No one would know what happened. She would not be regarded as the officers' whore!

When she turned the corner leading to the mess she saw it. Her vision was blurred, so she drew much nearer before the truth dawned. She halted, staring in horror. The body was tied upright to a wooden post, wrists fastened together behind it. A khaki blindfold covered those dark eyes. The short green jacket was torn and tattered, hanging open.

A silent scream rose in her throat. She had had sex with this man; had romped naked with him. Turning away from the terrible sight she vomited over a sign indicating where to find the visitors' car park.

The telephone woke Max Rydal at 5 a.m. He swore as he groped for the receiver, intent only on silencing that bloody row.

The brief information in clipped tones drove away the desire for sleep. He sat up, swinging his legs to the floor as he grunted that he'd be ready in twenty minutes. He swore again as he stubbed his toe against the unfamiliar furniture while padding to the kitchen to switch on the kettle. God, it was freezing! He hated sleeping in a stuffy atmosphere, so the central heating had gone off at midnight and was timed to start up at six. No point in advancing it. He'd be gone before the place warmed up.

He had arrived in Germany only two days ago to take command of 26 Section, Special Investigation Branch and his first case had to be the murder of a British officer! He had barely settled in, had had little time to assess his team or get to know senior staff at the various units based within his area of jurisdiction.

The one plus was that his deputy on many cases in the past was already established here as the second in command. They had always worked well in tandem: understood and respected each other. Unfortunately, Sergeant Major Tom Black also knew the truth about the tragedy in Max's life, which would not help his struggle through the healing process everyone promised was infallible.

Several mugs of strong black coffee and a hot shower stopped his shivers, and while he shaved, Max forced from his mind remnants of the familiar nightmare and concentrated on the job ahead. No accidental fatal punch-up between squaddies stoned out of their minds; an officer had been found shot dead outside the mess in the early hours. Suspects would be legion, and the media would make a three-course meal of it!

He pulled the third of his half-dozen 'duty' shirts from the shelf where he'd placed them two days ago, and reflected that he'd have to set up his laundering arrangement before he used the last of them. He tugged a plain tie from the rack on the back of the wardrobe door, swiftly knotted it, then shrugged into the jacket of his dark grey suit. A swift glance at the clock showed his twenty minutes were up. In the lift he put on his three-quarter-length topcoat, wondering what quirk of fate ensured that calls about serious crimes invariably came when he had finally fallen asleep after hours of tossing and turning.

Tom came up in a Land Rover as Max stepped out to the finger-numbing pre-dawn. It was warm inside the vehicle, and Tom wasted no time in pulling away from the kerb.

15

'In at the deep end, I'm afraid, sir,' said Tom by way of a greeting. 'Sounds like a messy one.'

'Par for the course,' grunted Max, the caffeine yet to kick in and do what it should to his sluggish system. 'Details?'

'Very few. Regimental Duty Officer called us after the Medical Officer certified the victim dead from a gunshot wound. The body's been left in situ; nothing's been touched. They've erected canvas around the scene. Only thing they didn't think of was to seal off the base. I set that up right away.'

'Good, although our man's almost certainly still on base. Best place for a military murderer to hide is amid the khaki horde.'

Tom nodded. 'Sounds like locking the stable door, but one murder can lead to another. Better to keep the scene uncluttered by new arrivals.'

Max studied his companion. Well-pressed dark suit, beautifully starched white shirt, regimental tie. Immaculate as if in uniform, whatever the time of day or night. Tom Black had a loyal, loving wife to wash, iron and care for him, but he had come up through the ranks learning the specifics of spit and polish from day one. From the old school of soldiering was Tom, with the same high values echoed in his private life. A dying breed, alas.

'Who's been sent ahead?' Max asked.

'Piercey and Beeny, with Staff Melly. All experienced with murder enquiries. The SOCO team likewise. You'll soon find they

16

don't come much better, sir.'

'How about the top brass of the victim's regiment?'

'I've only encountered them a couple of times on run-of-the-mill petty crimes. Nothing demanding their heavy cooperation, but they're much as you'd expect. Polite, but anxious to be rid of us. Angry that "one or two bad apples" have managed to enter their distinguished ranks.' He drew breath in through his teeth. 'This is going to knock them for six.'

'Not as badly as the next of kin. Does the victim have a wife and family here?'

'I've no details, not even a name. The corporal who took the message said the caller simply reported the fatality and demanded our immediate response; said he sounded deeply shocked.'

'As well he might. Not what you want to happen during the night watch of your spell of duty, is it? You're there to ensure all is quiet, secure and under control, yet an officer is gunned down and killed. Not in the secluded far reaches of the place, but right outside the officers' mess!'

'As I said, sounds like a messy one.'

'And all the possible motives are the stuff of tabloid sensationalism. Any whiff of scandal among the privileged ranks has editors licking their lips. I can imagine the giant headlines, can't you?'

'Especially if a woman features in it.' Tom adopted a coarse accent to quote. 'Regimental rumpy-pumpy leads to fatal sex duel.'

'I hope to God that isn't the case.'

'Wouldn't be the first time. Remember Cyprus five years ago?'

Max nodded. A squaddie bludgeoned to death a Cypriot who was secretly dating his fiancée. She was a Signals clerk two-timing them both. Three months later she married a rich local businessman.

When an hour later they reached the perimeter road of the large base housing several regiments and small ancillary attachments, mist was still hanging like a shroud. Lights showed muzzily through the gloom and ghostly figures were moving around as the daily routine got under way.

Tom eventually turned left along a narrower road between low brick buildings that looked like offices. Two hundred yards along it stood a tent enclosed by ropes and guarded by an armed soldier. He pulled up at ninety degrees to a flagstone path leading to a two-storey officers' mess fifty yards away.

Stepping out to the chilly dampness, Max glanced across at it. Death on the victim's very doorstep! The result of yet another sordid sex triangle? His heart sank. Investigation invariably uncovered human behaviour better left beneath the stones he was forced to overturn. The caffeine had now kicked in and his senses were raw.

Showing his ID to the guard, Max ducked his head to enter the crime scene lit by several lamps and immediately pulled up sharply. He had dealt with more violent, more gruesome killings, but there was something bizarre about the sight of this dark-haired man drooping lifelessly on a white-painted post bearing directional pointers to areas of the barracks.

'The work of an exhibitionist?' suggested Tom at his shoulder.

Max gazed thoughtfully at the khaki blindfold, the mess jacket hanging open, the neat bullet hole, the way the man's wrists had been tied behind the post. Curious.

'He certainly wanted early discovery of his crime. Must have killed his victim where the shot wouldn't have been heard, then brought the body here to tie up in clear view. Why? Assuming he used motorized transport, the safest course would be to pull up, shove the corpse out, then scarper. Body gets noticed just as quickly.'

'You think he didn't care about being caught in the act?'

'I think he's making some kind of statement. One important enough to risk discovery. He was bloody lucky to get away with it.'

'Or *she* was. Maybe this is a case of a woman and her lover deciding to get rid of hubby.'

'They didn't get rid of him, did they? They stuck the poor bastard up here for everyone to gawp at. There's something more complex than that behind this display. I suspect we have to understand the killer's message

19

before we can work out who had a burning need to make it.'

'Whoever's responsible would need an accomplice,' Tom pointed out. 'The victim's tall, muscular. Heavy enough when alive. It would take two to get him fastened upright to this post.'

Tom was stating the obvious, of course. The sight of the cadaver was getting to Max. He never liked psychological murders and his guts told him this was one.

He glanced at the four-man team in white coveralls already there at work. 'Cut the poor devil down ASAP, will you? When it grows light I'll instigate a search of the areas where the shooting might have taken place. Mr Black will know them better than I. He's familiar with this base.' He took one more look at the body before quitting the tent.

It was starting to grow lighter, although the mist kept the atmosphere grey and damp. The guard had a drip on the end of his nose. He looked cold and miserable. No doubt wondering when he'd be free to get his breakfast.

'They'll come in an ambulance to collect the body,' Max told him. 'No one else goes in there.'

'Yes, sir. I mean, no. No one, sir.'

'*Captain Rydal!*' A tall, thin officer was hurrying towards them. 'Sorry I wasn't here when you arrived. Wires got crossed. I'm James Harkness, 2IC.' He shook hands with Max and greeted Tom, with whom he'd had dealings before. 'I'm afraid Colonel Keegan

20

will be tied up until nine. Visiting top brass to entertain until they leave for their flight back to the UK.'

'Have they been on base overnight?' asked Max.

'As house guests of Colonel and Mrs Keegan, yes.' He frowned. 'You're not suggesting...'

'An officer was murdered during the night hours, Major. I need to know everyone's movements during that period,' Max explained. 'Purely routine for the purposes of elimination. I'd like to begin by talking to whoever found the body.' He raised his eyebrows. 'Unless you have the perpetrator locked up already?'

Major Harkness gave him a narrow-eyed look. 'Wouldn't have needed to call you if we had. It's a bloody awful business and I'd better put you in the picture before you start interviewing anyone. I've asked the Doc to meet us at my place. My wife will rustle up some bacon sandwiches and coffee while I reel off what we know, and attempt to give answers to your questions.'

'Thanks, coffee and sandwiches will be very welcome,' said Max, indicating their Land Rover.

As they drove to the Harkness's quarters, he said to Max, 'Tough for you to be faced with this the moment you arrive. Clive had an easy ride during the past year ... until his two boys were killed in that school-bus crash. God, what a terrible blow! I'll never forget how he

21

and Nell looked as they left here to fly home for the funeral. Couldn't help thinking what if it had been our two!' He dwelt on that for a moment or two then asked if Max knew Clive Bennett.

'I've met up with him now and again, that's all. Last thing I wanted was to step into his shoes in this situation.'

'Understandable. Now this! Nasty business. Grotesque! Right, here we are.'

Frances Harkness was a striking brunette who welcomed them with the ease of a woman used to entertaining all and sundry at short notice. The ideal army officer's wife! The room they entered was large and light, with several table lamps spreading warm yellow pools of brightness over the flowered covers of two sofas and a cluster of armchairs. The plain cream walls were adorned with paintings of battles fought by men in vivid uniforms covered with gold and embellishments. Max thought they were out of place in such a tasteful setting. However, each to his own, and the canvasses looked valuable. Harkness must be a collector of militaria.

Thick-set and toughly handsome, Tom Black appealed to most women and Frances Harkness was no exception. When he rose to take the heavy tray from her as she entered, she gave him a radiant smile.

'Thank you, Mr Black, it *was* rather heavy. Please help yourselves. I hear Jeremy knocking. I'll let him in then leave you to it.'

The Medical Officer was thin and milk-blond. His fair-skinned face was devoid of colour and dark circles emphasized large pale-blue eyes. Max studied him curiously. The man looked a physical wreck. There was surely a case here of 'physician, heal thyself'. Why was he still on duty?

'Jerry Fielding,' he said, offering Max his hand. 'Sorry we're being introduced under such shocking circumstances. Gross to kill him then tie him up like that.'

Max didn't elaborate on some grosser murders he had witnessed; instead he prompted their host to outline the facts while they ate.

'The facts *as we know them*,' Harkness pointed out crisply, as Tom handed round cups of coffee. 'The Duty Officer was woken shortly after 04:00 by Lieutenant Judith King, who claimed there was a dead body outside the mess. Peter Randolph went with her and saw someone he recognized as Major Leo Bekov tied to the signpost at the end of the approach path. He called Jeremy out to certify death. Then he informed Colonel Keegan. That's the point at which your unit was notified.'

'What was the victim's status here?' Max asked.

Harkness gave a small sigh. 'You're probably not yet aware that there was a high-profile meeting with the Russians yesterday over this emergency in Poland. Major Bekov was attached to General Pomeroy's staff as an interpreter. For greater security due to the tense political implications it was decided to

23

quarter our delegation here overnight, rather than in a hotel. It coincided with our annual celebration of a famous regimental victory: a formal dinner to which the visitors were invited out of courtesy. Hence why Major Bekov is in mess dress out there.'

Max's thoughts were racing. 'He was here for no more than a few hours? He's not a member of your staff?'

'That's right.'

'So it could only have been an opportunist killing.'

'Or Major Bekov was mistaken in the darkness for the intended victim,' Tom speculated.

'Mmm, possible, but the killer would have realized his mistake on seeing the body at close quarters. Why would he then have carried out the second part of his plan? More likely to have hidden the corpse where it wouldn't be found for some time. Or just panicked and run.'

Harkness gave Max a sharp-eyed look. 'The second part of his plan? How could he have planned to shoot an unknown officer just passing through? The delegates arrived on base at 17:30 with barely enough time to shower and dress for dinner. It was already dark when they reached us and they were taken directly to their respective hosts. No, no, it couldn't have been *planned*. It's obvious the killer was doped to the eyeballs and running amok with a rifle. Doped or deranged. Just fired at the first person he came upon. No *plan*. Just a bloody infernal cock-up.'

24

Max's initial reluctance to warm to the man deepened. He sensed that Harkness viewed the murder more as an annoying inconvenience rather than the tragic snuffing-out of a vital life long before the biblical span of three-score years and ten.

He turned his attention to Jeremy Fielding. 'Do you know of any men here who're suffering from depression? Any with complex family or personal problems? Anyone with a psychological hatred of officers?'

The MO gave a faint nod. 'Yes, to all of that. They're called squaddies. They get pissed on Saturdays and floor anyone trying to cheer them up. They go home and wallop the wife and the neighbour who's become too friendly with her, or they throw out the mother-in-law and rule the roost again. They become barrack-room lawyers cursing all commissioned ranks with foul-mouthed obscenities. But they don't murder men and put them up on display.'

'Someone did, sir,' said Tom quietly.

'And it's my guess he killed the right victim,' Max added, turning back to Harkness. 'I'll need to interview everyone who attended your dinner last night; find out who last saw the Major alive, and where. Discover who he spoke to during the evening, where he went on leaving the mess, and if anyone left with him.'

Harkness poured more coffee for them all, then leaned back in his chair. 'I've already warned Mark Ingham you'll want to talk to him. He was at Sandhurst with Major Bekov and offered to put him up overnight.'

Tom followed up on that. 'Close friends, were they, sir?'

'The mess was full – a number of our own officers had booked in, knowing the event was normally bibulous – and Mark mentioned that he knew Bekov.'

'And he volunteered to play host?'

'He was asked if he would oblige, Mr Black, and he readily agreed,' Harkness said in tones that suggested the subject was closed.

Had his arm well and truly twisted was Max's interpretation of that. An interesting line to pursue, but Ingham could wait. He said: 'I'd like to kick off by interviewing the woman who found the body. What was she doing out and about at that hour? You said she roused the Duty Officer, so she was not the one on call. I need to know her movements during the time the crime was committed.'

The MO spoke up swiftly. 'She was suffering from shock, so I gave her diazepam and suggested she get some sleep.'

'Her evidence could prove invaluable, Doctor. She was awake and walking around in the early hours. Why? Whom did she see, what did she hear? Incidentally, what was she wearing?'

'Well ... her mess dress,' he said hesitantly.

'Major Bekov was in his, which suggests he had an assignation when he left the mess. Ms King appears to have had a similar arrangement. I see that as highly significant.'

Fielding shook his head. 'What you're hinting at is way out. Judy's getting married in June. She wouldn't have a nocturnal tryst with someone merely in transit; a stranger.'

'Maybe she'd known Bekov before meeting her fiancé.'

Harkness stood up. 'You'll only learn the truth from Judith King herself. Jeremy, I suggest you check that she's now calm enough to give an account of how she came to discover the body, and I'll show Captain Rydal the room he can use for interviews.' He turned to Max, his blue eyes challenging. 'We've not yet had time to put out an official notice of the death, but we can make anyone available for questioning at short notice. We want this affair cleared up as swiftly and cleanly as possible, believe me.'

And the SIB out of our hair, Max added silently as he got to his feet. 'Of course. While I chat to mess members, Mr Black will check whether any rank and file have gone AWOL overnight. How about German civilians employed on the base?'

'They all leave by midnight. I've already checked. No problem. I can add to that. I left the mess around half twelve. Major Bekov was there participating in the usual high jinks.'

'And he was still there when I was called out to a lance-corporal who'd fallen asleep sucking a cough sweet and woke with it stuck in her oesophagus,' said Fielding.

'What time was that, sir?' asked Tom.

27

'About half an hour after Major Harkness left.'

'Did you return to the mess?'

He shook his head. 'Went home. My wife was glad to see me. Baby was having a bad night.'

'Do you live on base?' Max asked.

'In quarters, yes.'

'So what time did you arrive home?'

Fielding's eyes narrowed. 'Is this the third degree?'

Max smiled. 'We keep that for when we have a firm suspect. I need to establish where everyone who was moving around in the early hours was at the vital time. I want to know who else and what they might have seen. So far I know the victim was alive at 01:00 and found dead three hours later. I hope to narrow that window. Could you tell how long he had been dead before he was discovered? Was the body still warm?'

Fielding's pale face tensed. 'I didn't touch him. No point in checking for a pulse. It was bloody obvious that bullet through the heart had proved fatal. Pete Randolph and I were meticulous about not disturbing anything.'

'Very shrewd. Makes our job easier,' said Max, curious about the man's tetchiness. 'Maybe Ms King's information will give us an approximate time for the crime when you ask her to come along to the room Major Harkness will make available for us.' He began to follow the 2IC from the room, then turned back. 'By the way, you didn't actually tell me what time you arrived home after the medical emergency.'

There was real aggression now. 'The baby was screaming and my wife was at her wits' end.'

'Roughly?'

Fielding sighed. 'Do you have children?'

'No.' God, how long before questions like that stopped being so painful?

'So you've no notion how wearing a distressed baby can be. Post-natal depression makes it difficult for my wife to cope. When you're met with near-hysteria after a lengthy formal dinner and a medical emergency, the last thing you notice is the time.'

'So you can't help on that?'

'*No!*'

Max slowly nodded. 'Right. Well, perhaps you'd tell Ms King we need a preliminary statement from her as soon as she's ready.'

Max walked out beside Harkness to the Land Rover, wondering about a military doctor who could be so shaken over the sight of a dead body.

Two

The interview room was a small office at the end of one of the teaching blocks. There were no courses presently under way, so the classrooms were deserted. And cold. Two large convector heaters were produced, along with several soft cushioned armchairs to augment the functional office furniture.

Max did not plan to use these comfortable chairs during the coming interviews. In a murder enquiry he seldom applied the softly-softly approach, apart from sessions with the bereaved. A person's life had been taken by another who believed in the right to play God. Max knew the anguish and sense of rage caused by premature death; knew and could not forget.

In military uniform and heavy boots Judith King still managed to look sexily attractive. The thick webbing belt encircling a small waist emphasized her fully rounded breasts and hips. Natural-blonde hair was drawn back into a knot above her collar and large grey-green eyes, now dilated by shock, dominated sensual features. She must raise a few temperatures in the officers' mess, Max thought.

Pale and minus makeup, she sat on the edge of the wooden chair as if ready to take flight. Max's suspicion that she might have known the victim in the past grew. A young woman who had survived the rigours of Sandhurst and life within the chauvinist ranks of a mechanized regiment should not have been so shattered on finding the body of a virtual stranger.

'I'm Max Rydal,' he began. 'It's my job to find whoever killed Major Bekov and see they are rightly punished. When there is no obvious suspect I begin by interviewing the person who discovered the body, and build my case from there.'

She stared at him wordlessly. As the silence lengthened, Max wondered how strong a tranquillizer she had been given.

'I'm waiting for you to tell me what happened, Ms King,' he prompted quietly.

'On returning to the mess I saw a man tied to the signpost,' she began tonelessly. 'I thought it was a joke. The guys get up to some infantile stunts when they're tanked up. But when I got closer I saw that he'd been shot.'

'Murdered.'

'What? No!'

'You still thought it was a stunt: one that had gone wrong?'

'Of course not! I was in no state to think clearly, that's all.'

'Did you recognize the dead man?'

'No. His head was drooping and he was

31

blindfolded.'

Max instinctively knew she was lying. A faint sheen of perspiration glistened on her forehead, and she kept licking her lips nervously.

'So what happened then, Ms King?'

'I followed procedure and informed the Duty Officer.'

'Who told Major Harkness you were almost incoherent with shock.'

Her tongue ran over her lips again. 'That's rot! Pete was asleep. I had a job to wake him. He was probably still coming to.'

Max changed tack. 'Why were you returning to the mess alone at that hour?'

'As I said, the guys reach a stage when any women prefer to leave. My room is almost directly over the ante room and I knew the noise would stop me from sleeping. So I took a walk to pass some time and to clear my head. I'd drunk more than usual.'

'Why was that?'

'The dinner celebrated a famous victory. There were numerous toasts and I'd foolishly discounted the additional intake.'

'So you were fairly inebriated when you went for your walk?'

'I guess.'

'You weren't averse to strolling alone through a camp full of men in the early hours of a cold, misty morning?' he asked.

'I've done night patrols in Northern Ireland knowing I could be shot at,' she responded defiantly. 'As for a camp full of men, I'm a karate black belt. Anyone trying anything with me...'

'Would wish he hadn't.' He smiled. 'I get the picture. So what time did you leave the mess to go for your walk?'

Her mouth twisted. 'I'm sure you'll check with everyone. They'll tell you it was about 02:00. They'll also tell you Leo Bekov left at the same time.'

'I see. Did he go with you on your walk?'

'I've no idea what he did.'

Max grew impatient. 'You both went out through the main door and he then vanished into thin air? Is that what you're saying?'

Her eyes told him to drop dead.

'Ms King, did he follow or go ahead of you down the path? Did he turn away across the grass to the left or right?'

'I told you, I've no idea what he did.'

Max leaned back in his chair and fixed her with a steely glance. 'Shall we stop playing games? A distinguished, gifted officer passed an enjoyable evening in your mess, then someone decided to shoot him. He's dead! Robbed of life! No dignified end, either. He was strung up for all and sundry to gawp at. Something about that makes me bloody angry, and I didn't eat dinner in his company, as you did. Doesn't it make *you* angry?' He leaned forward. 'Where did Major Bekov go when he left the mess with you?'

She looked close to tears now. 'He was drunk. Pestered me. Refused to take no for an answer.'

'And?'

'He got the message eventually. And I went for my walk.'

'Leaving him where?'

'I don't know ... somewhere along the road outside this block, I think,' she invented wildly.

'So, after that annoying episode you walked around in the mist and cold, dressed in no more than an evening skirt and short mess jacket, *for two hours*? Most women would surely have retreated to a warm room and gone to bed with earplugs in place to combat the rumpus downstairs.'

The optical message was back to drop-dead. 'I'm not "most women". I've been on survival courses and slept in wet ditches, eaten worms, killed rabbits with my bare hands. I don't need to retire to bed because some lecherous sod tries it on. I'm a soldier. I'm tough.'

'So why did Major Fielding have to give you tranquillizers to combat the shock of what you found at the end of your long, chilly walk?'

Tom Black checked with the scene-of-crime team and was not surprised by their findings so far. The bullet was lodged in the body. The shot had been fired at close range, most probably from a 9mm Browning. Too many footprints and tyre tracks overlapped to be of any significance. The rope securing the body to the upright was standard army issue. The

34

chance of a possible absentee killer was also unproductive. There were none.

Tom's visit to Monmouth Company's offices brought him in contact with Sergeant Major Jim Galley, a former acquaintance from ten years back. After catching up with personal and professional news, Galley offered a desk where Tom could temporarily set up his laptop. On it he brought up on screen the victim's military details, reading with interest about the man whose life had ended at the age of thirty-five.

Leo Bekov had entered Sandhurst from Cambridge University and been commissioned into the Intelligence Corps. He was listed as being fluent in Russian, German and Serbo-Croat. Useful skills for an army career. They could bring an officer some interesting and advantageous assignments, such as the high-profile talks held yesterday.

Bekov had been married, then divorced eighteen months later. No mention of children. His next of kin was given as J. Marchant, solicitor, Bedford Chambers, Leicester. Both parents were dead. Tom's interest rose swiftly on noting that the dates of their demise tallied. Road accident? Rail crash? Air disaster? He'd follow up on that. If, by some unlikely chance, they had also been murdered this case could well be the last act of a family vendetta. One never knew with the Russians, Tom told himself.

Pushing aside his fanciful premise, Tom returned to his original belief that sex played a prominent part here. Bekov could have been playing around with someone's wife. Anger, jealousy and high alcohol intake had led to uncontrollable aggression. He had been lured from the mess, shot, then tied up there as the final bitter thumbing of the nose. Tom did not yet see the relevance of the blindfold, unless Bekov's eyes had been put out after death. A symbolic act? No longer would he look at other men's wives?

Max was hooked on the idea of a psychological killing; some obscure message in displaying the body thus. He was always averse to accepting sex triangles. Understandably so, but he would have eventually have to come to terms with his pregnant wife's death in a car driven by Corporal Cairns. The official story put out was that the pair had died in a crash during a thunderstorm, the NCO having offered Mrs Rydal a lift because her car had broken down by the roadside. True enough, but it was well known in the corporals' mess that 'something spicy' was going on between them. Scandal was rife in military establishments, but Tom had actually seen the lovers emerge from a small country hotel early one morning as he returned from an overnight interview with a suspect. Max would be a fool not to know what had been going on. A huge personal load to carry around and deal with!

Taking a gulp from the mug of tea a clerk had just brought him, Tom reviewed the possibilities in this present case. Top of his list of suspects right now were Mark Ingham, the victim's overnight host, and the Medical Officer, who had been moving around in the early hours. Both were married men whose wives might have had something going with the victim in the past. Because Bekov had flown in just yesterday, it seemed more than probable that the murder had been punishment for an earlier sin. Tom knew from experience that resentment and vengeance could simmer for a long time before coming to the boil over one final incident. Frequently, that incident was insignificant against the root cause; the last straw on the laden camel's back!

Staring at the screen revealing surface truths about a military officer who had ceased to exist some time in the early hours of a cheerless, misty morning, Tom discounted the notion of a random killing by a mixed-up soldier who loathed officers and had taken a pot shot at the first one who came within range. He also discounted a racial motive, in spite of the presence of Russians at yesterday's conference. If the killing had taken place outside the base it would have to be considered, but security had been tighter than usual and it was unlikely that an armed Russian would have managed to enter and leave undetected. A Russian would hardly use a Browning, either. So it was necessary to delve deeper into Bekov's career.

At that point Jim Galley came up and stood

by the desk. 'I've one of our MT corporals outside asking to speak to you. Says you'll want to hear some important evidence concerning the murder.' He shrugged. 'You know how it is, Tom. News gets around well before any official report.'

Tom switched off the laptop. 'Has he told *you* this evidence?'

'Says it's "delicate", whatever that means. He's a straight, honest bloke. Religious. Father's a vicar. I'm satisfied he's on the level. Shall I send him in?'

Tom stood. 'I'd rather go somewhere more private, Jim. There's people coming and going in the outer office. Could overhear.'

'Use my office. I'm off on rounds shortly, so you can take the laptop in there now.'

'Fine. Give me a coupla minutes then wheel him in.'

Corporal Gary Mitchum had the kind of clean, healthy looks that would successfully advertise prune-flavoured yoghurt or vitamin-enriched cereal. He also had blue eyes that gazed directly into Tom's brown ones as he accepted the invitation to sit. Jim Galley was right. This was a straight-up man.

'You have something to tell me concerning the death that hasn't yet been officially reported?'

'No, sir.'

Pulling a fast one after all! 'Then why the hell are you here?'

'Not about the death. About the officer who's been killed.'

Tom frowned. 'You knew Major Bekov?'

'No, sir, but I drove several officers from the airport to the conference yesterday, then back here when it ended. Major Bekov was in my car with two others. That's how I recognized him later.'

'Later?'

Mitchum's fair-skinned face flushed. 'I wouldn't say anything in the normal way. What people do is their affair. Gossip does a lot of harm. But ... well, it's all round the base the Major's been shot so I thought I should tell you, in private, what I saw in the early hours.'

Tom had perfected the art of hiding his re-actions when interviewing. He asked calmly, 'What did you see?'

The flush remained. 'It's ... it's rather *delicate*. I wouldn't want it circulating, sir.'

Wonder of wonders, a corporal with finer feelings! 'Anything we learn remains con-fidential unless it's required as evidence at trial. We have no control over that.' He saw he would have to prompt the man. 'You saw Major Bekov in the early hours? Alive, I take it?'

The flush deepened. 'Very much so, sir.'

'Where was this?'

'There's a dog that's attached hisself to the corporals' mess. Doesn't cause trouble so he's allowed to stay. One or two of us give him walks, play games with him.' The blue eyes lit up. 'He's a real Beckham with a football. Talk about laugh!'

39

Tom steered him firmly away from that. 'Has this dog anything to do with Major Bekov?'

The amusement faded. 'Bengo – that's the dog, sir – he sleeps in the little storeroom opposite our accommodation block. Last night about half two he set up a barking that woke me. It's not like him. He's usually good as gold. Well, he kept it up so long I thought there must be something wrong, so I pulled on my overalls and went across to him. Soon as I opened the door he was out and off. I suppose it was stupid to follow, all on me tod and half-dressed, but I did. He was on that bit of grass outside the gym. Something must've upset his stomach. He was getting shot of it both ends, poor little begger.'

Tom grew impatient. 'Are you giving me the runaround, Corporal?'

'No, sir. If it weren't for Bengo I wouldn't have seen them. In the gym!' The flush returned with a vengeance. 'She's nice. A good sport. But she was there with Major Bekov. I heard voices and faint laughter coming from the gym and I thought I should take a look at what was going on. The door was unlocked. Lieutenant King and Major Bekov were in there doing gymnastics. Sort of,' he finished lamely.

Oh God, thought Tom, guessing the kind of gymnastics they were doing. 'They were having sex?'

Mitchum was now looking uncomfortable. 'They were swinging on ropes, vaulting the

40

horse, climbing wall bars – all in the buff! Then they got on the trampoline for a bit. That's when I decided to go.'

'Were the lights on in the gym?'

'Only the small one by the door.'

'So how could you know who the naked man and woman were?'

'I know Lieutenant King's voice. It's sort of posh. And she would have access to the gym key, being the PT Officer.'

'And Major Bekov: how could you be certain he was the man?'

'By that Russian thing he shouted.'

'Explain.'

'He's half-Russian. He was translating for the General and his staff. I overheard that when I was driving them back and forth. Well, when they all came out from the conference they seemed very chuffed with how it went, and Major Bekov, he said a bit of Russian and laughed. Said it meant "bring on the vodka and the girls". Something like that. Well, he was laughing and chanting that same Russian as he was swinging on the ropes early this morning. Can't say it to you, sir, but I'd know it if I heard it again.' Mitchum sighed. 'I'm sure I did right telling you, although I wish I hadn't seen it. Who'd go and shoot him, sir? He seemed a pleasant, cheery sort of person.'

Tom's thoughts were racing. 'Can you be specific about when you saw him in the gym?'

'Sort of. I checked the time when I got back to bed after settling Bengo. Around 02:45.'

'I see. That's it?'

41

'Yes, sir.'

Pointless asking if he had heard a shot. This man would have volunteered the information. 'Keep this to yourself, Corporal.'

'Of course. As I said, I wouldn't want it circulating, sir.'

'No. Thank you for coming forward.'

As soon as the man had left the office Tom rang Max Rydal's mobile and entered ONE to indicate that the information was of top importance, and he should break into his interview to learn the facts.

Judith King had pressed her lips tightly together and refused to give any explanation of why she had been so deeply shocked on finding Bekov's body. Max had put the question three different ways, but she was saying nothing and trying to stare him down. He was glad when his mobile rang. He walked out to the corridor and closed the office door behind him.

'Yes?'

'I've just interviewed a corporal who says he saw the victim and Lieutenant King having it off in the gymnasium at roughly 02:30.'

Oh *ho*! 'He stood there and watched them?'

'Said they were doing gymnastics in the buff.'

'*What!*'

'Swinging on ropes, vaulting the horse – the lot. Naked. Claims he stopped watching when they moved to the trampoline and it got rather more personal.'

'Is this a load of hogwash?'

'Don't think so, sir. Religious bloke, reluctant to come forward but saw it as his duty. Says he won't spread it around, and I believe him.'

'Fair enough. Tell me later what he was doing up and about at that hour, but is he certain of the identity of this pair?'

'Says he recognized her posh voice, and some Russian the man quoted. The witness drove Major Bekov and others to and from the conference, which was when he heard the Russian phrase first.'

'Where are you now, Tom?'

'In Monmouth Company office, studying WAMI.'

'Right. When I've rounded this off I'll call you over to bring me up to date.'

When Max returned to the office Judith King was still sitting bolt upright, steely with determination. He allowed a short period of unnerving close study before saying quietly, 'You told me Major Bekov pestered you on leaving the mess, wouldn't take no for an answer. So how did you come to agree to go with him to the gymnasium?'

Colour drained from her cheeks; she no longer held his gaze. He now well understood why she had needed something to combat the shock of seeing her sexual partner hanging dead on a post only minutes later. Or had she helped put him there? Max had knocked around the world too much to dismiss the possibility of a woman copulating with a

43

man, then killing him. But there had to be a strong motive.

'Shall we go back to the point where you and the Major left the high jinks going on in the mess? You didn't go for a lonely two-hour walk, did you?'

She faced him again. 'I don't have to answer these questions.'

'Yes, you do,' he contradicted firmly. 'This is a murder enquiry. We have a witness who claims to have seen you and the victim performing gymnastics at 02:30. Around ninety minutes later you roused the Duty Officer to view Major Bekov's dead body ... which fixes the time of the murder quite finely and throws heavy suspicion on you, Ms King. You've done nothing but lie to me. That doesn't help your defence.'

'Defence?' she cried appalled. '*I* didn't kill him!'

'Did you aid and abet the person who did?'

'*No!*' It was a cry from the heart.

'Then why claim you saw no more of him after you went separate ways outside the mess until you found his body?'

She rose in agitation and, for a moment, Max thought she would walk out. But she instead went to the window behind him and stood gazing from it. If she thought this might earn his sympathy she was wasting her time. Max had knocked about the world too much for that, too. This woman had had the last known contact with Bekov, had the perfect opportunity to kill him, and was self-posses-

44

sed enough to do it. But two people were needed to fix the body to that post. There again came his conviction that there had been an undeniable need to make that public display of the murder. What motive lay behind that?

'Please sit down, Ms King. I mean to get the truth from you. I can chip away at it all day, or you can make it short by admitting what actually happened last night.'

She took her time returning to the chair. She looked haggard, the steel now missing from her eyes.

'Who saw us?' she asked heavily.

'Someone who swears he won't spread it around. But it'll be mentioned in evidence at trial, I imagine.'

'Oh *God*!' She fought for control momentarily. 'He must have slipped something into my drink. Doctored the wine. He ... well, he practically raped me.'

'You'll have to have a blood test and give a DNA sample. The first will show whether or not you were given a soporific. So whose idea was it to sneak off to the gym; his or yours?'

'You make it sound...'

'You said he was disgusting. Does that mean it was his suggestion?'

Her attitude changed drastically. In little more than a whisper she said, 'I'm getting married in June. There's been no one else since Peter and I got together. I can't *believe* that happened last night.'

'But it did, and he's now dead. You need to

give me all the facts if you want to clear yourself of his murder.'

'We were both drunk,' she said brokenly. 'He was pretty obvious about what he wanted when he followed me from the mess.'

'And?'

'I have the key to the small side door to the gym on a ring with some others. Unofficially, but it makes my life easier. It was cold outside, so we went there to talk.'

'But you knew he wanted sex, not conversation. You told me as much. Where are those keys kept, Ms King?'

'In my room.' She knew immediately that she had given herself away.

'So Major Bekov didn't follow you from the mess, pester you. I'm getting tired of your fictions. Isn't it a fact that you'd both had far too much to drink, fancied each other and sought somewhere private? Your room in the mess was too risky, and he was staying overnight with Captain Ingham. So you fetched the gymnasium key and led him there.'

'I can't explain my actions,' she said numbly. 'I've been drunk before, but this was different. I wasn't in control. It was as if he could persuade me to do *anything*. He had great charisma.'

Max forced himself not to interrupt. Although he thought what she said a load of girlie mush, Judith King was giving him an insight to Bekov's personality. A bloody knock-out with women, apparently.

'He was amazingly athletic. When he

started swinging on the ropes, chanting Russian and laughing, I ... I suppose I wanted to prove I could do better.' Her mouth twisted. 'Professional pride.'

'You'd had sex before these gymnastics?'

She nodded slowly.

'Then what happened?'

Her voice dropped further. 'He wanted it again. I tried to stop him, but I felt woozy and weak.'

'Are you saying he then raped you?'

She looked down avoiding an answer.

'What occurred between that point and your discovery of the body?'

After a shuddering sigh she told him she had woken alone on the trampoline.

'Major Bekov had left the gymnasium?'

'Yes.'

'Alone or with others?'

'*I don't know*,' she cried wearily. 'I was asleep quite a while. Or drugged.'

'You're persisting with that line?'

'Look, I've never felt so ill after drinking. I was so giddy it took a great effort just to pick up my clothes scattered around the floor. I was frozen and shivering, feeling ill. It was some time before I made my way back.' She swallowed. 'Then I found ... *that*.'

'*Him*,' Max corrected sharply. 'Have you any idea how long you were asleep. Or drugged?'

Some of her aggression returned. 'You have no time for me, have you? No understanding of how I feel.'

47

'It's my job to find out who murdered a man last night. I deal in facts, not emotions,' he said.

'Right, Captain Rydal, I looked at the gym clock while I was dressing. Fifteen minutes before four.'

'Any idea what time you fell asleep? Did you hear a shot? The sound of a vehicle racing past? Nothing?'

'If I had I would tell you.'

'Would you? So you went to the gym with Major Bekov at 02:00. A witness saw you settle on the trampoline thirty minutes later. You then fell asleep and woke after more than an hour had passed to find yourself alone. If that's true...'

'It *is* bloody true,' she cried hotly.

'We only have your word for it. If that's true, the victim was shot within a time slot for which you can't provide proof of your movements. That puts you in one hell of a spot. You'd better pray your DNA doesn't match any found at the murder scene.'

Three

Mark Ingham was badly hung over and in deep shock. James Harkness had just telephoned the news that he would shortly be called for interview by SIB detectives investigating the murder of Leo Bekov in the early hours of that morning. With shaking hands he poured himself a large measure of the hair of the dog and downed it rapidly, trying to tame his wildly rioting thoughts. What was he going to do? Why, in God's name, had that bastard once more invaded his life after all this time? Bekov, with a knowing smile, smug arrogance and bloody Slavic sensuality!

Mark's knees almost buckled when the doorbell rang. Christ, they were on his doorstep and he had had no time to *think*. He stayed where he was in the centre of the room, scarcely breathing. They would leave after a few minutes if he remained very quiet and still.

'Mark, open up! You're in big trouble, chum.'

It was the voice of his neighbour. Mark forced his legs to take him to where Andy Miles was shouting through the letterbox, and opened the door. Andy's face was flushed with animation.

'Have you heard? He was shot last night. Shot dead!'

Through a tight throat Mark said, 'James just rang me.'

'Ah. No wonder you look so bloody shaken. Wouldn't care to be in your shoes right now. SIB guys are already on the job. They'll want to grill you first. Bekov was your overnight guest.'

'He didn't sleep here,' Mark rasped.

'Don't we know it!' Brown eyes grew speculative. 'Why the hell didn't you let him in? He woke us and the kids, hammering on your door and yelling your name. Everyone in the close must have heard him. It was bloody three in the morning.'

'*What?*'

'Mind you, he was pissed to the eyeballs,' Andy ran on, unaware of the effect he was having on Mark. 'Swore at me in some foreign language when I told him to quieten it. He must have wandered off when you didn't open the door. Then someone jumped him. A psycho. Must have been, to put his body up on show like that.'

'*What?*'

'Didn't James tell you the corpse had been tied to the signpost outside our mess? Bloody weird, that. Judy found it and threw a fit. Could have been her hanging there. Some trigger-happy madman roaming around with a gun looking for a victim. Bekov was unlucky enough to cross his path on the one night he

50

was here. If that isn't a case of *if your number's up*!' He prepared to move off. 'No, I wouldn't like to be in your shoes, Mark. If you'd broken off your hectic session with Reena to let him in, the poor bastard would still be alive. Not something I'd like on my conscience.'

After shutting the door Mark rushed to the small cloakroom and threw up. The excessive retching left him shivering and exhausted sitting on the floor beside the lavatory, unable to believe what Andy had told him. No SIB investigator would credit he had not heard Bekov when half the surrounding families had been woken by the man's drunken demands to be let in. How the hell was he going to survive? He would have to admit he had not been in the house at the time. And that would land him in it right up to his neck. He threw up again.

After a while he stumbled to the kitchen to make black coffee. He still felt sick and panic-stricken. He knew he must very swiftly concoct a plausible story that even the most hard-nosed police officer would accept. Yet how could he clear himself of suspicion without confessing the truth? Think. *Think!*

A glance at the clock showed it was still early. The SIB would surely start their questioning with Judy, who had apparently found the body. What would she tell them? He had been certain she was too drunk to register what was going on last night, but what if he was wrong and she pointed the

51

finger at him? He gulped more coffee, his heart still hammering against his ribs. Concentrate! Start working out an alibi that would stand the test and get him through this appalling crisis.

Reena and Jane were in the kitchen eating cereal and toast in their dressing gowns. It was plain to Mark they had not heard the news. All to the good! Bobby Foyle was doing a stint in Northern Ireland right now so no one would have informed Jane. She would learn about it through the wives' grapevine.

Reena continued to munch toast, asking carelessly what he was doing there. 'Have you given your old buddy-buddy breakfast?'

'I was expecting you back to provide that.'

'Uhuh! I told you I won't stay in the same house with him. If you had more guts you'd have told James Harkness and forced him to find some other sucker to have Leo for the night.'

'Reena, shut up and listen! It's bloody important,' he said with urgency.

'Coffee?' asked Jane, holding up the cafetiere.

'No ... thanks,' he added more quietly. 'Reena, I'm in a jam. You two will have to get me out of it.'

'What sort of jam?' asked his wife with studied lack of interest.

'You don't look well, Mark,' commented Jane. 'Still hungover from last night? It takes Bobby twenty-four hours to recover from that

52

blasted annual dinner. Too many toasts, too much port, too much hair letting-down.'

Mark sunk onto a kitchen stool. Jane Foyle was an intelligent brunette who took army life as it came. Never made a song and dance like Reena. Right now Mark longed to shake some life into his pretty blonde wife, who was continuing with her breakfast as if he were not there.

'*Will you pay attention*,' he demanded, bending to speak in her ear. 'We've got to do this quickly.'

Her big blue eyes swivelled to look at him. 'Do what?'

'Get our story straight.'

'What story?'

'For God's sake, wake up, Reena! This is bloody important to me,' he snapped.

'You really are in a jam?' asked Jane with a hint of sympathy.

'Too bloody right!'

She turned to Reena. 'Come on, stop sulking. Mark's serious.'

Reena put down her toast and turned to face him. 'Right, I'm listening,' she said in bored tones.

'Last night Bekov made a play for Judy King.'

'Huh! He's welcome to that streak of health and muscle. I bet he got nowhere with Miss Vitamins.'

Mark trod carefully. 'He seemed to think he'd scored. Told me not to wait. He had other plans for the night.'

Pink crept into Reena's cheeks. 'You believed that?'

'Judy was giving him the come-on. We all saw the way it was going.'

Jane lowered her cup; said with surprise, 'Judy's crazy about Peter. She's always made that very clear.'

'Not last night, believe me,' Mark said with force. 'They left the mess together looking *very* cosy.'

'Well, well,' mused Jane. 'But how did that put you in a jam?'

'Because Bekov turned up at our place after all. Woke the neighbours, shouting and banging the knocker. Swore at them when they looked out to see what was going on. I've just had Andy, Justin and Phil round to complain.'

'What a nerve!' cried Reena. 'If their wives say anything to me I'll remind them of their rowdy parties that go on until the early hours.'

'I still don't see your problem,' said Jane.

Mark took a deep breath. 'The problem is that I wasn't there to let our guest in. Which is why he kept up the racket for so long.'

Reena's eyes narrowed. 'Where were you?'

'Look,' he began carefully, 'I'd had a skinful and wasn't thinking all that straight. I came here to have it out with you. You made me look a fool by walking out. I was going to persuade you to come back. When I got here all the lights were out, and I realized it was the middle of the night. So I sat on the doorstep to wait until you woke. Stupid thing to do on a night like that. I got so cold I finally made my way home.'

'You should have knocked. We'd have let you in,' said Jane.

She had played exactly the right card. 'That's what I want you to say; that I came here and had a long talk with Reena to mend our quarrel.'

'Why?' demanded his wife, always ready to argue.

'To explain why I wasn't at home when Bekov knocked.'

'Say what you've just told us.'

'And look a complete public fool?'

She shrugged. 'Why should we lie for you?'

'Because you're my wife.'

'Jane isn't.'

Mark lost his temper. 'There's just a chance you won't be soon unless you start growing up. This is deadly serious, Reena. I need you both to say I was here between half two and four this morning, because during that time someone shot and killed Leo Bekov.'

Jane was shocked, but Reena was clearly devastated. This proof of her feelings for the man drove him to add to her pain.

'After killing him they hung his body on the signpost outside the mess. Not such a glorious end for your hero, was it, but he got exactly what he deserved.'

'Did the lady corroborate Mitchum's story, sir?' asked Tom, settling in one of the chairs in the small office.

'Under duress. Suggested he must have doctored her drinks.'

'Think that's possible?'

'I doubt she'd have been lively enough to indulge in gymnastics, unless it was some kind of extreme stimulant. The short answer is, no, I don't. So what was this witness doing in the vicinity of the gym in the early hours?'

Max listened to the tale of a dog with diarrhoea and thought the case was becoming more bizarre by the minute. 'And he claims he left when the couple had sex on the trampoline, and got back to his room at 02:45? Can anyone vouch for that?'

Tom shook his head. 'Nor can anyone confirm his account of the dog with the squits. But if Lieutenant King admits to swinging on ropes with Major Bekov, Mitchum must have seen them.'

'Yes, it's unlikely he could dream up that scenario.' He cocked a wry glance at Tom. 'Major Bekov must have been unusually inventive.'

'And blessed with amazing stamina! Look, is there any chance they're both lying? Maybe she lured the victim there so Mitchum could kill him along the way. Then they took him to the officers' mess and tied him up.'

'Motive?'

'The Major insulted her in some way. Got too fresh earlier in the day. She phoned Mitchum because they had something going, and they planned to lead him on then finish him off.'

'Bit drastic. Why not just give him a hiding? He'd have got the message. You didn't meet Ms King. She's a karate black belt. If any man pushed his luck with her he'd end up very sore in a number of sensitive areas. She's not the sort to take up with a corporal, anyway.'

'We can't be sure of that.'

Max accepted that Tom wasn't being personally provocative; merely stating the obvious. It was necessary to consider every possibility, however unlikely. In their experience it frequently proved highly likely after all.

'Ms King had already washed her undies, but she's handed over her mess dress for examination. That should give us a lead on the activity in the gym,' Max said. 'I believe her story, up to the point where she reckons the victim left while she was asleep. The killers could have grabbed him in the gym and taken him off to where the execution was to take place. She has no alibi for the time between when Mitchum abandoned his salacious observations and when she woke the Duty Officer.'

Tom frowned. 'You think she's involved?'

'Not sure. She's genuinely shocked, but I suspect her remorse is for doing the dirty on her absent fiancé, not for taking a life. She showed no compassion for the victim. Referred to the body as "that". I'd say she's a pretty cool customer, but I don't see her as a killer.'

'An accomplice?'

'Quite likely. Until we have proof of where she was during the vital time, she remains a suspect.'

'The MO was moving around in the early hours. Maybe others were.'

'I've arranged to speak to the officers during their coffee break. A general chat. I'll then interrogate any who have no alibi for the time of the murder. I'll begin with a heavy session with Captain Ingham, who played host to the Major. He appears to have lain remarkably low about his guest who was absent all night. Didn't he wonder where the man was?'

'Not if he knew the Major's way with women. Maybe he returned after his gymnastics, then slipped out again unknown to his host for another rendezvous. One that turned nasty.'

Max nodded. 'It's possible. Something's been nagging at me; something about the body that should have registered. *Why* shoot a man then tie him to a post, risking exposure?'

'To make a statement. You said the killer was sending some kind of message with his actions.'

Max closed his eyes; visualized the sight that had met him several hours ago. Khaki blindfold, the body secured upright to a post, hands tied behind it; one shot neatly through the heart. Green jacket torn and hanging open, epaulettes ... There was a sudden rush of adrenaline as he surely translated the

58

killer's message.

'Picture the body, the way it was displayed,' he said urgently. 'What about his mess jacket?'

'Torn, unbuttoned.'

'Exactly! *There were no buttons on it!* They'd been removed along with the crowns on the epaulettes. Tom, a soldier is blindfolded, tied to a post and shot. What does that suggest to you?'

Tom's face lit with comprehension. 'Execution by firing squad.'

'Nail on the head,' declared Max with satisfaction. 'In the old days, when an officer was court-martialled and sentenced to death, some of the ultra-elite regiments forced him to put on full dress uniform for the execution. Then all insignia and embellishments were publicly sliced off with a sword in symbolic rejection of his honour and worthiness to be in their ranks, before he was shot.'

'By God, sir, how do we work our way through *that*?' Tom demanded.

'By looking into the past. I don't mean as far back as those quixotic times. I think this killing is someone's response to what he sees as a deed meriting the ultimate military punishment. As Major Bekov was here for only a few hours yesterday we shall have to delve into his career to unearth some action of his that could be regarded as treacherous, cowardly or highly dishonourable.'

'Conduct unbecoming?'

'In a nutshell!'

'Isn't it a bit kinky? Doesn't fit today's attitudes and thinking.'

'Of course it doesn't. Which means we're looking for someone who's hooked on the notion of chivalry. Someone who plays war games, not on a computer, but with model soldiers. Re-enacts famous battles from the past. Wellington at Waterloo. Roberts at Kandahar. Gordon at Khartoum.'

'But if Major Bekov had committed a serious crime, he would surely have been courtmartialled and punished.'

Max was feeling the buzz that told him he was on the right track. The session with Judith King had given him the wrong vibes. He was now intensely interested in Leo Bekov as a soldier.

'Maybe he was acquitted, and our killer didn't agree with the verdict.'

'Which means someone on this base knew the victim a while back,' said Tom.

'And had advance notice of his visit yesterday. This was no random killing, my friend, it was premeditated and brilliantly executed.'

'But pretty damn chancy. How could the perpetrator second guess his victim's movements last night?'

'That's what makes me certain one of his fellow officers carried it out. He was in the mess watching Bekov's every move.'

As Jeremy Fielding entered his house after telling Judy to dress and go for an interview with SIB, his brain and emotions were in

60

turmoil. He walked straight to the sideboard and poured himself a large whisky. Early morning, but he needed it. Apart from a few sips of coffee he had been unable to face the makeshift breakfast Frances had rustled up. God, what a nightmare twelve hours.

When Pete had called him out the second time, he said only that someone was dead outside the mess. Jeremy hoped to God he had not betrayed his true feelings on seeing that body dangling from the post. Pete had himself seemed curiously thrown, his normal sangfroid missing. So maybe he had not noticed a doctor's surprising reaction on seeing a dead man. Pray God he had not.

He poured another whisky. What the hell was he going to do? His life was falling around his ears: pressures piling one upon the other. Now this. He had deliberately spun a web of deceit, little realizing he would be held fast in it with no hope of escape.

Jeannie was revolted by the babe who puked over her and made stinking messes in her pants. The revulsion was sensed by the child, who shrieked constantly for the comfort and cuddles she was not getting from her mother. He was farming Briony out more and more frequently; had begun giving Jeannie Valium. She needed psychiatric help for severe post-natal depression, but she refused to agree to it.

He took another gulp of whisky. After qualifying, he had found life as a military doctor suited him perfectly. Too perfectly! So he had hastily married a colourless girl he had known since schooldays. He thought he had been so bloody clever, but Jeannie and her fruit of the womb were slowly driving him to the edge.

Then Leo Bekov had turned up to push him over!

The shrill note of the telephone made his nerves jump. He snatched up the receiver. *'Yes?'*

'Corporal Caine, sir. Will you be coming in, or shall I change all the appointments?'

Jeremy glanced at the clock. Morning surgery should have started thirty minutes ago. 'I'm tied up at the moment.'

'I'll admit one to sick bay, and give the others new times, shall I?'

'No, no,' he said wearily. 'I'll be there in twenty minutes.'

'Righto, sir.'

He replaced the receiver with a hand that shook. 'Pull yourself together,' he muttered. 'Bekov's dead. No way he can do anything. Just sort out Jeannie.'

He went up to the bedroom and pulled his drugged wife up to a sitting position, shaking her hard. 'You have to get dressed; have some breakfast. Jeannie, wake up,' he said harshly, shaking her hard until she opened her eyes to slits. 'It's eight thirty. You have to get dressed. I'll get Alice Foster to come and bath Briony, give her her bottle then take her out in the pram.' He shook her again. 'Did you hear me?'

She gave a dopey smile. 'Yes, Jerry. Alice will see to everything.'

'You have to do something in return.' Another shake. *'Listen* to me!'

'Something in return. Yes. It's just that I don't know what to *do* with babies. That's all it is,' she whined. 'I'll do anything. Really I will!'

'Then listen carefully! Last night I came in just before two fifteen, didn't I?'

'If you say so.'

'No, Jeannie, you looked at the clock because you'd been waiting for me to help with the baby, and you remember that it was two fifteen.'

'If you say so, Jerry,' she mumbled.

He began to shout at her. 'This is bloody important! If anyone comes here asking when I got back from that medical emergency, you'll tell them what I just said. *You recall looking at the clock and it was two fifteen.* Right?'

'It was two fifteen,' she recited muzzily.

He sighed. It sounded rehearsed, but it was the best he could hope for. 'If you get it wrong I won't ask Alice to help with Briony again. And I'll tell Roland Phipps to give you those psycho tests. I mean it!'

She came fully to her senses, crying in panic, 'It was two fifteen. I won't get it wrong. Promise, Jerry, promise.'

The sight of her sickened him. He turned away to cross to the nursery wondering how much longer he could maintain this farce of a marriage. He had encouraged her fear of getting pregnant again, thus relieving himself of the obligation to sleep with her, but he knew something would have to be done about her mental state before she became a danger to their child.

Just get through this first, he told himself. Bekov might be dead but he could still threaten. If Jeannie swore her husband had come in at two fifteen – an hour and a half before he had – all should be well.

Four

Max walked the short distance from their interview room to the officers' mess, leaving Tom to check out Leo Bekov's career movements then search for evidence that anyone present at last night's dinner had served with him in the past. Max was sure that was the right way to go on this.

The mist had lifted leaving a stark greyness unlikely to soften all day. Military establishments were never visually beautiful despite close-mown grassy areas and flower-beds outside offices, tended by green-fingered soldiers. But the leaden skies and bone-chilling temperature today gave an impression of an East European place of correction. One could easily imagine dank cellars, fetters, bread and water and harsh-faced interrogators below the looming pair of pre-war barrack blocks around which the base had expanded.

Max dismissed the fancy as he turned the bend leading to the mess. He'd watched too many black-and-white war films. 'Ve haff vays off making you talk!' He gave a wry smile. Had any Nazi ever really said that to anyone but John Mills, Trevor Howard, Dickie Attenborough and Co?

Turning his thoughts more productively, Max reflected on the information just phoned in from one of his team, who had accompanied Bekov's body to the morgue. The autopsy was about to get under way, but there were several interesting points about the deceased's clothing. The trousers were soaked with urine. The underpants, which were on back to front, also bore semen stains indicating that sexual intercourse had taken place shortly before death.

Buttons and badges of rank had been cut from the jacket with a sharp blade. It bore traces of fine dust and fibres that could be jute. These would be examined in detail, but it was possible the victim had been hooded with a sack at some point. Max was unhappy about that. It dismissed his theory of death by firing squad and smacked of the IRA. He sensed that the link was misleading, but if Bekov had served in Northern Ireland it would have to be considered.

There were two other important points. The

khaki blindfold was one of the large squares used as slings for arm and shoulder injuries, which could implicate Dr Fielding. Beneath the cloth Bekov's eyes had been wide open. Max translated that well enough. Fear, shock, the desire to peer through the hood. So had Bekov been shot without realizing he was about to die, or had his killer unhooded him to face his punishment for some past crime?

Max was pondering this as he entered the anteroom, where a group of uniformed men and women were discussing the astonishing drama at the conclusion of their regimental celebration. James Harkness spotted Max and crossed to greet him.

'Spoken to Judith King, have you? She's not a member of the regiment, of course. Physical Training Corps. Doubt she was of much help.'

Max let that pass. He never discussed a case before he more or less had it licked. 'There must have been quite a few guests last night who weren't in your regiment.'

Harkness gave a brief nod. 'Apart from General Pomeroy's team, they're all mess members and entitled to attend. The CO is very keen on non-discrimination in the mess. Come along, I'll introduce you.'

Colonel Jack Keegan, who had come from seeing the VIPs on their way, was tall and thin-featured with curly silver hair. He had a bone-crushing handshake and a steely gaze that warned Max to tread warily around him. 'Terrible business,' Keegan said crisply.

66

'General Pomeroy is extremely anxious that it be resolved as speedily as possible. Major Bekov was a gifted linguist who had several times acted as translator for him at high-level talks. He's particularly upset that the man should have fallen victim to a random killer on the one night he was with us.'

Max shook his head. 'We've eliminated the idea of a chance shooting, sir. There's reason to believe Major Bekov was the victim of a premeditated attack.'

'Premeditated! He was only here a few hours, man.'

'And a number of people would be aware in advance that he was coming. It's what the killer did with the body that I consider rules out death by mischance. We need to check everyone's whereabouts during the vital period. I imagine you were at home in bed, sir. I believe the General was your house guest. Were any of his team also hosted by you and your wife?'

'Yes. Brigadier Mostyn and Major Eames. They're on the General's permanent staff. And before you ask, Captain Rydal, they retired soon after midnight, as I did, and slept soundly until 06:00. They had had a heavy day of talks followed by our evening celebrations, with an early start this morning.' His mouth twisted. 'I promise you they were unlikely to have sneaked out in the early hours. A guard was on duty all night outside the house.'

Although Max was prepared to accept that

Keegan's guests had slept through until morning, he would still check their details in case they had served with Bekov in the past. If he had translated for Pomeroy on other occasions, he could have earned the enmity of another staff member who decided to exact retribution where suspicion would fall else-where.

'Major Harkness agreed to my request that your officers gather here so that I can check when and where each of them last saw Major Bekov. Speeds things up.'

'They're not all here. We have an important international exercise upcoming and field training has to continue as usual.' Keegan's keen gaze strayed from Max to fix on a subaltern who had burst into loud laughter over a companion's comment.

'I won't keep them long,' Max promised, drawing Keegan's attention back. 'Their evidence will help pinpoint the time of the murder more exactly.'

'And eliminate them from your enquiries.'

Max chose not to reply. He was almost certain one of them, with an accomplice, had put an end to the life of a man they believed deserved the ultimate penalty. His question-ing was mainly inconclusive, at first. A dozen of the younger officers lived in the mess, like Judith King, and were unable to prove they had gone to their rooms and stayed there until morning. The married men who lived in quarters and hirings could get verification from their wives, but that was always suspect.

Those already questioned started leaving on the word of their CO, and Max then approached a group of three captains talking intently in the far corner of the room where last night they had indulged in macho wildness.

Max said: 'I'm aware you have to get back to work, but I need your input to the events leading to the death of Major Bekov. When did each of you leave the mess?'

'We left together,' said one immediately. 'We live in neighbouring quarters.'

A shorter, dark-haired man gave a nervous grin. 'Thought it best to cause one disturbance rather than three at separate intervals.'

'Wives get stroppy, on occasion,' said the third.

Max smiled. 'Their prerogative, I guess. Recall what time you decided to call it a day?'

'Shortly after 01:30, I think. Pete called the Doc out on an emergency. We saw him drive off as we walked down the path to where...' He halted awkwardly. 'Bekov was still in mess then.'

'Sure?'

'Absolutely,' averred the shorter one. 'He was the kind of guy you notice.'

'Threw himself into the spirit of the evening,' agreed the third man caustically.

Experience told Max there was something strained about these three. They were quoting lines as if they'd been rehearsed. He asked for their names to add to the list in his hand. Andy Miles, Justin Cleeve and Philip Holt.

All about thirty, give or take a year or two, and looking distinctly uneasy.

'Had any of you met Major Bekov before yesterday? Served with him, or taken the same course, anything like that?'

All three firmly shook their heads. Well, that could be checked. Max adopted a more official tone. 'It's pretty obvious you're holding something back. I'm investigating the crime of cold-blooded murder. Right on your doorstep. If you know something that would throw light on it it's your duty to tell me, even if you suspect that it might incriminate one of your colleagues. Each piece of evidence is thoroughly checked. We're not in the game of making the innocent appear guilty in order to close a case.' He gave each man an interrogative stare. 'So which of you is going to be sensible?'

Andy Miles, who seemed the most authoritive, glanced at the others, then spoke hesitantly. 'We all feel uncomfortable in view of what happened. I guess the truth of it is just now hitting us. As I said, we left the mess at around 01:30 and walked home together.' He frowned. 'Strict rules about driving after a celebration like that. That's why officers book a room in the mess if they live on the far side of the base.'

'Or if they get grief from the wife when they return home the worse for wear,' put in Cleeve.

'Which means mess accommodation was full last night,' offered Philip Holt. 'And

Major Bekov was farmed out on—' He corrected himself swiftly. 'He was hosted by Mark Ingham, who'd been at Sandhurst with him.'

'We knew the situation,' admitted Andy Miles, 'which makes us now feel guilty about not taking him in.'

Despite not yet understanding what they were getting at, Max was feeling the familiar buzz. He waited for them to elaborate.

Miles continued. 'Look, Mark's wife is ... well, she's not a great fan of military life, so she was more than likely behind his decision to ignore the racket. I mean, Bekov was very drunk. And abusive.'

'It was a hell of a time to turn up,' added Holt. 'It's not as if he's a member of the regiment. Our battle honours are nothing to do with I Corps men, so it was bloody disgusting behaviour towards Mark, who played host under duress. He told me he couldn't stand Bekov from way back.'

'Phil!' said Miles warningly.

'You know very well the 2IC twisted his arm to have the bastard,' countered Holt.

'And the bastard is now dead,' Max reminded them coldly.

There was silence for a moment or two, then Andy Miles sighed heavily. 'Sorry. We didn't know the Major so we've no foundation for speaking ill of the man. Yes, he's dead ... and we could have prevented his murder.'

'Go on,' urged Max.

Miles appeared to be the natural spokesman. 'I suppose it took us around twenty minutes to reach our quarters. We were woken some time later by loud shouting and banging. It went on long enough to disturb my entire family, so I opened the window and looked out.'

'So did we,' said the other two.

'Major Bekov was outside Mark's door, kicking and banging it with his fists, roaring Mark's name and demanding to be let in. There was no response, which infuriated him even more. I called to him to shut it, but all I got was a tirade of what I took to be Russian expletives.'

'And?'

'I ... we,' Miles amended, indicating his companions, 'left him to it. When it eventually grew quiet I was puzzled because no lights had come on in Mark's house, opposite mine. So I took another look from the window. Bekov was walking away down the avenue, very unsteadily.' He frowned again. 'In retrospect I realize – we all do – that one of us should have done something. That we didn't we now see is indefensible. But we all have young kids who were already upset by the commotion he was making, so we were most reluctant to take him in.'

'No way was I exposing my family to that,' Holt protested. 'My wife was adamant that it was Mark's responsibility. He hasn't any kids. All he had to do was bunk him down on the settee and shut him up.'

Cleeve looked uncomfortable, nervously

72

running his fingers around the rim of his beret. 'I asked Mark earlier this morning why he hadn't let the bas— Major in. He told me to piss off. I guess he's feeling pretty bad. Worse than us. Bekov was his official guest, after all.'

Andy Miles said, 'I see now what I should have done was to ring Mark's number and tell him to open his door. I know Bekov was being a bloody nuisance and I can understand that Mark would want to ignore him, but it was his job to deal with the man.'

'Yes, and Mark was well aware mess accommodation was full,' Holt added. 'Where did he imagine the poor sod would spend the rest of the night?'

'I should have kept ringing his number until he answered,' Miles repeated heavily. 'One of us should have done *something*.'

Max fully understood why they had been loath to intervene, but their evidence put a new slant on the case because it must have happened *after* the session with Judith King.

He addressed Miles. 'What time did this occur?'

'Must have been around 03:00. I was in a deep sleep by then.'

So Bekov had gone to his overnight lodging straight from the gymnasium. Knowing he was a temporary member of General Pomeroy's staff, which made him a minor VIP, Ingham's denial of Bekov was most curious. He'd apparently hosted the Anglo-Russian 'under duress', so his subsequent behaviour

73

would have earned him a black mark regardless of what had happened. Why had he risked military censure so determinedly ... unless it was to lure his victim to his death? Punishment for something that happened at Sandhurst?

This was an intriguing development. Unless Miles, Cleeve and Holt were all lying, and Max could see no reason why they would, their evidence narrowed the time margin so drastically it suggested the killer had been at Bekov's heels waiting for the perfect moment to strike. And that had occurred after 03:00 and before 04:00, when his body had been seen by the Duty Officer. So had Mark Ingham and Judith King conspired in murder?

Drinking more coffee by now almost in isolation, Max reasoned that, denied entry to Ingham's house, Bekov would instinctively have headed back to the mess. So his team should search the route between the two for evidence of the shooting.

His introspection was broken by a blond captain resembling the young Robert Redford. 'Thought I should have a quick word before I leave. Due to give a lecture in fifteen,' he explained, offering his hand. 'Peter Randolph. Duty Officer last night.'

His handshake was firm and assured, his smile was dazzling, his eyes were the bluest Max had ever seen. He must flutter hearts wherever he went!

'Top marks for your prompt isolation of the body, and for leaving it undisturbed. Most people would have released it and taken it from public view,' said Max, thinking this man *must* be wearing tinted contact lenses.

The dazzling smile again. 'I'm an avid reader of whodunits. Know the scene of crime must be left as it is for forensic examination. Any valuable clues, were there?'

Max could do without an aspiring Hercule Poirot. 'The report isn't complete yet,' he said. 'Perhaps you'd give me a rough outline of the sequence of events. We'll take a formal statement later.'

'Naturally,' replied the whodunit expert suavely. 'I'd decided to do "rounds" just before midnight, fifteen before two and ten after five. I guess I was snatching a nap after the second sortie when Judy King woke me with a weird story. She was very drunk. Gibbering about a dead man hanging on a post. I thought it was some kind of lark, of course.'

'Tying dead bodies to signposts is what you do for fun in this regiment, is it?'

The smile vanished. 'Look, Judy was barely in control. I thought some of the lads had put up a facsimile of the CO for a dare.'

'But you dressed and went out to check.'

'Obliged to ... and I thought she'd wake everyone if I didn't. Hell of a shock. I called out Jerry Fielding, although I didn't doubt Tolstoy was dead.'

Max frowned. 'Tolstoy?'

'Did I say that?' He gave a sigh of a laugh. 'I was told the guy was Russian. I also wanted Jerry to see to Judy. Treat her for shock. She

75

looked bloody ill.'

'And then?'

'Called up the Duty Sergeant, told him to organize a tent and ropes to cordon off the area pronto. After that I informed the CO. It's all in my report.'

'Who was watching the body meanwhile?'

'I was. The window of the Duty Room gives a clear view of that signpost.'

'But it was dark, and the mess is at least fifty yards away.'

He was ready for that. 'The Duty Officer carries a powerful flashlight on "rounds". I left it trained on the body. I'd have seen any activity in the vicinity.'

'Mmm, your fiction reading paid off.'

He appeared not to notice the irony. 'Worrying to think some squaddie managed to get hold of a rifle and ammo so easily. He could instead have picked off Sergeant Squires or me.' The smile flashed again. 'My sister always said I have the luck of the devil.'

'Luck didn't enter into it ... neither did a rifle. You and the sergeant were quite safe.' He nodded at the large wall clock. 'You have five minutes to reach the venue for that lecture.'

Hot on the heels of the departing Randolph, James Harkness came up to Max. 'All done?'

'Yes, thanks, but I'd like the names of everyone who attended yesterday's talks and stayed here overnight. I'd also like a list of those people who would have known Major Bekov

76

was coming – mess staff, security, transport. And anyone who'd be in a position to get hold of the information secretly.'

Harkness looked annoyed. 'We do have a unit to run, you know.'

'Three of your officers have just now confirmed that the victim was alive at 03:00. An hour later, Ms King found his body. In the interim he had been grabbed, hooded, taken somewhere to be executed, then transported to this mess to be put on display. All that tells me the killer was efficient and fully prepared to commit the murder of that particular man. He knew in advance that Bekov would be at your celebration last night.'

After a short tense silence, Harkness nodded. 'I'll see you get that list.'

'And perhaps you'd track down Mark Ingham. I need to interview him in depth in the room you set aside for us. ASAP, please, Major.'

Peter Randolph's outer calm hid inner agitation and a continuing sense of disbelief. Rydal was going to prove a pain in the arse; too bloody smart for his copper's boots! For that's what he was; a plain and simple plod. Not an honest-to-God fighting man.

Peter had no time for SIB. He allowed that the Redcaps did a useful job breaking up pub brawls or catching absentees, but criminal investigations should be left to the civil police. Rydal must be smug with satisfaction. Because this murder was all-British, so to speak, the Krauts would be happy to let him deal with it. Back in the UK he would have to bow to pukka detectives on such a case.

Walking briskly to the drill hall, where he was to lecture on 'Booby-traps and how to recognize them', he berated himself for the slip Rydal had picked up. He had covered it swiftly, so the bloody man was unlikely to make anything of it. Peter and his close cronies had always referred to Bekov as Tolstoy in Bosnia. Among other names!

When Rory Hunter-Smyth had emailed that Tolstoy was about to grace the battalion with his presence, Peter had suffered a mixture of emotions. The first time they would come face to face since that day Peter would never forget. What an opportunity!

He now drew in his breath with renewed incredulity. Bekov had ignored him for the entire evening. The man *must* have recognized him. So it had been a few years ago, and there had been much water under the bridge since then, but the faces of those involved in the drama were imprinted on his memory. And on Rory's. And Mick's. So it must be the same for Tolstoy. Yet he had looked right through him. Lording it, as usual! Wearing that superior smile. Fancying himself.

That was what had riled them in Bosnia, because he, Rory and Mick were all better bred than the mongrel whelp of a Russian musician who defected during a cultural tour of Britain and a public-relations woman. Rory's people were distinguished Oxford academics, Mick's father and grandfather were senior judges, and his own family was listed in *Burke's Peerage*; a long line of titled generals.

His thoughts returned to last night. As Duty Officer he had been unable to drink and make merry. He had left the celebrations in time to change from mess dress ready for 'rounds' to check the armoury, CO's office, perimeter guards, etc. He had just returned to the Duty Room when he was told of the girl choking on a cough sweet, so he had pulled Jerry Fielding from the anteroom and sent him to the rescue.

That was when he had seen Bekov undoubtedly making it with Judy where every other hopeful, including himself, had failed. Peter had returned to the Duty Room seething. It was time Tolstoy paid up for that charmed life he led.

The lecture went smoothly. Peter had given it so many times no one would guess at his racing thoughts behind his air of inbred authority and cool command. He was not in the least cool. Shock still hovered under surface assurance. If Judy had not been pissed to the eyebrows she might have realized he was pretending to be asleep when she burst in on him.

She had given him one hell of a jolt. If she had been wandering around outside she could have seen him where he ought not to have been. He had not long ago stripped to vest and pants, taken a steadying nip from his

79

flask and got beneath the duvet when he heard the outer door crash open and a noisy approach. He had feigned unconsciousness – even snored – then had refused to take her seriously. Nothing had prepared him for what he found after following her outside. Thank God she was too drunk to register his reaction.

Rydal had interviewed her lengthily soon after his arrival. What might she have told him? She appeared to have taken the morning off to recover, so Peter would not know until they next met up whether or not she could drop him in it.

Yes, the handsome, immaculate officer addressing his troops in clipped, confident tones was a very worried man. Had he last night activated a booby-trap he had failed to recognize? Tolstoy was dead, but he still had the power to threaten.

Mark Ingham was going to brazen it out. Max recognized the underlying anxiety all too well, and this young officer with drawn features and ginger hair was suffering it. His eyes gave the game away; looking swiftly down after initial contact. Furtive, Max thought, but ready to trot out rehearsed lies.

He went straight to the core as soon as Ingham settled in the facing chair. 'Three of your colleagues dumped you in it in the mess just now, didn't they! Inconsiderate of a guest to return at that hour, drunk and rowdy, but on a special celebratory occasion surely not indefensible? Major Bekov could still be alive if you had answered his knock and let him in.'

Ingham said nothing, but his jaw tightened.

'So why didn't you?'

He raised his eyes, assumed an air of confidence. 'I wasn't actually there at the time.'

'Oh? Lieutenant Micheals told me he left the party a few minutes after you. That was an hour and a half before your guest hammered on the door to be let in.'

'Yes.'

'So it took you more than ninety minutes to go from the mess to your quarters?' Max asked in curiosity.

'I left the mess and went home,' Ingham said carefully. 'Look, this *is* all confidential, isn't it?'

'Any evidence bearing relevance to Major Bekov's murder could be made public at trial.'

'This is personal; nothing to do with his death. It's just ... I don't want it circulating.'

Max waited, fixing him with the unflinching gaze that frequently unnerved those he was questioning.

'My wife and I had had words.' Ingham forced a smile. 'She gets a bit worked up over dining-in nights, especially if they coincide with something she wants to do. You know how it is.'

(No! Susan had always welcomed his obligatory absences, Max afterwards realized. She could meet her lover!)

'Go on.'

'I suppose I said more than I should to her. She flung some things in a bag and said she'd stay with her friend until I came to my senses.'

'And the friend is?'

'Jane Foyle. Her husband Bobby is away right now. The girls spend a lot of time together.'

'Overnight?'

'Well, no, not as a rule.'

'So it was a serious row you had?'

'I didn't think so. I was stunned when Reena walked out.' He frowned. 'There was nothing I could do right then. Had to be in the mess pretty well straight after she left.'

'With your friend Leo.'

'He wasn't...' He pulled himself up; altered what he was about to say. 'Yes, we went together. But he was one of a team over here for a conference so he joined up with them when we arrived.'

'Even though you were hosting him? Maybe he felt *de trop* in view of your domestic situation.'

Ingham seized on that. Max had given him a fortunate prompt. 'He did. I mean, I felt bloody awkward about it, so he must have done. As usual, things started hotting up after midnight, but I was all for packing it in. He seemed to be in the thick of the fun and set to make a night of it. Didn't help my mood. Meant I had to hang around until he was ready to leave.'

'As a good friend does.'

The prod brought the result Max needed. 'I don't know where you got the idea Bekov's a friend. We were at Sandhurst together. I've had no contact with him since.'

'What, about twelve, thirteen years?'

Ingham nodded. 'As we were short of accommodation I agreed to put him up, that's all.'

'Mm, no wonder you felt bloody awkward about the row with your wife, with him in the house. Had Mrs Ingham met him before – during your Sandhurst days?'

'*No!*'

It was too quick, too emphatic, and his glance flickered nervously elsewhere. Oh *ho*, thought Max. Had Bekov ever performed naked gymnastics with the feisty Reena? 'So, although the acquaintance was so slight you were decent enough to wait until your guest was ready to leave the mess.'

Ingham was back on track. 'Naturally.'

'Go on.'

'I suppose it was just on one thirty when he came over and said he'd made other arrangements for the night. He'd been drinking heavily, but I had no reason to doubt what he said. I assumed he was planning to crash out in someone's room upstairs when the party eventually broke up. Suited me. I said goodnight and left.'

'And?'

'I went home, as I told you. But I couldn't stand the emptiness. I'd felt guilty all evening. Very upset. And I'd put a good few away, like

83

everyone else. Dutch courage persuaded me to go and see my wife, apologize, ask her to come back home.'

'In the early hours?'

Ingham coloured slightly. 'As I said, I'd put a few away. Booze spoke louder than sense. And Jane's quarters are only in the next avenue. Not far to walk.'

'So you left your house when?'

'Around half two, I guess.'

'Hardly a welcome caller at that hour, were you?' commented Max, unsure whether this man was a poor liar or simply a fool. Two women alone in a house would surely think twice about answering a ring at the doorbell in the early hours. Especially with a number of men who had wined and dined too well on the loose.

Adopting a rueful expression, Ingham said, 'I wouldn't have done it sober, but the girls were wonderful. They were still awake and talking. You know how they like long, girlie sessions moaning about men and our failings. They let me in and gave me black coffee. Then Jane left us alone to talk.'

'You apologized?'

'Mmm. Promised her a fun night out to compensate.'

'And your wife was mollified?'

'More or less. She promised to come home right after breakfast.'

'And you bedded down there for the rest of the night?'

'No. Couldn't expect Jane to make up a bed

at that hour.'

'Your wife wasn't so mollified she was prepared to let you share hers?'

Ingham ignored that. 'I went home, took a shower and several paracetamol, then got in a few hours' sleep. I'd no idea Bekov changed his plans and had been knocking the door while I was at Jane's. It was a terrible shock when my neighbours told me this morning.'

'I'm sure.' Max studied him closely for some moments. 'Will your wife and Mrs Foyle confirm your story?'

'It's not a story, it's the truth.'

'Will they confirm it?'

'Of course.'

'Good. Unfortunately, they can't do anything to make you feel better about the tragic result of your drunken decision to call on them in the middle of the night. You'll have to live with that as best you can.' Ingham looked set to go when Max added, 'Tell me about Leo Bekov. What did you make of him at Sandhurst?'

The jaw tightened further. 'I didn't have to make anything of him. I was just another cadet. Better ask the instructors there at the time. They were the ones who passed judgement on us all.'

'But they didn't mix with the cadets in their rooms, during recreational periods or away from the RMA.'

Ingham said nothing.

'You were swift to deny being a friend of the

deceased; you don't seem unduly concerned over the way in which his murder was made public. If Ms King had not been so late returning to the mess, the body would have been seen by a large number of people two or three hours later. Presumably what the killer hoped for. Now, I appreciate that your domestic set-to was uppermost in your mind – did your wife return home as promised, by the way?' At the man's nod, Max continued, 'But I still find it hard to accept your total lack of reaction to what has happened. Marital squabbles occur frequently and soon blow over, but murder ends a person's life. Kaput! Over! No reconciliation, no second chance, no fresh start. It's a hole in the ground or the incinerator.'

He stepped up the pressure. 'Leo Bekov was a former colleague, a guest in your house. But for your drunken decision to say sorry at half two in the morning, you would have opened your door when he thumped on it and shouted to be let in, and he would now be on a plane back to England healthy, happy and full of life. Why doesn't that bother you?'

Ingham's eyes grew shadowy and unreadable. 'You're wrong. It didn't happen through any of *my* actions, but because he said he'd made other plans then changed them. I'm not culpable. He sealed his own fate.'

'Over which you feel nothing?'

'I'm a soldier, trained to take death in my stride.'

Max gave a small derisory grunt. 'They trained you well!'

'Is that all?' demanded Ingham, who had gained confidence over his last few responses.

'You still haven't given an opinion on the kind of person the victim was.'

'That's because I hardly knew him.'

'You spent some months together at the RMA.'

'I had little to do with him. He wasn't one of my cronies.'

'How unfortunate, then, that you had your arm twisted over offering him a bed he never occupied because you'd quarrelled with your wife. I see now why you deny any sense of regret. If blame can be laid it should be on whoever forced you to play host to a man you so patently disliked.'

Ingham immediately reacted. 'I didn't say I disliked him.'

'You didn't have to. I'm used to reading unspoken messages. That's all for now, thank you, except to ask your permission to take a DNA sample.'

He looked alarmed. 'What for?'

'To compare with samples found at the scene of crime.'

'I didn't kill him,' he cried. 'I've just told you where I was while it was happening.'

'Then you have nothing to worry about, have you? We'll have a word with your wife and Mrs Foyle, then we might want to question you again.'

'They'll confirm what I've told you,' he said desperately.

'I'm sure they will. Like you, they'll have been well trained.'

Five

Mark headed back to the mess. He was sweating; his bowels were giving him urgent signals. Dare not go to his office until he had calmed down. He really needed a stiff drink, but there was no chance of that yet. Before lunch he had to write progress reports on two newly promoted corporals, inspect facilities in several accommodation blocks and preside on a charge brought against a pair of squaddies for brawling in the cookhouse. He had already postponed it from first thing this morning. He could not delay it further.

After ridding his innards of the results of nervous stomach churning, in the cloakroom, he brought his temperature down by dousing his face and hands with cold water. Only then did he indulge in relief. It was going to be all right. Judy could not have said anything; had not seen him last night. That cool bastard Rydal would have homed in on it. He was instead focusing on Bekov's movements after failing to gain admittance to their house. Mark was confident on that score. The girls would lie for him. They truly believed he had sat on the doorstep lacking the courage to ring the bell; believed he had gone there, tail between his legs, to apologize.

If only he could tell Reena what he had really been doing. She was shocked and upset, but would back his story because her ego wanted it to be true. But, oh boy, would he have a different approach from now on! No more 'punishments' in the spare room. She would be for it whether she wanted it or not. Her reaction to Bekov's murder had justified his long-held suspicions. She still lusted after the bastard. Well, her hero had met his certain fate. Time she had a new hero. Him.

Walking to his office Mark thought about Rydal's attempts to uncover a significant bond between himself and Bekov. His mouth twisted. He had handled that well. Ask the instructors! They would praise him to the skies, of course, but they had not known the real man.

They had had no sleep for thirty-six hours. The temperature was three below. The snow had frozen making progress hazardous. There seemed to be no end in sight. The white ridges of the Brecon Beacons stretched away in every direction.

They were all nearing the limit of their endurance. Alone, each might have decided to rest. Sleep and possible death could result. Each kept going because the others did.

Because Officer Cadet Bekov did.

He was out in front. It had not started that way, but as the trek took its toll the healthy competition to show leadership qualities and initiative had flagged. It was always like that. Bekov never pushed forward immediately. He waited for the right moment, then calmly stepped in to revive energies or offer an alternative solution.

Mark was suffering. The low temperature and high altitude had brought on a blinding headache. His teeth ached with the cold. His back, shoulders and thighs throbbed with anguish after trekking over uneven terrain all day and all night, carrying a heavy pack. The gash on his right calf was growing unbearably painful with every dogged step. Yesterday he had put on a field dressing, but blood had stuck to it and every movement pulled at the torn flesh.

Four hours later, now limping on his throbbing leg, Mark's boot slipped on the frozen rock and he fell heavily on his left side. The weight of his equipment tipped him over the edge of the track where he began to roll down the escarpment. His bulky pack made his descent uneven, so that his body thumped against the unyielding surface on every rotation.

His mind was too numb to register panic, but his torso felt the pain all too badly. He passed out momentarily. When awareness returned he lay gazing up at a formidable ice slope. Fear arrived in a rush, accelerating his heartbeat, weakening his limbs. His eyes swivelled, taking in all within his immediate vision. The peak vanished into low cloud. Everywhere else there was open space. Acres of it. A whole world of nothingness. One movement and he was a goner.

Scarcely daring to breathe, fear was replaced by a sense of failure. He had been careless enough to sustain an injury, he had rejected advice to call in asking to be airlifted, he had lost concentration and walked too near the edge. If he did not plunge to his death before medics winched him to safety, he would be thrown off the course for failing to reach required standards. His father would be deeply disappointed; his cocky half-brother would crow because he would not, after all, become a 'poncy officer'.

Through misty eyes Mark saw movement. A figure was being lowered on a rope. He called a fearful warning to stay away – his position was so precarious the slightest vibration could dislodge him – but his shout sounded little more than a hoarse whisper, and the figure drew nearer. He closed his eyes and prayed.

Utter silence sang around him for so long he opened his eyes again. Way above, he now saw a row of faces looking at him. The figure was no longer visible, but the rope was twitching. Where the hell was the idiot? Dangling over the void? He closed his eyes and prayed some more.

'Keep absolutely still,' said a calm, quiet

voice nearby. 'I'm going to tie a rope around your ankles. Can't risk getting any closer. If you should slip you'll be hanging upside down, but the lads will take the strain and you'll be safe.'

Mark felt careful hands looping something around his feet. He longed to scream an order to leave well alone, but he had recognized that voice. He would not show Bekov how terrified he was, counting his last moments on earth.

Those moments dragged on as the voice that sang so joyously spoke softly once more. 'You're now secure. The lads have requested a Casevac helo. It'll be here in an instant.'

It arrived as he spoke, and hung like a dark spider while the crew decided how to tackle the emergency. A winchman soon descended, stabilizing himself with his feet on the narrow ledge beside Mark's head while he asked questions to gauge his state of fitness to be moved. Reassured, Mark found he had no broken limbs, did not taste blood and could hear and understand all that was said.

In no time he was rising through the late afternoon sky, chest to chest with the winchman, and he knew he would see another dawn. Then Bekov was brought up to the cabin, and the aircraft moved across to land where the rest were waiting in a silent huddle.

Captain Bellamy, one of their instructors, had come in the helicopter. While the medics examined Mark's leg and gave him something to counteract shock, the officer tackled

Bekov.

'We don't look kindly on impulsive heroics at the Academy. The team radioed for Casevac and gave your position accurately. That's correct procedure. What you did was foolhardy and in no way enhanced your worth as a trainee officer. When leading a platoon, if one of your men lands in a dangerous situation you risk leaving the remainder without a commander by attempting an unnecessary single-handed rescue. You'll always have a support team to call on in an emergency.'

Bekov offered quiet defence. 'I wouldn't have done it if I'd been leading a platoon, sir. I was with fellow cadets acting without a commander.'

'Your action was the result of flawed judgement,' Bellamy insisted. 'Your fellow cadets are nearing total exhaustion from effort and lack of sleep. They are also combating sub-zero temperatures at high altitude. All that reduces the speed of their reactions and, therefore, their effectiveness in a crisis. You should not have relied on their ability to counteract the sudden jerk should Ingham have dropped from that ledge. Nor could you be certain your own rope wouldn't slide through hands stiffened by the cold. Your flamboyant rescue attempt could have resulted in two severe, if not fatal, casualties.' A pause to let the reprimand sink in. 'Are you an experienced mountaineer, Bekov?'

'No, sir.'

'Then you're not only headstrong, you're a fool. Casevac crews know exactly what they are doing in extreme situations. You don't. Remember that.'

'Yes, sir.'

'Right. Get out and rejoin the others.'

Bellamy climbed from the aircraft after him and addressed the grouped cadets. 'You now have less than three hours to reach the final RV, or you'll accumulate more penalty points to add to those earned by climbing the wrong peak last night. As Bekov appears to have an overwhelming desire to shine, he can set the pace at the front. Go to it, gentlemen.'

They looked acutely dismayed, believing they were all to be flown to the RV. Bekov marched off into the fast-approaching night casting Mark a look of dark fury. He could justifiably return it. Bellamy was right. Bekov could have killed them both.

Mark returned to Sandhurst fully recovered and determined to respond to the adverse comments in an otherwise good end-of-term interview. The instructors believed he should loosen up, express himself more freely, take the lead if he could offer a better solution to complex logistic or tactical problems. In other words, he had to convince them he could command men with the kind of judgement that would earn their trust and respect. A formidable aim.

Apparently not for Leo Bekov. Whatever had been said to him at his progress interview, he showed no sign of striving harder. Then why should he? thought Mark. The Anglo-Russian was agile and foxy on squash or tennis courts, a canny hockey player and reliable on a rugby pitch. His gymnastic skill was outstanding. He could mapread fast and accurately, was a decent shot and had great staying power on field exercises. He was popular with other cadets and oozed confidence. As if that were not enough, he spoke three other languages fluently. There was little doubt he would be an asset to the army.

At the mid-term party, Mark discovered that anyone immune to Bekov's personal charisma fell victim to the Russian folk music he played so brilliantly on his balalaika. The drinks were flowing, everyone letting their hair down. Mark's current girlfriend, Reena, looked sensational in a low-cut black lace top and the tightest stretch-satin trousers he had ever seen. Other men were eyeing her lasciviously, which gave Mark a pleasant sense of one-upmanship in this competitive life he was living.

When the group took a break, the revellers went outside to the fresher air of a warm summer evening. Mark was kissing Reena as she leaned back against a wall when he grew aware of distant music. People began to flow towards the sound. Reena stirred against him; angled her head away.

'What's that music, Mark?'

He turned her face back and opened his

mouth over hers again.

She pushed him away. 'Down, boy! I want to go where they're all going.'

Wearing a cream silk shirt, tight black trousers and a leather belt with a heavy silver buckle, Leo Bekov was sitting on an upended crate playing to a hushed audience. A shaft of moonlight fell on him like a theatre spot, accentuating the Slavic planes of his features and the dark gleam of his eyes.

Seeing Reena's response, Mark burned with a mix of resentment and jealousy. 'The Pied bloody Piper!'

'More like a satyr,' she replied softly. 'Look at those devilish eyes!'

When Mark returned with more drinks later in the evening, Reena was dancing with Bekov. They looked fantastic together; moved so sexily they seemed to be metaphorically copulating. One-upmanship faded fast.

Bekov began appearing at the pub, wine bar, disco, wherever Mark and Reena went at weekends. They were all places popular with the cadets, but Mark was sure the Anglo-Russian was dogging them. Reena told him he was paranoid.

For his twentieth-birthday celebration Mark splashed out by booking a table at a well-known London club, and a room at the Ritz. He was now seriously in love and planned to put a diamond on Reena's finger to stake his claim.

They had almost finished their starter when a small group was led to a nearby table by the head waiter. Mark stared in furious disbelief. It was too much of a coincidence that that bastard had arranged to eat here, of all places, on this particular date. There was only one way he could have known about this birthday meal. Turning to Reena, he saw the truth. She was exchanging optical messages with Bekov.

'You told him about tonight, didn't you,' he accused through his teeth, as Bekov approached wearing that smile that suggested he knew things others were ignorant of.

'Are you two following me around? Everywhere I go, there you are,' he greeted with infuriating bonhomie. 'I'm with a very merry group. Why don't you join us?'

'No, thanks,' Mark said bluntly. 'This is a private occasion.'

'Oh, what?'

'His *birthday*,' droned Reena, making it sound deadly dull.

'Great! We'll make it a celebration to remember. Party till dawn. Who knows where we'll be next year, Mark? On patrol in the Shankhill Road, tracking down illegals crossing into the New Territories, fighting rebels in some pestilent African state.' He punched Mark's shoulder matily. 'Eat, drink and be merry, for tomorrow we die. Maybe.' He laughed to show he took the prospect in his stride.

'Come on, Mark, it'll be fun,' urged Reena, getting to her feet.

Riven by jealousy and some even darker emotion, Mark said, 'I made it perfectly clear

I've planned something special for tonight. If you'd prefer to spend it with a bunch of Hooray Henrys, you'll do it without me.'

'Fine. You'd only put a damper on the fun if that's the mood you're in.' His girl walked away and was soon laughing and drinking with her satyr and his lusty friends.

As the course continued, Reena's grip on Mark's emotions made it difficult for him to concentrate on the demands on his mental and physical abilities. Growing desperate, he forced himself to contact and beg her to resume their relationship.

With his hormonal chaos calmed, Mark put his best efforts into the programme designed to drive cadets to their limits. He also tried to ignore Bekov's self-satisfied smiles whenever their glances met. He passed the physical and written tests successfully, but the instructors told him he was still holding back in team activities. It was essential that he gave them more evidence of the leadership qualities they knew he possessed if he hoped to gain a commission.

Worried, feeling stressed by the fear of failure, Mark knew he would be facing a decisive personal test during the major tactical exercise on Salisbury Plain. The cadets played Blue Force to wage war against Red Force who were, as usual, a company of experienced Gurkhas. The cadets were divided into Blues One, Two, Three and Four. On the second day, their mission was to drive the enemy from a large copse where their guns were concealed, then push forward to capture a farm being used as a divisional head-quarters.

Mark was nominated commander of Blue Two, who were to follow in rear of Blue One. When One signalled that they had gained and were holding ground to the west of the farm, and that Three and Four similarly command-ed ground to the east, Two was tasked to advance and capture the farm. Essential to success.

November had come in like a lion and stayed that way. Days of stormy rain had made the ground soft and sludgy; overnight fog frequently lingered during daylight hours. It could mask an advance, but it also hid the enemy ahead. Wars were fought in all climates and conditions, so bad weather was a bonus so far as the instructors were concerned.

Mark did not agree with them as he gazed at the thundering rain on that second day. The farm was out there swallowed up by the mist, somewhere north-west of their present position. In front of it was a copse in which enemy artillery was known to be concealed. Each leader had a plan showing the gun positions, based on supposed information from Intelligence. Their months of training told them not to take this for granted. Guns could be successfully camouflaged; bogus ones could look real in aerial photographs.

At the briefing the other three commanders had agreed first to take out the guns, then bring up their reserves to fight Red Force on even terms, driving them into the bag with a pincer movement while Mark's platoon attacked Red headquarters. Sounded simple, but the wily Gurkhas would have a strategy of their own that would take some outwitting.

As Mark waited with his men, that seemed disastrously apparent. Blue One, led by Bekov, had vanished into the mist an hour ago. Rifle fire, muffled by the damp air, had been heard for the past thirty minutes. There was a real struggle for the guns going on out there. Bekov was giving no sitreps, which Mark thought he should, so there was no way of telling progress. His own demands for information had been ignored.

Mark was feeling increasingly uneasy. The rain was showing no sign of lessening and, if there was much more delay, they would be trying to take the farmhouse in semi-darkness. Although this was only an exercise the eeriness of that foggy plain, combined with the sounds of distant battle, sent a shiver down Mark's spine. If this were for real would he find the courage to face it?

'Tackle the bastard again,' said one of his friends beside him. 'He's forgotten we're meant to take part in this.'

'Blue Two to Blue One, do you read me? Over,' Mark said urgently.

Nothing.

'Try again,' his friend insisted. 'I'm seizing up here.'

After a third attempt Bekov's calm voice

signalled the go-ahead. 'Blue One to Blue Two. Guns out of action. Enemy on the run. Advise you move up to position eight–zero–four *now*. Over.'

'Blue Two to Blue One. Message received. Wilco. Over and out.' Mark turned to his platoon with a grin. 'We're off, lads. Let's show the rest we don't take as long as them to gain our objective.'

He set off at a run through the swirling mist over soggy terrain scattered with stunted growth. It was hard going in boots weighty with mud. Stair-rod rain hindered visibility, but Mark was so charged up with adrenaline he raced on in the sudden certainty that he could lead men into battle if he had to.

They reached the copse, saw the unmanned guns and the watching instructors acting as marshals. A group of drenched 'killed and wounded' sat chatting on the muddy ground, their part in the day's fighting over. Ignoring them, Mark moved on to position 804 on his map, which lay on the far side of the copse. The farm was then around 250 yards ahead, no more than a blur on the horizon. To reach it they must cross an area of shallow dips and ridges. These, aided by the mist, would disguise their advance that would have to be on their bellies for most of the distance.

Mark swiftly outlined his strategy to his men, then contacted Blue One confirming that they were in position. Bekov told him to wait for his signal to go. Fleeting resentment over the imperious tone from the man he so deeply disliked had to be smothered. This was war. Personalities had to be set aside.

They all waited, keyed up, some biting their lower lips, others drumming fingers against rifles. Mark struggled with the urge to pee. His bladder could not be full. He had emptied it less than thirty minutes ago and had drunk nothing since then. It was nerves. God, would he wet himself in a real battle?

Suddenly: 'Blue One to Blue Two. Go, go, go!'

Mark forgot his bladder as he led the assault on the farm, snaking forward, dropping into the series of wide ruts then slithering fast over the ridges to reach the next dip. Several times he glanced back and was absurdly pleased that there was little evidence of thirty men following him. They were mounting a genuine surprise attack on enemy headquarters. *Yahoo!*

The 'farmhouse', which had been all manner of things in successive military exercises, was now clearly discernable. Mark waited until all his men were with him in the same hollow, then he gave them orders to approach and attack various parts of the stout-walled building with windows, doorways and several outhouses that were 'barns' today.

They were all hyped up and fully with him as he reported to Blue One that he was about to start the assault on headquarters, and requested supporting fire. Bekov acknowledged. Mark took a deep breath, then rose from cover in a crouching zigzag run, the fire of battle in his blood. Twenty-five yards on, with the sound of firing ahead signifying that the enemy had sighted them, Mark grew aware of gunfire to his rear. Blue One backing them up.

No, it was too close! He glanced over his shoulder and saw a line of Gurkhas wearing gleeful grins, coming up fast behind them. Where the hell had they sprung from? His heart plummeted to his boots. He had led them all into a trap! The marshals would declare a rout. Oh God, he had blown it. Not just the exercise but his hopes of a commission!

They held an inquest at the end of the day; Captain Bellamy and the other instructors. Blue Two had made a complete cock-up of the vital assault on enemy headquarters. What had gone wrong? Blue One leader said he had spotted the Gurkhas concealed behind a dummy haystack as they began to creep from it. He had warned Blue Two leader to halt his advance and deal with the menace on his flank. The warning had been ignored.

'I gave it twice, sir, then repeated it twice more even when I could see it was too late.' Bekov, muddy, sweating, face smeared with cam cream, looked genuinely troubled. 'Blue Two didn't acknowledge. There wasn't anything more I could do.'

Mark said forcefully, 'I didn't receive the warning. Of course I would have acted on it.'

Bellamy pursed his lips. 'Was your comms system switched off?'

'No, sir, I'd never do that in the middle of an attack.'

'So how was it you didn't hear Blue One's directive?'

Mark stayed silent. He dared not air his suspicions.

Bellamy asked Bekov if he was sure his own comms system was working.

'Very definitely, sir. I was in contact with Blues Three and Four throughout. I received Two's signal that the assault was about to begin, and I acknowledged.'

'Did you hear his acknowledgement?' Bellamy asked Mark.

'Yes, sir. Then I heard nothing more from him.'

'Are you saying your system malfunctioned immediately after that?'

'No, sir, I'm saying I didn't hear the warning to halt, or any info on a threat from the flank,' he asserted doggedly.

'You say you gave it several times?'

'Yes, sir,' said Bekov. 'Carter and Dodsworth can confirm. They were right beside me at the time.'

Bellamy turned once more to Mark. 'Is your system now working?'

Mark swallowed. 'Yes, sir.'

'Yet there appears to have been a major breakdown of communications at the most vital moment. Blue Two would have been slaughtered to a man if this had been for real.'

He laid into the rest of the weary cadets. 'For men with months of training behind them, expecting shortly to be given the privilege of leading troops in future conflicts, you have all put on a pretty tame showing today. If you hope to receive your commissions in two weeks' time, you'd better pull out all the stops from now on.'

The exercise continued for two more days. So did the rain. Mark battled, slogged and cursed with the rest, but his inner spark had died. He knew, he just *knew* Bekov had never transmitted a warning of those hidden Gurkhas. He had lied to the instructors. Carter and Dodsworth might have overheard him say the words but neither would have been able to tell whether or not the message was actually sent. Mark was certain Bekov had switched off his comms system deliberately.

During the final two days on Salisbury Plain Bekov kept smiling his knowing smile, showing he was aware Mark guessed but could do nothing.

Back at Sandhurst, Mark was called for interview. Captain Bellamy told him after a majority vote the instructors had decided to back-term him.

'Most of us agree you're worthy of a commission, Ingham, and that going through the term again will give you more self-assurance. You took our last comments too much to heart and tried too hard during the exercise. Your eagerness to impress overruled your discipline under pressure. I know this will be a disappointment, but the RMA undertakes to produce men ready to take command from the moment they join their regiments. We would be failing both you and your future colleagues if we allowed you to be commissioned too soon.'

It was a severe blow for Mark. He had to explain to his family why they would not be attending the Sovereign's Parade as they had expected. He also had to tell Reena why she would not be coming to the grand Commissioning Ball.

She was furious. 'I've spent bloody nearly three hundred pounds on a gorgeous posh frock for it!'

'You can wear it for the ball in the spring. It won't be wasted,' Mark told her miserably.

It wasn't. She wore it to the ball partnering Leo Bekov, and stood romantically with him beside the lake lit with fairy lights to watch the celebratory fireworks.

Mark spent the night in a shabby B&B bedroom, sick at heart and unable yet to face his disappointed father and cocky step-brother who had no time for 'poncy officers'.

As he walked to his office Mark thought of that conversation with Bekov last night.

'So Reena's walked out on you, Mark.'

'It's you she's walked out on. Not for the first time.'

A derisive laugh. 'You talking about twelve years ago? She was like chewing gum on the sole of my boot; difficult to discard. I knew from the day we met you'd be a runner-up all your life, in spite of your influential family. You're in this regiment when you wanted the Signals. I'm a major; you're still a captain.'

Mark had turned on him. 'And how have you got where you are? How often have you snatched kudos from others by refusing to give vital information? You never transmitted the warning on that exercise, did you?'

The knowing smile. 'Right on the button.'

'I was back-termed because of your lie.'

'I'm surprised they didn't kick you out completely.'

Mark's temper had flared. 'Why, you bastard? I've never understood why you were so vindictive to me.'

The smile turned to cold anger. 'I risked my life to save you on the Brecons. You showed no gratitude, ignored my courage. When Bellamy humiliated me in your presence you failed to support me; wouldn't confess how scared you were before I secured you. I don't forgive, I retaliate. It might take a while, but the opportunity comes.'

'You didn't save my life, the Casevac crew did! Why should I have sung false praises to Bellamy? You were so sure to pass the course, you didn't need help from anyone.'

'I deserved your recognition for the risk I took.'

'You're crazy!

'Survival is for the fittest, Ingham. That's why you'll always be second best. You haven't the guts to ensure you get exactly what you want from life.'

That last taunt had driven Mark to follow when Bekov went off with Judith King. He had retaliation in mind, not forgiveness.

Six

They found a place where Leo Bekov's life might have been so swiftly curtailed. It was a small copse bordering the perimeter road, close to the officers' married quarters and used by families for dog-walking, jogging and children's picnics. There were defined paths between the trees, and wooden-benched tables in clearings. The ideal spot for a nocturnal winter killing. And it was near enough to Mark Ingham's house to fit the tight timing.

After searching for two hours, one of the team came upon a button cut from the victim's jacket. The search was then concentrated on a smaller area, where the cartridge case was soon found. Undergrowth had been trampled around one of the picnic tables, and fibres were found on its rough edges. These would be compared with Bekov's clothes, his hair and the traces of jute on his jacket. DNA tests would reveal whether any of this evidence had come from the killers. No one doubted two people had been involved.

Tom drove across to check his team's findings. Mist still hung between bare, dripping trees, the gloom somehow echoing the last shocking moments of a man's life just a few hours earlier. Time had anaesthetized Tom's reactions to murder, yet he now suffered momentary empathy for someone Nemesis had descended on so fortuitously. Had Bekov been aware of why retribution was suddenly being dealt him in this foreign copse, or had hooding added to his punishment?

The police team was still combing the area for evidence. Tom hoped they would find the sack used to render the victim helpless, although the killers almost certainly disposed of it after transporting the body to where they put it up on display. That sack would provide excellent DNA, and it would reveal whether or not Bekov had died ignorant of the identity of his assailants. Had the blindfold replaced the hood before the fatal shot was fired? The covering of the eyes seemed significant to Tom; it strengthened his conviction that the Anglo-Russian had looked at another man's woman. Done a damned sight more than look, of course, but if they were considering symbolism in this murder that was surely as good an example as Max's firing-squad theory.

Feeling his feet turning numb from standing too long in the long wet grass, Tom detailed his two women sergeants, Connie Bush and Heather Johnson, to interview the girl who had supposedly almost choked on a cough sweet, and to check on the emergency treatment book in the surgery. The MO would hardly lie about something so easy to confirm, but he had seemed surprisingly shaken by a death; something a doctor should be used to.

Returning to the Land Rover, Tom telephoned Max with an update, then returned eagerly to his laptop. By the middle of the afternoon he was beginning to feel the familiar glow that came with the results of research narrowing a wide-open field of suspects to just a few. Whatever the truth behind the manner of this killing, Tom supported the belief that it had been committed by someone who had known the victim from the past. WAMI had produced three. Mark Ingham they already knew about. The MO, Jeremy Fielding, had been in the Gulf at the same time as Bekov, and last night's Duty Officer had served in Bosnia during the same period as the victim.

Peter Randolph and Fielding could have moved about freely last night without arousing suspicion. Both had had legitimate cause for doing so. The MO had been reluctant to confirm when he had returned to his quarter after attending the girl with the sweet stuck in her throat. Tom had not yet encountered Captain Randolph; he would learn his boss's assessment of him when they met for their résumé of the day's investigations.

He considered the three men. Two had

wives Bekov might have seduced. The bachelor Randolph could have lost a woman to him. Naked gymnastics! Tom knew his Nora would merely raise an eyebrow at the notion, but a fair number of women would be titillated by it ... and by any other erotic practices the half-Russian officer had pursued.

There was no regimental link to chase. The dead man had been commissioned into the Intelligence Corps. Ingham had not served with Bekov since leaving Sandhurst. A long time to wait for revenge, unless their paths had crossed briefly and aggressively in the interim. The MO had run a Casualty Clearing Station during the Gulf conflict. Had Bekov been a patient of his? Maybe the Doc had fancied a nurse who showed him she preferred sexual athletes to 'poultice wallopers'. Was that enough to warrant murder? Yes, lust drove men to extremes. But rarely once the passion cooled.

Of the three, Randolph had been most recently in Bekov's vicinity. Bosnia! Stressful, demanding, traumatic. 'Conduct unbecoming' could have gone unpunished there. He needed to meet Randolph, size him up. The same with Judith King. Women could be wilier than men; could lie more easily. They began as children: He hit me! He took my sweeties! He trod on my dolly and broke her arm! Accompanied by tears, these fibs brought cuddles, more sweets and a new Sindy to replace one whose novelty had faded. Tom had three daughters. He knew!

The jingle of his mobile interrupted these thoughts. He took it up. 'Sar'nt Major Black.'

'Tom, I want to talk to Captain Ingham's wife and the friend she spent last night with. He reckons they'll confirm his alibi. Then we'll call on Mrs Fielding. Pick me up here in ten.'

'Will do, sir.'

Tom disconnected his laptop and took it out to the Land Rover. If Fielding and Ingham had watertight alibis, things did not look good for Captain Randolph. On the other hand, the firing-squad angle might be too fanciful. Maybe things had simply got out of hand last night. Wine had been flowing, tempers became inflamed. Bang!

As Max climbed in beside him, Tom said, 'If your theory's right, the ladies we're about to interview could leave us with one strong suspect. Or is that too much to hope for?'

'Probably. Unfortunately, the word of a man's wife is very unreliable as evidence. Captain Ingham lied about his movements last night. Mrs Ingham will doubtless do the same. I shall concentrate on her friend. This first call is a formality.'

Reena Ingham wore too much makeup and too little clothing for a raw February day. The central heating was on full blast to compensate. Tom had met a number of wives like her. Petulant, bored; had entered the marriage willingly but hated the demands of army life. They frequently drove their husbands out of the profession they loved, or into the arms of someone more understanding. He could see the attraction here, though. Long blonde hair, curves where they should be, saucer eyes. Right now they were puffy and slightly bloodshot, as if she had been having a good weeping session. Knowing what her husband had said during his interview, Tom assumed the tears were the result of the quarrel that had driven her from the house last night.

She put on a bright smile for them. 'Mark said you'd be calling. Come in.'

They followed her through to the sitting room. Basic, colourless, it lacked the personal touch. No photographs or flowers, few ornaments, plain cushions and lampshades. She was clearly no homemaker. Or maybe she felt vibrant enough to enhance any room.

Waving her hand at the settee, she said, 'How about a drink? Scotch, G and T, beer?'

Neither man sat. 'This isn't a social call, Mrs Ingham. We simply want to ask you a few questions. Won't take more than a minute or two.'

Rydal's formal words left her untouched. She flopped into a chair and took up a glass containing a drink she had already started. 'Ask away, gentlemen. Don't mind if I finish this, do you?' She crossed her legs so that her short skirt slid further up her thighs. 'Wives aren't invited to their bloody formal dinner nights, so we have to have our own drinkies sessions.'

Tom realized she was three parts sozzled. Must have been some row the couple had.

Although, from the lascivious way she was eyeing him, it did not appear to have sapped her self-confidence. Receiving an optical nudge from Max, he opened the interview.

'Your husband told us you had decided to stay with Mrs Foyle last night after a quarrel. Would you tell us the cause of it, ma'am?'

She tossed back the rest of her drink, then got up to pour another from the bottle on the sideboard. Returning to her chair with a full glass, she took a long gulp before fixing them with a glassy look.

'Oasis were giving a concert. A one-night stand.' Her voice rose. 'On the same bloody night as their bloody celebration of something that happened a hundred bloody years ago! The army decides what we can and can't bloody do. Mark accepts it all; their stupid rules and regulations. If they told him to put his head in the oven and light the gas he'd do it!'

'So you had a row with your husband over the pop concert?' Tom prompted. 'And decided to stay with your friend to allow the situation to cool?'

'That's zackly it.' She giggled. 'You're smart, you know. You catch on quickly.'

'It didn't worry you that your husband had offered hospitality to an officer in transit?' asked Max.

'*Offered?* That's a laugh! The bloody army said he had to have him here, and Mark hadn't the guts to say no.'

'Why would he want to refuse, Mrs

114

Ingham?'

'Why?' It seemed to take her by surprise. 'Why? Well, he couldn't stand bloody Bekov, could he? Not after what happened at Sandhurst.'

'And what was that?'

Tardily realizing she had said too much, Reena Ingham buried her nose in her glass and drank noisily. Then she looked up with a sly smile. 'Mark was sorry afterwards. Soon as the dinner ended he came here ... No, came to *Jane's*, and told me it was all his fault. The lot! He's going to give me a week at the health farm after all. Isn't it sweet of him?'

Tom asked: 'What time did your husband arrive at your friend's house, ma'am?'

The saucer eyes became tea plates. 'When the dinner ended, I s'pose. How do I know? I was asleep, wasn't I.'

'Not sitting up chatting with Mrs Foyle?' put in Max.

She was silent for so long Tom thought she was refusing to answer. Then she got unsteadily to her feet. 'Look, he came to Jane's to 'pologize. Told me he was a mean beast. Would I forgive him? Give me anything I wanted if I did. Even the health farm, he said. Bugger the new car; go to the farm. So ... I'm going.' She peered mistily at them. 'Sure you won't have a drink?'

'Did your husband sleep at Mrs Foyle's house?' probed Max. 'After you'd forgiven him.'

She gave the sly smile again. 'I wasn't *that*

115

forgiving.'

'So he returned home in the early hours?'

The smile faded. 'Had to get bloody Bekov's breakfast, didn't he!' Her shoulders suddenly drooped; tears welled in her unfocused eyes as she whispered, 'Is he really dead? *Is* he?'

'I'm afraid so, ma'am,' Tom told her quietly, seeing evidence that sex very definitely played a part in this murder. This mixed-up woman had strong feelings for the victim which had been stirred by past encounters. Had the Inghams committed the crime together?

He put the question to his boss when they returned to the Land Rover. 'All that drinking is to cope with guilt ... or even grief. Women can destroy out of revenge, yet still love the victim. What d'you think, sir?'

'We need to know what happened at Sandhurst. Find out the names of the instructors at that time and we'll grill them. If it falls into the category of treachery, cowardice or dishonour, we could have a strong case against those two.'

'You're still going for the firing-squad theory?'

'Absolutely. Let's hear Mrs Foyle's version of last night's fiasco. If she's also knocking back the booze, we may have to add her to the list.'

Jane Foyle was level-headed and business-like. She did not offer even a cup of tea: there was no invitation to sit in the room with Oriental overtones. A set of carved tables, a

116

jade table lamp, embroidered silk pictures, a beautiful Chinese rug. The Foyles had clearly served in Hong Kong at some time. Tom saw evidence of a calm, confident personality in this room, and in the classic sweater and tailored black trousers on the woman they had come to question. Captain Foyle would have unconditional support from his wife. Lucky man! But however had she become a friend of Reena Ingham? Chalk and cheese ran them a close second.

She opened the conversation. 'Murder is always terrible, but when it happens in the midst of one's own close community it seems even more shocking. I didn't know Major Bekov and, so far as I'm aware, neither did my husband. So I can't be of any help with information about him – what he was like, why anyone could be driven to kill him. And in such a manner!'

'We'd like to hear about the events that took place in your house last night, Mrs Foyle.'

Tom wondered at his boss's stiff approach to this elegant woman, until it dawned on him that Jane Foyle was remarkably like Susan Rydal had been. Short dark hair, clear hazel eyes, undeniable style. This must be difficult for him.

Jane Foyle gave a faint smile. 'I'd hardly call them events. Reena Ingham came here asking to stay overnight because she'd had a barney with Mark. He was committed to being in the mess by seven, so they had no time to sort things out.' Her smile broadened slightly. 'On

117

formal occasions the demands of the mess come before anyone and anything, as you'll be well aware. Are you married, Captain Rydal?'

'No.' It sounded bleak.

She continued. 'Reena and I ate a light meal, then watched *Inspector Morse* on TV. We had a nightcap and went to bed shortly before midnight. I sleep fitfully whenever my husband is in Northern Ireland. He was quite severely wounded on patrol six years ago. So I was lying awake at half two when I heard the doorbell. It was so insistent I thought someone had come with bad news. It was a relief to find Mark on the doorstep instead.'

'Was he drunk?'

'Not aggressively so, or I wouldn't have let him in.'

'Did he say why he'd come, ma'am?' asked Tom.

'Of course. He was upset; had been worrying all evening about having to leave the quarrel unresolved. Luckily, Major Bekov told him he had made other sleeping arrangements, so Mark came to sort things out with his wife.'

'And you were tolerant enough to allow him in at that unsocial hour?'

'Captain Rydal, in this curious life we lead, where our husbands can be sent away at a moment's notice, where they can be maimed, blinded, blown apart at any time, it's vital for misunderstandings or quarrels to be ironed out at the earliest opportunity.'

'And was Mrs Ingham eager to talk to her husband in the middle of the night?' asked Tom.

She avoided a direct answer. 'I made coffee for us all, then took mine upstairs to drink while reading, leaving them to make their peace.'

'And did they, ma'am?'

'Apparently. Mrs Ingham looked in to say all was well as she returned to bed.'

'Her husband didn't accompany her?' probed Max Rydal.

'That would have been very bad-mannered, don't you think?'

'Worse than waking you at an ungodly hour?'

'Mark needed to sober up and prepare for a working day. There was also the probability that his house guest would return for the same reasons, and for breakfast. Instead, the poor man had been killed.'

'In the copse close at hand. While you were reading had you heard a sound like a shot, Mrs Foyle?'

'Sorry, no.'

'What time was it when Mrs Ingham told you she had patched up the quarrel with her husband, ma'am?'

'I believe it must have been just after four.'

She was looking from one to the other as they alternated the questioning. It was a tactic they frequently used in the hope of unsettling the witness. Max continued it.

'So he was here for around an hour and a

half?'

'Yes.'

'And when did Mrs Ingham return to her home, ma'am?'

'After breakfast.'

'She didn't feel obliged to go back and cook it for her repentant husband, and their guest?'

'I can't answer for how she felt. You must ask her.' It was calm and unflustered.

Tom tried a new approach. 'When did news of the murder reach you?'

'Captain Ingham came to tell us. He was very upset to learn that Major Bekov had changed his plans again and had been knocking at their door while he had been here mending the quarrel.'

'What time was it then?'

She looked back frankly at Max. 'I've no idea. We were eating breakfast after a very disturbed night, when we heard some shocking news. It didn't occur to me to look at the clock. Would anyone, in similar circumstances?'

'Possibly not.' Max gave a faint smile. 'Thank you, Mrs Foyle, we won't trouble you any longer.' As they all walked along the corridor, he added, 'Mrs Ingham told us you were a great comfort to her. As you said, murder is always terrible. When the victim is someone you knew well it can be devastating. She was still upset about his sudden death when we left her just now.'

'Understandable ... but it *was* twelve years ago. She'll bounce back. She always does.'

It was already growing dark, and Max could see no point in returning to the chilly office set aside for them. 'Home, James,' he announced, getting in the Land Rover. 'Can't do much more here until we've checked data with the rest of the team, and it'll be a bloody sight warmer back at base. We'll stop for coffee and a sandwich en route. That should keep us going until we get a meal.'

Tom sighed. He had been looking forward to a family evening; games with the girls followed by a quiet period with Nora. Fat chance of that now! All the same, this was an intriguing case certain to throw up surprises all the way along.

He glanced at Max as they drove away. 'I wonder how long those two women will remain friends once Mrs Ingham discovers the other let slip the fact that she knew the victim twelve years ago.'

'I'm amazed they are friends. Hardly compatible. Ingham denied his wife's earlier knowledge of Bekov, but I suspect his entire story's fabricated. He bribed his wife with a week at a health farm. I'd like to know how he persuaded Mrs Foyle to cover for him. Her husband's away. Maybe she's playing around and Ingham threatened to tell unless she cooperated.'

'Unlikely. Not a nice woman like her.'

'That nice woman was lying in her teeth, my friend.'

During the sixty-minute drive Max called

Section Headquarters with a directive to get details of instructors and supporting staff at Sandhurst for the year Mark had undertaken his training. The reply had been emailed by the time they got back. Scanning the list Max found a name he knew. David Hanson had been in Hong Kong seven years ago when Max had worked on a brutal murder case. WAMI now revealed where the man was presently serving, and within a short time Max was speaking to him at his home in Shropshire. After the usual pleasantries, Max explained why he had called.

'I remember Bekov very well, Max. Excellent all-round candidate. Pretty good at everything. Popular with his peers. Son of a Russian professor of music, he could play a balalaika like a professional. Athletic! My God, he could leap around like those Cossack dancers that come over here on tour.'

'Why wasn't he awarded the Sword of Honour, if he was so bloody marvellous?'

'Because he knew far too well that he was.'

'Ah!'

'The other man you mentioned; give me the name again.'

'Mark Ingham.'

'Ingham? Yes ... of course, should have got it first time. We back-termed him two weeks before commissioning. Bright chap. Came from an influential family. Had money. The family, I mean.'

'The reason for the back-terming?'

'You're asking me to cast my mind back

122

twelve, thirteen years,' he protested.

'Didn't seem a problem with Leo Bekov.'

A short laugh. 'Not a man you'd easily forget. Why d'you want this info, by the way?'

'He was murdered in the early hours of this morning.'

'Bloody hell, was he? And Ingham's a suspect? Right, give me a mo to refresh my memory. We didn't back-term very often. It was usually due to illness or injury. Occasionally through a misdemeanour.'

'And Ingham?'

'Yes, got it now. Bit slow to take the lead. Knew what to do, but allowed others to seize command far too often. He was warned to buck his ideas up and he tried too hard. Made a balls-up of an attack during an exercise. Claimed his comms system failed at the vital moment: never received an instruction to halt and deal with enemy advancing from the flank. Pushed on and led his men into—' He broke off and gave a low whistle. 'Would you believe it was Bekov who gave the signal to halt? Swore he'd warned Ingham several times.'

'And Bekov was believed rather than Ingham?'

Hanson must have detected a note of criticism. 'Look, he really wasn't ready. Ingham needed more time to develop his latent talent for command.'

'But it was that episode that prompted the back-terming?'

'*Confirmed* the decision. Max, you're not

suggesting … It was many years ago, for God's sake! Half the British army would be bumped off if men committed murder over something like that. I can think of a few who've dropped me in it over the years.'

'*Moi aussi,* as the Frogs say, but maybe Ingham's latent talent for command prevailed over this. His wife looks to be part of whatever happened between him and Bekov.'

'A *crime passionelle,* as we're talking Frog?'

'No … but she could have provided the spur into action last night.'

'Well, you've more experience in that area than I have. How was Bekov killed?'

'Shot at close range.' He would not give details of the more bizarre aspect of the case before an official statement had been issued.

'A swift, merciful end,' Hanson mused. 'Still, it's a rotten way to end a military career. Shot by one of your own side rather than the enemy.'

'Whoever shot him *was* the enemy.'

They chatted a few minutes more, then Max thanked him and prepared to disconnect.

'Hold on a mo, just remembered something else,' Hanson said urgently. 'Might give you a bit more on Bekov; the kind of man he was.' He then outlined how Ingham had fallen in the Brecon Beacons. 'Before the Casevac guys arrived, Bekov went down to fix a securing rope around Ingham's ankles. Bloody risky. He was censured for taking unnecessary action, of course. But that was Bekov –

124

flamboyant, extrovert, hogging the limelight. All the same, it took guts and could have saved Ingham from slipping in those minutes before the helo arrived. I wouldn't have had the nerve to do it.'

Max caught up on some routine paperwork before calling one of the duty drivers to take him the short distance to the apartment he had not yet occupied long enough to think of as home. In fact, he had not had a 'home' since Susan was killed. He had immediately put the house they had bought together on the market, auctioned the furniture. Since then he had rented basic accommodation.

The smell of paint greeted him as he opened the front door halfway along a row of similar doors. The apartment had been renovated prior to his arrival, which left it filled with the combined odours of emulsion, putty, unseasoned wood and carpet fresh from a warehouse. The furniture was ultra-modern and virtually featureless, the decor unimaginative. For Max it was merely a place to eat and sleep, so it fulfilled its purpose adequately.

He went straight to the kitchen, where he poured a large whisky, then took a prepared meal from the refrigerator Nora Black had stocked for him and put it in the microwave. He drank deeply while watching it revolving for the required four minutes, took it out, then walked away. He had eaten little all day, but he could not face this concoction.

It was the Foyle woman, of course. So strongly reminiscent of Susan. He returned to the main room taking the whisky bottle with him, and sank on the mock-leather sofa lost in the past. He had been investigating a claim by a sergeant's wife that the local chemist had given her the wrong pills, which led her to collapse in the street. The pharmacist he went to see was a striking, dark-haired young woman with calm manner and a husky voice. He had succumbed there and then. Susan had taken no interest in the six-foot, well-built detective until he had discovered a child had emptied two containers of pills to play with and put them back in the wrong bottles.

They had married three months later and moved into a married quarter at a bleak, wind-blasted military establishment on the east coast. When Max was later posted to Salisbury Plain they had bought a cottage and began collecting antique furniture with delight and enthusiasm for their first real home together. Susan had tackled gardening in a big way, and Max believed his wife to be perfectly fulfilled.

Investigations frequently took him away for several days at a time, and he was often called out at unsocial hours. That had ruined their lovemaking more than once! Had that been behind Susan's search for...? For what? Excitement, danger, *sex*! She could not have been in love with Cairns. Had she merely wanted a bit of rough? Because that was what he was, a big, brash mechanic with audacious eyes and oil beneath his fingernails, who had once fixed her car when it broke down in the camp confines.

Max poured more whisky but it did nothing to anaesthetize the ever-simmering rage, as he recalled returning from Scotland to learn the MO had confirmed that Susan was pregnant. He had been unprepared for the mixture of emotions he felt at the news. Joy, apprehension, *awe*. A small living creature to rear, teach and protect. There had actually been tears in his eyes as he had acknowledged he had everything a man could possibly want.

Brooding well into the night, Max was eventually brought from the past by the slamming of a front door next to his own. Male and female voices laughing, excited. Soon there would be the rhythmic squeak of bed springs on the other side of the bedroom wall, no doubt. Is that all life was about, in the end? Sex!

It was as if he could persuade me to do anything. Judith King could not believe what she had done in the gym with Bekov an hour before he was shot dead. A man who was flamboyant, extrovert, hogging the limelight. Yet he had been popular with his peers, although that Slavic charisma had probably charmed the pants off numerous women. So what could he have done to prompt the ultimate military punishment? It was surely something greater than causing a doubtful cadet to be back-termed. Even so, Mark

Ingham was lying about his own movements last night. Why?

Reena Ingham had known Bekov from twelve years back; she was grieving for him. A former lover? Yet she was now lying for her husband. So was Jane Foyle. If Ingham was not a decisive enough person to commit murder, what had he really been doing during those vital hours? Could he actually have been in his quarters the whole time and not admitted Bekov out of bloody-mindedness? If so, he was unlikely to sleep peacefully for a while.

When Max eventually turned in it was to dream that he was interviewing a woman in a house filled with Oriental treasures, and found the vital witness was really Susan. He awoke sweating, limbs stiff with tension, to see there had been a heavy snowfall overnight prohibiting a further search of the murder scene.

Breakfasting on egg and bacon rolls, with several cups of black coffee, Max drove his own car to Section Headquarters, where he held a progress conference with his team, furthering his knowledge of them in the process. Outlining his theory on the manner of the killing, he received some inscrutable looks that would have done credit to a few Chinese he had encountered in Hong Kong. Well, they would grow accustomed to his gut feelings as time passed.

The autopsy report on Bekov arrived shortly after the meeting broke up. Max studied it.

No real surprises. The bullet wounds and powder burns on the surrounding skin were conducive with a 9mm Browning being the murder weapon. The deceased had imbibed a great deal of alcohol along with a heavy meal before death. He had also been sexually active. There were several fine strands of rope fibres in the semen on his inner thighs. (Naked gymnastics, of course!) Bruises on the knuckles were consistent with heavy contact with a wooden object. Slight bruising on the right toes suggested the deceased had kicked against something hard. (Trying to gain entry to the Ingham quarters!)

More bruises on the upper torso where the victim had been tightly secured to the sign-post, and around the wrists that had been lashed together behind it. In the hair, mouth and nostrils were particles of fibres used in coarse sacking. These matched fibres found on the mess jacket, and upheld the belief that the victim had been hooded with a large sack before death.

Digesting these facts, Max deduced that Bekov had abandoned his attempt to get in the Ingham house; had wandered off so high on alcohol and sexual stimulation he had not known he was being followed. His assailants had come up behind him, pulled the sack over his head and shoulders, then forced him to walk through the copse to be killed in cold blood.

Max felt sure the sack had been removed first. The ritual behind this shooting demanded that the condemned man should face the contempt of those who had found him guilty. It therefore followed that Bekov would have recognized the reason for the retribution. Or had he been too drunk to understand what was happening? Max would only know the answer when he apprehended those who had taken Leo Bekov's life.

On the heels of the autopsy report came another, revealing a totally unexpected angle on a case that was threatening to bring to the surface truths the main players would lie like crazy to keep hidden.

Max now reluctantly conceded that Tom Black might be right in saying sex dominated the motive for killing the Anglo-Russian officer.

Seven

Judith King wore a red tracksuit and white trainers. She had come direct from a physical-training session in response to Max's summons. That she had more colour today was probably due to the exertions of a demanding workout, but there was a bruised look about her eyes that betrayed deep inner turmoil. By God, so there should be, thought Max.

She stood behind the chair in an attitude of impatience. 'I told you all I know yesterday. This is disrupting my programme. Couldn't you have waited until I was free?'

'No. I need immediate answers from you, and I'm not in the mood for another performance like yesterday's. I want the truth at first shot,' he said crisply. 'I'm investigating a murder. That's more important than anyone's programme.'

Her healthy flush began to fade. She sat, facing him across the desk, and said firmly, 'I didn't kill him!'

'I have here the report on the forensic examination of your mess dress. There were traces of the dead man's semen on the skirt, and that of another man. Who else did you

131

have sex with that night?'

Jumping to her feet she said explosively, '*What?* What the hell are you suggesting? That I serviced the entire officers' mess? You bastard! I don't have to take this.'

'It's not a suggestion; there's irrefutable evidence of sexual activity with Major Bekov and a second man that night. Who was he?'

Her eyes narrowed; her mouth twisted. 'We're trained to deal with interrogation. I'm familiar with these humiliating tactics. If you think you can rattle me into confessing to murder, think again. How would I have got him from the copse? How would I have secured him to that post? Answer that!'

'With the help of your second lover.'

After a moment of optical vitriol she turned away. 'I'm not listening to any more of this.'

Max let her get as far as the door. 'You've admitted to having sex and romping naked with the victim. We've a witness who supports that and establishes an approximate time. We have evidence that suggests the murder was executed during an hour for which you have no solid alibi. You say you were asleep in the gym; you can't prove that. Do you understand the predicament you're in, Ms King?'

While she stared back speechlessly, Max waved his hand at the chair. 'I told you I'm in no mood for another performance. This is not a simulation of interrogation by an enemy, it's an investigation into the violent death of a British officer on this base. I suggest you start telling me the truth about your movements that night.'

From the doorway she said, in a voice shaking with emotion, 'It's a mistake.'

'No mistake. Two distinct DNA traces.'

'There *couldn't* be!'

'Are you denying intimacy with another man before or after your interlude with Major Bekov?'

'Of course I'm bloody well denying it!'

'Forensic evidence proves otherwise.'

'*No!*' She began advancing on him. 'No, no, no!'

'You want to protect both your reputations, but he could provide you with an alibi for that vital time. Unless you carried out the murder together.' When she gave no response, he leaned back in his chair and studied her. 'By checking the blood group of everyone on the base we could reduce the possibles to a few hundred. After that we would have to resort to asking for DNA samples. It would take a great deal of time and expense. It would also interfere with the coming NATO exercise everyone's getting geared up for. Colonel Keegan wouldn't be too happy about that. On the other hand, if you give me his name I can interview him right away. Your liaison wouldn't necessarily become public knowledge.'

Gripping the back of the chair, she said carefully, 'There ... was ... no ... other ... man.'

'After Major Bekov left the gym he went to Captain Ingham's quarters. You could have

133

met your lover, followed the Major and killed him. After tying him to the post, the man drove off leaving you to wake the Duty Officer and put on a suitable act to suggest you were in shock. It all ties in very neatly, doesn't it?'

If she was acting now she deserved an Oscar, thought Max as he watched her sink on to the chair to gaze at him in distress. 'I don't understand any of this. It's absurd. Bizarre! I've admitted to acting totally out of character that night. I still can't believe I did what I did.'

'There was no trace of any kind of drug in your blood sample, by the way. High percentage of alcohol, that's all.'

'Oh, God!'

He waited a moment. 'Are you ready to tell me the man's name?'

'There *was* no other man. I'm not a whore,' she said brokenly.

'I've not suggested you are. I'm simply following up on forensic evidence.' This was said more quietly. Max was beginning to believe this young woman was genuinely confused.

'They *have* made a mistake,' she said. 'I swear there was no one else. I'm getting married in June. That business with ... I told you, since meeting Peter there's been no one. It was a one-off. Madness of some kind. I know I can't prove I was in the gym until just before four, but I woke on that trampoline feeling ill and icy cold. I pulled on my clothes, headed

134

for my room ... and found *that*.'

'*Him*,' Max corrected automatically, his mind dabbling with vague theories.

'Look, if you do what you threaten – check every man – the truth would emerge. I'd lose everything,' she said urgently. 'Colonel Keegan would relish the chance to slag me off. So would a few more I could name. My career would go downhill fast, I'd be the target of any man who thought I dropped my knickers on request. The army is a close-knit family. Things get around. You know that. I'd be driven to resign my commission. Worst of all, I'd lose Peter.'

'He wouldn't stand by you?'

'In his place, would you?' She gave a deep sigh. 'How can I convince you I'm telling the truth. I had sex with Leo Bekov. That's all.'

The strands of several ideas began to meld, and he checked his files. 'You said in the first interview he wanted a second session. "I tried to stop him but I felt woozy and weak",' he quoted, then glanced up at her. 'When I asked if he raped you, you chose not to reply. Would you care to now?'

She shook her head, looking utterly miserable.

'It wasn't rape? You didn't try to stop him?'

She shrugged. 'He didn't overpower me. I was just so tired and giddy after leaping and swinging on the ropes, I was half asleep when he suggested it.'

'You didn't actually say no?'

'I don't know. Can't remember much about

it,' she conceded wearily. 'Don't remember him getting dressed and leaving, so I must have fallen asleep in the middle of it. I think I gave him a bit of a push at one stage; thought he was getting a bit too enthusiastic. But the drink and gymnastics had put me out for the count.'

Max paused fractionally before sounding her out. 'Is it possible that another person could have had sex with you while you were in that state?'

Her head jerked up. *'What?'*

'Are you certain it was Major Bekov both times?'

'Of course,' she said hotly. 'We'd been trampolining and fell in a heap. We were laughing. Then he said something about not wasting it.'

Max did not have to ask what that meant. He was ready to conclude the interview; wanted to pursue his theory. Judith King was looking haggard. He would get nothing useful from her with further questions.

'That's all for now. I may need to speak to you again later.'

She did not get up immediately; seemed confused by the abrupt dismissal. 'What about those DNA samples?'

'I'll put that on hold while I investigate further.'

'I see. Right.' She stood. 'You'll let me know if you're going to do it? Tell me before you start?'

Max nodded. 'I wish you'd play equally

136

straight with me.'

'I have. There was no other man, and I didn't kill Leo. I just wish he'd never come here.'

The moment she left, Max rang Tom Black. 'That MT corporal – the voyeur. Get hold of him pronto and bring him here. He has some explaining to do.'

He disconnected and reread the statement made by Gary Mitchum, his anger rising further. Then he got up and stood gazing blindly from the window. In the distance a drill squad was rehearsing for a ceremonial parade; trucks, Land Rovers and groups of lively soldiers passed along the road outside. All Max saw was his CO and the Padre walking up the path to his office to tell him his wife had been killed alongside Corporal Cairns, who had apparently offered her a lift during the flash storm.

The unborn boy child had also been killed. Alexander Rydal. They had already decided on his name. The active foetus they had seen on the scanner had had no identifying features; no way of telling if he should rightly be called Alexander Cairns. No way of ever telling now. DNA would have settled the question. Had he been a fool over that? Would certainty have been a greater torment than this unending doubt?

A knock on the door broke his intro-spection. Tom Black entered to say he had the NCO witness outside. 'Something new emerged, sir?'

'Ms King swears Major Bekov was her only partner that night. I believe she's certain she's telling the truth.'

Tom looked puzzled. 'Not sure what you're getting at.'

'If I'm right about this, she has grounds for a charge of rape.'

The penny dropped. 'The other man did it without her knowledge?'

'While she was so drunk she had no idea it wasn't the same man throughout.'

Tom nodded. 'That would constitute rape. Almost impossible to prove, though.'

'Agreed. She's unlikely to pursue it in court, even if we get a confession.'

'From Corporal Mitchum? No, sir, I can't see it. Wouldn't treat a woman that way. He was very low-key about what he says he saw going on. Only came forward because Major Bekov was killed soon after. So far as I know he hasn't spread the tale around.'

'He wouldn't if he took part in it. Wheel him in. We'll hear his defence then settle the question with DNA,' Max said unequivocally.

Gary Mitchum was in his mechanic's overalls and beret. He halted with a great stamp of boots, saluted and quoted his name, rank and number.

Max was irritated, not only by this but because he saw a young man who looked supremely unlikely to have done what was suspected. Over the years Max had learned to recognize types. This fresh-faced, well-spoken vicar's son was non-aggressive; would almost certainly be happier driving and repairing vehicles than toting an SA80. So what was he doing in the army?

'No need for name, rank and number. You're not on a charge, Corporal,' he told him. 'There are a few points arising from your statement that I need to clear with you. Sit down.'

'Yes sir.' His fair skin turned pink; he perched on the very edge of the chair.

'You said you left the gymnasium on the night before last *when things began to get private*. By that you meant when the couple began to have sex?'

The blush deepened. 'It seemed that way, sir.'

'Why go? You'd watched them romping around naked. Enough to make any healthy young man very excited, I'd have thought. Excited enough to want to watch the rest. Watch, and imagine himself in Major Bekov's place.'

Corporal Mitchum's cheeks grew as red as peonies. 'I'm not like that, sir.'

'Why? Are you gay?'

'*No*, sir.'

'Yet you didn't respond like a normal red-blooded, twenty-two-year-old male while secretly watching erotic sexual behaviour?'

'I wasn't *secretly watching*, sir.' It was a protest.

'You told them you were there?'

'Of course not. I heard voices in the gym and thought I should check it out. Maybe tell

139

the Duty Sergeant. That's the only reason I went in.'

'And you stayed because you'd never before seen Ms King without clothes on and you couldn't take your eyes off her. Do you fancy her?'

The Corporal's blue eyes avoided direct contact for the first time.

'Answer the officer's question, Corporal Mitchum,' said Tom with a gentleness that told Max he did not approve of the way the interview was going.

Looking at his hands linked in his lap, Gary Mitchum mumbled, 'She's a nice person. Friendly. Treats everyone the same.'

Max went for the kill. 'And you wanted her to do that in the gymnasium. Did you stay there watching until Major Bekov dressed and departed, leaving Ms King asleep on the trampoline? Did you then go to her and demand the same as she'd given him?'

Mitchum's head jerked up. The colour had drained from his cheeks; there was anger in his eyes. 'I'd never do anything like that. *Never.* Ask anyone, sir. I wish I'd never gone in there. I wish I'd not come forward to say I'd seen the Major just before he was killed. Never thought I'd be accused of something like this.'

'You've not been accused of anything. You were asked if that's what you did, and you've denied it.' Max leaned back to regard him shrewdly. 'Do you object to giving my team a DNA sample?'

'No, sir.' It was immediate, confident.

Tom Black said: 'Right, that's all, Corporal Mitchum.'

When they were alone Max turned to the man beside him and grimaced. 'Save me from saintly corporals! Now we're right up the creek without a paddle.'

Jeremy Fielding was stressed to the hilt. The SIB team had checked with Lance-Corporal Myers that she had been treated for an obstruction in her throat. They had also checked the time logged in the admissions book. Reena and Jane had been questioned yesterday to confirm Mark's statement, so why hadn't they visited Jeannie?

Leaving the surgery in the early hours of that terrible night, Jeremy had driven along empty roads to his destination. He was certain no one had seen him. It was on his return to his quarters much later that it worried him. He had been so worked up, could he have passed someone without noticing? At that hour it was surely unlikely, yet Judy King had been out then.

Mess gossip about her was rife. Her detractors had secretly dubbed her 'the black widow', as in the female spider which kills its mate, because it was universally agreed she surely had sex with Leo Bekov that night. And then what? Much as he liked Judy, Jeremy was too desperate to concern himself with her problems. His own were threatening to break his future irrevocably.

When he had eventually returned home that night, Jeannie was practically hysterical, sitting on a chair gazing in horror at Briony lying in a mess of diarrhoea in her cot. The child's harrassed activity meant she was covered in liquid excreta. She was shrieking in great distress. Jeannie had rushed to cling to him, demanding to know why he had left her alone all night. His control had snapped. For several mad moments he considered ridding himself of these unbearable burdens: strangling Jeannie and smothering the screaming, stinking baby with a pillow. Sanity had prevailed. A tranquillizer for his loathsome wife; warm water, a clean pad and sleepsuit for the little girl.

In the resulting blessed silence he had had to face the bleak facts. Seeing Leo again had brought things to a head. It had been a terrible shock to learn he would overnight at the base, and attend the dinner. Jeremy had prayed for a medical emergency that would save him from being there, but the call-out had come too late.

After a gap of ten years he had come face to face with a man he would never forget, and Leo had ignored him. Walked past as if they were strangers! But all through that evening he had smiled his provocative smile whenever their glances met, telling Jeremy he well remembered the desert and could break his silence any time.

When Peter Randolph had called him out later, to certify a death, Jeremy had then to stage the performance of his life. He had known he needed Jeannie as never before. She *must* cover for him.

The SIB team had arrived soon after nine this morning. It was now almost lunchtime. Had they already lined someone up for the murder? Was there a chance they would show no interest in him, despite Rydal's probing questions on his movements over breakfast in the Harkness house yesterday?

Restless, worried, he abandoned his case notes, picked up his cap and headed for his house. Briony was with Alice Foster again today. The sergeant's wife who used to be a nursery nurse loved having the baby, and what Jeremy paid her went towards her fund to set up a nursery school when she returned to England. She was a godsend, but it was no solution. Jeannie must be made to care for her child. Once this present crisis was resolved he would take steps to deal with the problem. For now, his main concern was that she would lie with conviction when they questioned her. Why were they taking so long?

When he saw a Land Rover parked in the snow right outside the house his heart raced. Had Jeannie already landed him in it? He had rehearsed her again at breakfast, but if she quoted it parrot-fashion she would fool no one.

It appeared Rydal and his deputy had only just arrived, because Jeannie was offering them coffee in her best hostess manner when Jeremy walked down the hall to the sitting room. Before they could reply, she looked up and smiled. 'Jerry, you're early! How nice. Captain Rydal and Mr Black would like to ask us some questions about the murder. I've already told them I didn't know Major Bekov, but that you did.'

'Why on earth did you say that?' he asked sharply.

'You were talking on the phone last week to someone, and I heard you say Leo Bekov was the last man you ever wanted to see again. I only remembered that when Captain Rydal mentioned the victim's name.'

She could be so bloody normal when Briony was out of the house. In a blue wool dress, with her hair caught back in a fancy clip, no one would equate this classy-looking girl with the hysterical slut she was most of the time. She had just dropped a bombshell proving she eavesdropped on his private calls. Dear God, what else had she overheard?

Max Rydal turned to him. 'We already know you both served during the Gulf War and could have met up. Will you explain why you were loath to renew the acquaintance, Doctor?'

Seething, Jeremy said: 'He was brought in to me after a "friendly fire" incident on the Iraqi border, suffering from shock and hypothermia. Nothing serious. He was very young and fit, but he piled on the agony to prevent being discharged when he should have been.

144

Typical malingerer! Enjoyed being the centre of attention. I've no time for men like that. But he was a crafty devil; managed to get away with anything.'

'Not this time.'

'No. Well ... I'm afraid that's all I can tell you about him.' He glanced at Jeannie. 'Is lunch near enough ready?' Turning back to the detectives, he explained. 'I hold a pre-natal clinic on Thursday afternoons. Makes it a bit of a rush.'

Rydal did not take the hint and leave. 'We can get through this fairly swiftly. We have corroboration from those concerned with the emergency you dealt with. The Duty Orderly says you told him to keep the girl in for the rest of the night, then left shortly after 02:00. Then Captain Randolph called you out again at 04:10 to certify that the man Ms King discovered was dead. Where were you between leaving the surgery and that call?'

'Here. I told you that yesterday.'

'But you couldn't say what time you got back.'

'I explained why.' He turned to Jeannie with a silent prayer. 'Did you notice the time, darling?'

'It was four fifteen.'

'No! That was when I went out,' he corrected forcefully. 'What was the time when I came in?'

'Yes. Sorry, Jerry, I got muddled. I remember it now. I looked at the clock and saw that it was two fifteen,' she recited.

145

She had blown it!

Rydal pounced. 'You happened to look at the clock even though you were very distressed because the baby wouldn't stop crying, and you'd been up all night?'

Jeannie fell for it. 'All it does is scream and scream. When Jerry's not here I don't know what to *do*.' Her voice was adopting the familiar whine; her personality was rapidly changing. 'He has so many long night calls. It's not fair. I need him with me. I can't cope with it all alone. He knows that. I keep asking him to get an assistant for the night calls, but he says the army won't wear it.'

Into the brief silence, Sergeant Major Black said quietly, 'You offered us coffee, ma'am. Can I give you a hand in the kitchen?'

'Oh ... yes ... coffee.' Jeannie returned to being the polite hostess as if a switch had been tripped. 'That's very thoughtful of you.'

They walked through to the kitchen, and Jeremy braced himself. He was now in one hell of a fix. He should have left Jeannie out of it and stuck to his original story that the situation was too stressful to record exact timing. Why couldn't Rydal accept that? Truth was, he had just had time to sedate Jeannie and clean up the baby before Peter Randolph had summoned him to view Bekov's body. Thank God he had got back in time to field that call or the situation would be even stickier right now.

'Why did you instruct your wife to lie for you, Doctor?'

He trod carefully. 'She's suffering from post-natal depression. Gets very anxious when I'm not here. The obligatory dinner and two emergency calls meant I was away a lot that night, and she keeps insisting I didn't return from the mess until four fifteen. That was when I left again to examine the body, of course. Knowing one of your team was likely to question her, I tried to straighten her out, that's all.'

'So you did notice the time when you returned from the surgery?'

'No. As I said yesterday, it was like all hell let loose here when I got in. But I left there about 02:00 and it normally takes fifteen minutes or so to get here.'

'So how long did it take you the night before last?'

Jeremy felt his temper rising. 'The usual time. I didn't kill Leo Bekov, you know.'

'Has anyone suggested you did?'

'Why else would you keep on and on about timings?'

'These numerous night calls you get. Is that usual?'

His heart began to thump with anxiety. What was he getting at now? 'My wife tends to exaggerate. They're the normal accidents, drunken punch-ups you get in any military establishment.' He tried a light laugh. 'Silly girls sucking sweets in bed and damn near choking.'

'Maybe your wife thought that an unlikely tale. Is she inclined to be jealous? I believe some women after giving birth lose their self-confidence and suspect their husbands of straying.'

He was thrown. What was Rydal hinting? It was impossible to read him. An intense man: dark hair, eyes as uncompromising as the grey-green Atlantic, tight mouth. Dangerous! Jeremy decided to pass on that oblique question.

'Are you?'

'Am I what?'

'Straying?'

To cover his rising nervousness Jeremy walked to a chair and flopped into it, forcing another light laugh. 'You're joking, of course. I'm struggling to deal with a sick wife, and a tiny daughter. You've no idea of the chaos a baby can create during its first months of life.'

Rydal's mouth tightened further, setting Jeremy wondering what the hell the man had read into that. 'Seems quiet enough now.'

'The baby's with Sergeant Foster's wife. She's a trained child nurse. Jeannie needed a break.'

'Don't you need one? Some light relief, at least.'

Oh God, he was back to that! 'I'm due long leave next month. Thinking of Spain. Chill out.'

'Won't you be merely relocating the chaos? Or are you planning to leave your wife and child here?'

'No. A change of scene will probably sort everything out,' he said with assumed confidence, although the change of scene he planned for Jeannie was the psychiatric wing of the military hospital. He would head for a destination more isolated and tropical than Spain. And not alone!

'Look, I need to eat if I'm to get any lunch before taking the clinic. There's really nothing useful I can contribute,' he said, again hinting that the man should leave.

Rydal did not budge. 'Oh, but there is. Ms King believed her drinks had been spiked, because she felt so ill after leaving the mess. The blood sample you took showed a very high alcohol content; enough to make even a tough squaddie soft-kneed, I'd say. When you saw her after confirming that Major Bekov was dead, what state was she in? "Shocked", you said earlier. Does that mean dumbstruck, unaware of your presence; or babbling in-coherently? Was she still vomiting; trembling, tearful, aggressive, defensive?'

Jeremy tried to hide his annoyance. 'Bekov was dead. Her reaction to the fact surely has no relevance.'

'Just answer the question, please.'

He gave a hefty sigh. 'She was hypothermic, withdrawn, curled into the foetal position beneath her duvet and resistant to my per-suasion. As I said, *in shock*,' he added with emphasis.

Rydal clearly had a thick skin. He con-tinued unabashed. 'Yet you managed to administer a tranquillizer.'

'I held out diazepam and a glass of water.

149

She took them automatically.'

'She trusts you?'

Jeremy frowned. 'Why wouldn't she?'

'How well do you know her, Doctor?'

'Sorry?'

'You're concerned with medical health, she's promoting physical health. You must liaise quite frequently; have common professional interests. How about your personal interests?'

Seeing the way this man's mind was working, Jeremy was about to reply when he made a sudden about turn. This could work to his advantage. 'We're both country and western music aficionados. Jeannie's into Brahms and Mozart; not my scene at all. And I suppose Judy and I are cuckoos in the nest.' He forced a smile. 'Not pukka members of the regiment whose mess we use.'

'She's engaged. Wedding in June, I understand.'

'That's right. He's in Brunei.'

'Out of sight, out of mind! When I suggested she could have been returning from an assignation when she came upon the body, you claimed it was a ridiculous assumption. Quite heatedly, as I recall.'

'Because Judy's not that type.'

'You have proof of that?'

'Now, look...'

'Any notion of what she *had* been doing?'

He was growing really irritated. 'Haven't you asked her?'

'Oh, yes.'

150

'And?'

'And I'd like your input.'

'I haven't any, and I'd be glad if you'd leave me to have my lunch. I'll be cutting things really fine now.'

Jeannie came in at that moment carrying a plate of biscuits, followed by Sergeant Major Black with a tray bearing a cafetiere and their second-best china.

'Sorry we've been so long,' Jeannie said with winning charm. 'We were distracted by the antics of two red squirrels in the snow, weren't we, Mr Black? Such a pity the greys drove them out of England. They're so much the prettier.'

'I'm afraid we have to move on, Mrs Fielding,' said Rydal. 'Your husband is running late. I'm sure he'll appreciate the coffee after his hurried lunch.' He glanced across at Jeremy. 'Are you willing to provide us with a DNA sample, Doctor?'

His heart suddenly raced. 'For what purpose?'

The detective gave what masqueraded as a reassuring smile. 'Elimination. We shall be asking the same of anyone who previously served with Major Bekov and who was moving about the base after the regimental dinner. I'll send one of my team along to your surgery. That's assuming we have your go-ahead.'

He left with his deputy before Jeremy could say yea or nay.

Jeannie chattered brightly while he hastily

151

consumed tinned pea soup and several ham and tomato baps. He heard none of her words because his mind was uneasily elsewhere. Rydal thought he lusted after Judy. Fine! He had given the man veiled encouragement on that score, but the request for a DNA sample had set alarm bells ringing.

Why the emphasis on men who had previously served with Leo? Surely he had not left documents to be read in the event of his death. No, it was too soon for that, even if they existed. Max Rydal was shrewd, foxy. Yet there was no way he could learn about what had taken place in the desert just over ten years ago. Was there?

Eight

Tropical sunsets were reputed to be incomparable, but watching the day end in the desert was also pretty awesome. For once it made no impression on Jeremy. He was recovering from a shock similar to a hefty punch in the solar plexus, seeing not sundown over rows of tents and an endless stockpile of equipment for war but an amazing dawn.

There had been girls, of course. Medical students were renowned for being lusty, and Jeremy had gone with the flow. Hectic

152

parties, student rags, locking of horns over the currently desired 'hind'. It had been vital to give hormones their head; satisfying release from the stress of intense study.

Joining the army had freed him from the alternative of general practice. During the first eighteen months in a military hospital he had settled happily in his mainly masculine world. Being in a battle zone was exciting. Living and working among men engaged in the demanding business of waging war offered a 'high' his civilian counterparts would never experience. Now, at the age of twenty-five, dormant desires had awoken. With a vengeance!

This morning Casevac had flown in with a young Intelligence Corps subaltern who had been trapped all night beneath an overturned Land Rover. Lieutenant Leo Bekov was hypothermic, exhausted and lucky to be alive. One of the paramedics who brought him in had given Jeremy what they knew of the accident.

'He was on a covert mission along the border, sir. I Corps bods get up to all manner of tricks no one's supposed to know about. The Yanks certainly didn't. One of their helos shot 'em up. Bloody Yanks! Trigger happy, some of 'em! Anything moves in a question-mark zone at night, they don't wait to give the benefit of doubt. The driver copped it. Mr Bekov was pinned down under the vehicle. Lucky for him he was in the seat well or he'd have been crushed. As it was, the wheel was pressing so hard against his chest he couldn't reach his SARBE to activate it. Seems he spent all night scooping at the soft sand with his fingers and heels, shifting his position inch by inch, until he could reach across for his rescue beacon. His unit sent us out for him soon as they got his signal.' He had grinned. 'A very tenacious individual, I'd say. The sort who could find a bloody needle in a haystack after everyone else had given up.'

The Intelligence major who had gone out with the Casevac helicopter attempted to debrief the patient on their arrival at this Casualty Clearing Station, but he had fallen asleep. Or pretended to!

'He may have vital information that could influence our strategy. I need to hear it. Urgently, Doctor!'

Major Carpenter had looked set to stay beside the bed. Irked by the man's superior attitude, Jeremy had moved him on.

'You're welcome to wait outside on the sand for as long as you wish, but my staff have little enough room here without healthy bodies getting in their way. And since a vast army has been sitting around for weeks without decisive action, I doubt one of your junior officers will be instrumental in getting it up off its backside overnight, Major.'

So Jeremy was put under strict orders to call Carpenter as soon as the patient surfaced from his sleep of exhaustion and exposure to the bitter night temperature. It lasted for eight hours. Thirty minutes ago he had

154

opened his eyes and requested a urine bottle most urgently. Jeremy had been alerted and left the writing-up of case notes to enter the small ward.

'Hallo, you look more lively now,' he greeted with a smile. 'You've caused a stir among your colleagues. Major Carpenter believes you may hold the key to launch our land offensive.'

'The name's Bekov, not Schwarzkopf.' He grinned. 'Tell you what, Doc, before I launch the invasion I could murder a good square meal.'

In that moment, gazing down at a tanned face darkened by stubble, and glowing black eyes, the scales had fallen from Jeremy's own. So here he was, in the purple-rose shadow of dusk, trying to accept that he had just fallen in love. The fast-dropping temperature set him shivering. He was in a fever: outer chill, inner burning. He had never suspected this wayward gene. It had not manifested itself before. Relationships had been straightforward, although he had always been happiest in male company. Girls had been there for sex, nothing more. Not one of them had aroused the powerful attraction he presently felt.

He prayed he had acted normally; hoped desperately there had been no sign of his emotional turmoil as he checked out his patient before informing Giles Carpenter he could come over. The Major was there now, asking questions while Bekov tucked into soup and a hearty omelette. Jeremy felt ridiculously jealous of Carpenter. Dear God, how must he handle this?

Jeremy slept little. Well used to the constant thunder of aircraft on bombing raids, he usually found no difficulty in dropping off. It did not disturb him that night; he was kept awake by excitement and apprehension.

After Carpenter departed, Jeremy had sat talking to Leo Bekov for an hour or more. The patient was disinclined to settle for sleep again so soon, and it was perfectly natural for the two officers to engage in personal conversation. Working with a sergeant and two lance-corporal orderlies, Jeremy welcomed commissioned patients he could relax with for a while. They were never there long enough for him to get to know them well. He gave emergency treatment before onwarding them to a field hospital, or back to their unit if the problem was only minor. In Bekov's case the normal procedure would be to discharge him in the morning with orders not to resume full duties for two days.

Jeremy already knew he intended to keep him for a further twenty-four hours. The difficulty was how to prevent his staff seeing through whatever pretext he came up with. No matter. He *had* to spend more time with the Anglo-Russian. There was already a satisfying rapport between them; a further day could provide the foundation for an ongoing friendship. They were the same age and had discovered several similar interests. Chess, cryptic puzzles and fishing – the only sport Jeremy had any interest in, although the other man loved every aspect of it. Jeremy had confessed to a passion for country and western music, impulsively adding that he had bought a guitar in his teens.

'Strummed at it endlessly, doing Willie Nelson impersonations and driving everyone in the vicinity spare. Thought I was Grand Ole Opry material.'

'My father's a professor of music. Taught me to play the balalaika. Goes everywhere with me. You still got your guitar? We could play a duet.'

'It's in my parents' attic somewhere,' he had said regretfully, recognizing a missed opportunity. 'Tell me about the balalaika.'

So Jeremy had sat there in the low yellow light, falling deeper and deeper beneath the spell of a man who seemed dynamic even in the wake of a narrow escape from American bullets on the lonely sands. Now he was in bed remembering every moment with Leo and fighting the twin tugs of common sense and desire, knowing which he would allow to win.

With his sleep pattern disturbed, Leo did not wake until late morning, which gave Jeremy the excuse to keep him until the following day. The staff had little to do. Patients were thin on the ground, as yet. Once the advance into Kuwait began they would be working flat out, although the generals were predicting minimal casualties on the Allied side. Sited as they were near the border, Jeremy guessed they would be treating more enemy wounded than their own.

That day strengthened the bond between the two youthful officers, although the patient remained ignorant of what ailed the doctor. Indeed, the patient was so lively he seemed out of place in the ward. Which meant the staff did not think it strange for Jeremy to invite him to his own quarters to eat dinner brought over from a nearby mess. Leo had persuaded someone to collect his balalaika and, after they had eaten, he began to play. Jeremy then thanked his stars his guitar was in England. Leo produced musical magic that completed his host's downfall.

When the final notes of the haunting Russian folk tunes died away, the sound of clapping made Jeremy aware of a sizeable audience sitting cross-legged on the sand outside his tent. Leo got up, his face alive with elation, and walked to them.

'Sorry, guys, end of performance. I'm a sick man.' He turned a laughing face to Jeremy. 'Aren't I, Doc?'

He was too emotional to reply for a moment or two. 'Yes. That's enough excitement for now.'

'Couldn't you give us a concert, sir?' asked a soldier eagerly. 'DLB would sanction it for sure. He's hot on morale-boosting.'

At that point the next wave of aircraft roared overhead, vibrating their eardrums.

When they had passed, Leo laughed. 'The Yanks have it in for me. If I arranged a concert they'd sure as hell drown me out from start to finish.' He waved as he crossed to the medical tent. *'Do svidanya!'*

An hour after Leo's departure the following morning Jeremy sat at his desk doodling, his mind occupied with how he could see him again. The Intelligence unit was forty-five minutes' drive away. Difficult to claim he had been passing. After half a day struggling with the problem, it dawned on Jeremy there *was* no problem. Men were cadging lifts all the time in order to visit someone in another regiment or unit. A mate. He was making a mountain from a molehill because his fondness for Leo was vastly different from that of a friend. Yet he was the only one who knew, thank God. It was perfectly possible to see him as often as he wished without raising eyebrows.

Over the next three weeks the pair met up frequently, always in some neutral spot because Giles Carpenter heavily discouraged 'outsiders' on his turf.

'Are you really doing top-secret work the whole time?' Jeremy had asked early on, as they drank cold beer in an infantry mess tent where Leo appeared to be welcome. In fact, he was welcomed in most regimental messes, which aroused in Jeremy a jealousy he was ashamed of. Yet he could not deny it.

'Of course we are,' Leo had replied with a

cheeky grin. 'Not for your inquisitive little eyes and ears, Comrade Doctor!'

His frequent teasing made Jeremy long to respond as he would if Leo were a woman – a tweak of his hair, a playful slap on his buttocks. A masterful kiss! Each meeting left Jeremy restless, unable to sleep, dissatisfied with his daily routine. He knew he would be unable to restrain his true feelings much longer.

He tried to analyse Leo's attitude towards him. He liked to provoke the way a lover did; appeared eager to meet up and was never in a hurry to leave. However, they were never alone together for long. Leo seemed to attract people to his side without trying. The balalaika was a great magnet, of course, yet his all-embracing smile was for Jeremy whenever he glanced up from the strings. Hour after hour Jeremy asked himself if Leo could possibly be in love, too. Was he waiting for a sign that would bring his confession? Jeremy held back from giving it for fear of destroying what they now had.

Then everything changed. The invasion got under way. The relatively relaxed scene outside the medical tents became loudly, feverishly mobile. Engines roared into life as lines of parked trucks moved out laden with supplies in support of the spearhead troops. The stacks of ammunition, fuel, vehicle and communications spares, drinking water, protective clothing, emergency first-aid supplies and food had storemen in forklifts swarming around them. Casevac trucks conspicuously marked as ambulances were fuelled up ready to go. Relentless waves of bombers continued to fill the sky above it all.

Jeremy stood with his three-man team watching the start of a mammoth invasion of an occupied country; a country that was mostly barren desert dotted with oil wells. The general opinion was that the Iraqi army had been so decimated by the air bombardment, the Allies would race through to Kuwait City meeting little resistance. No one but the politicians and generals knew what would happen when the tanks reached the Iraqi border. The prediction of light casualties might change if they swept on in a bid to unseat Saddam Hussein.

Gazing at the brown haze stirred up by moving columns way out beyond the Kuwait border, Jeremy knew this would be his first encounter with the kind of wounds inflicted by war. Demands would be made on his knowledge and capabilities. His staff would rely on him for diagnoses and decisions. Men's lives could be saved or lost within these tents. The weight of his professional responsibility descended on him as the tanks rolled forward over the sands.

The advance was swifter than even optimists had forecast. The Casualty Clearing Station moved forward on the heels of the troops, giving emergency treatment before sending patients further back to the hospitals, rest areas or PoW centres. Jeremy and his team worked continuously, splinting fractures, staunching haemorrhages, dressing minor wounds, treating burns. Severe casualties were urgently airlifted back to Saudi.

Most of their patients were Iraqis, young boys among them, thin and demoralized, with fear or despair in their eyes. Jeremy was shaken by his reaction to these haunted creatures. They had stood no chance against the might of the West, poor devils. In a moment of unexpected perspicacity he knew why he was a doctor, not a fighting soldier. He could never deliberately take a life.

It was over in four days. Kuwait was liberated, but the oil wells had been sabotaged. Poisonous, oily black smoke hung in a choking blanket over the country now littered with the corpses of tanks, trucks, guns ... and men.

As soon as the pressure eased, Jeremy tried to trace the whereabouts of Leo's unit. Fears for his safety had been at the back of his mind when working; they had plagued him during off-duty periods. At the height of the battle it had been impossible to get news of the part Intelligence was playing. Something vital, without doubt. Jeremy's guess that they were now in Kuwait City proved correct. Everyone was waiting for a decision on whether or not the war was over.

Unable to visit Leo, Jeremy used the comms system to put through a call to him. Vocal contact was better than none. After a series of connections punctuated by long pauses, a sergeant informed him that Lieutenant Bekov was presently at a conference.

Deeply frustrated, although thankful Leo was clearly safe and well, Jeremy said, 'Leave a message for him to contact Captain Fielding soonest.'

Twenty-four nerve-jangling hours passed. He put through a second call. Same sergeant. Same information. Same message left for Leo. Another day of silence. Jeremy grew desperate. Two weeks since their last wonderful meeting. Days of professional pressure, of long, demanding hours dealing with torn bodies, blood, and human flesh hideously burned. He was stressed out. Curiously, the silence now planes no longer roared overhead was also an irritant; it increased his sense of deprivation. He needed Leo. Badly.

He called the Intelligence unit three more times and almost sighed with relief when he was finally put through to Leo's extension.

'Lieutenant Bekov.'

'At last! I've been trying to get you for four days.'

'Sorry, who is this?'

'Me, you high and mighty bastard. *Jerry*.'

'Oh. Jerry.'

Leo's cool manner registered. 'Is something wrong? Why haven't you been in touch? I left several messages to call me. Didn't they reach you?'

'*Nein, nein*, Herr Doktor.'

Jeremy's taut nerves jangled. 'Cut that out,

163

Leo! I'm not in the mood. I've been up to my eyes in gore and dressings, and bloody anguished about your safety.'

'Have you? Why?'

It was colder than cool. 'What's the matter, for God's sake? Is there someone with you? Can't you speak freely?'

After a fractional pause, Leo said cuttingly, 'Haven't you any idea what's going on here, how many considerations are hanging in the balance? The next few days will affect the future of the entire Mid East. If we decide to invade Iraq you'll be *wallowing* in gore and dressings, Comrade.'

Hurt and angry, Jeremy snapped, 'Decided your name is Schwarzkopf after all, have you? OK, go ahead and make world history, you pompous shit, but if you're the victim of a second blue on blue you'll welcome the attentions of a lowly doctor again.'

He got drunk that night, something he was not prone to do. Luckily, there was no emergency that Sergeant Cornish, who was on duty, could not handle. A serious case was admitted during the day, and Jeremy failed to spot the obvious until one of his orderlies drew his attention to it before he administered the wrong drug. He was deeply shaken.

In the midst of drowning his sorrows again that night, he decided he must instead repair the rift between himself and the man who meant so much to him. He blamed himself for the quarrel. Leo handled sensitive information in foreign languages. The demand for

164

accuracy when decoding encrypted material must put great pressure on him, even more so in this present crucial period. Small wonder he had been distracted, offhand. An apology was essential before the rift widened to a bridgeless chasm.

Wangling a couple of days' R&R, Jeremy bent the ear of a helicopter pilot, who agreed to take him as a passenger on a supply trip to the capital. The wells were still belching out smoke. The acrid stench penetrated the aircraft. The roads running arrow-straight across desolation were still littered with broken enemy guns, transports and bodies not yet collected. The waste of war!

The friendly pilot chatted during the short flight, but Jeremy was not listening. At the airport he cadged a lift to where Leo's unit was presently located. The streets were teeming with people and traffic; as much of it military as Kuwaiti. Heavy black boots and desert gear mingled with sandals and flowing robes. The liberators and the liberated.

The I Corps unit had installed its equipment on the top floor of one of the luxury hotels. Tourists were nonexistent; the armed forces occupied them for now. Jeremy had no problem reaching the outer office manned by a sergeant.

'Captain Fielding, hoping to see Lieutenant Bekov,' he announced.

The NCO smiled. 'Oh, hallo, sir. You're in luck today. He's just got back from a meeting. I'll patch through to him. There's a room across the corridor we use for visitors. He'll be along in a few minutes.'

It was actually one of the hotel's bedrooms, but the twin beds had been pushed against the walls and dotted with cushions to resemble sofas. A round table and a couple of padded chairs completed the waiting-room look. From the large window it was possible to see a panorama of burning oil wells.

The sound of heavy footsteps approaching. Jeremy swung to face the open door, excitement mounting. There was no smile of greeting from Leo. He stood in the doorway, legs firmly apart, hands deep in his pockets and studied Jeremy with something astonishingly akin to disparagement.

'Well, well, well! So where's the big bunch of flowers?'

'What?' he murmured, caught off balance.

'The peace offering. Come to apologize, haven't you?'

'Well ... yes.'

'You're sorry you called me a high and mighty bastard. You truly didn't mean it when you said I'm a pompous shit. You've been upset and worried about me. Unable to sleep. That's what made you so petulant.' His eyebrows arched questioningly. 'Have I got it about right, Jerry?'

Confused, thrown by this curious aggression, he moved towards Leo. 'We've both been stressed; not our usual selves. I thought we could maybe have a few drinks together. A meal. Talk. Get back to normal.'

166

'Normal? That's rich coming from you, Jerry boy! You queers make me want to *puke*,' he said with quiet venom. 'At Cambridge I was raped by one of your kind when I was too drunk to fight him off. He claimed he'd never buggered a Russki. Wanted to know if we were different. Well, we are. We don't accept humiliation of any kind. We retaliate. My abuser was caught concealing data on his person during exams – cheating, in fact. He was sent down. He never understood how the info got concealed in his clothing, but he understood bloody well why, and who was responsible.'

Stunned, nauseous, Jeremy said, 'God, Leo, that has nothing to do with...'

'We retaliate,' he repeated. 'I knew what you were up to right from the start. Saw the look in your eyes while you touched my bare body, checking me over, you slimy creep! So I decided to use the gift of power you offered me.' He gave a mocking smile. 'It was immensely gratifying to watch you almost pissing yourself with ecstasy each time I smiled at you across the balalaika, and to see you get a hard-on when I put my arm along the back of your seat or my leg happened to brush against yours.'

He walked up to Jeremy, his black eyes fiery with loathing.

'First time for you, is it? Shy as a cock virgin and suffering agonies of frustration the more I teased and provoked. Well, here's another facet of my power over you, Jerry boy. I can end your career any time I like. The army won't tolerate your kind in its ranks, especially a doctor who can get his perverted kicks under the guise of a "thorough examination". So run along home like a good boy and stop bothering me ... or else!'

Driven by intolerable mortification, Jeremy grabbed at Leo's throat to cease the flow of wounding words. He forgot he was attacking an athlete. A knee was thrust into his genitals with sickening force. A killing punch to his stomach sent him staggering backwards into the table and chairs, which scattered under the impetus. He lost his balance and fell.

The sergeant appeared at the door. 'Problem, sir?'

Leo nodded. 'Captain Fielding just collapsed. Fever, I imagine. I've advised him to see a doctor.'

He walked off leaving Jeremy to struggle painfully into a sitting position, facing a man who would certainly recognize a punch-up when he came upon one. As it was between officers, he wisely withdrew, but Jeremy knew he must first have seen the tears rolling down his cheeks.

Nine

It began to snow again. Real heavy stuff. Four of the SIB team were continuing their dogged check to discover if anyone on the base had been awake or moving around from midnight onward on the night of the murder. Had someone seen or heard anything significant? Two sergeants were again questioning mess staff who had been on duty for the celebration dinner and who would have returned to their rooms in the early hours.

Max considered these long shots. He was hooked on his theory and had three strong leads. He reviewed these with Tom after lunch in their interview room.

'Ingham and the MO are clearly lying about their movements on leaving the mess. And they're withholding facts about their earlier encounter with Bekov. Through David Hanson we know the victim was responsible for tipping the scales against Ingham that resulted in back-terming. Surely not enough to warrant murder thirteen years later.'

'Mrs Ingham has been involved with him in the past. A stronger motive there for her husband.'

'I agree. Do we have the date of the Ingham

marriage?'

Tom referred to his file. 'Six months after commissioning.'

'Mmm. Did Reena have an affair with Bekov before meeting Ingham or after the wedding?'

'Maybe it began before the marriage, then there was a sneaky revival after the ring was on her finger. Would explain a lot.'

'Certainly would. When she walked out on him that evening, Ingham would have been made to look a fool in front of the rival he was hosting under duress. Then, when Bekov told him he'd made alternative sleeping arrangements, Ingham imagined he intended to bunk up with his wife. Which is why he went to the Foyle house to check on her.'

Tom got up and moved to stand beside one of the heaters, rubbing his hands together. 'It's bloody freezing in here. Temperature's dropping fast. So you believe Ingham went to the house, and the women let him in even knowing he'd had a skinful?'

Max sighed. 'No, I don't. They're *all* lying, but I've no idea why. If Ingham wasn't at home when Bekov turned up, where the hell was he? We don't rate him as the killer, but he was doing something we should know about or why the transparent lie?'

He joined Tom by the heater. 'Look at what we know of him. He allowed his arm to be twisted over hosting a man he must have heartily disliked. His wife clearly wears the pants. He's prepared to spin us a yarn that portrays him as a wimp who'd go to another woman's house in the middle of the night to apologize for something he didn't believe was his fault. He was back-termed at Sandhurst because they considered he was rather slow to take command. He's too bloody unassertive to conceive and carry out this murder.'

Tom nodded. 'Remember that case in Singapore when the lance-corporal confessed to raping a pair of prossies? Hadn't been near them, but he confessed simply to raise his cred with his mates.'

'And?'

'Maybe Ingham's creating this elaborate and unlikely story for the same reason. Wants to wipe his reputation for greyness; his inability to dazzle.'

'The way Bekov did? So he knows we can't prove he's guilty, because he isn't, but he takes on an aura of mystery as a suspect. His wife, his colleagues will view him differently. Well, you could be right.'

'On that premise, he could actually have gone straight home after the dinner, been there when Bekov knocked, and deliberately refused to let him in. A small triumph that wouldn't take too much assertion to carry out. Would have been a shock to learn the poor devil had been shot dead as a result, of course.'

Watching large snowflakes swirling around outside the window, Max considered the theory. 'No, I don't go for that. Why rope in those women to cover for him during the vital

171

period? He had to bribe his wife with a week at a health farm. Damned expensive. And why would the Foyle woman participate in the deception?'

Tom was struck by sudden inspiration. 'Because she *knew* what he was really doing. Look, Reena goes up to bed and settles for the night. Probably had her share of booze during the evening and goes out like a light. Jane Foyle then calls Ingham on his mobile. He leaves the mess and goes home, where she joins him. Ingham has no intention of letting the Major in when he hammers on the door, because he's in bed with the wife's best friend – literally! They set the alarm so she can return to her house before anyone's around – she lives in the adjacent avenue, remember – and the flighty Reena is none the wiser.'

Max shook his head. 'Jane Foyle wouldn't play around with a guy like Ingham. He's too lightweight for a classy woman like her.'

'So they both like it kinky. She plays the punishing nanny; he's the naughty boy. Appearances are deceptive.'

Max was away on bruising reminiscences. A captain's wife and a corporal! Had Susan wanted it kinky? Had she ordered Cairns around so that he got his kicks from obeying? 'Yes, ma'am.' With a smart salute. Stark naked!

'What d'you think, sir?'

He turned with a frown. 'What?'

'Ingham having it away with Mrs Foyle. Her husband's in Northern Ireland. Perfect

172

opportunity.'

'Let's get Captain Foyle's details up on screen when we get back tonight. Point of interest only. Unless Jane Foyle aided the murder of Bekov, what she does and with whom is not our concern. Ingham is. I want another crack at him tomorrow. Wherever he was that night he might have seen something he won't reveal because it'll blow his cover story.'

He went back to the chair behind the desk and referred to the file. 'We also need to re-interview the MO. His testimony has as many holes as a shower nozzle. He's clearly a man under extreme pressure, screwed up so tight one more turn will break him. That makes him interesting. Being called out to certify the death of a man he knew – only slightly, if he's to be believed – shocked him so much he couldn't think straight. Earlier today he said it usually took fifteen minutes from the surgery to his quarter, which pinpointed when he had returned from the emergency with the cough sweet. Why didn't he say that two days ago? Then, he claimed his wife was in such a state with a screaming baby he hadn't looked at the clock. Got hot under the collar; refused to offer even an approximate time.'

Tom pursed his lips. 'He's got his hands full with that wife of his. I reckon she needs psychiatric help. Nora says some women get that way after giving birth. It's all the more curious that he relied on her to give him an

173

alibi today.'

'Let's hope he has his wits more about him when dealing with patients.'

'I've been asking around. Seems he knows his stuff well enough. The rank and file like him. "A decent bloke" is what I heard repeatedly. Popular in the mess, too, according to some of the caterers. But there's no doubt he was up to something that night.'

Max slipped his arms in the sleeves of his sheepskin jacket. 'Christ, it's like the inside of a fridge in here! Those heaters are next to useless.' He frowned up at Tom. 'Was the Doc the other man in the gym with Ms King? Light relief from a neurotic wife and screaming baby?'

Tom shrugged his own topcoat on. 'He admitted to having some common interests with the lady. If he had sex with her after Bekov left it would explain his reaction to being called to certify his death minutes later.'

'Unless he'd killed Bekov only minutes earlier.'

'Motive?'

'Jealous lover.'

'DNA will settle the question ... and that would kick out your firing-squad theory, sir.'

Max sighed and got to his feet. 'We're getting bloody nowhere, and if we stay here much longer we'll be too cold to do anything useful. I'd like another word with Captain Randolph. In his office, which I bet will be warmer than this.'

It was. Not so their reception. Peter Randolph made his annoyance very obvious. 'I've to finish these reports by four thirty, then cut across to the mess for an extraordinary meeting called by the CO. Come back in the morning, around ten.'

Max took off his thick coat and sat in the chair beside Randolph's desk. 'We're investigating a murder. We don't come back in the morning when an interviewee is available now. Why did you keep quiet about your encounter with Leo Bekov in Bosnia?'

'Sorry, not with you,' he drawled, still studying the screen.

This second encounter did nothing to improve Max's reaction to a handsome man with the in-bred assurance of being the latest in a long line of very distinguished soldiers. If Bekov had been too well aware of his own worth, this man could beat him hands down. It suggested there'd have been no love lost had they been thrown together in a combat situation.

'Leo Bekov. The man murdered and tied to a post on the night you were Duty Officer. The man you called Tolstoy in a Freudian slip you clumsily tried to cover up. Are you with me now, Captain Randolph?' he asked caustically. 'Why didn't you admit to knowing him in Bosnia?'

Randolph clearly guessed this was a shot in the dark. 'Because I didn't. If he served out there our paths are unlikely to have crossed. He was I Corps. Intercepts; interrogation.

That was his thing. He wouldn't have been involved in the real nitty-gritty like me.'

Tom took up the questioning. 'Major Bekov served in the same sector as your squadron during a corresponding period, sir. He was fluent in Serbo-Croat, which suggests he could have acted as interpreter for officers like yourself in the field.'

A smile played around Randolph's mouth. 'You could check that out with his corps headquarters, Sar'nt Major.'

'We've someone already on it, sir.'

Max could see they were wasting their time. This man was no Ingham; he was supremely assertive and smoothly confident. He stood.

'This extraordinary mess meeting; anything to do with the murder?'

'I should think so, wouldn't you?' It was *so* superior!

'Then I'm sure you'll contribute usefully from all those whodunits you read,' Max returned coolly. 'By the way, we'd like a DNA sample from you, if you're agreeable.'

Oh *ho*! Some reaction at last!

'DNA? Why? I was in the Duty Room asleep until Judy King woke me to view the body.'

'You decline, sir?' asked Tom in exactly the right tone.

Randolph's urbanity was recovering. 'I just don't see the point.'

Wonderfully po-faced, Tom said, 'Purposes of elimination.'

'Elimination from what?'

176

'Our list of suspects, sir.'

Randolph overdid it this time. *'Suspects?* Dear me, I suggest it's time you called the Home Office; got them to send out some genuine detectives. You're clearly scratching around trying to pin this on anyone – even the man who has the most obvious alibi of all.'

'Humour us,' invited Max. 'We have to learn by experience, and as you know you have the perfect alibi we can't possibly pin anything on you even if, in our ham-fisted, amateurish way, we imagine your DNA matches some found at the scene of the crime. I'll send one of my team to take a sample while you're finishing those reports. Thank you for your valuable time.'

They crunched across the deepening layer of snow to their vehicle and got in it. Tom started the engine and set the wipers swishing.

'He's got a point, sir. Duty Officer has to be on call through the night.'

'Yes, but he can be reached anywhere on base through his radio. Doesn't mean he's snug under the duvet when he answers. Far from having the perfect alibi, that guy had the opportunity to track down the man he knew as Tolstoy and put an end to him. In addition, he's far more likely to do it in this quixotic fashion than either Ingham or Fielding. He's a descendant of men steeped in concepts of honour and chivalry.'

'He was none too chivalrous just now,' Tom

177

pointed out drily.

'He sees us as amateurish plods, that's why.' Max turned to Tom. 'You've been out here for more than a year. You must have crossed his path before.'

'No, in fact. This regiment behaves itself reasonably well, which is usually a sign of good leadership. We had a case of mess supplies going missing in large quantities. Two storemen had an arrangement with the owner of a small bistro in town. We got them within twenty-four hours. Another time, a female clerk reckoned one of the lads had touched her up in the swimming pool. Turned out he'd given her the heave-ho after a brief affair, and she wanted revenge. Her claim couldn't be proved; he denied it. End of story. Captain Randolph played no part in either investigation.'

'Mmm, if that's all they normally get up to, no wonder this affair has prompted an extra-ordinary mess meeting. Think I should gatecrash; hear their theories?'

Tom grinned. 'I doubt they'd allow an amateurish plod to sit in, sir.'

By then they had driven to where the rest of the team had gathered ready to leave. Tom pulled up and got out to organize a pair to collect the DNA from Peter Randolph. In the warmth of the vehicle Max let his mind wander back to Tom's theory on Ingham and Jane Foyle. It was not too difficult to imagine Ingham going for the matron and naughty boy technique. He could be the type who was

excited by being caned for imagined misbehaviour, and to perform submissive tricks
on command.

No, the Foyle woman would never be party
to sexual degradation, he would swear to that.
But what if she did it for payment because
her husband was in deep financial trouble?
The men mostly achieved orgasm through
pain and humiliation; had no need to enter
the woman. Would Bobby Foyle be prepared
to go along with it just to get them out of
debt?

If Susan had been doing it with her sandy-
haired corporal *he* would never have acqui-
esced. It was sexual betrayal however one
looked at it. He jumped nervously when Tom
pulled open the door and slid in. Tom had
been with him when he heard that Susan had
been killed. Knowing it was commonly believed she was having an affair with Cairns
was humiliation enough for Max. He needed
no whipping of the bare buttocks to invite
pain. The difference was the pain *he* suffered
was not a twisted brand of pleasure. It was
pure anguish.

They drove to the main gate in silence.
Once the barrier had lowered behind them,
Tom said, 'This Tolstoy business. You reckon
it relates to Bosnia, do you?'

'Certain of it. But Randolph's a hard nut to
crack. We'll get nothing from him unless we
produce undeniable facts. Put Johnson and
Pepperidge on to checking with I Corps who
Bekov served with in Bosnia. And do the

same for his time in the Gulf. Someone could give us a lead; someone must know who Bekov knew or became friendly with. A charismatic guy like him would draw people who would always remember him. David Hanson immediately recalled that one cadet among hundreds from thirteen years ago. Had to be prompted on Ingham, even though his had been one of only a few instances of back-terming.'

There was a lengthy silence broken only by the swish of windscreen wipers and the squeak of compressed snow beneath their tyres. Then Tom said: 'Wish I'd met Major Bekov. He sounds the type of officer the men either love or hate, yet would follow without question. They usually finish up as commanders-in-chief.'

'Mmm. *Someone* we've been talking to over the last couple of days made sure he would not.'

'But if your theory's right, somewhere along the way he did something that deserved being deprived of a distinguished future.'

'He was deprived of *life*, Tom. No trial; no chance to mount a defence, try to put things right. No man deserves that.'

Tom shot him a glance. 'Someone else steeped in concepts of honour and chivalry?'

'No, just hell bent on dispensing justice.'

Back at their own section base they learned that Peter Randolph had left his office before the DNA sample could be taken. He had retreated to the officers' mess. The two SIB sergeants had been told the meeting was about to start and Captain Randolph would be unavailable for the rest of the evening.

'Showing his refusal to take us seriously,' said Tom in disgust.

Max smiled with satisfaction. 'No, he's showing weakness and uncertainty. He's read enough detective fiction to know that a refusal to cooperate will suggest guilt, but he's unsure what to do about it. We'll be at him first thing tomorrow armed with more facts. I want everyone tonight on digging into his career, and even those of his renowned family. We'll surely come up with *something* that'll wipe that superior smile from his chops.'

Tom relished that thought while he checked reports on concurrent investigations: a burglary at a married quarters and a road-rage incident. He then went home before the plummeting temperature made driving too hazardous.

Warmth and laughter greeted him as he entered from the garage. As usual, he felt the loving atmosphere of his home instantly easing his tension. He was a man richly blessed, he knew. The profession he had chosen revealed the seedy, the greedy, the violent aspects of life. It was good to step away to a cocoon of the sweeter, gentler human traits.

As he walked down the hallway, three giggling girls in varied sizes scuttled past, heading for the stairs.

'Hi, Dad. Hi, Dad. Hi, Dad,' they chorused. 'We've bought a new video of Brad Pitt. *Ooooh!* Mum says we can watch it until bed-time. See you then.'

They vanished upward in a flurry of legs clad in sweatpants, leaving Tom smiling. Nora was putting the ironing board away as he walked in the kitchen.

'Who the hell is Brad Pitt Oooh?'

'You don't want to know, love. It'll be some-one new next week. Your nose is like an ice cube,' she complained as she kissed him.

'It's well below freezing out there.' He sniffed. 'What's that delicious smell?'

Nora biffed him gently. 'As if you don't know it's your favourite steak and onion pie.'

'Great! You're so good at feeding me I might make an honest woman of you one day,' he said, shrugging off his topcoat.

'I'm as honest now as you'll ever make me. You, or any other man. Time for a beer first, if you want one.'

'No, let's eat. I only had soup and a few stringy lamb sandwiches for lunch. I'm starving.'

Nora donned oven gloves. 'So were your daughters. If I hadn't made a second pie for us you might have had soup and sandwiches for dinner, too.'

'You'd have been in deep trouble if,' Tom warned.

Blue eyes twinkled as his wife looked up from the pie she was bringing from the oven.

'I was hoping for that later tonight.'

Tom grinned acknowledgement of her invitation, yet while they ate their meal, saw their girls off to bed and relaxed with another glass of wine as they watched a black-and-white British film on TV, Tom found his mind still on the Bekov murder. The timing was so tight it would be a hard nut to crack.

The big problem with military detecting was that the khaki community was constantly on the move. All over the world. Tracing witnesses, gathering evidence, trying to solve the crime could become an international affair if the motive sprang from past actions. He shared Max Rydal's certainty that the victim had been punished for something he had done way back, which meant the killer must have served with him at one time. He must also be cool, assured and able to plan at short notice an opportunistic murder. Yet why wait for this chance reunion? Had it been impossible to wreak vengeance at the time of the perceived evil act?

Unaware of the TV screen turning blank, Tom started when Nora's hand gripped his arm. 'Would it help to talk about it?'

Unlike civilian policemen, their military counterparts operated among closely linked groups, often living cheek-by-jowl as an alien nucleus in a foreign country. The comfort of discussing problems with sympathetic partners was denied because confidentiality had to be strictly maintained when everyone knew everyone else. Gossip and rumour ran through a brigade, a unit, an accommodation block like wildfire. A case could easily be ruined by careless talk.

Tom frowned, then said after a pause, 'Jeff and Margaret are our close friends, aren't they? Suppose I was away on a case and she turned up on our doorstep with a small bag, saying they'd had a row and could she overnight with you. And suppose Jeff came in the morning asking you both to say he'd been with you here in the early hours attempting to repair the quarrel, because there'd been a bit of trouble and he wanted to keep clear of it. What would you do?'

'Would I lie to the army authorities? That's a tough one, love. I'd want to be certain he wasn't mixed up in the bit of trouble, and I'd want to know why he needed an alibi for the early hours; where he'd really been.'

'If his answers were satisfactory?'

'I'd have to think of you and the girls. You come before friends, however close, and I wouldn't have anything rebounding on us. In any case, Tom, if Margaret turned up here begging a bed for the night, first thing I'd do is try to mediate between them. If you were away and unable to tackle Jeff, I'd still do what I could to patch things up and get them back together before bedtime.'

Tom held up his hands. 'OK, let's not get bogged down with it. Suffice to say you wouldn't calmly lie your socks off without hesitation.'

She studied him shrewdly. 'Whoever has,

has more than friendship as a motive. Sounds like she could be in love with the man herself.'

'To understand a woman's behaviour, ask another of the species,' he said thoughtfully.

'Ready for bed now?'

'Mmm. Go on up. I'll slip the bolts and set the alarm.'

As he made the house secure, Tom dismissed the notion of Jane Foyle being in love with Ingham. Kinky sex was still a possibility. Maybe they should search Inham's home for canes, bottles labelled castor oil and a nanny's outfit.

The next hour with Nora was not in the least kinky, just pleasurable, satisfying and warmly loving. As they lay entwined ready for sleep, Tom murmured, 'So who *is* Brad Pitt Ooooh?'

'Not a patch on you, love, take my word.'

There were heart-shaped balloons tied to the door next to his when Max reached his new flat after a long period spent writing up his reports. A Valentine's party was already noisily under way in the adjoining apartment. Max's heart sank as the booming sounds of German pop music assaulted his ears. Why was it always played at such deafening volume? The party guests surely could not hear each other speaking!

Useless to put on any of his own CDs. Their mellow sounds wouldn't compete. He had a sudden memory of Susan asking his taste in

185

music on their second date. She had just admitted to being a lover of opera and the classical composers, so he confessed with some reluctance his fondness for guitar, mandolin, balalaika pieces. 'And especially Paraguayan harps. Anything that can be plucked, I suppose.'

'Like chickens?' she'd teased.

He'd known in that minute that he wanted to spend the rest of his life with her.

He poured a whisky to help him ride out the pain that recollection brought. It didn't, so he poured another. Soon the wall was practically shaking from the bass beat, and he knew he had to get away. Putting his overcoat on again, he took the lift to the ground floor and left the building.

It had stopped snowing, but the sub-zero temperature had frozen the surface so hard it would be folly to drive in his search for peace. He set out on foot. There was no wind, little traffic. It was virginly white, and still. Balm to his troubled spirit.

As he trudged through hushed streets Max faced the fact that he had a problem more insuperable than incompatible neighbours. At the start of his career he had been one of a group at all times. Marriage to Susan had changed that, but he had happily settled in the twosome he had believed would last his lifetime. 'Until death do us part' had occurred too soon. In view of his risky profession, the Grim Reaper had got it wrong by taking Susan first.

He was immediately lost in painful speculation on what the situation would be if Cairns' car hadn't skidded and hit a wall. Would Susan have run off with her lover or come to her senses and asked his forgiveness? Would he have been able to give it? The car crash had left those questions unanswered. How long would it be before he no longer cared about the answers? How long before he adjusted to being a widower?

He was presently neither a husband nor a carefree bachelor. Young singles now seemed to him a breed apart; married couples no longer sent invitations unless they had uneven numbers at the last minute and needed another unattached male.

He was wary of eleventh-hour telephone calls, so his social life was pretty much at a standstill. His hope of a fresh start here in Germany had had no time to get off the ground.

He was not good at living alone; had never been domesticated. Max Rydal was not a 'new man'. He had no ambition to become a superchef dazzling guests with his culinary genius. There was no garden over which to wax enthusiastic and bore people with botanical superlatives. As a young bachelor he had thrown himself into the usual passions; as a husband he had cherished the joys of what he had believed to be a close marriage. Now he was adrift on a troubled sea with no chart to help him steer a new course. He would find it, in time. Until then his work filled the void.

As he plodded onward he mentally reviewed what they knew about the three men who
had served with Bekov before. Ingham and
Fielding were hiding the truth about their
movements on the night of the murder. Peter
Randolph was avoiding the need to lie by
making himself unavailable. Which made him
as strong a suspect as the others.

But what of Jane Foyle? Max didn't go
along with Tom's theory of kinky sex with
Ingham, yet he would not rule out her
possible adultery. With Fielding? Had she and
the doctor committed the crime together?
No, the Foyle woman would not lie to clear
Ingham if she had done it herself. Why was
she offering false evidence? What hold had
Ingham over her? Her affair with Fielding?
Was he threatening to tell her absent husband? Judith King was doing the dirty on her
man during his foreign tour, so why not Jane
Foyle? Susan Rydal had, but no one had
given away her guilty secret. Her husband
had had to discover it the hard way.

Max trudged on, lost in a crime that was
not the murder of Bekov, but the theft of his
wife and unborn child. By the time his pain
and anger had eased he was exhausted. It was
then he saw the illuminated sign of a small
Gasthof, and walked in to secure a room for
the night. Stripping off his clothes he slid
gratefully beneath the thick duvet and fell
instantly asleep.

The shrill tone of his mobile brought him

awake. Max couldn't fathom where he was. His brain was still getting to grips with the problem when he grunted a response into the tiny telephone.

'Tom Black, sir. Will you be coming in this morning?'

Max read the green numbers on the digital clock beside his bed. It was 09:30.

'Oh God, had a late night, Tom. Send someone to pick me up, will you? Left my car at the apartment.'

'Where exactly are you?'

Max scrambled heavy-limbed from the bed to take up a brochure from the chest across the room. He read aloud: 'Der Rote Löwe. It's a small inn. I've no idea of its location.'

'I have. Be there in twenty-five.'

'No, send out one of the drivers.'

'I've some news. Report just in gives us our first breakthrough. Be there in twenty-five.'

Ten

They were at it again. They had done nothing but row for the past three days. Mark's nerves were ragged at the edges; growing more so as time passed. He told himself everything would settle once the SIB cleared up the case and departed, yet in solitary moments he knew he would never again be the person he was before that night.

He was sleeping badly, jumping at his own shadow, short-tempered with his NCOs, forgetful and ineffective in his daily routine. Worst of all was his complete reversal of feeling for Reena. This morning she was like a bird, twittering on and on about the health farm until he could take no more. He brought his clenched fists down hard on the breakfast bar, making her and the checked pottery jump.

'If you say one more word about that bloody place I'll send you to a funny farm instead!'

Her thin face hardened; her eyes iced over. 'Don't you shout at me! You owe me, don't forget. Would you like me to spread it around that you really sat on the doorstep like a downcast dog that night – that you got me and Jane to lie about letting you in because the truth would show you up as a pathetic wimp?'

He stood so suddenly the tall stool fell to the floor. 'The truth would show *you* as the washed-up little tart you are. D'you really imagine I sat outside Jane's house on a freezing night because you'd decided to sleep there? Oh, no! I was *far* more pleasantly occupied,' he added wildly.

'Really? Came home and jerked yourself off because I didn't let you have it for a week? Is that what you were doing when Leo knocked and rang the bell?' Her voice began to crack. 'That what you were bloody doing when he walked off and got himself shot?'

'He got what he deserved,' Mark snapped.

'No, he didn't. He *didn't*, you bastard! He was a real man, not an apology for one, like you. You always hated Leo because you knew you'd never measure up to him in any way. You never will. You'll always be second best.'

This echo of Bekov's same words increased Mark's fury. 'According to him you weren't even that, my stupid little wife! He told me that night you were as difficult to get rid of as chewing gum on the sole of his boot.' He turned and headed for the door. 'You didn't walk out on me when you spent the night at Jane's. It was because you knew he only had to lift his foot and you'd fasten yourself to his sole again,'

Reena grabbed a mug and threw it at him. A plate followed. Both missed Mark by many

inches. 'Bastard, bastard, *bastard*!' she shrieked, then fell across the remains of breakfast
and began to sob.

Mark snatched up his parka and beret, then
slammed out of the house. He backed the car
ferociously on to the short avenue leading to
the perimeter road, then headed for his office
following tracks impressed in the frozen
snow. He had long yearned for a 4x4, but the
car-fund money was now going to be blued
on seven days of pampering and self-in-
dulgence. It was the price of an alibi. Unfortunately, peace of mind was not even an
optional extra on the deal.

He was drinking a welcome mug of tea in
his office with Sergeant Bicester as they
reviewed the day ahead when Tom Black
tapped on the open door and entered. Mark's
heart missed a beat then raced for several
moments, until common sense took over. He
had nothing to fear. He had not killed Leo
Bekov. They could not prove otherwise.

'Good morning, Mr Black. Care for some
tea?' he said as pleasantly as he could.

No smile. 'No, thank you, sir. Captain
Rydal wants to speak to you in our interview
room. I've a Land Rover outside.'

Mark shook his head. 'I've a lecture to give
in fifteen, followed by an NCOs' strategy
meeting.'

'This isn't a request, sir.'

Seeing curious hostility in the man's dark
eyes, Mark's temper started to rise again. 'I've
already told you all I can and normal routine

has to continue, you know. We have a NATO exercise coming up next week.'

'We're investigating the murder of a British officer. Not an exercise, the real thing ... sir. I'll wait for you in the vehicle.'

Sergeant Bicester murmured, 'I'll tell them to hold on the lecture, and we can reschedule the NCOs' meeting.'

Mark barely heard him. Something was wrong. Surely ... no, Judy would not at this stage add to her testimony. For a start, she would never have confessed to her sexual overdrive with the man she had found dead shortly afterwards. What she had said to explain why she was wandering around at that hour was anyone's guess. There had been great speculation among the officers on her activity that night. They had seen her go off with Bekov, clearly set for sex. What had occurred between then and the moment she had discovered his body no one could imagine, but the notion of her being involved in murder was under discussion. Judy was saying nothing; keeping well away from them all.

Mark's own lie to explain why he had not been there to let Bekov in when he knocked had been generally accepted in the mess. He knew it portrayed him as somewhat spineless. Better that than the truth!

During the short drive Mark remained silent, telling himself this would be no more than a check on the exact timing of his movements that fatal night. Or maybe they wanted him to confirm some information they had gleaned on Bekov himself. Yet, why the intense hostility of the man beside him?

That hostility was equally apparent in Max Rydal. It burned in his gaze that had been cold before. He offered no greeting, just waited for Mark to sit facing him across the desk.

'Captain Ingham, you claimed that on the night of Major Bekov's murder you went from your quarters to the house of Mrs Foyle at 02:30 to mend a quarrel with your wife, who was spending the night there. Mrs Foyle said you stayed for around ninety minutes before returning home.'

'Yes.' He swallowed and repeated it more clearly. 'Yes, that's correct.'

Silence. Twin expressions of accusation boring into him. A cold, bare room. Hostile interrogation!

'Now tell us the truth about your movements that night,' Rydal challenged.

He swallowed again. 'That is the truth.'

'When this case goes to trial you'll be giving evidence under oath,' Tom Black said harshly.

Oh God, what was happening here?

Rydal's voice grew icier. 'At 02:00 Lieutenant King went with Major Bekov to the gymnasium, where she admits they had sex. They were seen there half an hour later by a witness. Ms King claims Major Bekov left while she was asleep. She also claims she woke at around 03:45, dressed and returned to the mess, where she discovered his body.

194

Forensics found traces of the victim's semen on her skirt. And that of another man. She swears she had no second sexual partner. Captain Ingham, the DNA of that semen matches the sample you gave us.'

Mark's world caved in. This was worse, far worse than anything he had ever faced. There seemed no way out, yet he must find one. With his heart hammering against his ribs he mentally travelled back to that night.

Everyone saw the way Judy was responding to Bekov. They were even laying bets on his getting inside her knickers before morning, and when the pair sneaked out there was a general feeling of sour grapes. The luscious Judy had played the loyal, untouchable fiancée when some of the lads had tried their luck with her. Yet she had flaunted her perfectly toned body, sending unmistakable messages to Bekov from her tits to her toes. He had acknowledged them with a supremely confident smile.

Seeing that smile again inflamed Mark and sent him in pursuit. It was the response to an alcohol-induced impulse, but the fire of resentment and hostility had been fanned tonight from embers that had been glowing for a long time. Mark had no real purpose in mind. He was more like a man with an aching tooth driven to bite on it to induce more pain. Yet the sight of Bekov's hand fondling Judy's buttocks as they walked, and of hers running up and down his spine beneath his short mess jacket, began to excite rather than hurt.

Reena had been 'punishing' him again over the past few days because he was refusing to let her go with friends to a health farm for a week. It cost the bloody earth, and they needed the money to replace their car, he kept telling her. So she had moved his things to the spare room – she seemed able to go without sex far longer than he – and had thrown a tantrum when he ruled they should sleep together tonight because of their guest.

Mark was damned sure he would not let Bekov be aware of the situation. He had insisted he would return to their double bed whether or not Reena liked it. She had promptly packed her things and decamped to Jane's house, making it obvious to Bekov that her husband was being cold-shouldered by a girl who had once been one of *his* retinue. Watching Bekov work his charm on Judy, Mark was suddenly convinced Reena had quit the house because she still fancied her 'satyr' and would not lie in bed with Mark when he was just the other side of the bedroom wall.

Following the pair in to the gym, Mark stood in the shadows watching them tug off their clothes before falling on a soft-landing mattress and going at it hammer and tongs. Bekov gave her the full works: Judy cried out and moaned in ecstasy. Mark got an erection just watching, and hostility burned even hotter as he imagined Reena beneath this thrusting bastard.

He was then astonished to see Bekov push himself off the girl and begin climbing the wall bars, laughing triumphantly. Judy scrambled after him, calling out to him and laughing, too. In the dim light her naked body looked fantastic. Mark could not drag his gaze from it, and his erection became acutely painful. At that point he grew aware of someone standing in the doorway, intent on the two nude gymnasts. Mark drew further into the shadows.

The two silent watchers then saw a performance of uninhibited grace as the pair swung back and forth on ropes, hanging upside down, turning somersaults, going hand-over-hand from rope to rope; she laughing, he chanting something incomprehensible but clearly arrogant. Then Bekov climbed on the large trampoline and began to jump higher and higher. Judy joined him, breasts bouncing tantalizingly, until he pulled her hard against him and their bodies melded.

They lost the rhythm and fell to the canvas. Mark's hyper-aroused state then took a further beating as Bekov embarked on a repeat performance. Christ, what stamina! Is that what Reena expected from him? All-night bonking, with athletics!

Mark was so consumed with bitter speculation he only grew aware that the other person had gone when Bekov rolled clear and dropped to the floor, where he began drunkenly to dress. He shook Judy, but she appeared to be in a post-coital world of her own. Even when he tried to sit her up she gave little response. Bekov gave a manual gesture indicating that he gave up trying, spread her skirt and jacket over her, then left on unsteady legs. He did not see Mark well back in the dark corner.

Bastard, thought Mark. Shaft her out of her senses, then bugger off. He had probably done that to Reena. The stupid cows all lapped it up; thought he was God's gift!

He moved cautiously to the trampoline. Judy was either asleep or dead drunk. She was breathing out enough alcoholic fumes to do justice to a brewery. Two-faced bitch! She had dropped her touch-me-not attitude along with her knickers for a guy who was just passing through. A stranger. Pete Harrison, whom she planned to marry when he returned from Brunei, little knew what a tramp she was. Little knew his future wife would continue to lust after Bekov; compare him unfavourably with that Anglo-Russian stud. As Reena did with him!

He reached out, pulled the monkey jacket and long skirt from the naked girl. Judy's nipples were still enlarged and hard; her blonde pubic hair glistened wetly. Her skin was hot to the touch and smelled of copulation. His inflamed desire told Mark he had one of Bekov's leftovers at home. Why not have another of them now? He was primed and ready, after all.

She half-roused as he straddled her; muttered faintly that he should go away. She even pushed weakly at his thick mess jacket.

Typical female foreplay, pretending reluctance! They loved to tease, to stimulate; wanting the rough, tough approach. He had seen Bekov give it to her. He did the same, and swiftly climaxed.

Four hours later, sobering fast in the cold light of dawn, Mark felt uncertain. Guilty, even. But, Christ, Judy had been doing it with gusto with Bekov. Loving it. Holding nothing back. He had simply continued feeding her appetite for it, hadn't he? No reason to have doubts. No reason at all.

Coming back from the mental flashback to that bizarre night, Mark faced two pairs of damning eyes and knew they would not give up until satisfied. He felt like a drowning man. He had believed his DNA sample was for comparison with some found at the murder scene. It had never occurred to him that Judy's clothes would be subjected to any tests. Tests that produced irrefutable results. He was in deep, deep trouble.

'When you had sex with Lieutenant King in the gymnasium in the early hours of February twelfth, was it with her knowledge and consent?' demanded Tom Black.

'No!'

'You raped her?'

'*No!*' he cried. 'I meant, no I didn't have sex with her.'

'Then how do you explain the fact that there were traces of your semen on her skirt?'

Oh God, this was terrible! Think! *Think,*

Mark! 'It must have been when I picked up her clothes.'

Rydal's eyebrows rose. 'What exactly did you pick them up with?'

'I don't appreciate your cheap wit,' Mark snapped, and instantly regretted it. Riling them would only worsen his case.

'So you admit to being in the gymnasium, *not* in Mrs Foyle's house placating your wife?'

He nodded. Useless to deny it.

'Ms King swears only Major Bekov was there with her.'

Mark began to relax a little. Judy recalled nothing of the affair, thank God. 'They didn't know I'd followed them, that's why.'

Rydal fixed Mark with a steady look. 'Did you and Ms King lure Major Bekov to the gym, where she was prepared to have sex with him, and when he was exhausted as well as heavily intoxicated did you both allow him to wander away in unfamiliar surroundings so that you could follow and kill him?'

Mark was horrified. They were trying to pin a murder charge on him instead of rape. 'That's crazy. Utterly crazy! *I* didn't kill him. If Judy says I did, she's lying.'

'*You've* been lying, sir,' Tom Black pointed out. 'And persuaded two women to back up that lie.'

Unable to get his brain around this shocking development, Mark repeated, 'I didn't kill him. Why would I?'

'Because of what happened at Sandhurst.'

He was bewildered. 'Sandhurst?'

'Wasn't Leo Bekov partially responsible for your being back-termed?'

'Who told you that?'

'We're investigators, sir. We search out facts.'

'That was more than thirteen years ago. If I was going to kill him for that, wouldn't I have done it then?'

Max Rydal jumped in. 'Why go to the gym that night if it wasn't to follow a murder plan?'

Mark knew the near truth would humiliate him, but he had no option if he was to clear himself of the greater charge. So he told how he had followed the pair because he could not believe Judy King would do the dirty on her fiancé with a man she knew nothing of.

'You've already discovered I have no cause to think much of Bekov. Although he didn't actually tell me he had made other sleeping arrangements, as I said earlier, he *was* supposed to be a guest in my house and he went off with her in the early hours without a word of explanation or apology to me. I was bloody annoyed, so I set off after them.'

'You entered the gym and watched them having sex,' Rydal said coldly. 'Are you a regular voyeur?'

'Of course not! I wouldn't have been then except that someone else arrived and stood in the doorway. It meant I couldn't leave.'

'Go on,' prompted Tom Black.

'They began doing gymnastics. Naked. The other man – I saw no more than a dim figure

201

– vanished when Judy and Bekov settled on the trampoline.'

'But you stayed for further titillation.'

'It wasn't like that,' he protested, knowing he did not sound convincing. 'It would have been difficult to leave without their becoming aware of my presence.'

'And you were waiting for your turn on the trampoline with Ms King. After all, she was being pretty free with her body.'

Christ, they were back to that now! He avoided their scrutiny, but knew this had to be said if he was to wriggle out of this.

'Look, I'd had a skinful and my wife had walked out to spend the night with Jane. Watching them having it off like crazy, and swinging naked on ropes ... it was bloody erotic stuff. I became highly aroused. Any man would.'

'And?'

'And so when Bekov walked away leaving Judy naked on the trampoline, I was in such a state I had to get relief by the usual means.' He forced a chummy, one-of-the-boys smile. 'You know how it is.'

'Then how did your semen get on Ms King's skirt?'

'I said just now. When I picked it up. Judy was out cold; exhausted, blind drunk. So I covered her up with her clothes. It was a very cold night.'

'You didn't try to rouse her; get her to dress and leave?'

'Bekov had failed to do that ... and I didn't

want her to know I'd been watching. I simply covered her up and left.'

'To go where?'

'Home. I later realized I must have arrived at the house only a few minutes after Bekov knocked on the door.'

Tom Black referred to a file. 'Let's get the timing fixed on this new version of your story, shall we?' He ran through what Mark had just said, adding evidence of the time given by the unnamed witness.

In the subsequent silence Mark was driven to say, 'Yes, that must be about right.'

'You say you probably arrived several minutes after Major Bekov tried to gain admittance, which would put the time at about 03:10. So what did you do between then and 04:00?'

'Went to bed.'

Rydal came in to bat again. 'You weren't concerned about where your house guest might be wandering, drunk and in unfamiliar territory?'

Mark failed to keep the acid from his voice. 'Bekov could look after himself. He always fell on his feet.'

'So you went to bed leaving a fellow officer sparsely covered against the bitter cold in the gym, and your guest roaming blindly around the base on a night of freezing temperatures? Can you prove that was what happened?'

'What? Of course not! My wife was with Jane Foyle.'

'And she told us you were with her between

half two and 04:00. Why did you persuade her to lie?'

'Isn't it obvious? When I learned Bekov had been here I knew it would be apparent I wasn't in the house, and I was afraid I'd be suspected of killing him. I didn't want to admit what I'd really been doing – things are bad enough with Reena, as it is – so I ... Stupid, I suppose, but there seemed to be one shock after another that night.'

Tom Black asked: 'What lie did you tell your wife to persuade *her* to lie?'

They never gave up, the bloody SIB! He told them about sitting on the doorstep.

'And she believed it?'

It was highly sceptical, which rattled Mark even more. 'My wife has a high opinion of herself. She'll believe anything flattering, however far-fetched.'

'Mrs Foyle the same?' asked Rydal.

'What?'

'What persuaded her to lie?'

'She's thick as thieves with Reena.'

There was a long silence during which the two detectives stared uncompromisingly at Mark until he averted his gaze. Then Max Rydal said coldly, 'Are you offering this evidence as the true account of your movements on the night of February twelfth, Captain Ingham?'

'Yes,' he said swiftly.

'You wish your previous statement to be completely disregarded?'

'That's right. Look, I'm sorry about that.'

He thought an apology would soften their attitude, and relief began to creep through him. It appeared the interview was over. He had sidled out of that business with Judy very well. Saints be praised, she had been unaware that he was there, much less that he had...

As Mark stood ready to leave, Rydal got to his feet and delivered a body blow. 'Mark Ingham, you will be reported for conduct unbecoming and for attempting to pervert the course of justice. You do not have to say anything, but it may harm your defence if you do not mention now something which you later rely on in court. Anything you do say may be given in evidence.'

Tom Black circled the desk to face him. 'You cannot provide proof of when you returned to your quarters from the gym, nor that you were in bed there when Major Bekov was shot dead. You have admitted to lying to us during earlier questioning. You could be lying again. The victim conspired to set back your career at Sandhurst, and there was a link between him and your wife in the past. Men have killed for far less, Captain Ingham. You may be called for further questioning in the course of our enquiries.'

Mark left the classroom knowing his world had caved in. A police report to Colonel Keegan would lead to an in-depth enquiry, if not a full court martial. One moment of madness prompted by a provoking encounter with Bekov would put paid to his future career and bring public humiliation. He would be known as a wanker who got his kicks from voyeurism. Dear Christ, Bekov's retaliation was even greater than the bastard intended!

Trudging blindly along the frozen road, murderous rage welled up in him. He was still under suspicion of shooting Bekov. He wished he had. It would go some way to mitigating his coming punishment. His whirlwind thoughts completely lost sight of the rape he had committed against a young woman in no condition to be aware of it.

As the door closed behind Ingham, Max looked at Tom. 'Well?'

'He's no killer.'

'I agree. *But!* His wife makes him look a fool in the eyes of a man he detests but envies. He's drunk, and high on mess night machismo. Bekov makes off with a pseudo-virgin others have failed to bed, and he follows because he can't help himself. He watches his arch-rival have rampant sex, frolic naked with this desirable woman, then go for a second helping. He then staggers off leaving her in post-coital dreamland and completely vulnerable. Ingham crosses to her: he has an unbearably painful erection. She's lying there invitingly; she's just been going at it like crazy with Bekov, who's doubtless done the same with Reena in his time. Is he really likely to solve the problem manually?'

'It's rape, no matter the circumstances that

led to it,' Tom ruled harshly.

'Of course it's bloody rape! He knew it the moment he sobered up. Hence the desperate alibi. But he wouldn't have seen it that way at the time. It's like taking towels from a hotel. Everyone does it so it's not really theft.'

'Bad simile, sir.' Tom was hot on rape. He had three daughters fast growing up.

Max sighed heavily. 'Ms King is unaware of what took place: we can't prove he actually entered her.'

'Do we tell her this?'

'Unless she demands enlightenment I suggest we leave it for the moment and stick to the main issue.'

'Ingham may be called to give evidence as to the time Bekov left the gymnasium. He's the only witness to that.'

'And to the fact that Ms King was still there when *he* left fifteen minutes later.' Max was gazing out at the icy scene and musing. 'You're still not one hundred per cent with me on the firing-squad theory, are you?'

'I understand the logic of it. It's the timing that queers the pitch for me. Victim knocks on the Inghams' door at roughly 03:00 and...'

'Unless the neighbours are lying to cover their own guilt.'

Tom frowned. 'We'll consider that when other avenues turn into blind alleys. Within an hour from then, the victim is hooded, marched into the copse, shot dead, driven a mile or so then tied up blindfolded and minus badges of rank.'

'An hour's time enough.'

'Only if the killer knew exactly where Bekov would be at any given time that evening.'

'No one would have known *exactly* where he would be. The plan has to be fluid. He follows the pair when they leave the mess. He sees Ingham also following; sees him enter the gym several minutes after them. He waits. Bekov comes out alone, but something prevents the killer from hooding and grabbing him then. Too well illuminated; a car passes? But he knows Bekov will be denied entry to Ingham's house, because the man is still with Ms King. That works in his favour. Bekov is sure to head back to the mess, seeking a makeshift bed for what remains of the night. Perfect opportunity to nobble him en route.'

Tom greeted that with silence and an expression of strong doubt. Max had to convince him. 'Look, someone on this base had advance knowledge of Bekov's visit. He recognizes he's being offered the chance to avenge a wrong so grievous the guilty man must pay with his life. He has a single night in which to carry this out. It happens to be a night when there will be mess celebrations well into the early hours; every excuse for officers to be out and about later than usual. Great! He knows Leo Bekov's penchant for booze and women. Even better. If his victim drinks heavily it'll be easier to catch him unawares. He's going to get the bastard come hell or high water. He's a first-class tactician. Cool under fire. Supremely sure of himself.

He patiently waits for the right moment, then pounces. Got him! The punishment is carried out as planned, and the perpetrator resumes his normal military routine.'

Tom's eyes narrowed speculatively. 'You've just described Captain Peter Randolph.'

Eleven

James Harkness rang to say he had the lists Max had requested, and invited him to the mess for coffee. Tom said he would get on with checking out Bobby Foyle on WAMI.

'I think we have to investigate his wife,' advised Max on the point of leaving. 'That woman and Reena Ingham thick as thieves? They'd have nothing in common save husbands in the same regiment. So what made Jane Foyle lie for Ingham in a murder investigation? She's too level-headed to accept that crap about his sitting on her doorstep afraid to ring the bell, so why was she so confident he didn't kill Bekov? We now know it wasn't because she was spanking him and forcing him to take his nasty medicine, because he was in the gym raping Ms King.'

'Maybe he likes it both ways; went from one to the other.'

Max departed burdened by the image of a

naked corporal obeying degrading commands from the captain's wife. *Yes, ma'am, at the double!* Had that been the attraction? Had Susan secretly yearned to dominate?

Welcome warmth greeted him as he entered the mess. The 2IC, immaculate and assured, poured coffee, said how bloody cold it was and expressed the hope that the thaw would not set in until after the NATO exercise.

'Once this melts the ground will be a quagmire. Our vehicles will be sucked down, rendered ineffective. Bloody things need updating but our defence budget won't cover it. Makes us look poor relations against our NATO partners, who all seem able to afford the latest version of battle equipment.'

'A workman is only as good as his tools,' agreed Max. 'If the PM's going to continue his policy of offering to send troops we haven't got every time there's a politically important squabble anywhere in the world, he'll have to put his hand in his pocket to equip them adequately, or lose face.'

'Tell me about it,' groaned Harkness.

They spent a few minutes indulging in the usual military grievances, then Harkness produced the lists – one with the names of members of the visiting deputation, the other showing those who would have had advance knowledge of Leo Bekov's visit.

'You've got nowhere, I take it?' The bonhomie vanished. 'Your people are disrupting routine. Lectures are being delayed, parades cancelled, classes poorly attended. In the run-up to this exercise we need our personnel on top line.'

'We're investigating a murder, Major. So far, we've been able to suppress the more bizarre aspects of the case from the media, but a leak is sure to occur before long. You could possibly speed things up by persuading your officers to stop giving false statements. Mark Ingham has just admitted the truth in the face of irrefutable evidence. He wasted a lot of our time.'

'Questioning our officers *is* a waste of time,' Harkness said crisply. 'You'd do far better to look for an unstable squaddie. Jeremy Fielding could help you there.'

Max set down his empty cup. 'According to him none of them are killers. I hope, for your regiment's sake, he's wrong, or you'll quickly be defeated in battle.'

It was as if Max had blasphemed before the Pope. 'This regiment has *never* suffered a defeat! We've been involved in major setbacks like Colenso, Passchendaele, Tobruk as part of a large combined force, but our regimental battle honours are legion and we've spawned eleven VCs.' Colour suffused the man's thin cheeks. 'You'd not understand the strength of regimental pride, having no comparable history, but—'

'The office of Provost Marshal was established several centuries before your regiment came into existence,' Max reminded him swiftly. 'Don't underestimate us, Major.'

'But you haven't advanced at all in this

211

shocking affair, have you,' Harkness snapped.

Max got to his feet. 'We don't yet know who killed Major Bekov, but we've uncovered some pretty unsavoury evidence. You may have spawned eleven VCs, but right now you have a rather grubby bunch in this mess. Thanks for the lists.' He walked out muttering, 'Save me from men wedded to their regiments!'

It was snowing again. He had requested that the heating be put on in their class-cum-interview room, and was given the inevitable reply. Defence cuts mean we can't heat an entire block for the sake of one room. He had been offered another portable radiator. It was better than nothing.

There was a woman sitting with Tom beside one of the heaters, drinking coffee and engaging him in what looked to be earnest conversation. She glanced up as Max entered. He put her age at around twenty-seven and she was truly beautiful in the way few women are. A mass of dark hair, silvery-green eyes, clear creamy complexion, apricot-tinted mouth. She wore a full-length black coat with a fur collar, and high tan leather boots. She did not smile as Tom introduced her.

'This is Mrs Caroline Bekov, sir.'

Max was rarely lost for words, yet he was now. Tom explained further. 'Major Bekov's solicitor informed her of his death. She arrived at Section Headquarters this morning with a request to see you. Corporal Headley drove her over here; thought it the best thing. I told him he should have notified us before coming.'

'Yes.' Max cleared his throat and belatedly offered his hand. 'How do you do, Mrs Bekov. We have far more comfortable facilities at our headquarters. I'm sorry you've been subjected to a long drive in this weather only to sit in this icebox.' He reached for the phone. 'I'll arrange for us to talk in the officers' mess.'

'Please don't bother,' she said quietly. 'Mr Black has made me very welcome and the coffee has warmed me. I've just a few questions to ask, then I'd like to see Leo's body. I believe you have to give me permission to do that.'

Still unusually thrown by this development, Max waved away Tom's offer of coffee and dragged another chair forward to sit beside her. Divorcée or widow, he decided not to divulge the bizarre nature of her former husband's death. The marriage ended seven years ago – she must have been a teenage bride – so what on earth had prompted this mission to view his body?

Max trod carefully. 'You've been divorced for some time, I believe.'

'Seven years, yes.' She had a very direct gaze. 'Does that mean you won't let me see him?'

He avoided an answer. 'You haven't remarried.'

'I'm still in love with Leo.' No drama, no

213

dabbing at misty eyes, just a sincere statement of fact.

Conscious of Tom's matching fascination with this development, Max said, 'You were not named as Major Bekov's next of kin, so why did his solicitor notify you of his death?'

'Leo left instructions that he should.'

Max frowned. 'The pair of you kept in touch after the divorce?'

A faint smile accompanied the denial. 'Oh, no. You didn't know Leo.'

'Tell us about him. Please,' he added, believing any information about the victim would aid his thinking on the case.

'We met on a train. I'd spent five days with my sister in St Mawgan; he'd been scaling cliffs all along the Cornish coast. He burst into the carriage like a pack mule.' Her smile was sunny with recollection. 'Enormous backpack, ropes and tackle looped over his shoulders, boots hanging from their laces. And a curiously shaped leather case in his hand. I asked why he hadn't taken all the equipment by road. He said the route to the West Country was clogged with vehicles crammed with families, screaming kids, buckets and spades, and obese people thrusting triple cheeseburgers in their mouths as they sat in traffic jams. He said he could relax and sleep on a train. But he didn't.

'After a while we were the only ones left in the compartment. That was when I asked about the leather case. He said it contained his balalaika, took it out and began to play the

214

most exciting music as if there was nothing unusual about doing it on a train. There were soon people standing around listening.' She looked from Max to Tom, and back. 'He was proud of his Russian ancestry. Never tried to dismiss the bloodline, no matter who we were with.'

'His name would be a giveaway,' offered Max.

'We married three weeks later at a register office. My parents kicked up merry hell. It was too hasty, I was too young, I knew nothing about him and he was *Russian*. Leo made an all-night dash to Sunderland and won them over. He always could, you know. He was—' She broke off, searching for words. 'He was like a beacon drawing people to its light.'

'His people welcomed the marriage?' asked Tom.

'Yes. Boris was a lovely man. He had come to England on tour with an orchestra. Leo's mother was one of the PR team handling the arrangements. When the tour ended, Boris defected. He couldn't bear to leave Vera. He embraced everything British, but instilled in his son a love of Russian music and the advantages of being multilingual. They accepted me without reservations. And I them, because Leo loved us all with equal passion.'

'Yet your marriage ended only eighteen months later,' Max said. 'Mind if I ask why?'

Caroline Bekov's face grew shadowed. 'I'm

not one of those people who believe their lives are mapped out from birth to death; that nothing they do will change their destiny. Yet the fates truly conspired to drive us apart. The nature of Leo's work meant he didn't have lengthy postings. He would be away for just a few weeks. Often less. I transferred to the local branch of the finance company I was working for when we met, so I was well occupied during his absences. He was doing a short, intense stint in Northern Ireland when several of my former colleagues came from Head Office for a three-day attachment. We planned a night out together.' Her gaze remained steady as she said, 'The partying got out of hand. We all drank too much, then piled in a car to drive up to a viewpoint giving a fantastic panorama of the city. The driver lost control, shot a red light, then mounted the pavement just as a police car was cruising past.'

She paused to ask Tom if she could have another coffee. Max could see she needed the break to gain her composure, and joined Tom at the side table.

'When she's ready, I'll take her across to the mortuary, then sort out overnight accommodation for her,' he said quietly. 'Warn the hospital we're on our way when we leave here.'

'Will do. I'll check in with you later.'

They all had fresh mugs of coffee when Caroline Bekov continued. 'We were kept in the cells overnight because the guys had been abusive to the panda-car crew. Next morning we were all charged with being drunk and disorderly. The driver faced more serious charges, of course. We were all shocked at the way an enjoyable get-together had turned out. I was so hungover, I didn't attempt to go in the office and went straight home.'

She took a long drink from the mug held in both hands for warmth. 'The light was flashing on the answer machine. The tape was full of frantic messages from Leo. He had been calling since seven the previous evening.' She took a deep breath and let it out slowly. 'In the last message before the tape ran out he said he was in Coventry. In the hospital where his parents' bodies had been taken. "Where the hell are you when I most need you?" he cried before he was cut off.'

Tom leaned forward with a frown. '*Both* parents had been killed? A road accident?'

'A seven-vehicle pile-up on the motorway. Caused by a sales rep driving recklessly after a too-liquid lunch.' She studied the steam rising from her coffee. 'No need to elaborate on the way things deteriorated. Leo was shattered by their deaths. A tanker had been involved; cars and occupants badly burned. I lied to him about where I'd spent the night. Then the court summons revealed the truth. At the very time his mother and father were burning to death, his wife was drunk and careering around in a car like their murderer. He walked out. I never saw him again.'

'The divorce proceedings?' asked Max, the

217

talk of car smashes getting beneath his guard.

'All done through his solicitor. Leo was a proud man and utterly unforgiving. No one was ever given a second chance. As he saw it, I had abandoned him at his moment of most need.'

Max once more took in the beauty of her. How could any man walk away so finally from someone like this? '*You* made no attempt at reconciliation?'

'No.'

'Although you loved him?' She said nothing. 'These past seven years must have been very difficult for you.'

She passed on that. 'Press reports said only that Leo had been shot, and an investigation was under way. Can you give me any more details?'

This was tricky. She was neither family nor next of kin, officially. Yet she *cared*. Bekov had been wrong. His wife had not abandoned him seven years ago. She still had not.

'One bullet through the heart. Death would have been immediate.'

She got to her feet. 'I really want to see him. Please tell me where he is.'

Max stood slowly. 'You're sure about this?'

'Oh, yes. Seven years ago he left our house one morning knowing he had no intention of coming back. I had no chance to say goodbye, and I need to.'

The British Military Hospital was five kilometres away; not too arduous a drive. The

Land Rover could cope with present road conditions, but it was not the vehicle in which Max would have chosen to take someone who was a grieving widow, however one looked at it, to view her loved one's body.

While driving to the main gate they were silent, Max brooding on Caroline's last words. He had not said goodbye to Susan on her last morning as his wife. She had still been asleep when he left the house. He had formally identified her body; he had prayed for her soul and that of the unborn infant at the funeral. But he had never bidden her farewell. On his next leave he could visit the crematorium, wander in the Garden of Remembrance, murmur appropriate words. That might put the demons to flight. As for forgiveness...! He glanced at the lovely woman beside him. Had she made her peace with Bekov during the last seven years, or had only his death made that possible? Was that her true reason for coming here?

Once on the main road Max followed the tracks made by other vehicles. He drove slowly to allow mortuary staff time to prepare for their visit. Leo Bekov would look serene and unblemished, unlike many murder victims Max had seen. Unlike the grotesquely broken body of his wife he had gazed at in numb horror!

'This must be irksome for you,' Caroline said quietly. 'Surely one of your drivers should be doing this duty.'

'One of my drivers should never have

brought you here in the first place. Had I been told of your arrival, I'd have returned to headquarters to meet you.' He gave her a swift glance. 'You must have travelled overnight from England.'

She managed a faint smile. 'Remember that old song about boats and trains and planes? As soon as that solicitor phoned me with the news I was working out the quickest means of getting here.'

'Mmm, the legal man was swift off the mark! We notified him promptly as he was registered as next of kin, but how did he know where to contact you? Have you stayed in that same house?'

She shook her head. 'We were renting it. I bought a flat near my parents' home and dealt with the divorce correspondence at that address. I would have been traced had I moved from there, but it would have taken time and Leo might have been ... Captain Rydal, his will apparently gives no instructions about his funeral. At the time he made it – shortly after he left me – I suppose he was only considering possible death in action. He was young and superbly fit, but he was a soldier.'

Max guessed what was coming. 'You're not the declared next of kin and, legally, you're no longer related to him by marriage. In cases where there are no kith or kin a body can be released to a friend, employer or other sympathetic person for burial on application to the coroner.' He hesitated momentarily.

'During those seven years your ex-husband might have grown close to someone who could also come forward with the same desire.'

'No,' she declared confidently. 'Among the things he said before abandoning our marriage, he swore he would never again trust a woman enough to love her. I believe he meant that.'

They entered the hospital gates and Max drove to the mortuary, reflecting that she was probably right. The Major had clearly been a man who conquered then swiftly departed, leaving women with their unrealized dreams.

He pulled up outside the low red-brick building, and turned to her. 'As his ex-wife you should have no problem with your application. I'll intercede on your behalf.'

She gathered up her large travelling bag. 'You're very kind.'

Max forestalled her. 'Please wait here while I check that they are aware of our visit. It won't take long.'

He strode through the heavy swing doors, pushing away the memories that threatened each time he entered one of these storehouses of the dead. No way would he let them have her stand by while they pulled out a metal drawer containing the empty shell of a man she had never stopped loving. This was not just an official identification. This was to be an emotional reunion and farewell. He wanted the body decently laid out on a table draped with dark cloth in the private room set

221

aside for the bereaved. He found Tom had organized just that. Good man!

Max fetched his passenger and escorted her to the door of the room. 'Take as long as you like. There's no time limit on these occasions. Leave your bag with me. When you're ready I'll take you to the Gasthof just across the road from the gates and book you a room for the night.'

She turned to him, tension now in every muscle of her face. 'Please don't wait. I'm likely to be some time. There are a lot of things I have to tell him, things he gave me no opportunity to say. They have to be expressed before the chance is lost forever.' She put her hand lightly on his arm. 'Can you possibly understand that?'

Oh, yes, he understood that too bloody well! He cleared his throat. 'If that's what you'd prefer. However, please let me take that heavy bag across to the Gasthof to fix up a room and dinner for you. I'll arrange for a driver to collect you in the morning and take you to our headquarters where you can complete the application I mentioned.'

'How long will it be before...?'

'Difficult to say. But unless you have other things to do in Germany, I advise you to go home and wait there. Welfare will organize Major Bekov's return to England and inform you of flight times, and so on. They'll also offer any other help or support you might need.'

For the first time she looked close to tears.

'I never dreamed it would end this way. He was so *vital*, so talented. He had so much to give to life. Why would anyone take it from him?'

'That's what we have to discover, Mrs Bekov. Because your husband was merely overnighting here, finding a motive is difficult.'

Visibly holding on to her self-control, she said, 'Leo not only never forgave, he retaliated. My punishment was seven years of silence. I loved him, so I accepted his terms. Look for someone who hated him, and couldn't.'

Jeremy Fielding pulled up a short distance from the copse, leaving the engine running for warmth. He stared at the place where Leo had been murdered. It was one of the worst nights he could remember. His hands now trembled on the wheel, nausea hovered, his entire body registered the heightened thudding of his heart. He recognized the signs of hyperarousal; had suffered it once before during a potholing adventure, when a sudden torrent had rushed through the subterranean catacomb. The water then had stopped at just below shoulder level. It now threatened totally to engulf him. He lowered his aching head to his hands gripping the wheel, unable to look at that copse a moment longer.

The terrible humiliation Leo had dealt him in Kuwait had driven Jeremy to deny his instincts for almost two years. Then he had met Joe in a pub in Catterick. Joe was a scenery designer for a theatrical props company, and he had made all the running. Well experienced, Joe was enchanted by the opportunity to initiate a virgin. Jeremy's posting to Northern Ireland brought an abrupt end to the mutually enjoyable relationship. Joe had kissed him goodbye, said it had been fun and walked away without a backward glance.

Jeremy had been bereft, until his gaze fell upon a young orderly in the new hospital. The situation was far more tricky this time. So tricky, nothing came of what was clearly mutual attraction. Frustrated, Jeremy had decided a wife would be an advantageous cover for a man in his position. By then, he had accepted what he was and wanted freedom to enjoy its pleasures. Releasing his sexual needs with Jeannie, he had then drastically limited his freedom. Suddenly, he had to play devoted husband and father; toe the family line.

Then came the posting to Germany. Ben had been admitted to sick bay three months later with an allergic reaction to raw fish – he had sampled sushi. Ben had a lean, muscular body, intense blue eyes and a great sense of humour, but Ben was a lance corporal and a patient, to boot. Highly risky on both counts. Yet Jeremy was in love and seeking escape from the miseries of married life, so he cautiously pursued the unmistakable signals from a like spirit.

Ben confessed that he wanted to put on a show for Christmas; maybe a pantomime. He had always loved dressing up and larking about on stage. He said lots of the lads enjoyed making props, painting scenery, thinking up topical gags, arsing around in lewd sketches. Kept them out of mischief. A panto was British. Something they could not get in Krautland. Ben was given the go-ahead from Colonel Keegan.

Jeremy then told Ben about his close friend in Catterick who designed theatrical scenery; said he had become interested in the art. Maybe he could put in a bit of work for the coming show. He did, and Ben made his interest as obvious as possible in the presence of others.

They stored large pieces of scenery or props in the sports pavilion, and one late evening Jeremy contrived to stay there with Ben when the others had left. The young ranker was experienced and enthusiastic, acting like a drug on Jeremy who invented medical emergencies so they could meet in the pavilion. Ben had had a copy of the key made, and it was one of the few places on the base where they would be safe from discovery. Daytime assignations there were out of the question, so they had occasionally managed to meet in motels on corresponding days off; even once or twice deep in the forest. Jeremy had found that wildly exciting – passion surrounded by birdsong and rustlings in the undergrowth – but Ben liked his comforts.

With Jeannie growing more and more unstable, and poor little Briony perpetually distressed, Jeremy devised a desperate plan. Both he and Ben had leave due. He would have Jeannie admitted for psychiatric treatment, let Alice Foster have the baby for two weeks, then take his lover to the Seychelles. Their own cabin on a deserted shore. Sunshine, warmth, nude bathing, watching the sun go down while getting irresponsibly drunk. Ben wholly his for fourteen glorious days!

The regimental dinner had offered the perfect opportunity for a rendezvous. Jeremy had been delayed by the choking girl, but he called Ben on his mobile, as usual, to say he was on his way. Ben had been in a deep sleep by then, and asked what the hell time Jerry thought it was. It was too late, and too bloody cold. Forget it! Jeremy could not. Seeing Leo again had revived memories that drove him to seek comfort from the only possible source. He needed to see Ben. Please. *Please*.

So they had met, and had a monumental row. Ben was irritable, haughty and dismissive. Jeremy's confidence had been undermined by the realization that Leo's magnetic charm still had the power to get under his guard. He therefore sought gentleness, affection and warm understanding. Ben had simply wanted instant gratification as a reward for leaving his snug bed on a freezing night. Words flew between them, frank and deeply wounding to a man whose humiliation ten years earlier now seemed as raw as it had been then.

Ben had stormed out, chillingly reminding his lover that it would take just one word in the right ear to end his career as an officer and as a doctor. Misbehaviour with a subordinate and a patient! 'Bear that in mind, chuck,' he had warned, then added a parting shot. 'There's plenty of fish in the sea, and I'm out to catch bigger and better than the likes of you.'

Shock had piled upon shock. At home, he had found a hysterical wife and a screaming, malodorous baby. Less than half an hour later, he had been called out to examine a body tied to a signpost.

Jeremy's hands on the wheel grew wet with his silent tears as the vision of Leo's body hanging there like an executed prisoner rose vividly in his mind yet again. It would not go away. He had been so vital, so energetic. It was still impossible to believe that compelling personality could have been brutally extinguished just yards from where he now sat.

His sense of loss was physical pain he must ease. Not at home. No comfort, no love there. Only one hope and he was desperate enough to pursue it. Keeping his gaze from the snow-covered copse looming starkly in the darkness, Jeremy punched out the number of Ben's mobile on his own.

Finally, Ben's voice. Cold. 'So what is it?'

'I need to see you.'

'I don't think so, chuck.'

'Ben, please!'

'After last time? You've got a hope.'

'We can't leave things as they are.'

'Suits me.'

Jeremy said swiftly, 'It doesn't suit *me*. Look, I can explain my mood the other night. And I've something very exciting to tell you. It'll prove how important a part of my life you've become.'

'It's too bloody cold.'

'I know ... but I've another place in mind. Very warm. Very private. All the trimmings. Please come. I'm ... I'm feeling rather desperate.'

'Need a quickie, do you?'

'I'll be there in ten minutes,' he said, trying to keep his gaze from the copse. 'You'll be glad you came, believe me.'

Ben disconnected, leaving Jeremy unsure of his intentions as he put the vehicle in motion and headed for the sports pavilion. He was shivering with cold and a sense of foundering on rocks offering minimal safety: the pressure of the vehicle's tyres set the frozen surface squeaking as he drove to the little pavilion. A 'quickie' was not what he needed; it was human warmth, a sign of caring, a hand reaching out in the darkness to hold him steady as the water rose higher and higher.

He parked in the usual place near a block of women's quarters, then walked swiftly in the shadows to the wooden structure where he had found intermittent happiness over the past three months. He let himself in with the key he had had copied from Ben's, and stood in darkness to watch from the window. Ben sidled in within minutes, the blast of air from outside hardly lowering the chill temperature inside. Jeremy turned instinctively to this human contact.

'Don't bother bending over,' Ben rasped by way of greeting. 'I've only come to get this sorted. I've had it with you, Jerry. I told you last time, but the message doesn't seem to have got through.'

'We both said a lot of things we didn't mean that night,' he responded tightly.

'No, chuck, I *meant* what I said.'

'Don't call me chuck! You know I hate it.'

Ben closed on him. 'Know what I hate? Midnight lust with a middle-aged major where the only hope of a bit of excitement is a spanking with a cricket bat. I want spice and variety; young, freewheeling guys who don't whinge on about wives and babies. Guys I can meet openly. Guys with rooms in town.'

'You want to play the field all of a sudden?'

'I've *been* playing the field,' Ben said with relish. 'You were just an experimental side-line.'

'*What?*'

'I met Rolf a month or so before Christmas. He organizes weekend parties in his apartment. The kind where anything goes. Know what I mean? No, course you don't! Scampering naked in the forest was your idea of a major thrill. These guys have invented the kind of excitement you'd never come up with in a lifetime.'

Jeremy grew even colder. 'You've been indulging in this the whole time we've known each other?'

'Yeah. Oh, I admit it was a turn-on, at the start, to have an officer at my beck and call, and I really appreciated the presents you gave me. But this little game has run its course, Jerry lad. Don't call me up any more. Understood?'

As Ben turned away, Jeremy unfroze enough to say fiercely, 'You bloody heedless fool! Don't you realize what risks you've been exposed to at those parties *where anything goes*? What you've exposed *me* to? Christ, Ben, you might have a throbbing organ between your legs, but haven't you *anything* between your ears?' He paused, fighting for control, before adding, 'I want you in my surgery first thing to give a sample of blood. That's an order! From a middle-aged officer to a dickhead corporal!'

Jeremy stayed among the sports gear long after Ben departed. Leo Bekov had started him out along this road: he was now in a dark cul de sac.

Twelve

When Mark got home after somehow sur-
viving the demands of the day, he found
Reena drunk and abusive. Her makeup was
too thick, her voice too shrill and her free
language no longer came over as smartly
modern. He decided she looked and sounded
like a slut.

He poured a stiff whisky and downed it
swiftly before pouring himself another. His
future was on the skids. No way to reverse the
plunge. He had no idea how soon SIB would
submit the report; when Jack Keegan would
call him to face the charges against him.
Reena's voice washed over him as he tried to
steady himself with slugs of spirit. Instead of
deadening his fears it made him hotly
aggressive. He rounded on his wife.

'For God's sake, shut up! I've had one hell
of a day. I don't need your self-obsessed
whining when I get home. Don't you ever
think of anyone but yourself?'

'What kind of day d'you think *I've* had, you
pig?' she retaliated. ''S all right for you. Got
things to do. All your palsy-walsys in the mess
to laugh and joke with. Yes, sir, no, sir, three
bags full, sir, wherever you go. I'm stuck here

day in, day out. Phoned Jane. Said she had to go out. Knew she was lying; her car was there all morning.'

Mark looked her over with something stronger than distaste and barely short of loathing. 'If you're drinking at this rate no wonder she avoids you. Jane's a really nice woman.'

'Meaning I'm not?' She gave a twisted smile. 'You won't care that I've moved your stuff to the spare room, then.'

'No, and I'll bloody stay there from now on. Want the truth? I'd rather be alone than share a bed with a selfish bitch stinking of gin.' He moved towards her, wagging his empty glass warningly. 'You can forget the health farm. I'm going to need that money.'

'*No!* You promised.'

'I've now *un*promised,' he declared wildly.

'Then I'll tell the Redcaps you made me lie about going to Jane's that night.'

'They already know you lied. You're for it, same as me. They plan to charge us with perverting the course of justice. You'll be in court instead of at the health farm.'

'*What!*'

'SIB are on to us, my tarty little wife. Bang goes my promotion, bang goes your privileged life out here, bang go all my hopes for the future. All because someone decided bang goes Leo bloody Bekov. I hope whoever put a bullet in him gets away with it. They deserve a bloody medal!'

'You *bastard!*' she cried, ashen-faced. 'He's

232

worth *ten* of you.'

Mark gave a grim smile. 'He's worth no more than a hole in the ground now. Best place for him.'

Subsiding on the sofa, Reena tearfully recited the charms and virtues of her former lover. 'Compared to him you're no better than a pile of *shit*!' she shrieked. 'You got me into this. They can't make me go to court. I've done nothing wrong. You *told* me what to say. *You* made me lie. I'll tell them that. I'll tell them you're so spineless you haven't enough bottle to own up to why you weren't here to let poor Leo in that night. Oh God, I can't believe he's *dead*. I can't believe...' Further words were smothered by her racking sobs as her grief grew too great to bear.

Unable to take any more, Mark snatched up his car keys, left the house and drove in to town. Even as early as this the bars had customers. Mark toured the more popular venues, drinking steadily as he contemplated the appalling collapse of his ordered life. Then, inevitably, he found himself in a more lively bar where girls wearing G-strings, and tassels on their nipples, gyrated around poles on the counter. He knew that he had come to the wrong place. Their long bare legs, rounded buttocks and full breasts swaying before his unfocused gaze drove home the enormity of what he had done.

Judy had been dead to the world, and he had been too drunk to consider the possibility of leaving incriminating evidence on her clothes. All the same, no one would have been any the wiser if Bekov had not met his certain fate just afterwards, because no one would have done DNA tests. Come to that, if Leo bloody Bekov had not made a play for Judy and hauled her off to the gym so he could show off, as usual, he would not have followed them and done what he had. It was all that Russian bastard's fault, not his!

He ordered another beer, gazing moodily at the dancing girls' near-nakedness. Judy had a sexier, more exciting body than these tatty fräuleins. But even there, Bekov had gone one better. She had responded eagerly; had gratified him without reservations. Mark Ingham had had to make do with the leftovers from Bekov's feast. He drained the glass and nodded at the barman to give him another.

Would that cold bugger Rydal tell Judy what he had discovered? She apparently had no recollection of his assault on her. He found it difficult enough now to be in her presence. How would he handle the situation once he was formally charged and the enquiry under way; when he was forced to admit he had watched the pair throughout their private cavorting, then was obliged to masturbate for relief? So would he appear in a better light by admitting the truth? No way! A charge of rape would follow.

His confidence plunged to rock-bottom. How *could* he have done that? He was not a vicious brute. He had always treated women with respect; had never fantasized about violation, bondage or male mastery. His appetite was that of any normal healthy man, and he had been true to Reena ... until that night.

All at once, the atmosphere in the bar seemed sordid, unhealthy. He looked around at the men ogling the girls. Men with red shiny faces and goggling eyes. Fat men, bald men, skinny, shifty-looking men, brutish youths with tattooed arms and rings in ears, noses and mouths. Lust emanated from them all as thick wet lips closed over the rims of glasses, and eyes narrowed with appreciation of this penis-fodder. Mark knew he had sunk to their level now.

Blundering through the noisy mass, he stepped out on the frozen snow and immediately threw up. Shivering in the bitter night chill, still nauseous, he staggered and stumbled over the many ridges in the icy surface to reach his car. He dropped his keys twice before successfully finding the lock. Starting the engine, he moved off with no idea of where to go. Just keep driving. Stay on the move. Escape the demons.

Lights along the street swung crazily. People loomed out of the neon brilliance; elongated, staring, mouthing at him. Ugly, each and every one. The din beat against his ears. Every driver was blasting on his horn. Raucous music spilled from every building. Someone was playing a bass drum. No, it was the thudding of his heart.

He reached the autobahn. Oncoming

235

headlights blinded him. They came straight at him. He tugged the wheel over. The car began to slide on the ice. It continued to slide. He lost control of it.

There was a deafening bang.

Mark returned to consciousness to find he was lying across the wheel. The car was on its side. Through the gap left by the shattered windscreen he could see rotating lights against the darkness. There was an ambulance and a car with POLIZEI along its side. He was in pain and all around him there appeared to be a vast void. He closed his eyes.

There was no Bekov to descend with a rope to tie around his ankles in case he slipped into everlasting blackness. Not this time. He began silently to cry, and his tears mingled with the blood across his face.

Breakfast in the Black household was a noisy but ordered routine. Getting girls of eight, ten and twelve out of bed, showered and healthily fed in time to catch the school bus was admirably managed by Nora.

This morning, as Tom fed bread into the toaster four slices at a time, he was aware of an unusual hush above stairs. No rushing feet, no high-pitched squabbling over hair clips or socks, no chivvying by a firm maternal voice. He glanced at the clock. They should be starting on their cereal by now. Putting his bacon to grill, he walked to the foot of the stairs.

'You're running late, girls. Put your skates on!'

Subdued giggles as a response. No suggestion of movement. Shrugging, he returned to the kitchen in time to turn the bacon before it became too crisp. The water in the poacher had come to the boil, so he dropped four eggs in the greased cups. Nora would not allow fried eggs. Bad cholesterol! Tom humoured her at home, but enjoyed a fry-up when he had the chance of it elsewhere. He was about to return to shout another warning when Nora appeared.

'Carry on with yours, love. Female emergency. Maggie's first period! She's acting like a tragedy queen; the other two are ridiculously jealous. They'll soon discover what a curse it can be when it occurs on a special date.' She gave a rueful smile and kissed him on the cheek. 'Or when it prevents a night of passion.' Returning upstairs, she called over her shoulder, 'I'll run them to school. They'll never get the bus.'

The bacon burned, the eggs poached into small rocks while Tom stood facing the unpalatable truth. His little girls were developing into young women far too soon. Beth, Gina and Maggie would gradually grow away from him, turning into creatures who became more and difficult to understand. Then there would be *boys*! It did not bear thinking about. If only one of them had been a son.

He knew he was fortunate to have a devoted wife and well-adjusted children. The credit

237

must go to Nora, for the demands of his work limited the time he could spend with them. He was doubly fortunate in having a loving atmosphere to return to after dealing with the darker side of humanity. Two of his sergeants had selfish wives; another was going through a messy divorce. A corporal had got himself involved with a German girl and was frantically trying to disentangle himself. Then there was Max Rydal; alone, haunted by black doubts.

Munching toast, Tom forced his thoughts away from family and on to the complex murder they were trying to make sense of. Three men had known the victim before and had had the opportunity to kill him. Tom's money was on Peter Randolph, who had eluded the pair seeking DNA because he was at an all-day combined-services strategy meeting for the upcoming NATO exercise. They would nab him today for certain.

Arriving at Headquarters, Tom was met almost at the door by Sergeant Boyle – he of the messy divorce – with information that had just been relayed.

'Sir, we have a witness who says she saw Major Fielding enter the sports pavilion on the night of the murder.'

'Why didn't she come forward earlier?'

'Seems the boyfriend broke it off when she told him she might be pregnant. She was up all night crying. That's when she saw the Doc, but she was too miserable to think much of it. She's now discovered she isn't pregnant and thinks the sighting might be important.'

'For God's sake, give me factual reports, not Mills and Boon sob stories. All you needed to say was that personal problems prevented her from saying something before.'

'Sorry, sir. Private Fawcett says it was quite a while after 02:00 when she spotted him.'

Tom frowned. 'How could she positively identify anyone in the darkness, and from a distance?'

'Her room overlooks the sports ground. She gets a good view of all the matches. She says she was in the Christmas show, and they kept scenery and suchlike in the pavilion. Major Fielding helped out backstage, so she knows him pretty well.'

'OK, check it out. Did she see this person leave again?'

'No. She fell asleep.'

'Huh, very helpful!' He moved across to Sergeant Flynn and asked her if she had managed to get any information from Intelligence on Leo Bekov's activities in Kuwait and Bosnia. The answer was no.

'Chase 'em up! Tell them to stop being obstructive.'

'They're protecting their own, sir.'

'It's one of theirs who's been murdered!'

He crossed to his desk and studied the plan of the base. The sports ground, with small pavilion, was sited about a kilometre from the surgery and bordering the perimeter road. A block of women's living quarters stood along a side road also housing Admin offices. If the girl's room was on the west side she would easily see the pavilion, even at night. A street lamp illuminated the junction, but at that distance identification would be subject to doubt. Her claim would have to be tested under similar conditions.

This evidence supported the theory that Fielding was lying about his movements that night. He could have gone to the pavilion with a lover or fellow conspirator. The witness claimed he was there well after 02:00. Bekov had then been embarking on his second helping of Judith King, watched by the envious Ingham. Corporal Mitchum had very properly been hastening back to bed, dog tucked under his arm, no doubt. His quarters lay in the opposite direction to the pavilion so he wouldn't have seen anyone entering it.

The MO suddenly seemed the prime suspect for the murder. The timing worked, and the lover he met could also have been his partner in crime. She could have helped Fielding drive the body to the mess and tie him up, after killing him. The timing exonerated Lieutenant King and left Jane Foyle in the frame.

Max rose early after an unusually calm sleep and cooked a substantial breakfast. It was quiet next door, so he listened to a CD of Russian folk tunes played by a balalaika orchestra while he ate. Caroline Bekov's account of how she met the man she had married had caught Max's imagination.

Anyone who began to play a balalaika like a pro on a train in England would, of course, draw people. It wasn't the done thing!

He smiled as he pictured the tut-tutting of elderly fogies fading as they fell beneath the spell of the music; teenagers abandoning hissing Walkmans to watch the flying fingers of a man producing alien magic on a triangular keyboard; babies falling silent lulled by the dulcet sounds. And a beautiful girl succumbing to the lure of haunting melodies created by a charismatic musician.

While Max listened to his CD he found himself beginning to understand the personality so recently extinguished. Physically attractive, sexually beckoning, intelligent, multilingual, assured to the point of arrogance, highly gifted. Such a man must often invoke envy to overshadow admiration.

Someone had taken that to the extreme whereby he could only cope with life if Bekov was removed from it. But he was controlled enough to wait for the perfect opportunity, and daring enough to risk taking it. Peter Randolph filled the bill exactly. Another attractive, sexually beckoning, intelligent, arrogant male who had been legitimately cruising around the base that night. And Max was damned sure his path had crossed Bekov's in Bosnia. That slightly derisive use of 'Tolstoy' had betrayed the fact. Time they pinned down that elusive blue-blood.

After showering and further reducing his supply of clean shirts, Max put through a call to the Gasthof asking them to inform Mrs Bekov that someone would be coming to see her about funeral arrangements in around an hour's time. He then finished dressing, stacked his breakfast dishes in the dishwasher and left the apartment suspecting his neighbours must be away. It was still far too quiet.

The air outside was bitterly cold. Driving conditions were bad. Below-zero temperatures overnight had hardened the packed snow so that even the earlier wheel-tracks were now hazardous. Without the chains Max had fitted to his wheels, his car would have failed to find purchase on the icy surface.

His intention of making only a brief call at Section Headquarters was foiled. As he entered, Tom called to him and came forward.

'Good morning, sir. Some new evidence on the Bekov murder.'

Max opened the door of his office and motioned Tom to follow him in. He perched on the edge of his desk to listen.

'We have a witness who claims she saw Major Fielding enter the sports pavilion in the early hours of that morning. Her evidence could prove he was lying about returning directly from his surgery to his quarters.' Tom added fuller details, then gave his theory on a meeting with a lover/accomplice to way-lay then kill Bekov. 'It could prove to be the break-through we need.'

'It could also be a load of codswallop, Tom. Why the hell would he meet a lover in the

242

sports pavilion on a freezing cold night?'

'Same reason as Ms King and the Major,' he returned drily. 'Maybe the Doc's another sexual athlete; likes kicking a football or swinging a cricket bat in the nude, while she watches admiringly.'

Max laughed. 'Most women I know grumble incessantly if they're asked to stand warmly wrapped up on the sidelines to watch their man perform in sports gear. Never come across one willing to turn blue with cold just to watch him do it naked in the early hours.'

It brought a return smile from Tom. 'One of the pleasures of this job is discovering how many nutters we have around us.'

'Fielding isn't a nutter, my friend, he's a man on the brink of a precipice. Meeting Bekov again could have threatened to tip him over. We'll go after him when I get back.'

'From where?'

Max stood. 'I promised Mrs Bekov I'd support her claim to her ex-husband's body for burial. Has Sergeant Bush prepared the form for her to sign?'

'I told her about it yesterday and she never forgets important things like that. I'll get it from her. You plan to be away long?'

'As long as it takes. Can't rush something like that.'

Caroline Bekov was sitting in the small lounge area where a log fire added attractive visual comfort to that from the central heating. She looked pale but as beautiful as Max remembered, today in dark velvet trousers and a heavy cream polo-neck. Her surprise as she stood was evident.

'Captain Rydal! I was expecting one of your staff. They didn't tell me you were coming yourself.'

He shook the hand she offered. 'I wanted to go through the formalities with you and to show you the letter I've written in support of your claim.' He took off his topcoat and hung it on one of the stout hooks along the wall. 'I've asked them to bring us coffee. This might take a little time.'

He sat in a chair beside hers and took papers from his briefcase to lay on top of it while he asked if she had been comfortable there.

'Thank you, yes, but I confess I spent most of the night wrapped in the duvet in a chair by the window, looking out at the snow.' She studied the fireglow. 'Seeing him again – after what happened all those years ago – well, it was ... unnerving.' She glanced back at Max. 'I wasn't prepared for the evidence that he'd finally gone away. I began to tell him all the things I came here to say. Then I realized how pointless it was. Captain Rydal...'

'Max,' he prompted swiftly, identifying far too well with what she was telling him. 'It wasn't pointless, because *you* needed to do it.'

'From the day he walked out knowing he was leaving me, I saw nothing of him for seven interminable years. I knew he would never forgive me and return, yet he was still a part of me. Still alive and vital. Can you understand that it was somehow comforting to know that?'

Max tried to imagine his own feelings if Susan had simply walked out on him. Would he have been comforted by the fact that she was alive and pursuing her dreams? Halfway through telling himself there was no comparison here, Caroline spoke again.

'Seeing that pale face, his expressive dark eyes irrevocably lidded, his utter *stillness*, was a worse blow than I'd expected. He'd gone from me more finally than on that unforgettable day. It seemed impossible that his fire and energy had been extinguished. That he'd never laugh, and dance, and ... *love* again. Never play his balalaika and draw people around him to listen enchanted.' She gazed at the fire once more, her voice growing so quiet Max had a job to hear her. 'I suddenly knew he wouldn't want me – wouldn't want *anyone* – to see him as no more than a lifeless shell.'

Max put a comforting hand on her shoulder. Thank God she didn't yet know the killer had intended his lifeless victim to be seen by as many people as possible. He said gently, 'Do you still want to go ahead with this claim?'

She glanced up swiftly. 'Oh, *of course*. His parents are long dead, and I was closer to him than anyone else.' Her lovely eyes appealed to him. 'Why else would he have instructed his solicitor to inform me of his death?'

245

In a bid to ease her grief Max took up the papers he had brought and began to explain the necessary procedures. He then gave her a copy of his covering letter to the coroner. While she was reading this a waiter brought a tray of coffee. Max poured for them both and handed her a cup. In spite of the heat from the fire, Caroline curled her hands around the elegant china as if seeking warmth to counteract the chill of the stark subject they were discussing.

She looked across at him. 'You've been very kind, Captain...'

'Max,' he corrected.

Her smile was little more than the ghost of one. 'Max. It's very good of you to devote time to me when you must be wanting to get on with your investigation. Have you any idea who was responsible for this *senseless* killing?'

'We're following three leads. I promise you we'll find who did it.' He drank some coffee, wondering again how any man could walk away so resolutely from this lovely woman; not find it in his heart eventually to forgive her for what had been a cruel twist of fate. 'You suggested yesterday that we look for someone who hated him and couldn't accept his terms of retaliation. Do you know of any instances in the past when Major Bekov had cause to avenge some real or imagined wrong committed by a military colleague?'

Still tightly gripping her cup she slowly shook her head. 'Leo rarely discussed his work with me. Much of it was confidential, of

246

course, but he liked to have fun when he was out of uniform. We'd travel miles to concerts or exhibitions. He loved London nightlife, so we spent many weekends in his parents' apartment, even if they were away. He discovered a Russian restaurant and thought nothing of driving sixty miles there and back for a meal several times a month.'

'Were you equally enthusiastic?' Max asked.

Her smile was wide now. 'Oh, yes! He made everything larger than life, wildly exciting, pushing at the boundaries. I've never known anyone so charged with vitality. And when he played his balalaika he seemed to become filled with the passion and tragedy of those wonderful old folk tunes. Those were some of the most precious moments of our time together.' Her eyes grew glassy with moisture. 'I'd give anything to have that balalaika. It was so much a part of him. I can't bear the thought—'

'His personal effects will be sent to his solicitor,' Max interrupted gently. 'There's sure to be a will of sorts. I suggest you contact him when you get home to see if that would be possible.' He held up the coffee pot questioningly, and she gave him her cup for a refill. As he poured he asked, 'When do you plan to leave?'

'I've booked a seat on this evening's flight to Heathrow. I'll take the noon train to the airport.' She gazed at the full cup he pushed along the table towards her. 'There's nothing here for me now.'

'I'll drive you to the station,' he said impulsively.

Her eyes met his. Tears had vanished, but they remained extra bright. 'Thank you, but I've already organized a taxi. I really appreciate your help, especially as I'm merely an ex-widow, so to speak.'

That hurt him in a manner he didn't expect. 'You're the one person who cared enough to come here and claim him. That doesn't make you *ex* anything where Leo Bekov is concerned. I'm only sorry you were unable to say what you wanted to him yesterday.'

'But I did, Max. Last night, as I sat by the window looking out at the snowy scene. It conjured up memories of the vivid tales he told me of the icy expanses of Russia which had generated the emotive tunes he used to play. I knew then that his spirit was out there, no longer with what I saw at the hospital.' She smiled. 'I might have guessed at the start. Although he was passionately loyal to the country of his birth, the blood of his ancestors pulsed through his veins to make him perpetually restless. I spoke to him and made my peace before he moved off to seek them.'

Jeremy Fielding drew blood from Ben's arm, then applied a cottonwool pad and strip of plaster, all the time refusing to meet those brown eyes that had teased him so often. 'The result should be here tomorrow. I'll put an URGENT sticker on it.' He wrote Ben's details on a label attached to the plastic envelope into which he dropped the sample. 'That's it. You can go,' he said coldly.

As the door clicked shut behind his former lover he lowered his aching head on his hands. All night he had been facing the truth of what a bloody fool he had been. He had been well aware of the dangers, but had surrendered to temptation. The affair with Joe had been warm and mutually loyal. He now saw that a similar relationship with Ben had never been possible. It had been a crazy infatuation on his part; merely an experimental sideline for Ben. Gay weekend parties, cottaging, cruising, whatever one called it, meant sexual gratification without commitment. He wanted friendship, sharing and caring with just one person.

He thought back on those few unforgettable weeks in the desert. If Leo had been gay they could have become the perfect partners. Now Leo was dead, and he was facing a possible long, painful journey towards the same end.

He grew aware that Corporal Minns was in the doorway telling him something. He peered at the man through blurred eyes. 'Say again.'

'Captain Rydal and Mr Black are here to speak to you, sir.'

They came in and stood silent until Minns closed the door. Then Rydal said, 'We could do this in your quarters, but we thought you'd prefer your wife not to be present.'

Jeremy stared listlessly; waited for the other

man to continue.

'Major Fielding, a witness has come forward claiming she saw you entering the sports pavilion some time soon after 02:00 on the night Leo Bekov was murdered. Would you care to comment on that?'

'What?' he asked in disbelief.

'You told us you returned home straight after dealing with the medical emergency.'

'Yes.'

'You didn't stop off at the sports pavilion?'

'No.'

The two detectives pulled out chairs and sat. 'Had you arranged to meet someone there, sir?' asked Tom Black.

Jeremy could not get his mind around this. How *could* someone have seen him at that hour? The road had been deserted. He had passed no one along the way.

Rydal's next words drilled into him. 'When you learned Major Bekov would be visiting the base, did you see an opportunity to avenge something that happened when your paths crossed in the desert? Did you plan his death with an accomplice who waited in the pavilion with a sack and some rope? Did you meet him there bringing a gun, and one of those squares of cloth you use for a sling to act as a blindfold? Did you then both follow your victim from Captain Ingham's house, throw the sack over him, then frogmarch him to where you shot him dead?'

Jeremy looked from one to the other of his accusers. 'You're surely not serious.'

250

'We now know you lied to us about your movements that night, so you are high on our list of suspects,' Rydal told him. 'How much more serious would you like us to be?'

Fighting his way through the fog of mental confusion, Jeremy said haltingly, 'I wouldn't ... *couldn't* kill Leo. He was ... a friend.'

'You told us he had been no more than a patient; a malingerer you had little time for.'

'Did I?' He ran a hand through his hair. 'Look, I'm not having a very good day. Can we do this later?'

'We need answers now,' the Sergeant Major insisted.

Jeremy gazed at his linked hands on the desk. This was one long, continuing nightmare with little prospect of waking from it. 'He *was* a patient. Another officer to talk to. I got to know him.'

'So why not tell us that before? There's nothing secret about a short-term friendship in wartime, is there?'

'Of course not!' He had sounded too defensive, so he attempted to gloss over that swift denial. 'It had been a hell of a night for me. I never enjoy celebrations of past deeds by a regiment I don't belong to. I usually slide out of them, but because we had VIP guests I was obliged to attend.'

'And you renewed your acquaintance with Major Bekov,' said Tom Black.

'Actually, no. He was with the General's entourage, kept pretty well entertained by James Harkness and the regimental stalwarts.

Anyway, ten years had passed. Water under the bridge.'

'So you didn't exchange words?'

'No opportunity.' Jeremy leaned back in his chair and regarded them through weary eyes. 'Just as I thought I could decently slip away, Pete Randolph came to tell me there was an emergency call. The patient was frightened, so simple treatment took longer than it should have. Then, when I reached home, I faced another emergency.'

He told them the details. 'I'd no sooner calmed Jeannie, cleaned up my little daughter, then rolled into bed, than Pete called me out to certify death in one of our official guests.' He studied his hands again. 'That's all he told me, so what I saw when I got there came as something of a shock. Leo looked so ... so...'

'Punished?' suggested Rydal.

Jeremy looked up swiftly. 'I suppose ... He'd been so full of life only an hour or so before.'

'But you must be accustomed to sudden death,' reasoned Tom Black. 'You were there in the Gulf.'

'That was *war*. Cause and effect follow an accepted pattern. Leo's murder seemed so ... gross,' he finished with uncheckable sadness.

After a brief pause, Rydal said, 'You haven't answered our question.'

Jeremy frowned. 'What question?'

'Whom did you meet in the sports pavilion that night?'

It was like being caught in a web with two

spiders watching his struggles to be free. 'I didn't *go* to the pavilion.

'We have a witness who swears you did.'

'Your witness is mistaken.'

Rydal took a different line. 'When we spoke to your wife, she complained of the frequent night-time emergency calls you had to deal with. You explained them away as punch-ups, accidental injuries; the normal medley of military mishaps. We've checked your records. Over the past three months you've had just two emergencies after midnight, one being the girl choking on a cough sweet. Where did you go on all those other occasions, Doctor?'

His stomach muscles tightened, his throat grew dryer still. 'My wife exaggerated. She's in a very nervous state at present. Hates being alone in the house. If I'm absent for ten minutes, it's an hour to her.'

The Sergeant Major asked, 'Have you had secret meetings in the pavilion before, sir?'

'Don't you *listen*?' he demanded heatedly. 'My wife is not responsible for what she says. She needs help to work through her depression. I've already spoken to Major Phipps about fixing a series of consultations.' He looked pointedly at the large wall clock, and got to his feet. 'I should have gone home for coffee ten minutes ago. She'll be growing agitated.'

Neither detective moved. Max Rydal continued by intensifying the pressure. 'We believe your dealings with Leo Bekov were more complex than you say they were, and we have a witness who places you on the perimeter road on the night of his murder. We shall seek permission to search your quarters, and two of my team are presently looking for evidence in the pavilion. By your own admission your wife should not be relied upon to make accurate statements, so it would seem you have no way of proving where you were at the time the murder took place. We may eventually have to conduct a search of these premises.'

Tom Black turned the screw further. 'If you confirmed the assignation in the pavilion, and the person you met there came forward to support your statement, we could sort things out much easier, sir.'

The Devil and the deep blue sea! No way could he ever admit to those meetings with Ben, so the searches would take place and he would be damaged by inference. They would find nothing to link him with Leo's death, but Jeannie would grow more agitated by the invasion of their home and his professional integrity would suffer if they took the surgery apart looking for a gun or the sack Leo's killer used to hood him.

He said woodenly: 'I shall insist on being present if you decide to search here. There are confidential records, drugs and valuable equipment which are all my responsibility. If you search my quarters my wife's fragile nerves will suffer further. You won't find anything incriminating at either place, I swear. *I did not kill Major Bekov.'*

Rydal's calm gaze held his. 'Why don't you prove it by telling us the facts about your rendezvous in the sports pavilion. It would be much simpler that way.'

No, it would not! Jeremy rose and walked to the hook where his cap hung by the door. 'I suppose you have to do what you imagine is your duty, despite my denial of any complicity in the murder of a fellow officer. I have my duty, too, gentlemen. I promised to visit one of the wives who is due to give birth any day now. Her quarters are on my way home.' He held the door open. 'After you.'

Thirteen

Drinking coffee beside the heaters in their interview room fifteen minutes later, Max stared moodily through the window. Witness statements were useless without solid evidence, and Private Fawcett's claim to have seen the MO from her window in the dead of night was too lightweight. Even if a reconstruction by the team proved it possible to identify someone under those conditions, unless proof of his presence in the pavilion was found he could deny it till kingdom come!

He had just promised Caroline Bekov a

certain result, but the case was going no-where. Snowfall had put paid to scene-of-crime searching; the DNA match only proved Ingham had participated in the sexual capers in the gym. Forensics had found no link with any on the victim's clothing or body, so Ingham was off the hook for the murder.

Fielding was surely hiding *something*. He had appeared highly stressed before; today he looked positively ill. Under relentless questioning he might crack and confess the truth about that night.

Then there was Peter Randolph. Too clever, too slick and all too likely to have master-minded the elimination of the man he had dubbed 'Tolstoy'. Getting to grips with him would be a contest of wits and wills, no doubt.

The section had three other investigations currently under way – an accusation of wife-beating, the theft of cutlery from a corporals' mess and a claim by a German that his underage daughter had been seduced by a British soldier – but Max had delegated so that he could concentrate on this murder. The initial sense of challenge had turned into a personal quest; the victim was fast be-coming too vitally human to remain focused.

'We should talk again to Mrs Foyle,' Tom said into the brooding silence, dragging Max back from visions of snowy wastes, balalaikas and a dark-haired girl with misty green eyes.

He returned to the reality of a basic class-room and the solid bulk of a man who knew him well. 'Yes. As you suggested, Reena Ingham probably drank a fair amount before retiring, and slept soundly. Jane Foyle could then have slipped from the house and returned before her guest emerged for breakfast. Ingham's request to provide him with an alibi could have suited her to a tee.'

'You think *she* met Fielding in the pavilion?'

'Possibly. But not for amorous reasons. Groping amid nets of footballs and hockey sticks wouldn't be her scene.'

'I checked her husband out. Good record. He's specializing in anti-terrorist tactics. Had tours in Oman and Hong Kong. Frequent spells in Northern Ireland. No indication he ever served with Bekov.'

'They could've met up in Ulster on an anti-terrorist course. Bekov was Intelligence, don't forget.'

'You're suggesting Jane Foyle could have killed the Major on behalf of her husband?'

Max sighed. 'Just letting ideas float around in my mind, Tom. It bothers me why she should befriend a woman like Reena Ingham, then be prepared to lie for the woman's husband in a murder investigation. I like things to add up. Jane Foyle's behaviour doesn't.'

'No more than the former Mrs Bekov's. How could she accept his terms, as she put it, then race over here after seven years of total estrangement to say goodbye to his lifeless body?'

'If you don't understand why after talking to her yesterday, you never will,' Max said, more sharply than he intended. 'It has no bearing on the case. Jane Foyle's lies *have*!'

The telephone rang. Max took it up, hoping to hear of a positive result from the search of the pavilion, but it was a request for him to see the CO right away. There had been no time to submit the charges he meant to bring against Ingham and his wife, so Max could only think he was to be given a pep talk about solving the case before eighty per cent of personnel were due to depart on the multi-national exercise.

He was irritated to find James Harkness in the overheated office with Jack Keegan. After bidding both men good morning, he swiftly asked if they had information for him.

'Captain Ingham was involved in a serious road accident last night,' Keegan said with the touch of steel Max suspected he possessed. 'His condition is critical enough to warrant round-the-clock observation. His wife is at his side.'

Although not what he had expected to be told, Max was not thrown by the news. 'I'm sorry to hear that.'

'I imagine you might be. On top of deep regret that he was not at home when Major Bekov returned unexpectedly to his quarter, Mark has been under pressure preparing for this important NATO exercise. This is what results when men are subjected to lengthy and unnecessary interrogations, to say nothing of having their wives distressed by questioning.'

Max waited a moment or two before saying quietly, 'Are you laying his car accident at my door, sir?'

James Harkness answered that. 'Because Major Bekov's body was found outside our mess, you've concentrated on hounding the officers. You asked me for a list of all personnel who would be aware of the Major's pending visit, yet you haven't followed up on it. Why?'

'None of those mentioned on the list served with the victim in the past, save three officers. All three have been unable to give a satisfactory account of their movements on the night the crime was committed. Ingham gave us a statement backed by his wife and Mrs Foyle. We then found forensic evidence that he was elsewhere. When challenged yesterday he confessed he had lied. His latest version claims he was back in his quarters at the time Bekov was killed. He can't prove that. He lied once. He may be lying again.'

He turned his attention back to the CO. 'Major Fielding's statements vary from day to day, and we now have a witness who saw him elsewhere when he says he was at home with his wife and screaming baby. Mrs Fielding is an unreliable witness. Fielding told us that himself.'

'She's a sick woman, needs specialist treatment.'

His dismissive tone told Max of Colonel Keegan's diluted interest. The medical officer was not a member of his regiment and, therefore, far more likely to have transgressed than one of his own mechanized stalwarts! Max went ahead and committed total sacrilege.

'We need to interview Captain Randolph in depth today.'

'*Why?*' demanded Harkness. 'He was Duty Officer that night. Dealt with the discovery of the body, and so on, with commendable efficiency and discretion.'

Oh *ho*, the blue-eyed boy here, was he? His distinguished antecedents would stand him in good stead with die-hards like this pair.

'Yes, *I* was impressed by his efficiency and discretion,' Max said equably. 'A man who is invariably calm and controlled, I imagine.'

'Absolutely,' said Harkness.

'As Duty Officer, he would have been out and about that night, yet he appears to have seen nothing suspicious while others spotted all manner of things from their windows. I find that curious. He's one of the three who served with Bekov before. He denies knowing the Major, but he let slip a nickname that puts the lie to that. We have to get to the bottom of his denial.'

Keegan looked greatly annoyed. 'How much longer is it going to take before you clear these officers and concentrate on tracing an unstable character among the rank and file? That's where you'll find the killer, mark my words.'

Max's temper was slipping out of control. 'If people lie to us it wastes valuable time. A word from you to your officers about telling the truth might hurry things up, sir.' He edged to the door, addressing Harkness. 'Was anyone else involved in Ingham's accident?'

'He swerved to avoid an oncoming car. Skidded on ice and hit trees. The other driver called an ambulance.'

'He was lucky. Driving under the influence *and* smashing into a German vehicle could have added to the stress he's under.'

Tom had news when Max got back to the interview room. A cufflink bearing the badge of the Royal Army Medical Corps had been found in the sports pavilion. Members of the team were now at the Fielding house seeking the matching link.

Max gave a tight smile. 'I've just been telling the CO and his faithful henchman we'd be further advanced in this case if their officers stopped lying.' He stood warming his rear just inches from one of the heaters. 'His partner in crime meets the MO in the pavilion with the necessary gear. That girl witness says Fielding wasn't carrying anything, but he could have had the sling cloth folded in his pocket and the gun stuffed in his waistband. The other one had the rope and sack.'

'Acting as stooge?'

'Yes. Simply there to hood and tie the victim. Fielding does the refinements.'

'If the killing was for a past sin, why does the other person participate? What's the motive?'

261

'Maybe there were two different motives. What if the accomplice was Ingham, who had his own reasons to hate Bekov?'

'At the time the Doc was seen entering the pavilion, Ingham was doing the dirty on Lieutenant King in the gym.'

'Bugger it, so he was!'

As if she had heard her name mentioned, Judith King walked in seconds later. Her eyes were today darkly circled, her cheeks slightly hollowed. The radiance of health had dimmed over the past few days. They waited for her to speak, but her usual forthrightness appeared to have deserted her.

'Good morning, ma'am,' said Tom eventually. 'What can we do for you?'

She addressed Max. 'I've been wondering ... you did say you'd let me know about taking DNA samples.'

Max thought quickly. It would be a while before his damning report on Ingham was received by the CO, and a court of inquiry would not be set up until the man was out of hospital and deemed fit to answer the charges against him. A matter of several months, at least, before this young woman was made aware of the sordid facts concerning the second lover they claimed she had that night. Max decided it would serve no useful purpose to burden her with the truth at this point. She had been a victim, after all.

'I suggest you relax on that one, Ms King,' he said.

She caught her breath in relief. 'I told you

they'd made a mistake.'

'I'm not saying forensics made a mistake.'

'But...'

'We're concentrating on other evidence at the moment,' said Tom.

Her eyes brightened slightly. 'Have you discovered who did it?'

'Until you can produce a witness to prove you were asleep in the gym when the crime took place, *you're* still on our list of suspects,' Max pointed out quietly.

Apprehension battled with caution as she digested that statement. 'You already know I can't do that.' Into the ensuing silence, she said, 'I'm not taking part in the NATO exercise, so I'll be on-base when you realize who murdered him.' She turned for the door, but paused with one hand against the frame. 'Leo Bekov might have been a bastard, but I've known worse ones. He didn't deserve what they did to him.'

As she left the room, Tom murmured, 'I guess he cast his spell over her, too.'

'Why else would she have behaved as she did with him?' asked Max, recalling Caroline Bekov's eager words on how he made everything seem larger than life; irresistibly exciting. 'But that young woman didn't deserve what happened later.'

'We've made bloody sure Ingham will pay for what he did,' Tom said grimly.

'The CO just now told me our man wrapped his car round a tree last night. Now in hospital with Reena dutifully beside the bed.'

'Well, well! Was he badly hurt?'

'Not badly enough. No one mentioned his balls were crushed beyond recognition.'

'Pity.'

'Keegan and Harkness believe he was stressed out by our remorseless questioning at a time when he was dealing with the demands of the coming exercise. When they read our report they'll know better.'

Tom finished his coffee and put aside the mug. 'More info came in while you were with the CO. Beeny and Piercey still haven't got DNA from Captain Randolph. He's not in his office and his sergeant says he's unsure where he is right now.'

'Bollocks! They have to know where everyone is throughout the day, particularly the officers, when terrorist attacks are a real threat.'

Tom grimaced. 'I told him that in words a sergeant would feel right at home with. He's loyal, I'll give him that. It's going to take a word from you to open him up.'

Max snatched up the telephone. The sergeant opened up! Within minutes the two detectives were driving from the base to a heathland area used for tank and weapons training, where Peter Randolph was checking his company's firepower. Sunshine was still glittering the frozen snow; trees lining the road were laden with it. Together with a clear, pale-blue sky the scene might have charmed travellers on more innocuous journeys.

The military men scarcely noticed the

264

winter beauty. Tom was brooding over the inevitability of his sweet young daughters facing the temptations and dangers of puberty. Max was speculating on what lay behind the nickname 'Tolstoy' used so disparagingly by the regiment's blue-eyed boy. From what he had learned of Leo Bekov, it was not difficult to guess his maverick personality would clash with that of an upright son of the colours like Randolph. The Robert Redford lookalike should attract women like a magnet, yet he was unmarried. Why? Playing the field?

Max knew enough about human nature to guess Randolph lacked the charisma the Anglo-Russian possessed and which had endeared him to men as well as women. Corporal Mitchum had thought Bekov 'a pleasant, cheery person' from just a brief encounter driving him to and from the conference, and David Hanson remembered him clearly at Sandhurst from thirteen years back. Jeremy Fielding had finally admitted he had counted Bekov a friend, and Ingham's dislike was so patently rooted in envious admiration. So what lay behind Peter Randolph's attitude towards a fellow officer whose path he had certainly crossed in Bosnia?

As soon as they turned on to the track leading to the military restricted area, the boom of firing could be heard in the still air. The Land Rover bumped over the uneven ground for five or six minutes until they reached a pair of wooden huts where several officers were studying a chart, deep in heated argument. Tom pulled up and they left the vehicle to approach the small group. Max let them continue their absorbed planning for a minute or two, then interrupted it.

'We're here to speak to Captain Randolph. Where will we find him?'

They all glanced up. One face was familiar: Andy Miles, Ingham's neighbour who had revealed Bekov's attempt to enter an un-occupied house.

He smiled his recognition. 'Hello again! I'm afraid Pete's out there in the middle of the heath testing his Warriors' guns,' he said with more assurance than he had shown at their last meeting. 'Can't tell you how long he'll be out there. Bloody important to get things up to speed before we go to war next week.' He grinned and explained about the exercise. 'Can't have our NATO allies regarding us as poor relations.'

Max regarded him frankly. 'We also have to get things "up to speed" before the exercise takes most of you away from the scene of crime. When investigating a murder, we have authority to interview anyone at *any* time. Even during a real war. Please radio Captain Randolph and tell him to come in pronto. His gunners can carry on without him. They must know their stuff well enough.'

For a split second Andy Miles looked set to defy the order, then he switched on his two-way radio and spoke rapidly. Max headed back to the comparative warmth of the Land

266

Rover, Tom following. Once settled inside, he nodded towards the young men in Arctic combat gear.

'They'll have to fight any future war whether or not they agree with the cause they're ordered to defend. They'll make a hell of a good job of it, whether or not others look on them as NATO's poor relations. Unfortunately, they look on us as troublemakers, not fighting soldiers. They tend to forget we're also in action during wars.'

'And our lads get killed,' Tom added heavily, thinking of two brothers who had been caught in an ambush in Kosovo.

The boom and lighter rattle of gunfire continued as they sat in silence watching the armoured vehicles that resembled toys crisscrossing way out on the frozen heathland. Then they saw one pull out of the contrived mêlée and head towards them. Max knew Randolph's attitude would harden further at this disruptive summons. He reflected that an irate man might be easier to trip up, although the Warrior was approaching so slowly it was clear he was giving himself time to prepare his story.

'Do we take him in for questioning?' asked Tom.

'Depends on what we get from him here. If we have to get tough, we will.'

'He's unlikely to confess. He's too canny.'

'It's that I'm banking on. He's been avoiding direct interrogation, but he's too smart not to know it highlights the fact that he has something to hide. He's been playing for time, which hatches the unwelcome supposition that he hoped we'd find the killer before he was forced to reveal whatever happened between him and the victim in Bosnia.'

'A chargeable offence?'

'Certainly something he doesn't want to make available to us; something that'll ruin his squeaky clean image.'

The Warrior stopped about fifty yards away. They saw its commander exchange a few words with the man standing beside him, before climbing down and crunching over the snow towards them as the vehicle swung round to head back across the heath.

Rosy-cheeked from the chill, tall and impressive in combat gear, Peter Randolph looked the ideal image for an army recruitment poster. JOIN US AND BECOME LIKE HIM!

Watched by the group with the chart, the young captain walked to Max and Tom, who stood beside the Land Rover. His keen blue gaze raked them both as he halted a few feet away.

'You're like dogs worrying at a bone.'

'We've been likened to worse beasts,' Max returned evenly. 'Right now you happen to be the most interesting bit of the bone. Why are you dodging our request for a DNA sample?'

'You surely haven't driven way out here, interrupting a vital check, just to collect my saliva.' The coolness bordering on insolence in his tone was at odds with the undeniable signs of tension around his mouth. When there was no response from the SIB men, he said, 'We'd better continue this inside.'

They followed him in to a basic office fitted up for military operations with a large square table, a dozen chairs, a radio transmitter and a long wall-hung blackboard. Randolph gazed from the window at the activity outside for perhaps a full minute before turning to break the silence. His stress was now apparent in the set of his shoulders, his facial muscles and his strained tone.

'I had intended making a statement before leaving for the NATO exercise ... if it became necessary.'

'A statement concerning Major Bekov's murder, sir?' asked Tom.

'Concerning the period immediately before that. He was still alive when I left him in the copse with a sack over his head.'

Max had long ago ceased to be surprised by human behaviour, but this was unexpected. 'Can you offer evidence to support that?'

'The Duty Sergeant called me up at 03:40 to report that he had caught one of the two-man patrols having a smoke in the cinema doorway, leaving a stretch of perimeter fence vulnerable. We discussed the action we'd take over the incident and he ended the call by assuring me he'd inspected the fence and it was secure. I then returned to the Duty Room. There's a full account in my report.'

'And?' demanded Max.

'And I couldn't have done that if I was in

the middle of transporting and tying to a post a man I'd just killed. You also have my word that Tolstoy was alive when I left him. That should be enough.'

'Several of your fellow officers have given us a pack of lies. We tend not to rely on any man's *word*, Captain Randolph. On more than one occasion you denied having met Leo Bekov before, and I imagine you are now about to tell us the reverse.'

Randolph stared belligerently for several moments, then pulled out a chair and sat heavily. The detectives also sat.

'Before you begin I must ask you to refer to Major Bekov by his real name throughout.'

Randolph gave a brief nod. 'I'll explain why we called him Tolstoy. *We* being myself, Rory Hunter-Smyth and Michael Farringdon. We were all lieutenants in the second battalion, which was serving with the UN, struggling to bring some kind of humanity to the brutal conflict in Bosnia.' He gave a bitter exclamation. 'A thankless, futile brief. Wherever else I may be deployed during my career, Bosnia is certain to haunt my old age the most. Battle casualties I understand. What went on there was beyond understanding.'

Max made no attempt to interrupt. He was glimpsing the man beneath the assured soldier. What he was about to hear would surely cast significant light on the personality of Leo Bekov. But would it reveal why he had been given the ultimate military punishment?

The hint of emotion vanished when Randolph continued. 'Captain Bekov was loosely designated a liaison officer, but he acted on orders from his own corps's bosses. We considered him a maverick, not altogether to be trusted.'

'Oh?'

'He sported a three-quarter sheepskin coat over his uniform, and a fur hat. He also kept dark stubble on his jowls and wore his hair longer than regs permit, deliberately enhancing his Slavic appearance. He seemed able to get away with anything. I mean, he resembled a bloody Serb!'

'For good reasons, I imagine,' inserted Tom.

A sneer. 'He spoke Serbo-Croat like a native. Russian, too, but that wasn't surprising. His father was a music teacher from St Petersburg. Bekov was more bloody Russki than British ... and the Ivans made no secret of their sympathy with the Serbs, did they? We had no time for him.'

'Because he was a maverick, or because he wasn't a true-blue Brit?' asked Max drily.

Randolph rose to that. 'He was an arrogant, freelance shit, who pranced around like some kind of Balkan T. E. Lawrence, impressing the troops.'

'He was popular with the men?' Max thought of Tom's guess that Bekov would be either loved or hated. It seemed he had aroused both emotions in Bosnia.

'He acted the clown. He was forever playing his balalaika and singing bawdy Russian songs. They lapped it up.'

271

'Troops welcome light relief on active service,' Tom pointed out.

'The service we were on was *passive*,' Randolph said bitterly.

Max thought it time to get back to what lay behind Randolph's confession. 'You said you left Major Bekov hooded but alive in the copse on the night of February the twelfth. That would have been some time after 03:00?'

'Yes.'

'So tell us what prompted that. Another dinner-night jape?'

He took that on the chin. 'You could call it that. Rory Hunter-Smyth emailed that Tols—Bekov was coming with General Pomeroy's deputation. He and I sounded off a bit about the business in Bosnia, and I said I'd like to show the bastard he couldn't always get away scot-free with bloody arbitrary behaviour. When he subsequently ignored me in the mess, I went ahead with my tentative plan to put the fear of God in him if the opportunity came my way.'

'Tell us what happened in Bosnia, sir,' invited Tom.

Fourteen

A bitter wind whistled down from the hills. Early afternoon, yet the greyness hung above them like approaching night as the five-vehicle convoy bumped over the snow-covered road. Two ambulances sandwiched between three Warriors heading for the outskirts of the small town that had been repeatedly shelled. Their brief was to bring out patients and nurses from a children's hospital so badly damaged it could no longer function. There was no electricity, pitifully few medicines, hardly any food, and water was having to be hauled from a nearby stream now badly polluted. A clear-cut case for UN humanitarian aid. Permission to move the children to a safe place where they could receive treatment had been sought, and given. The UN troops knew that counted for little with the roaming bands of armed Serbs conducting their own war on their own terms.

Peter gazed from the Warrior at the grim, desolate scene, raging inwardly at what he was doing. This was not soldiering. They should not be asked to stand by while civilians were murdered, their homes torched. They should not have to be abused and

273

humiliated by lawless ruffians far too trigger-happy, and not retaliate. They were highly trained members of a venerated regiment in the finest army in the world. They drove impressive armed vehicles; they carried guns. Yet they were forbidden to use them.

Peter was sick to his stomach. His father, his grandfather, were appalled by his role here. All those heroic ancestors must be turning in their graves over the old regiment being so demeaned. Three months into a six-month tour, and Peter wondered how he would get through the second half without breaking neutrality rules. Rory and Mick felt the same way. They were in the two Warriors ahead of him.

In the first was Tolstoy, ostensibly to smooth their passage. Peter scowled. The bastard had been excessively chummy with a Russian detachment they had encountered several weeks ago, and his liaison with the Serbs, who frequently challenged them, more often than not involved smiles and nods of collusion. How could they be sure of what he was telling those savage brutes? Why was an Anglo-Russian so highly thought of by the top brass?

'Here we go,' Peter murmured to his crew as a bend revealed yet another road block manned by a rag-tag, bearded group with Kalashnikovs. 'This lot have been armed by the Ivans, too. Easy does it when we go through. Annoy them now and they'll be obstructive on the way back.'

'I'd annoy them all right, if I could get my hands on them,' muttered Private Casey from within the Warrior.

They halted at the rear of the column. Peter watched Bekov climb from Rory's vehicle and saunter over to where mines lay across the road ten yards ahead of a rough barrier. The Serbs took precautions against would-be heroes who might run the gauntlet and crash through it.

'What's the problem?' Peter asked of Rory.

'Dickheads who think they own the road,' came his friend's bitter response. 'Captain Bekov is showing them the permit to pass signed by their area commander. Should do the trick.'

'Do these thugs know who the area commander is?'

'They will by the time our liaison officer explains.'

Peter closed his mouth over the opinion he would have given if they were not being overheard by their crews. But Private Willard beside him murmured, 'They'll regard that permit as a bit of paper to wipe their bums with, that's all.'

Scepticism soon vanished when the Serbs began shifting the mines to the roadside, and the barrier was lifted. Bekov even got a gesture vaguely between a wave and a salute as he walked back to the Warrior. Peter grunted derisively. How the hell had he persuaded them so swiftly?

That thought occupied him until they

reached the outskirts of what remained of the town. The sight of burnt-out houses, snow blackened by ash or darkened by blood, piles of rubble that had been a school or a church, torn and filthy material fluttering in the wind, and silent huddles of humanity seeking shelter where they could, grew no easier to accept no matter how often Peter came across ethnic barbarism. He knew they all burned with impotence while they did what little the UN terms permitted beneath the hostility in the eyes of these victims.

They turned left to make the slight climb towards the damaged hospital standing in several acres of grounds. Flags bearing red crosses had been hung against the cream walls. Two had been shot to pieces. There were gaping holes in the twin buildings; their pale walls blackened. Littering the snow around them was the debris of sickness and death, deposited there to prevent pollution and infection inside the wards.

Peter stared at the stark scene with the familiar suppressed anger. From within the Warrior came Lance-Corporal Packer's quiet oath.

'They should be hung by their balls over an open fire for doing that to helpless kids.'

The column pulled up outside what used to be the main entrance. Peter jumped to the ground and walked to join Rory, Mick and Leo Bekov. The orderlies opened the doors of their ambulances and waited for the word to load up. The Warrior crews remained where they were. This was to be a swift operation. Permission to be there did not guarantee their safety, as they had learned to their cost on their last mission. One of their transports had been shelled; two men wounded. They wanted to effect the transfer of patients and get away in the shortest time possible.

The four officers climbed the broken steps then saw fully the state of what had been a solid portico.

'We can't bring them out through here,' said Rory, gazing at the heaped rubble blocking the entrance hall.

'Looks like the first floor collapsed. Let's fan out and go around the sides until we find somewhere safe,' said Mick.

They turned and descended, Peter saying, 'They're sure to have moved everyone near an exit. The staff have to go back and forth with the water from that river.'

Bekov held up a warning hand, and halted. 'I don't like it. It's too quiet. They must have heard the column arrive. Why hasn't someone come out to meet us?'

'Why would they leave here?' reasoned Mick. 'Where else could they go?'

'I think I should check the place out first.'

'We'll all check it out,' said Peter, resenting the high-handed attitude. Bekov was only one rank higher, not a bloody general.

Rory and Mick began walking to the right, leaving him to go with Bekov, who merely shrugged and muttered something incomprehensible. Peter advanced with caution, however. There was certainly an unsettling hush hanging over the entire complex. The crunch on snow made by their boots sounded unnaturally loud. They should not have been apprehensive. Wherever they went in this doomed country the only sounds were gunfire, the roar of conflagrations, the crash of falling masonry. The people were mute with despair; children silenced by trauma. No dogs barked; they were shot on sight. Birds had flown deep into the forest. In the trees around the hospital nothing moved.

The rear was more damaged than the front. Peter said: 'They won't be here. That wall's likely to cave in at any time.'

The words were hardly out when Bekov jumped lightly to a broken veranda beneath the teetering wall, and began shouting through a gap large enough to climb through. He repeated his call three times, then turned to beckon Peter.

'They're in here. They tell us to take great care.'

'There must be a better way through,' he said, holding back.

Bekov gave him a knowing smile. 'There is a Russian folk tale about Timid Peter. I'll tell it to you sometime.' He climbed dextrously through the gap and vanished.

Peter trotted alongside the rear wall looking for access and found it just as Rory and Mick had begun clambering over broken glass and splintered wood in a long, dim corridor.

'This seems to be the only hope for bringing out stretchers,' said Rory. 'Where's Tolstoy?'

'Already inside. Took a stupid risk. He shouted and heard a response, so they are still here. Christ, you can't see what you might be treading on.'

'Just as well,' Mick remarked, from grim experience.

'We should turn here,' Peter advised, as they reached a junction. 'Tolstoy located them in an area to the right of where we just came in.'

They advanced slowly, alert for the unexpected: booby traps, concealed snipers, antipersonnel mines. Rory said quietly, 'Get that terrible smell?'

They got it! It was now familiar and it warned of what to expect to see. Turning a corner they discovered the glimmer of candles dotted around a large square room. In the faint grey light from high windows, Peter made out rows of high-sided cots packed close together and filled with infants. Beneath the cots, older children lay on bare mattresses. None of them moved. None made a sound. There was just a sea of dark eyes staring at the military intruders. It was unnerving. Overall was the stench of urine, vomit and the outpouring of diarrhoea. The normal hospital smell was absent. Disinfectant had run out days ago.

Peter looked with dismay. It was impossible to guess exact numbers, but there were far more here than they had been led to believe. He edged closer to Rory. 'Which of Tolstoy's corps's spies counted this lot and got it wrong?'

Rory grunted. 'Half of them look so frail they'll break if we pick them up.'

Mick wanted action. 'Come on. It'll be dark on that road back unless we make a start.'

'OK, show the stretcher-bearers the way in and warn them about numbers, Mick.'

Peter nodded towards the far end of the ward. 'Tolstoy's having a serious session with someone who's probably the senior nurse. I hope he's telling her about the limited space we have.'

Rory gave an impatient grunt. 'It's an Intelligence cock-up. All we can do is put the worst cases in the ambulances and the rest in the Warriors. They'll throw up and crap all over them, and I'll insist on the prick who miscounted cleaning up afterwards. Our guys shouldn't have the job to do.'

Bekov was walking carefully between the cots bringing his companion across to them. 'This is Sister Marcia. She wishes to thank you for what you're doing.'

The woman nodded her agreement. She was of indeterminate age and wore a stained, torn overall that had been white, and a scarf around her head. She was hollow-eyed with fear and lack of sleep. Small wonder she regarded them as saviours.

'The situation is pretty straightforward,' Bekov told them. 'Half these children will remain here. The journey would kill them. Only two of the nurses will come with us.

One in each ambulance. I've told Sister Marcia we'll leave her all our spare drugs and medical supplies from the ambulances, and I'll personally arrange for a helicopter drop of further supplies. It's the best we can do, under the circumstances.'

A clatter of boots heralded the army orderlies, with Mick. Bekov explained that the nurses would indicate which children should be stretchered, and which could be carried. Then he told the men to hand over everything they would not need for the journey back to base.

'They're desperate even for bandages. The women have torn up their own clothes to use. They now only have the overalls they're wearing.'

'Aren't they coming with us, sir?' asked a red-haired orderly.

'Half these mites are dying. The women will stay to make their end as painless and comfortable as possible.'

'We can't leave them here,' protested another. 'There's rats everywhere, and the first gale will blow this building down on top of them.'

Bekov ignored that to have a short interchange with Sister Marcia. Then he rounded on the men. 'Get started! The nurses will carry out as many as they can. The officers will move the cots outside. That way, we can shift greater numbers in a shorter time.'

'These are *our* men he's ordering around,' Rory said under his breath as he walked with

Peter to lift the nearest cot. It contained four babies lying crosswise. 'The cocky bastard's right, though. This is the way to move them out.'

'Where are their mothers, d'you reckon?'

'Dead. Otherwise they'd be here tending them, wouldn't they.'

It was a silent progress back and forth those ruined corridors now illuminated by military flashlights. It had begun to snow heavily, which added to their urgency. Throughout the transfer from hospital to vehicle not one child or baby made a sound. As Peter looked into their emaciated faces, their blank eyes, he wondered if they would ever smile again. He saw Bekov talking encouragingly to those he carried in his arms, smiling at them, tapping their noses gently, tickling them – a surprising facet of the man – but even he received no response.

'Wonder he didn't bring his balalaika to get 'em going,' muttered Mick sourly as he passed with undeniable twins in his arms.

They stood in the blizzard handing babies from cots to the orderlies, who had to fit them in head to toe, literally like sardines in a tin. There were twenty-five remaining to settle in the Warriors. The youngsters showed no resistance, listening impassively to Bekov and their nurses explaining where they were being taken. They shed no tears on parting from the women who had been caring for them; there were no smiles for the men in blue helmets rescuing them from the misery of their surroundings.

All over the world British soldiers took pity on children, did whatever they could for them, tried to establish brief rapport. It was never enough. It was not enough now. There was no guarantee that where these patients eventually ended up would not later be over-run by Serbs.

Peter's crew were unhappy about leaving the nurses and so many dying children. They said so with the anger their present role aroused. He let them sound off. They needed to ease their frustration. They ranted and raved, but obeyed him. They were good men. They knew he shared their feelings, and he had faith in them. There was little else to have faith in in this benighted country.

They moved off into the snowstorm. Peter tugged his scarf higher around his neck; pulled down his goggles. They had constantly to be wiped but without them his eyes would be lacerated by the driving sleet. Visibility had deteriorated. The road ahead ran alongside the river, cutting through hills. It would be highly hazardous if the blizzard raged on. He concentrated on the hot shower awaiting him, the substantial meal, the bottle of whisky in his quarters.

Suddenly, these thoughts were blasted away by several hefty explosions. *One, two, three.* There were shouts from his crew; terse instructions from Rory in the leading Warrior. Peter swung round. The hospital buildings had been hit with accuracy. *One, two, three.*

The front entrance flew apart as Peter watched. Where they had been loading the children was now a crater. *One, two, three.* The side walls folded and fell. The ward would be beneath them. One more salvo, and what remained of the hospital disintegrated completely.

The earlier curses and oaths, the urging to turn back for the others ceased as the column drove on, away from yet another human tragedy they could do nothing to avenge. Artillerymen in the hills must have seen them leave and finished the job they had begun days before. Peter stared blindly through snow-covered goggles, visualizing that stinking ward, dying youth and brave women. His brain told him they had been doomed anyway. His emotions protested that they had posed no threat, had been fighting no enemy but sickness.

The snow gradually abated until there were large flakes drifting lazily. The usual intercom chatter was missing. It was a column of grim-faced soldiers and mute children that reached the road block. Nothing so simple as acknowledgement of their return by moving the mines and raising the barrier. The five vehicles were forced to halt. Bekov once more jumped down to cross to two men huddled inside the crude sentry box. An unknown number sheltered in a nearby shell-blasted house.

After some minutes of fierce conversation between Bekov and the guards, which involved much pointing at the column, Peter asked Rory what was going on.

'From where I am it looks like they're refusing to accept the pass. These brutes have bloody-mindedness down to a fine art. I think it's time for back-up, guys.'

Peter jumped to the ground to join Rory and Mick as they approached the barrier. He said loudly to Bekov, 'We're authorized to pass through. Don't stand any nonsense from them.'

Bekov spun round. 'Don't faze the situation with aggression!'

'So what the hell are they showing?' he returned.

Rory challenged Bekov. 'What *is* the situation? They knew we went through earlier to fetch these children. You did tell them that, didn't you?'

'Of course I bloody told them,' Bekov snapped. 'They're accusing us of harbouring the enemy.'

'They're kids!' cried Mick explosively. 'Ask if they're scared of sick toddlers. Ask if they're afraid of puking babies.'

Bekov's mouth tightened; his black eyes grew hostile. 'You think insults will get us through?'

'You don't seem to be getting far with your method.'

'OK, so take over from me, Farringdon.'

'All I'm saying is...'

'All you're saying is hotheaded and dangerous. We're facing a tricky confrontation.

285

Leave me to handle it ... unless you speak Serbo-Croat, too.'

'Calm down,' said Rory. 'We're getting nowhere by arguing.'

Bekov's glance was contemptuous. 'Neither are these kids we've pledged to help. You three are my supporting officers, not judge advocates. Just back off!'

Peter spotted reinforcements coming from the house, led by a bearded giant. All carried Kalashnikovs. 'This looks like the boss man. Maybe we'll now get somewhere.'

The subalterns stood solidly behind him as Bekov held an intense conversation with this apparent chief. It dragged on and on. Bekov kept shaking his head, referring frequently to the pass in his hand. The Serb looked surly and immovable, refused even to glance at the signed paper.

Mick muttered: 'What I'd give for the chance to mow this lot down and charge through. We have overwhelming firepower.'

'We're forbidden to involve ourselves in this war unless we are attacked,' Rory reminded him bitterly.

'We *are* involved in it,' said Peter. 'These ragged bastards are confronting us with live mines to prevent our progress. That's as close to attacking us as I need to justify having a go at them.'

Leo Bekov turned from the Serb. His dark-jowelled face was working with anger; a muscle twitched beside his mouth. 'This great sod of a human garbage pile is claiming we have with us the son of a Croatian commander whose unit killed both his own sons. He says until we hand over this boy, we'll stay right where we are. He means what he says.'

'So we blast our way through,' said Mick, knowing it was a futile comment.

'That's definitely not on,' ruled Rory, who was the senior of the three subalterns. 'We're not handing anyone over on his say-so. We're UN, and take orders only from them.'

'We're also in a no-win situation,' Bekov said frankly. 'He can keep us here indefinitely.'

'Does he know this boy by sight?' asked Peter.

'I gather not.'

'Then we say we left him at the hospital they've just flattened. He's now almost certainly dead.'

'I've already tried that. He asked how I would know a boy I'd never seen or heard of before.' He studied them all. 'I know these people. We won't be moving from here until we comply.'

Rory was as angry as Bekov. 'You're saying we have to give them a boy – any boy – as a kind of payment for being allowed to pass? Definitely not! They'll kill him.'

'Undoubtedly. But how many of these children would survive even overnight here? We've no food for them; no milk. We haven't enough blankets to prevent the weakest going under with hypothermia. And what if we're

287

still here tomorrow night? We could sit it out for quite a while, but those kids won't survive. They're ill and badly undernourished.'

'So you're advocating we meekly hand over some poor little devil to these inhuman brutes?'

Peter's protest was ignored. Bekov addressed Rory. 'We have to balance many lives against one. We really have no option.'

'We have the option of calling their bluff, and that's what we're going to do,' said Rory with finality.

The three mechanized officers turned and walked back to the leading Warrior, leaving Bekov to explain their decision. Rory immediately called up their base to give a sitrep. He was pressed for more details. Then he listened to instructions from their colonel, his expression hardening as the authoratative voice once more outlined the narrow confines of their role.

'Yes, sir, understood,' he said coldly, and clicked off.

Peter read his friend's face too well. 'You've been told to hand him over.'

'In theory, we can be accused of assisting Croatians. Giving them UN protection. That's contrary to the rules of the agreement.'

'Bloody hell, some of those kids are no more than *weeks* old,' raged Mick.

Rory vented his anger on Mick. 'We're forbidden to take sides. You know we're no more than bloody eunuchs in blue hats out here.

When are you going to accept that?'

Peter said heavily, 'Mick's right.'

Rory had swung round to gaze across the white, frozen landscape where the hospital lay as an enormous broken eyesore against the natural beauty of this area. Gaining control, he said: 'When we get home I'm going to resign my commission. What we're doing here is an insult to everything I joined and trained for.'

Peter stood silently beside Mick, feeling a protest growing like an inflating balloon inside him. They then became aware of what was happening beside one of the ambulances. Bekov was questioning the nurses more and more insistently as they stood like pillars staring at him.

Peter walked across. 'What's going on?'

Without looking at him, Bekov said, 'I asked if that boy is here with us. They said he is, but they refuse to identify him.'

'Did you tell them what you intend to do with him?'

Black eyes bored into his. 'What *we* intend to do. This is a combined authority decision. Don't pin it on me.'

'It's the decision of higher authority, Bekov. I'm not accepting *any* responsibility for the murder of an innocent child.'

The other man spat out what was probably a Russian oath. 'Innocent kids are being murdered wholesale *on both sides*. Wars do that! Haven't your toffee-nosed ancestors taught you soldiering is no profession for ingenues like you, unable to make tough decisions without sentimentality? You're supposed to be a commander of men. For God's sake show some sign of it now, instead of washing your hands of the job. We have to sacrifice one to save sixty-two. That's the score, whether we like it or not!' He turned back to the ashen-faced nurses and resumed his questioning.

Peter strode back to his friends, seething with anger and determined to tackle Bekov head on when they reached base.

'What's he doing?' asked Rory.

'Those women won't identify the sacrificial lamb.'

'Someone has to,' Rory pointed out dully.

'We can't ask another kid to betray—' He broke off as his attention was drawn to what Bekov was now doing.

Along with his unorthodox dress, the Anglo-Russian carried a Smith and Wesson revolver he had picked up in the Balkans, in preference to the more usual Browning automatic. He was holding it in front of the nurses as he emptied the bullets into his palm. Then he inserted just one and spun the chamber.

'Christ, he's going to shoot one of them to make the other talk,' breathed Peter.

He was wrong. Bekov opened the door of Mick's Warrior and drew a toddler from it to hold the gun to its temple. The three officers were rooted to the spot with disbelief as Bekov squeezed the trigger. *Click!* He spoke intently to the nurses. He squeezed again.

Click! The women began crying, pleading with him. A third click. The child defecated with terror, turning the snow brown by its feet. Bekov stared unblinking at the women, prepared to play the game out to its grim conclusion. But they could not let it happen. A stream of words flowed from them as one reached for the toddler and the other pointed inside the vehicle with a hand that shook.

'I'll have him for that!' vowed Mick in strangled tones. 'I'll put him in shit so deep he'll choke on it.'

Peter struggled to come to terms with what he had witnessed and been unable to stop. 'We can get him arraigned. That was unspeakably callous.'

Bekov emerged from the Warrior carrying a boy whose leg was in plaster from ankle to hip; a boy he had earlier been soothing with comforting smiles and assurances of safety. He crunched across snow that was hardening further as night lowered the temperature, and then he carefully set the child down by the sentry box. In silence, the guards pushed the mines aside and began to raise the barrier. Engines roared as the column prepared to move forward. The three officers returned to their Warriors knowing they would never forget what they had just experienced. Of the many terrible things they had come across, this had brought home the savagery of the region more than any other ... and, in their opinion, the savagery had been committed by a man in a British uniform.

Peter was so swamped by dark thoughts he was unaware that Bekov had walked some yards beyond the barrier and was waiting by a bend in the track, with the intention of climbing aboard the last vehicle after it had successfully cleared the road block. Peter Warrior.

As Lance-Corporal Packer drew up momentarily to allow their liaison officer on, Peter was shocked from his introspection by the sound of a shot. Turning swiftly to look back at the Serbs, he could just make out through the fast-gathering dusk a small inert body lying on the snow beside the sentry box.

Rory's voice said in his ear, 'Christ, the bastards didn't waste any time! At least they didn't torture him first.'

But Peter was certain he knew who had fired the bullet guaranteeing a clean, swift execution.

'So you and the other regimental officers submitted damaging reports on Bekov?'

Peter came from thoughts of the one aspect of that day he had not mentioned to these detectives. His account had recreated it so vividly he had forgotten he was sitting in a chilly classroom in Germany.

'Sorry?'

Max Rydal repeated his question.

'Actually, no. Not officially. The children were collected by Red Cross ambulances and driven to their neutral compound. We were congratulated on managing to save as many as sixty-two.' He sighed. 'Somehow ... I don't know ... It was over. We were stressed out. All we wanted was to have a meal, get our heads down and put the whole affair behind us. Dozens had been killed during the shelling of the hospital. Dozens more would die when we weren't around to see. Rory, Mick and I had a discussion and agreed to report just that we had checked with the CO, then carried out his ruling.

'The following morning at breakfast we had revived somewhat and decided we couldn't let Tol— Bekov get away with what he had done to force the nurses to betray the identity of the boy. So we asked for an unofficial meeting with Colonel Anderson and expressed our concerns over the maverick behaviour.'

'And the outcome?'

'The CO promised to look into our claims. Three days later he sent for Rory and told him he was satisfied Captain Bekov had been driven to resolve a very difficult situation. The women would not have named the boy without taking such drastic action. Rory was assured the child had been in no danger, because there had been no ammunition in the revolver. Bekov had explained it was one of his "party tricks". It looks as if he replaces one bullet, but he actually palms it. He demonstrated this to Colonel Anderson and his own CO by holding the gun to his own temple while he seemingly played Russian roulette.'

'So no action was taken against him?'

'No. I told you he appeared to get away with anything.'

'But you decided it was time that stopped, and killed him after the regimental dinner on February the twelfth,' Tom Black said.

'Oh, no. I did to him what he had done to that kid in Bosnia. Scared the shit out of him.'

'Go on,' said Rydal into the silence.

Peter saw once more the region that had produced inhumanity at extreme level. Would he ever be rid of those images? 'Bekov remained in his capacity as Intelligence/Liaison Officer, although we had no further close dealings with him during our tour. He continued to play his bloody balalaika and dazzle the rank and file.'

'Did no one else protest over his solution to the impasse at the road block?' asked Rydal

'I doubt any of them saw his "party trick".'

'Except the orderlies in the ambulance,' Tom Black suggested.

'They might have ... but the overriding feeling at the conclusion of that mission was relief that we got so many out before the hospital was flattened. Minds tended to grow numbed when faced with ethnic cleansing on a massive scale, you know.'

'So you had no further contact with Leo Bekov until he came here with the British deputation?'

'That's right.' He had recovered from the time-slip back to Bosnia, and spoke with his usual air of confidence. 'I saw his visit as an opportunity to show my contempt, and the fact that I was Duty Officer that night seemed providential. It allowed me the freedom to move around the base without arousing curiosity.'

'Agreed, but how could you be certain of carrying out your intention?'

'I couldn't. His visit gave me an opportunity, not a certainty, but when he subsequently ignored me in the mess my resolve hardened. In Bosnia I had also picked up a Smith and Wesson. There was a huge variety of weapons in use by the warring factions, and by the multinational UN forces. I began acquiring them. My grandfather has a formidable collection of firearms. I had it in mind to do the same.

'I decided to play Russian roulette with Bekov using my revolver. Hooding him first would make the business even more frightening. I knew the hope of bringing it off was chancy. He was deeply involved in the hijinks when I went off on my first "rounds", and he was still enjoying himself when I dragged Jerry Fielding out to a med emergency. I watched from the window of the Duty Room; eventually saw Bekov leave the mess around 02:00, cursed when Judy King walked off with him. Next minute, Mark Ingham set off on their heels. Curious, I followed, making sure he wasn't aware of my vehicle tagging him.

'Mystified as to why Ingham went in the gym, I was about to investigate when I spotted a guy in mechanic's overalls also go in there with a dog under his arm. Totally baffled, I thought I had stumbled upon some questionable activity, but Sergeant Squires came through to me at that moment to say a prowler had been spotted near the sports ground. We had VIPs on base, so I was obliged to cruise the southern half while he did the same around the other sector.

'After fruitlessly combing the area for half an hour, and checking with the patrols, I was returning to the gym when I came upon my man wandering alone near the copse. He was clearly tanked up; staggering uncertainly in the direction of the mess. I doused my head-lamps, left the vehicle and followed on foot with the sack and revolver, telling myself Nemesis was hand-in-glove with me on this.

'Bekov stumbled over to the trees and began fumbling with his fly. He had no idea what was happening when I shoved the sack over his head, pinioned his arms with a webbing belt and forced him along that path through the copse. He was scared bloody stiff, pissing himself and grunting with fear.'

'As the child had,' said Tom Black softly.

'Yes. I wanted him to know what that kid had gone through. When we reached a barbecue table I pushed him face down on it and put the barrel to his temple. I told him there was just one bullet in the chamber and we were going to play a little game.'

'How did he react to that?' asked Rydal.

'With silence. He made no attempt to

bargain, or ask why I was doing it.'

'Maybe he guessed. Although he ignored you in the mess, he would have recognized you from that time. You felt he was confident there was no ammunition in the gun?'

'No, I thought he was so terrified it had rendered him speechless. I squeezed the trigger five times. *Click, click, click, click, click!* Then I slipped a blank in and fired close beside his head. He then found his voice, believing he had been shot. Auto-suggestion! His yell was full of imagined pain. I unbuckled the belt, releasing his arms, and left him slowly to accept that he was still alive. It was a hell of a shock to walk outside shortly afterwards and find him hanging dead on that post.' He frowned. 'Whoever killed him must have been watching in that copse until I left. But I saw no one.'

'You were too engrossed in meting out your own punishment of a man who believed he could get away with anything,' Rydal suggested.

'I wanted to put the fear of God in him, and that's all I did, I swear. You'd find my DNA would probably match some found on that table, but I did not kill Leo Bekov. If you compare the striations on the bullet with the barrel of my revolver...'

'The murder weapon was a 9mm Browning. Do you have one in your personal collection, sir?' asked Tom Black.

'No. Too ordinary. I'm using them all the time.'

There was a short pause, then Rydal said, 'You left the victim lying on the table hooded?'

'The sack was loose. He could easily remove and discard it.'

'What did you do then?'

'Returned to my vehicle, where Sergeant Squires almost immediately called me up to report the two guards smoking. I drove back to the Duty Room and had just got beneath the duvet when Judy King arrived to report her discovery of a body. You know the rest.'

'You returned to the Duty Room *minutes* before Ms King burst in with the news? How was it you didn't see the body there?' asked Tom.

'I drove in from a southerly direction. Entered by the side door to the mess. No chance of seeing it from there.'

After agreeing to submit a written statement later that day, Peter was officially admonished for hampering the investigation by withholding vital evidence, and warned he would be questioned again. He left the semi-warmth for the freezing air outside, where he stood alone staring at the scene that revived memories of the place he had been talking about. Snow, bitter cold, the sound of gunfire and the sight of Warriors pushing across barren landscape. Relating those events again brought them vividly alive in his mind's eye. They would surely realize why he had kept quiet until they pushed for a DNA sample. He had expected the killer would be swiftly traced; that the investigation would be wound up by now. None of this would then have to have been made public.

Telling those two hostile men what he had done to Bekov, in retrospect and the cold light of day, it had come over as puerile. School-boy revenge. Seven years had passed since Bosnia. In that time he had served in Belfast, Kosovo and, briefly, in Sierra Leone. He thought himself a first-rate commander. His record confirmed it. That impulsive act of retribution had been unworthy of him.

For several days now he had lived with the knowledge that he had surely contributed to Leo Bekov's death. The killers had to have been watching the copse. All they then had to do was pounce on the hooded man attempting to recover from a severe fright, and deliver the coup de grace. In truth, Peter faced the fact that he had marched Bekov to the perfect murder site and reduced him to a state of helplessness, unable to fight off his attackers. He had led the lamb to the slaughter.

Still staring at the stark winter scene, Peter mentally recalled that road block in Bosnia. He saw again the man whose appearance resembled old photographs of Russian artists and writers, whom they had dubbed Tolstoy, and he suddenly sensed what it might have cost that man to act as he had. He thought of his own certainty that the Anglo-Russian had fired the shot that saved the boy from a gruesome death at the hands of those Serbs.

In the intervening years Peter had witnessed death and bestiality in other countries – children whose hands or entire arms had been sliced off in Sierra Leone; small charred bodies piled high in Kosovo. So why had he been so set on gaining dominance over that particular man, or so melodramatically demonstrating his contempt?

Peter Randolph, latest in a long line of decorated heroes whom he was obliged to emulate, had secretly envied Tolstoy's military élan and resourcefulness; his ease in establishing rapport with all and sundry. Captain P. W. L. Randolph had an unblemished record because he followed rules to the letter, demanded obedience from his men without getting close to them, said all the right things to the right people. Family expectations ruled his every word, every action. The burden of meeting them was growing ever heavier. An inner rebellious spirit longed to break out, but he had determinedly crushed it.

He thought back to that fatal night. Tolstoy had ignored him because he categorized him as one of a group of uniformed automatons. A toy soldier in a box of identical ones. It now became blindingly clear that he had not punished the man for what he had done in Bosnia, but because he was all Peter Randolph secretly longed to be.

Fifteen

'I could do with a beer,' said Tom as a door slammed and the sound of Randolph's studded boots in the corridor ceased.

'I'd settle for a hot toddy.' Max rose and walked to stand by the window, where the sound of gunfire and armoured vehicles trundling across a frozen landscape made the Bosnian drama they had just heard seem all too tragically real. He thanked God he had never been forced to make such a heart-rending decision. Tom joined him to gaze morosely at the young captain, who now stood as if in a trance, making no attempt to get back on the job.

'Think he's on the up and up, sir?'

Max came from his introspection. 'What did you make of his evidence?'

'It didn't endear him to me, but I think he's too intelligent to offer us that unless it's true. He can't prove the victim was alive when he left the copse, but I've been through the duty reports for that night and there *was* a conversation between him and the Duty Sergeant regarding the perimeter guards at 03:45. Due to VIP presence they checked everything with extra diligence that night. He's right. He couldn't have been transporting and tying up the victim at that vital time. His comment about seeing a mechanic with a dog under his arm also ties in with our timetable of evidence.'

Max grunted a laugh. 'I wonder what he thought the "questionable activity" in the gym might be!'

'Mmm, one woman, three men ... and a dog! If only that little dog had barked in the gymnasium, the night would have ended very differently. It's quite a thought, isn't it?'

'No, Tom, I think Randolph got it right. Nemesis was playing a hand in the game. Bekov's time was up.'

'That mention of a prowler near the sports ground didn't strike me as particularly significant when I first read the report. Now it makes sense. It must have been Major Fielding.'

'Or the person he was meeting there. I agree Randolph is probably telling the truth at last. Which leaves the Doctor as prime suspect. The RAMC cufflink must be his. Once we have the matching one we'll grill him in earnest.' He checked his watch. 'Let's get back and grab some lunch. After it, we'll call on Jane Foyle. We need to know why she lied for Ingham. Then we'll return to HQ. We have to review all the evidence before we tackle Fielding, and I'm not sitting in that ice-house to do it.'

Tom's bleak mood didn't improve much with

a hot meal and a pint in the sergeants' mess. He sat next to a man who had served in Bosnia and was still trying to get the experience out of his system by constantly talking about it. Listening to him, Tom found himself better understanding the cruel dilemma Peter Randolph and his fellows had faced at the road block. If Bekov had not taken the brutal initiative, how would the other three officers have solved it? Why had Randolph seen fit to punish the man who had relieved him and his friends of taking an unpalatable step?

Draining his pint, Tom wondered how he, himself, would have resolved such a situation, and he thanked God he had never served with a peace-keeping force divested of the power to do just that.

Max ate lunch sitting alone at the end of a long polished table, but he welcomed the chance to think while he ate. Peter Randolph had added a further dimension to this complex case. The killers must have been close behind Bekov from the moment he left the mess with Judith King, awaiting their chance. Randolph had unwittingly made it easier for them ... and 'they' must have been Jeremy Fielding and the accomplice he met in the sports pavilion.

Of the three who had served with Leo Bekov in the past, Fielding's link was still a mystery. Ingham had been back-termed through Bekov's connivance during a vital exercise: Randolph's inflexible military correctness had been outraged by Bekov's maverick tactics. But how had the Anglo-Russian earned the ultimate punishment from the doctor?

Chewing his pork chop, Max pondered that with reservations. He could believe Randolph capable of the bizarre aspect of the murder, but Jeremy Fielding did not come over as wildly imaginative, nor was there any suggestion of a hot, uncontrollable temper. He appeared to be coping with a very difficult domestic situation, which would goad many men to violent outbursts. Not necessarily physical, but certainly verbal. The Fieldings' neighbours, when questioned, had shown sympathy with him – a nice man who didn't deserve such a silly wife – and denied hearing rows between the couple.

All the same, Fielding looked deeply haunted, and Max knew from experience that quiet, controlled men eventually snapped beneath an intolerable burden. Bekov's visit after a long gap of time must have tipped the scales.

Max declined the pudding and walked through to the anteroom for coffee, still thoughtful. Past experience had also shown that having killed, quiet, controlled men reverted to type. Getting a confession from Fielding would not be easy. The damning facts might have to be drawn from his accomplice. Jane Foyle?

He visualized the woman they were about to visit. Would she assist with the murder of someone she claimed never to have met? Maybe. Like Fielding, she was calm and controlled, but in a partnership with him she would surely be the mastermind. There was more steel in her than in the doctor. Max could not believe she was lovestruck enough to help him kill a stranger, so if she had met Fielding that night for such a deadly purpose, it must have been because Bekov had touched her life in some way in the past.

Yet women whose paths crossed his remembered him with warmth and not a little yearning, regardless of his cavalier treatment. Strange creatures, women!

Judith noticed Max Rydal sitting alone to eat. Another cuckoo in the nest. A most exclusive nest! She sat halfway down the table in her own cocoon of isolation. The bastards gathered at the top continued their 'blokey' conversation as if she were not there. Fast-talking baritones discussed the vitally important work they had been engaged in during the morning. They were so bloody full of themselves, so certain of their own worth, so totally part of the band of brothers far beyond her reach.

She had deliberately come late for lunch, so it was not long before she was the only diner left at the table. She picked at a meal she didn't really want, and drank a lot of water as she contemplated what she was about to do. Glancing through to the anteroom, she noted that Max Rydal was still isolated. He gazed from a window while he drank coffee in a corner well away from the eager beavers anticipating the NATO exercise. Intuition told her he was not averse to solitary contemplation in the midst of others. She was, and had reached a decision she was shortly to act upon.

To pass some time she flicked through newspapers and magazines that held no interest for her. Then, checking her watch, she rose and walked briskly to the Commanding Officer's office.

Jack Keegan glanced up impatiently as if Judith had burst in on him without first lodging a request. She saluted and thanked him for agreeing to see her.

'Yes ... well, I'm fearfully busy with this exercise almost upon us, so please make it brief.'

She did. 'I want to apply for a transfer to another unit, sir.'

He leaned back, eyes narrowing. 'When eighty per cent of personnel are preparing to move out for four and a half weeks, and a murder investigation is under way? Bad timing, Judith.'

'If it doesn't go through by Friday there'll be a delay of up to two months before any action can be taken.'

'Why the flaming hurry?'

She had known what his reaction would be. From the moment she had joined them direct from the Physical Training School she had been fighting the CO and James Harkness for acceptance, and the rest of the 'boys' for sexual equality. She had lost on both counts. Maybe if she wore the same badge, drove a Warrior, manned a gun, squirmed around in the mud on exercises with them, it might be different. But a woman who spent most of her days in a track suit, shorts and T-shirt, or a swimsuit, was not considered their equal. Add blonde good looks and a shapely figure, and the average male had just one thought in mind.

'I'm planning to get married in June, so I'd like to be settled elsewhere by then.'

'There's plenty of time. Come and see me again after the exercise.'

'I'd like you to put it through right away, please.'

Keegan sighed heavily. 'Judith, this NATO exercise is vitally important. There's unrest in a number of areas around the globe, and the situation in the Middle East is explosive. We could be drawn into another conflict at any time, at short notice. Wouldn't you agree that training and preparation for that is more important than your marital arrangements?'

'My wedding plans aren't behind this request. It's the way I'm being treated by my colleagues since the night of the murder.'

His greying eyebrows rose. 'My officers are accusing you of killing Major Bekov?'

He was being deliberately obtuse. He had several days ago questioned her on why she had been out and about alone at the time she had discovered the body; a commanding officer checking on the unwelcome behaviour of a mess member. Still in shock, she had been obliged to confess the partial truth knowing it would all be made public at the eventual trial.

Keegan had been bitingly condemnatory, reading her a lecture on the misuse of military premises for which she was responsible and held the key. There had been a lot more about an officer's duty to set examples to lower ranks in both professional and private behaviour, which she had lamentably failed to do.

Remembering his words now, her colour rose. 'There are all manner of stories circulating about what I did after the dinner. I can take normal baiting as well as any of them, but it's gone beyond an acceptable level for so-called gentlemen. Last night, a note was pushed beneath my door suggesting I might care to perform an extremely indecent act with the writer at some time between two and four this morning.'

Keegan's mouth tightened. 'And the author of this note was?'

'Anonymous. Like the others who've stuck lewd messages on my car windscreen, or sent vile texts to my mobile.'

'So you have no actual proof that your commissioned colleagues are responsible?'

'I know who they are,' she declared with heat. 'They leer at me in the mess, and they wink knowingly when we pass each other around the base. I want a swift transfer, sir.'

He studied her shrewdly for several moments. 'Judith, I regret to say you have never tried to understand the spirit of this regiment; the demands it makes on its officers and men. You have consistently held aloof from us and all we stand for. Our celebration of a famous victory is naturally a time for vigorous enjoyment. Nevertheless, there are acceptable standards of behaviour which you exceeded. Your colleagues not surprisingly disapprove, but I can take no action on your vague accusations since you have no proof to back them up. I will, however, forward your application for a transfer. The move will benefit us all. You may go.'

Throughout an exercise session with a platoon of unenthusiastic men and women, followed by forty-five minutes of indoor hockey, Judith struggled to contain her rage. Forgoing her usual equipment check, she went to her room to shower and put on her uniform. Once there, she gave vent to her feelings and burst into tears. She had given this job her best shot, but the bloody regiment had won.

At Sandhurst she had mixed in well and almost enjoyed the tougher, more exhausting aspects of the course. She had opted to join an infantry regiment, but soon found serving with a predominantly male unit vastly different from roughing it with an all-girl platoon. Tense night patrols around the hostile streets of Northern Ireland had caused her to rethink her career. An excellent sportswoman, she had applied for a transfer.

Second Lieutenant Judith King passed the course with top marks. She was then selected to train a team to perform a gymnastic display at the Remembrance Day service at the Royal Albert Hall. It was there she had met Captain Peter Harrison, in command of a team of Royal Engineers simulating the stealthy construction of a pontoon bridge at night just below an enemy position.

Her posting to this present regiment had suited them both because they had then been just a ninety-minute drive apart. Six months later, Peter had been seconded to Brunei for a year and they had decided to marry when he returned. When Judith travelled to Germany with the regiment, things had begun going downhill. Her relations with the CO, never very easy, had now dropped to an all-time low, and she was facing taunts and general derision from the men she lived and worked with. Yet, dear God, had she not provided fuel for their lascivious speculations?

Lying on her bed, she closed her eyes as the haunting images returned. Flashing dark eyes challenging her to cast aside her humdrum life and temporary celibacy. A smile that promised alien excitement. A superb, athletic body performing with speed and daring on equipment she used daily, supercharging her to follow. His triumphant laughter still rang in her ears: it had added intoxication to the wild episode. Then there rose up the vision of his lifeless body hanging on that post, eyes bound, hands tied behind him, and the tears sliding down her cheeks were for him.

Slowly, Judith faced the truth. She could not marry Peter in June. He was decent, kind, affectionate. Life with a man whose sights were set on achieving high rank after years of dedicated service would be secure and order-ed. They would move house many times; she would be left alone at regular intervals due to the demands of his career. She would rear their children, become a standard army wife, attend obligatory cocktail parties, pay lip service to bastards like Jack Keegan for her husband's sake. What a dreary prospect.

She craved the freedom to live at full throttle; yearned to cast aside all inhibitions and become the woman who had been dormant until Leo Bekov had beckoned. That would be impossible as Mrs Peter Harrison.

Developing this revelation further, Judith realized military rules and regulations would dictate her life even if she remained single. She then saw that the application she was about to submit should not be a request to move, but to resign her commission. Then she could take off and really live.

'Get a decent lunch?' Max asked as he climb-ed in the Land Rover.

'Nice warming soup, followed by fishcakes and chips. Nora tells me to keep off chips. Bad for the heart, she says.'

'Men don't come much fitter than you, Tom.'

'Tell Nora that, sir.'

The vehicle slewed on an icy patch as Tom turned into the road where the Foyles' quarters were located. 'Driving conditions are worsening. That's another reason why we'll head back after this interview. They were all cheering in the mess because their exercise will be easier in snow than in mud and slush, but we're not in a Warrior.' As Tom drew up with care, Max added, 'I hope to God she isn't comforting Mrs Ingham over her husband's drink-drive injuries. We need to pin Jane Foyle down, and we won't do that with a weepy Reena there.'

'If she is, I'll get her on making tea, leaving you alone with the lady of the house.'

Jane Foyle wore black trousers, a pale-green angora sweater and an antique silver pendant. She seemed unworried to find them on her doorstep. Max was again struck by her similarity to Susan. It was slightly unnerving.

'You'd better come in out of that bitter wind,' she said calmly.

The living room looked serene and immaculate, a glow from artificial coals and a tall vase of bright holly berries brightening the hearth. Was it as tidy as this when Bobby Foyle was here? Max wondered. Perhaps she was one of those women who go around after their husbands, picking up scattered pages of newspapers and putting them in order before folding them neatly. Did Jane Foyle snatch up dirty socks and shirts as her man discarded them, and immediately mop up the drips when he poured his beer? Was that why she made no offer of coffee or tea? Too great a risk of marks on the table! There was no invitation to sit, either. They all stood in the centre of the patterned silver-grey carpet.

Max was happy to keep things formal. 'Do you have a second set of lies ready for us, Mrs Foyle?'

Her gaze did not waver from his. 'Reena told me Mark has now confessed he wasn't here when we said he was. I don't know the truth, because he's presently in a serious condition in hospital. However, as you haven't charged him with the murder, his real explanation must have satisfied you of his innocence. Surely, that's all that matters.'

'What matters, Mrs Foyle, is that someone on this base ended a man's life a few nights ago, and you lied to give Captain Ingham an alibi. You're far too intelligent to believe his tale of sitting on your doorstep on a freezing night, so why were you willing to help him divert suspicion? We have two possible answers to that. Either you were with him during the crucial period, or you needed an alibi yourself.'

She frowned. 'Reena was with me all night.'

'And was presumably in your spare room from around midnight,' said Tom. 'You could have slipped out without her knowledge. Can you prove that you didn't leave the house?'

Her composure was finally ruffled. 'Are you suggesting *I* shot that poor man?'

'We're suggesting reasons why you might have done as Mark Ingham asked, that's all,' Max put in coolly. 'If we're wrong, put us right.'

After a moment or two she sank with a sigh onto a large padded footstool. 'Reena Ingham is vain, spoilt and immature. At one time or another she has fallen out with most of the wives here, which leaves her without friends. Her only interests are her personal appearance and having a good time, so she soon grows bored.

'My husband and Mark are good chums. They go speed cycling, and play soldiers.' She glanced at the ceiling. 'In our boxroom there's a huge table on which they set up the relevant terrain for the battle they're currently engaged in. They try to outwit each other to produce a reverse victory in famous engagements.'

Tossing Max a significant glance at this revelation, Tom said, 'So that leaves you having to entertain Mrs Ingham?'

Also alert to the information that Bobby Foyle was fascinated by past military exploits, Max asked, 'What has that to do with the fact that you lied to us?'

She had recovered her composure and refused to be drawn. 'Reena turned up with an overnight bag on the night of the dinner, deeply upset because Mark had been shanghai-ed into hosting an officer in transit, much against his will, and she had walked out. When I tried to persuade her to go back she

314

told me she had had a hot affair with their guest way back, so it was impossible for her to stay beneath the same roof with him. She was furious with Mark for agreeing to play host; hinted that the two men had fallen out badly at Sandhurst. But I know the pressures James Harkness exerts over our husbands, and I guessed Mark had been put in an impossible position by him. I thought having Reena overnight was the least I could do to ease the situation for him.'

Max thought it time to force the issue. 'So, once Mrs Ingham was asleep, did you slip out to meet someone in the sports pavilion?'

Her astonishment was genuine. 'What?'

Tom explained. 'We have a witness statement concerning a rendezvous in the pavilion just prior to the murder. Evidence found there almost certainly identifies one person. Were you the other one, ma'am?'

'Why on earth would I meet someone in the early hours of the morning there, of all places?'

'To finalize the plan to kill Major Bekov,' Max suggested.

She turned her attention back to him. 'I've never met Major Bekov; knew nothing of the man until he was found dead here.'

'But the man seen entering the pavilion knew him well. Perhaps you collaborated for his sake.'

'Captain Rydal, I love my husband dearly. We have an extremely happy marriage,' she said with a hint of frost in her tone. 'Your

315

supposition is ludicrous.'

He believed her. There was an unshakable dignity about her that made nonsense of the notion she would conspire to murder. Yet he had been duped by the dignity of a woman he had lived with for four years and thought he understood.

'You're a devoted wife; you have an ideal marriage. Why, then, did you so readily lie for another man desperate to establish an alibi? You risked the charge of attempting to pervert the course of justice I could very well bring against you. Surely it wasn't only because Mark Ingham plays soldiers with your husband.'

She got to her feet to look him more fully in the eye. 'Mark is one of those people who never quite get the good things they deserve because they're too *nice*. Reena makes demands on him and offers nothing in return. Fellow officers take advantage of his good nature to switch leave periods or palm off unpopular duties, borrow the lawnmower, tools – anything. He's one of life's givers. In your time I'm sure you've come across others like that.'

She appeared to expect an answer, so Max nodded.

'And those people don't commit murder.'

'Ah, but they do,' put in Tom. 'The worm finally turns.'

It angered her. 'Mark Ingham is not a worm. He's a thoroughly nice man who wouldn't kill unless on a battlefield. That's why I helped him out when he said he was in a jam.'

'Would you do the same for all your husband's friends?' Max asked.

There was a significant pause before she said quietly, 'Possibly not.'

'So why for him? Aren't the others "thoroughly nice men"?'

She fought an obvious battle with herself, then said with clear reluctance, 'Two years ago Bobby landed himself in a serious military predicament. It could have damaged his career. Mark covered for him; took a risk with his own career. We both owe him a lot.'

Max gave her a long look. 'When your husband gets back from Ireland, and Captain Ingham recovers enough to face the charges that we mean to bring against him, you'll discover what your good friend actually did on the night of February the twelfth. It led him to hit the bottle last night and drive out suicidally on ice-bound roads. Then you can decide whether or not you owed this "thoroughly nice man" that much.'

Sixteen

The only welcoming aspect of the apartment was the warmth, Max thought as he surveyed the uncluttered lines of furniture and fittings so new they bore no signs of occupation. Even the lighting was starkly white. It reached every corner and plane with an in-your-face brightness that defied mood or temper.

Taking off his topcoat and snow-coated boots, he padded across the sterile room in his thick socks feeling such perfection was somehow being vandalized by his intrusion. At the kitchen door he stopped. The glistening white surfaces, crimson utensils and pots were too suggestive of blood on snow. It wasn't often a case got too great a grip on him, but Peter Randolph's account of those children in Bosnia had stayed with him all day.

Shaking himself mentally, he walked across to the large freezer and reviewed its contents. Microwavable beef, lamb, chicken, fish, stew, cauliflower cheese, pizzas. He fancied none of it. Pouring a large whisky he took it back to the living room and sat in one of the chairs that still smelled of cleaning fluid. Even with lighting reduced to a single wall-bracket, it was still harsh, allowing no shadows or contrasts.

He recalled the elegance of the Foyles' quarters. Scrupulously tidy they might be, but they were cosily beckoning and spoke of the occupiers' personalities. Those days and nights spent alone would still hold for Jane Foyle evidence of her husband's presence. His clothes in a wardrobe, shaving gear in the bathroom, his favourites alongside hers in the bookcase. The aura of him wherever she went about the house.

The woman Jane Foyle so strongly resembled had made a lovely home for himself and her to share. Max remembered it with the familiar pain. Had his own aura not been strong enough for her on his frequent absences? Was that why Susan had sought comfort elsewhere?

Draining the glass swiftly he forced his thoughts from the question to which he'd never find the answer, and concentrated on the interview with Mrs Foyle. If he felt bloody-minded he could charge her with perverting the course of justice but, in truth, she hadn't because he and Tom had known all along Mark Ingham was lying. Her substantiation of his lies had done no harm to the course of justice.

The reason for her loyalty was much more to the point, Max felt. Repaying a good turn? Ingham must have risked a lot covering for Bobby Foyle to deserve in return the offering of false evidence in a murder enquiry. Most wives would surely have needed to satisfy themselves as to what he had really been doing that required an alibi. No way could Max accept Jane Foyle's belief in Ingham's supposed vigil on her doorstep in the early hours. So why had she so readily supported him? That her husband would was more understandable, but would Bobby be happy about his wife's putting herself at risk of prosecution for his friend's sake? The serious military predicament referred to must have been a career-busting one to earn such generous repayment.

Max walked over to pour himself a second whisky, pondering what mess Captain Robert Foyle had got himself into a year or so back. Presumably, Ingham's 'cover' had sorted the matter to the satisfaction of their superiors, and the incident was long closed. No concern of SIB.

He stood with the glass in his hand, reluctant to return to the pungent-smelling chair. To the Foyles, Ingham was a thoroughly nice man who never got what he really deserved. Did that include those things he envied Bekov for getting so easily? Envy which the Anglo-Russian's sudden intrusion into his life again made so uncontainable he struck out at the injustice of it all?

Gazing with narrowed eyes at the curious black landscape print on the wall, Max wondered if they had got it wrong after all. Ingham re-enacted historic battles with Bobby Foyle. So he was into the romance of cavalry, cannon and infantry squares. Into past traditions of élite regiments. The kind of man who would deem death by firing squad a fitting punishment? The pulsebeat in Max's temples quickened. What if Ingham had told the truth about events in the gymnasium? What if instead of raping Judith King, his sexual excitement had been expressed by killing the object of his envy? Suppose he had followed Bekov from the gym, watched him banging and kicking the door knowing he must seek shelter elsewhere, then tailed him until Peter Randolph turned up to make the job a hell of a lot easier?

His concentration was rudely shattered by pulsating bass sounds and raucous vocals from the adjoining apartment. Oh God, the neighbours had arrived home! There would be no more peace. Pulling on his boots, Max grabbed his coat and hastened from the apartment. He needed to think.

It was cold and still outside. And glistening. The sky had cleared and a brilliant moon silvered everything. A myriad stars were so bright they appeared to be fizzing like sparklers at a heavenly fireworks display. Max breathed in relief as he coiled his scarf several times around his neck and drew on his gloves. Passing traffic made little noise on the frozen snow; pedestrians walked cautiously, their breath clouding like Max's as he headed towards a restaurant he had intended trying sometime. Sometime had come earlier than expected.

As he walked, Max elaborated on the supposition that his judgements so far had been up the creek. As Tom had told Jane Foyle just a few hours ago, worms finally turned. She had fired up in Ingham's defence. Too passionate a defence for a husband's best friend? Had she and Ingham really had something going? It would have been easy to get the disgruntled Reena drunk enough to sleep deeply, then slip from the house at a call from Ingham's mobile to help him transport and tie up the body. If so, she would have to have taken her own car to the copse to meet her partner. A forensic search of the vehicle might produce supporting evidence.

Even as he was deciding to put that in motion tomorrow, he recalled the lack of Ingham's DNA at the crime scene. No, no, Max, you got it right first time, he told himself impatiently. Turned worm or not, Ingham is no killer.

He then realized he had passed the restaurant and had to retrace his steps for two hundred yards. The ground floor was full, so he was conducted to the mezzanine and a table for two beside a window. A legend along the wall told how the building had once been a hunting lodge owned by the local land-owner. The original wood panelling had been preserved, and there were mounted stags' heads alongside ancient rifles to reflect its history. Rather too rusticly Bavarian for Max's taste, but there was thankfully no musak!

After ordering a substantial meal and a large carafe of wine, Max gazed at the snowy scene outside thinking again of Randolph's heartrending story. Had that upright son of the regiment really felt Bekov's strategy on that occasion deserved such retribution? On active service – and that *had* been despite the peacekeeping tag – men often had to make painfully difficult instant decisions; sometimes sacrifice a few lives to save a much larger number. It was just one aspect of a soldier's job. Surely Randolph and his snooty friends had understood that? It seemed to Max more likely that dislike of the Anglo-Russian had been at the root of the decision to frighten and humiliate him.

The waiter brought his meal at that point. The veal fricassée tasted good. Max ate with relish and made short work of half the carafe of wine while he reflected on the character of the man who had aroused such strong emotions in many people. Curiously, as widely different as Randolph and Ingham were, they had certainly felt matching bitter resentment and envy of a man who made them seem in some way inadequate.

So what of Jeremy Fielding? Had something happened in Kuwait that had affected him the same way? Bekov had ignored him in the mess on that significant evening, as he had the other two. Salt rubbed in an old wound?

Revived by the excellent food, Max settled slowly to empty the carafe before deciding how to round off the meal. The mezzanine was now full; the waiters scurrying back and forth. They were unlikely to pester him until he was ready to order. He had noticed he was the only sole diner. Nothing in that. He had grown used to being surrounded by couples and groups.

As he sipped his wine, he suddenly caught himself imagining Caroline Bekov occupying the empty chair facing him. She would fit in well with these surroundings. Stylish and striking, she had a definite European flair. Due to her husband's Slavic influence? Max could well understand why the womanizing Bekov had been captivated by her, but not how he could be so ruthlessly unforgiving as to abandon her.

'I loved him so I accepted his terms. Find someone who hated him and couldn't.'

Mulling over Caroline's words, Max turned full circle to see Fielding as the only possible suspect. Randolph and Ingham had felt demeaned by Bekov, but they hadn't *hated* him. The Medical Corps major must have good reason to. He was already so badly stressed it should be easy enough to break him under intense questioning. The cufflink proved he had been in the sports pavilion that night, not at home pacifying his wife and child. They would get at the truth in the morning.

Pouring the last of the wine into his glass, Max cleared his mind of professional demands and allowed thoughts of Caroline Bekov to wander along erotic byways as he gazed out at the white night.

It was late when Max returned to the unfriendly apartment, but he fell almost instantly asleep for the first time in many nights. Instead of the usual nightmares, his dreams were a confusion of bizarre scenes. Horsemen hunting stags across icy wastes, silently screaming children being mown down and killed by the racing horses and a beautiful dark-haired woman kneeling in grief beside the body of a blindfolded man tossed out on the snow.

The result of Ben's blood test came in halfway through the morning. Jeremy read it unemotionally. He had guessed his lover could not indulge in the group sex he apparently found so irresistible and escape the consequences. Ben would have to be told, and questioned about any other military partners who must also be tested. God, what a prospect!

It was now essential to get himself checked. The chances of Ben having passed on the infection were strong. If necessary, he could resign his commission without the truth being revealed. But how would Ben react to the grim news? That was his real fear. He would have nothing to lose by naming his commissioned partner. Might he see that as the ultimate in an NCO's power over an officer – the apparent basis of his sexual indulgence in the pavilion.

He could deny it; suggest Ben was psychologically attempting to punish him for being the instrument of proving something so unwelcome. Yet, SIB had found a cufflink in the pavilion – Christ knew when he had lost it during that shattering row they had had – and were certain to demand an explanation.

He got to his feet restlessly and stared from the window. His future was looking ever bleaker. If Ben named him, and provided evidence to support his claim, it would lead to a court martial. What he had believed to be a loyal, fond relationship would be publicly exposed as exploitation of an NCO by a senior officer. The press would link it with Leo's murder – sure to – and the tabloid headlines would announce his shame to the world. He could imagine them: MAJOR'S GAY SEX AMID SPORTS GEAR AT MURDER BASE.

Resting his forehead against the icy pane, Jeremy faced his possible fate. He could be kicked out in disgrace from the army. His medical career would be in doubt. His family would never understand his sexuality. They would cut themselves out of his life. If Ben had infected him, that life could become a slow death.

The telephone rang, making his nerves jangle. He crossed slowly to his desk; took up the receiver. 'Yes?'

'Sir, Sar'nt Major Black is here. Convenient to talk to him?'

No, his nerves screamed. 'Send him in.'

He sat behind his desk where the HIV test result lay, and prepared to fight. The detective came in bringing a waft of icy air from outside. His cheeks were rosy from the bitter wind. Despite much stamping of feet in the outer office some snow remained on his boots. He was not smiling.

'Good morning, sir. Surgery over?'

'It is, yes. Are you after some medical advice?'

Tom Black did not consider that worthy of a reply. 'Captain Rydal would like you to come across to our interview room.'

'For what purpose?'

'An in-depth investigation into your movements on the night of February the twelfth. I have a vehicle outside.'

'Mr Black, I have twice outlined what I did on the night of the murder. I'm disinclined to go over it again,' he said, remaining firmly seated.

'We have forensic confirmation that the cufflink found in the pavilion is the match of one your wife surrendered to us yesterday.'

Jeremy had his answer ready. 'Quite possibly. Are you aware that I helped backstage for the Christmas pantomime? We stored scenery and props there. I was in and out frequently.'

'In mess dress, sir?'

'Well ... I believe I did once call in to see how things were going after a dining-in night.'

'Two of our sergeants are presently interviewing Lance-Corporal Snaith, who apparently masterminded the panto. I'll ask them

327

to get verification of that from him, sir.' He stepped to the open door. 'Captain Rydal won't keep you any longer than necessary.'

He would have to go. What was Ben saying right now? Would he protect their relationship and go along with the lie just offered? Jeremy slid the HIV test result in the centre desk drawer and locked it. Pocketing the key, he took up his coat and cap. The net was closing fast, leaving him no escape route.

Next minute, there was one. The telephone rang when he was almost at the outer door. Then a shout halted him.

'*Sir!* Emergency call! Accident in number two store. Pallet collapsed under a load. Two storemen badly crushed.'

A medical emergency took priority over anything else. Jeremy left Tom Black standing and prepared to follow the ambulance across the base. Dealing with the critical period during which the pallet was winched off the seriously injured men drove other thoughts to the back of his mind, but once the ambulance set off with them the symbolic comparison of being crushed by an intolerable weight returned to him.

When he could no longer stay in the store without good cause, he crunched over the snow to his car and sat in it, battling an impulse to turn out through the main gate and just keep driving. Reason told him running was no answer. He would look guilty.

SIB were after him for Leo's murder. A witness had seen him enter the pavilion that night; they had found the incriminating cufflink. They knew he had lied about returning directly home from the surgery: Jeannie had made it too obvious he had tried to concoct an alibi. And SIB knew there had been a past encounter with Leo in the Gulf. They would probe and probe until they discovered the truth about that night, even if Ben kept quiet about their relationship. So why not drive away? Go to ground somewhere. Change his identity. Start a new life.

His pager bleeped. He stared at it, returning from the moment of wildness, then took up his mobile. 'Yes, Sergeant Phipps?'

'Free to speak, sir?'

'Yes, they're on the way to hospital.'

'Thought you should know Mrs Freeman went into labour very fast. I sent the other ambulance. Time it got to her, birth was imminent. Corporal Ryan delivered a six-pound-four-ounce-boy in the vehicle. Mother and baby fine, sir.'

'Ah ... good,' he replied tonelessly.

A slight pause. 'Everything all right, sir?'

'Yes ... yes, I'm going for an early lunch. I'll be at home if I'm needed.'

He drove automatically along the ruts left by a succession of vehicles. That boy who had just entered the world would wish he had never left the womb. It was a savage place out here.

Letting himself in the house he was met with the sounds of the TV blaring and Briony screaming in paroxysms of distress. Almost

329

noon. She should have been napping contentedly after her bathtime feed. And where the hell was Jeannie? Lounge was deserted; TV off. In the kitchen no lunch was cooking on the stove. He trod heavily up the stairs. The nursery door was closed. He made to open it, but it would not budge.

Jeannie was still in her dressing gown, sitting in bed staring at the TV blasting out a German pop song. He silenced it by tugging the plug from the socket.

'Where's the key to the nursery?' he demanded. *'Where is it?'* he yelled, advancing on her.

'It wouldn't stop, Jerry. I kept telling it to. Then it did disgusting things all over my dress. Filthy! Stinking! It was very, very naughty. So I gave it a smack and locked it away. It had to be punished, Jerry, like I was. Locked in my room without any tea. Then it'll be sorry and won't do it again.'

Jeremy seized her shoulders and shook her. *'Where's the bloody key?'*

She looked frightened. 'I don't know. Truly I don't, Jerry. I ... I think I threw it away.'

He flung her down on her side, then strode across ready to kick the door in, fearful of what might have been done to the baby. When he reached the landing he spotted the key on the floor, half under a small table. Snatching it up, he entered the nursery which reeked of faeces. Briony was scarlet-faced and squirming in discomfort and fright. He examined her gently, speaking words of comfort. She did not appear to have been harmed, just badly scared.

He lifted her from the cot and set about making her clean. She recognized love and gentleness. Her crying grew less frenzied, eventually dying away. Jeremy held her close, the baby's cheek against his soft and smelling of talcum powder. She had been created through his basic need, not through love. He owed her a better life than this to compensate for his careless seed.

Carrying his daughter downstairs, he telephoned Alice Foster. She said she could be there in fifteen minutes. Tucked up in her pram, Briony soon fell into an exhausted sleep. Jeremy then went upstairs to see to Jeannie. She was also sleeping peacefully when Alice collected the baby.

'Just ring when you'd like me to bring her back,' she said. 'I've some of her formula left, so I'll give her her evening feed and have her ready for bed, if you like. You know I love having her.'

He watched Alice push the pram down the front path, then he turned back and poured himself a stiff drink. He made a ham sandwich to eat with another double whisky while he sat at the writing desk. Thirty minutes later, he rang Sergeant Phipps.

'Bit of a problem at home. Would you get through to Mr Black and explain? Ask if he and Captain Rydal would mind coming here to talk to me instead. Thanks.'

He disconnected and sank back in his chair

with another hefty drink. Best to get it over with.

After another isolated lunch in the officers' mess, Max returned to the chilly classroom to find Tom waiting with his coat on. He relayed Sergeant Phipps' message.

'Fair enough. It'll be a damn sight warmer there.'

Tom drove the short distance to the Fieldings' quarters and parked behind their car. 'I guess he sorted the emergency well enough.'

'Mmm. Unless another crops up we'll pin him down and force a confession. With any luck, we can wind this case up by the end of the week,' said Max.

The front door was ajar. Tom rang the bell, then called for permission to enter. Silence. They went in. Fielding was in an armchair. There was a glass beside him with a quarter-inch of spirit in it. He was dead.

Max picked up the sheet of paper beneath the crystal glass and read aloud to Tom: "'I can't let this dangerous situation go on any longer. My unstable wife has been put beyond doing irreparable damage to our child. You'll find her upstairs.

"'It's my dying wish that my parents, John and Cathleen Fielding, should become Briony's guardians, or that they should make arrangements for the very best foster care if they feel unable to rear her.

"'I state categorically that I did not kill Leo Bekov, nor did I aid the person who did.'"

Max studied the signature written with a perfectly steady hand. Three words near the bottom of the page were askew and must have been scrawled as an afterthought when it was almost too late. *I loved him.*

Seventeen

Someone broke the rules and sold to a journalist all he knew about Jeremy Fielding's suicide after giving his wife a lethal injection. The same informant also divulged the facts about the treatment of Leo Bekov's body, which had been kept from the press. Even the broadsheets went to town on the two dramas, particularly those with no love for the establishment and the amount spent on defence.

The tabloids declared Jeannie Fielding had been suffering a total mental breakdown after giving birth, so the child had been cared for by a sergeant's wife to prevent the little girl being harmed. Speculation on why the doctor had terminated both their lives centred on the murder of Leo Bekov. What was the connection between the Fieldings and the Anglo-Russian linguist?

With the bit between their teeth, newsmen dug out details of all three lives. The Fielding woman had been whiter than white until her breakdown, so interest was focused on the two military officers. Much better left-wing scope there!

The link was unearthed. During the war to free Kuwait, Fielding and Bekov had been close friends, yet they had not once been in contact since then. Had they fallen foul of each other in the course of their duty? Had the confrontation been so bitter it drove the doctor to kill Bekov when they came face to face again? They had publicly ignored each other in the officers' mess, and several hours later, Bekov's body was found blindfolded and tied upright to a post like a condemned man executed by firing squad. Military Police sources claimed the murder investigation was still ongoing, but Major Fielding had been called out on an emergency and could have crossed paths with Bekov in the early hours. Could that encounter have turned fatally violent?

Photographs were rooted out by determined reporters. Bekov as a Sandhurst cadet, Bekov with his balalaika and with his beautiful ex-wife Caroline. There were youthful pictures of the Fieldings, but the son of a Russian asylum-seeker, who had spent just one doomed night in Germany, provided the most fertile copy.

Colonel Keegan thankfully took the bulk of his battalion off to participate in the NATO exercise, charging Max with the task of finding who had betrayed his fellows and the regiment by blabbing to the Press.

SIB had more pressing matters on their

hands. Fielding's suicide note was a signed confession to the murder of his wife, but reports on both deaths had to be prepared for the coroner. The Home Office handled the sensitive duty of informing both sets of parents. The senior Fieldings flew out to collect the baby so disastrously left to their care. Army welfare personnel then worked hard to deflect aggression from the other grief-stricken grandparents, who arrived to demand custody of their darling daughter's child. Frustrated, they swore to take the Fieldings to court over the issue, and poured out to any and every journalist their sense of outrage that an innocent babe should be placed in the hands of a couple who had produced a deranged murderer.

A week after the tragic discovery in the Fieldings' quarters, when the base was populated by only those few not taking part in the exercise, Max addressed his team. After thanking them for their good work on the Fielding case, he spoke about the Bekov murder.

'I want all stops pulled out on this. The press are enjoying a field day at the moment, making wild suppositions damaging not only to us but to the service as a whole. We need a swift solution. Fielding's dying declaration of innocence puts the focus on Peter Randolph, if my theory of punishment for a past deed is correct.'

'What if your theory's wrong, sir?' asked

Staff Sergeant Melly, who had been cynical all along.

'Then God help us,' Max replied heavily. 'It'll mean any one of the seven thousand plus on that base grabbed a Browning and took a pot shot at the first poor bugger who crossed his path.'

Connie Bush spoke up. 'If your theory's right, we've not yet checked which of the rank and file might have served with Major Bekov in the past.'

Max nodded. 'A good point. Unfortunately, they're all out on a mock battlefield now, so although we can check them out on WAMI we can't question them until we feel they could be suspects.'

Tom Black said, 'If we could find the murder weapon it would narrow the field. And the sack Randolph says he used must have been taken away by the killers. That would be useful evidence.'

Sergeant Piercey said, 'Are we convinced by the Fielding suicide note? He had the opportunity; he was seen entering the pavilion at the vital time. He lied about his movements that night. His batty wife could have helped him tie the body to the post. That's why he killed her too.'

Tom shook his head. 'He was taking an irrevocable step that morning. He had nothing to lose. A dying man's confession has to be the truth.'

'Balls,' said Piercey under his breath.

Tom heard him, said bitingly, 'You have

336

something more to contribute?'

Unabashed, he said, 'His suicide note made no mention of what he was doing in the sports pavilion, or who he was meeting there. He surely didn't go to be alone. Suppose Ms King went there after her nooky in the gym, met the Doc and went to the copse to help him do the deed? Being the PT Officer, she'd know her way around that pavilion. And she'd be pretty thick with the MO. Sports injuries, and so on. I think we should have another go at her.'

Connie Bush added to that. 'Maybe the Doc was keen on Judith King, saw Bekov making a meal of her in the gym – seems to have been quite an audience there – and killed him through jealousy.'

'So why didn't the note read I loved *her* rather than *him*?' argued Melly.

'Because the Doc was gay,' ventured Sergeant Beeny, a newcomer to the team. 'He meant he loved Bekov.'

'That doesn't necessarily make him gay,' said Tom. 'From what we've learned of the victim he was either resented or greatly admired by other men, and not in any carnal sense. He was a colourful, charismatic character.'

'I've already checked out the gay angle,' revealed Connie Bush. 'Discreetly, of course. No one appears to have been propositioned by the MO. There's no evidence that he took too long examining male patients, or that he asked them to strip off unnecessarily. He was generally regarded as a right-on guy. If he was playing around, I'd put my money on another woman. His wife surely drove him to seek consolation elsewhere.'

'Do we believe Jane Foyle's evidence?' asked Sergeant Heather Johnson. 'Perhaps she was the Doc's bit on the side.'

Max had had enough. 'You're all clutching at straws! When you find conclusive evidence of who killed Leo Bekov, come and tell me.'

He vanished into his office and shut the door firmly, knowing he was allowing the case to get on top of him. Everything just said had been spinning round and around in his head for the past two weeks, and he was no nearer to seeing light at the end of this perplexing tunnel. A persistent inner conviction that his theory was correct was being undermined by the gradual bowing out of the obvious suspects. Ingham had cracked up. Fielding was dead. Randolph had an alibi. For the rest of that morning he tried to deal with reports on other cases they were handling, but Bekov was never fully out of his thoughts.

Restless, unable to concentrate, he quit his office by the rear door and drove the short distance to his apartment for a sandwich lunch. Both neighbours were out all day, so it was quiet. Layering cheese, tomato and ham on long soft rolls, he decided it would be worth investigating Bobby Foyle. Although WAMI had not shown the man as serving on any station with Bekov it didn't mean they had never met up on a short course at

338

some time.

Knowing he was clutching at straws – something he had accused his team of doing – his thoughts turned to Caroline Bekov. How was she coping with the bizarre truth about the murder, and with the media sensationalism surrounding the man she loved so deeply? He had a strong urge to write to her; an official letter to soften the crude exaggerations in the tabloids. He resisted it because he suspected his motive was not in the least official. He regretted the fact that the reverential funeral she had doubtless planned would now be overrun by ghoulish reporters. Dignity would be destroyed by flashing cameras and intrusive interviewers. Poor Caroline.

Tom went home for lunch, taking Nora totally by surprise. An accredited dressmaker, she was engaged in making a wedding gown and three bridesmaid's dresses for a sergeant about to marry her male counterpart. The dining room was festooned with pink satin and handmade rosebuds. He took one look at Nora's dismayed expression and laughed.

'So much for delight at the unexpected arrival of your old man! You couldn't look more shattered if I'd caught you in bed with a toyboy.'

'Huh, fat chance of that! I have to finish this lot in four days, and it's parents' night at the school tomorrow. Unlike you, I can't plead pressure of work to get out of it. What are you doing here at this hour?'

'Not what I'd like to take the chance of doing while the girls are out of the house, that's obvious.'

'One-track mind, yours,' she said, laying aside the strapless boned bodice she was working on and coming round the table to him. 'Problems, love?'

He kissed her. 'What makes you ask?'

'I've known you a long time, Tom Black. Soup and sandwiches?'

'Fine, but I'll do it. You carry on until it's ready.'

'Actually, I could do with a break.' She walked through to the kitchen and took a can of soup from a cupboard to push along the worktop towards him. 'See to that while I do the rest.'

As he heated the soup Tom watched his wife slice cold beef from the remains of yesterday's joint. How different his life was from Jeremy Fielding's. Marriage could be bliss or hell. That poor sod had been driven to kill himself rather than face what his had become.

'I'm such a lucky man,' he said quietly.

Nora glanced across at him. 'It's only a few beef sandwiches.' She continued buttering bread, then said with understanding, 'It's the Fieldings, isn't it? They've got to you. The whole business out at that base.'

'Not only me. Max said his piece this morning, then shut himself in his office,' Tom told her, stirring soup automatically. 'He's demanding results, but we've no leads and the bulk of the regiment is a hundred Ks away on a bloody NATO exercise. No way we can question umpteen men engaged in mock warfare in the hope of finding answers to questions we're not aware exist.'

She cut the sandwiches diagonally across and arranged them on two plates. 'It's all that trash in the papers. Whoever sold the facts to a journalist deserves to be hung! It can't harm the dead, but their poor families are suffering. As for that baby being fought over by her grandparents, what a legacy for life she has! Her father killed her psychiatric mother, then himself. She'll be branded with that for the rest of her days.'

They sat at the breakfast bar to eat, both thinking of Briony Fielding in comparison with the love and security their three girls enjoyed. When Tom finished his soup he pushed the bowl aside.

'I've no idea where to go now on this one, love. All morning I've reviewed what we've got; looked at it every which way. Some of the team are sceptical, but I have to agree with Max that Bekov was killed by someone he'd known in the past. While the exercise lasts we can't question the entire rank and file. There's only Captain Randolph left of the commissioned suspects. The events of that night and the very tight timing points to the killer being present at the regimental dinner, but he has a watertight alibi.'

The breaking of the story in the papers meant Tom felt able to discuss the case with

Nora. It had become public knowledge now. So he told her of Randolph's confession to conducting a mock execution in the copse.

'He swears he left the victim alive. There's no proof of that, but he couldn't have transported and tied up the body because he was having an involved conversation on security with the Duty Sergeant at that specific time.'

'How d'you know he was?'

Tom munched his sandwich. 'It's in his report and in Sergeant Squires'.'

'Is he Betty Squires' husband?'

'No idea. His name's Eric.'

'That's him. She's a member of the PTA. Always referring to her Eric as if he's the Oracle. How well d'you know him?'

'Hardly at all.'

Nora brushed crumbs from her fingers. 'So how d'you know he can be trusted not to falsify his report?'

'What?' Tom's hand paused halfway to his mouth with his last sandwich.

'Couldn't he and Captain Randolph have together moved the body from the copse and lied about their supposed conversation?'

The beef sandwich was lowered to the plate as Tom took in the import of what Nora was suggesting. He'd talked to Eric Squires about the various incidents mentioned in the duty reports. He had seemed conscientious and straightforward; no hint of evasion in his manner. But Nora had a point.

A DNA match would link Randolph to the scene of crime and prove bodily contact with the victim. He would be aware of that, hence his claim of a *mock* shooting. Only confirmation of a detailed telephone conversation with the Duty Sergeant would show it to have been impossible for him to carry out the second stage of the murder within the time frame. Christ, why hadn't any of them considered collusion between two men who had legitimate cause to be anywhere on that base during the night hours, and who could give each other an apparently official alibi?

'And Squires was almost certainly in Bosnia with Randolph,' Tom breathed, putting thoughts into words. 'What if he was in one of the Warriors carrying those sick kids!'

The door to Max's office was still closed when Tom returned. Only two members of the team were present in the large room and they immediately feigned intense concentration on work. Where the rest were was anyone's guess. Pulling out all the stops, as their officer commanded? What stops? Feet of snow prevented scene of crime searching, and the base was empty of all but ancillary staff. Tom was eager to explore this new theory, however, and went directly to his office.

Entering his password, Tom soon brought up on screen the information he wanted. Sergeant Eric Squires *had* been with the regiment in Bosnia, so he could well have come across Leo Bekov even if he had not been part of that dramatic rescue mission. He sat back in his chair, thoughts racing. Luck, chance – in Bekov's case, Nemesis – had played a big role in that killing, but it seemed just too providential that Squires and Randolph should *happen* to be on duty together if they had planned murder.

After a moment's reflection he picked up the telephone and punched out a number. He was soon through to the Admin section, whose staff were still functioning while the operational companies were away. Tom made himself known to the female sergeant at the end of the line and asked for her help.

'I'm checking the duty roster for February 12th. Can you tell me if either Captain Randolph or Sergeant Squires swapped duty with someone that day?'

'Just a moment, sir.' The sound of fingernails clicking on a keyboard. 'Feb 12, you said? No. Ah, half a mo. Yes, there were some changes.'

'Go on,' urged Tom.

'Two days earlier Sar'nt Bryn had a forty-eight-hour compassionate – wife having twins sooner than expected – so Sar'nt Collyer stood in at the last moment. But he was on the regular roster two days ahead so, as there was top security that night, Captain Symes switched him with Sar'nt Squires.'

'Did Squires volunteer for it?'

'No idea, sir. The computer doesn't show that kind of thing.'

More's the pity, thought Tom.

'Anything else, sir?'

'Tell me which company Sar'nt Squires is

in, and the name of the officer commanding.'

When he had the information Tom then asked for the contact number being used by Central Operations during the exercise. 'I need to speak to Squires urgently.'

'He's not gone on the exercise. Broke his ankle during training.' A giggle entered her voice. 'He's on light duties in Belmont Company office being waited on by Lance-Corporal Cynthia Hall. We all reckon he arranged the accident on purpose.'

Ready to bawl her out for gossiping on an official call, Tom held his peace. She had just given him an unexpected bonus and he was anxious to be on his way. Cutting the connection, he shrugged on his topcoat and left the office. Max's door was still firmly shut, but he had anyway decided to pursue this lead solo. If it was a dead end only he would be frustrated. On the other hand, it would be good to confront his boss with a result. Truth to tell, Tom was slightly put out over the morning's review when Max had expressed his opinion of the team then retired to his office without having the usual short private conversation with his 2IC.

The cold spell was continuing. Fresh snow had fallen overnight and the lowering sky looked ready to shed more at any minute. During the hour long drive Tom's sense of hopeful anticipation was tempered with disgust that no one in the team, especially himself, had considered what had been Nora's instant reaction to Randolph's alibi. They

345

needed to sharpen up. All right, *he* did!

He had been thinking too much lately about the girls turning into young women, with the attendant worries and problems. The onset of Maggie's menstruation cycle had shaken him badly – erected a frail barrier between them. Their relationship had subtly altered. She was less boisterous; he felt vaguely awkward in her company. All the 'little girl' things he used to do – pulling her plaits, giving her a bear hug, tickling her until she begged for mercy – now seemed forbidden. Nora told him he'd get over it, and by the time their youngest started 'the Curse' he'd wonder what all the fuss was about.

He had always wanted a son. He now wished all three children were boys. There'd be no secret whispering in corners, no anguished glances at Nora when he said what appeared to be the wrong thing, no bedroom walls covered with posters of freakish-looking males who inspired shrieks or sighs. They all looked pretty wet and wimpy to Tom.

He was fantasizing about playing football with his three sons when he reached the base and checked through the main gate. His mind immediately snapped into professional mode as he drove the perimeter of what had become almost a ghost establishment.

Belmont Company office was fifty yards along a transverse road and looked deserted as Tom approached. There was a car parked alongside the squat brick building, however, and lights shone from the rear windows.

When he entered, Tom understood why his informant had giggled about Eric Squires' predicament. Lance-Corporal Hall was the loveliest soldier Tom had ever seen. Dark auburn hair, large velvety-brown eyes, flawless complexion. And what a smile! Until told this impressively masculine 'civilian' was an SIB sergeant major. The smile turned to a defensive mask as she got to her feet beside her computer.

'There's only me here, sir. They're all on manoeuvres.'

'You're running the show single-handed? I find that hard to believe.'

'Well, no, sir. Lieutenant Troy's on hand to deal with anything outside normal routine. You'd probably do best to drive over to Admin. He'll be able to help you.'

'Sergeant Squires is the person who can help me. I understand he's doing light duties here.'

She blurted out, 'Who told you that?'

Tom's expression hardened. 'Where will I find him?'

'I'll ... patch through to him, sir,' she said, colour heightened as she picked up the telephone.

'If he's really at home skiving, tell me how to reach his quarters,' Tom commanded, growing irritated with this pretty bamboozler.

'No, he's here.' She began punching out an extension number. 'I'll get him for you. Oh, *Sergeant Squires*,' she said with emphasis. 'Sar'nt Major Black is in the front office to see you. Says it's urgent.' The brown eyes fastened on Tom as she said into the receiver, 'That's right. You will? I'll tell him.'

She replaced the receiver. 'He's coming, sir. Said would I explain it might take a while because his ankle's in plaster.'

'So where is he?'

'Oh ... checking things in Records. He has to lock away the files before he can leave. Security.'

Really annoyed by now, Tom snapped, 'I know all about security, girl, and I'll make it easier by going to Records to speak to him. Direct me!'

Hesitating momentarily, she then led Tom to the inner door and pointed along a corridor. 'It's the room right at the end. But you have to know the code to get in. Much better wait for him here, sir.'

Tom was already on his way and knocking on the door before the girl had time to telephone a warning to Squires. When he rapped sharply a second time, the door was jerked open.

'Tell him I'm ... oh, it's you, sir,' said a red-faced Squires. 'I'm hampered by the plaster on my foot. Takes twice as long to do everything.'

'Like coming back in here with me to answer some questions?' Tom walked past him into the room fitted with filing cabinets and stacked boxes. Beside the microfilm viewer stood a TV set. Half hidden behind a stack of files was a six-pack, and in the waste basket pushed well towards the wall in the kneehole were three empty cans. It was apparent what form of 'light duties' Squires had been engaged in. Under other circumstances Tom might have asked pointedly what the latest score was, but he was here on very serious business. This NCO might well be an accomplice in murder.

'I'm still investigating the death of Major Bekov. Evidence has come to light that several people were out and about during the critical hours of that night. I've been going through the duty reports submitted by the Duty Officer and yourself. Apart from the prowler someone thought they saw near the sports ground, neither of you mentioned other activity in the early hours. How was that?'

Squires had recovered his poise. 'Because we didn't see it. If we had, it would have been recorded. We were on extra alert that night, sir. If people were moving around they must have hidden from our vehicles, or been in different areas when we passed.'

'Some *tight security*!' said Tom coldly.

Squires bridled. 'We had the perimeter well and truly covered by patrols with dogs. You know it's impossible to keep an eye on the internal areas of an entire base. Whoever killed the Major knew his way around, that's for sure, but he still took a hell of a risk of being caught tying him up.'

Tom changed direction sharply. 'You must have come across the victim in Bosnia.'

Now Squires grew evasive. 'Was he out there?'

'You know bloody well he was. He acted as a translator and general liaison officer for your regiment. According to Captain Randolph he was highly popular with the men. Entertained them with his balalaika and bawdy Russian songs.'

'Oh, *him!*' exclaimed Squires with affected surprise. 'I never knew his name. I'm not one for that kind of music, anyway.'

'And all the newspaper publicity surrounding his murder didn't make the connection for you? Come on, man, you can't be *that* thick.' At the sergeant's silence Tom turned the screws. 'Evidence now throws suspicion on those who knew him in the past. You're one.'

'*What?*' He looked alarmed. 'There's a whole bloody battalion was out there in Bosnia with him.'

Satisfied that Squires was now rattled, Tom pushed home his point. 'But *you* were the person on duty the night he was killed. That gave you the perfect opportunity for revenge.'

'*Revenge?* Look, you can't pin this on me. I didn't *know* the bloke.'

'I only have your word on that. Tell me about Bosnia. That mission to bring sick children from a hospital before it was turned to rubble; were you part of it?'

'No. I knew about it. We all did.'

'And about Major Bekov's participation?'

It was clear Squires had no idea what he

350

was being asked. 'I guess he went along to mediate. He spoke Serbo-Croat.' Apprehension was turning into aggression. 'I don't know why you've come here like this. You can't fabricate things that didn't happen just because you haven't found who did him in. It wasn't me. You can't prove it was.'

'Can you prove it wasn't?' Tom countered.

'My duty report. Read it. It's all in there what I was doing that night. You've already questioned me once and were satisfied. Why aren't you now?'

'New evidence.' Tom regarded Squires' nondescript features, pale eyes and the twitching nerve beside his mouth. 'The Oracle'? His wife must wear rose-tinted glasses. 'You claim to have called up Captain Randolph at 03:40 to report having caught a two-man patrol elsewhere than along their stretch of perimeter wire.'

'Yes. Johnson and Pitkin having a crafty fag. I slapped them on a charge. Had a spell behind bars for it, they did.'

'You told Captain Randolph this when you'd ensured the patrol was back in action?'

'That's right.'

'You're certain it was 03:40?'

Squires grew mulish. 'It's there in my report.'

'How did the Duty Officer sound?'

'*Sound?* Don't know what you mean.'

Tom was losing patience. 'Don't play the fool with me! Did he answer the call immediately? Was he calm, angry? Was he at all out of breath?'

'What's this all about, sir? Surely no one hopped over that unguarded stretch of wire and killed the Major?'

'How well d'you know Captain Randolph?'

'How well? I've occasionally done duties with him, and I've spoken to him when he lectures the platoons in my company. Apart from that I don't come across him much. He's always pleasant enough, but not the kind to ask you about yourself or take an interest in you like some of the officers. But he's well respected.'

Tom felt the impetus was being lost and put things bluntly. 'On the surface those duty reports give you and Captain Randolph alibis for the time of the murder, which we have deduced was around 03:35. I said *on the surface*, but they could have been concocted between you to cover the time you committed the crime together then drove the body to the officers' mess to tie it up. Was that what happened? Did you assist in the murder of Major Leo Bekov?'

Eric Squires now knew he was on firm ground. 'No, I did not! I called up the Duty Officer at 03:40 after I'd sent Johnson and Pitkin back on their beat. I told him what had occurred and assured him the stretch of wire was again covered. I then decided to check the other patrols once more, to be on the safe side. I drove right round the perimeter and spoke to them all. I'll give you their names. You can check with them.'

Tom felt as deflated as a punctured balloon. His team had spoken to all the guards at the very start of the investigation, but they would only have asked if anything unusual had been seen. This infallible evidence would not have been offered because the patrols would have regarded it as routine.

Halfway back to Section Headquarters, snow began falling thick and fast, bringing dusk early. Tom decided to go straight home. He had worked late often enough on this case. He deserved some time with his family. As he was planning a cosy evening with Nora he remembered the bridesmaid's dresses and grew more depressed. She would be buried beneath pink satin and rosebuds until bedtime. Wrong moment then to tell her about his wild-goose chase.

Straining to see the road ahead through the white flurries, Tom told himself this was the one case that was set to defeat them.

The afternoon was boring and seemingly endless. But for the state of the roads Max would have taken a long drive in the hope of lightening his spirits, and to hell with paperwork. Several irritating phone calls concerning documentation deepened his gloom, driving him from his chair to gaze restlessly from the window.

Snow was the problem, he told himself. It prevented further searching of the crime scene. And a few thousand possible suspects were now away fighting mock battles with their allies. His theory must have been wrong, which left the field open for any person on base that night to have killed Bekov.

Watching large flakes tumbling to settle on the white layer that covered everything in sight, Max acknowledged that snow was the root cause of his fierce mood. He could not rid his inner vision of pictures of a hospital sheltering dying children and a few courageous nurses being blown apart, while a military convoy attempting to take many to safety was being held to ransom by a few thugs with rifles and landmines. Peter Randolph had a way with words that had made that bleak frozen scene all too real. And the actions of Leo Bekov.

Leo Bekov was inexorably linked with Caroline, whose enduring love for the man aroused in Max curious envy. Each moment of his two meetings with her were somehow overshadowed by images of snowbound Russia conjured up by the sound of the balalaika Bekov had apparently played with such seductive flair.

These overriding mind pictures, enhanced by the wintry atmosphere around him, made his inability to find who had put an end to the enigmatic Bekov too personal a sense of failure. He desperately wanted to make good his promise to Caroline to find and punish the killer. She would be suffering the pain of the newspaper revelations: he needed to show her that at least justice would be done.

Dusk came early and Max decided to call it

a day. He had vented his spleen on his team this morning and departed leaving them in peace. He did look in at Tom's office on his way out, but it was empty. Just as well, perhaps. Tom was as frustrated over this case as he.

Walking from the lift to his apartment it was immediately clear no peace would be found there tonight. A card pinned to his neighbour's door told him Frau Bauer was hosting a lingerie party at the cocktail hour. From the sound of things, one or two guests had arrived early. Elated female voices punctuated by shrieks of laughter already reached Max through the dividing wall. As wine flowed and the underwear on sale became ever sexier, the hubbub would be more than he could accept in his present state of mind.

He swiftly downed a warming whisky, slipped a small book from the table into his pocket, then left the apartment knowing he must search out new living quarters at the weekend. This knicker party was the last straw. He needed a place that was cosy, more lived-in, more relaxing, even if it was further from Section Headquarters.

Head bowed to avoid the stinging blizzard, Max trudged through several back streets to a small hotel he knew offered a decent dinner menu, and whose lounge was quiet and comfortable. Warmth, peace and restful decor greeted him on the other side of the glass-panelled door. A huge log fire gave out a welcoming glow to those who had braved the elements to get there. Not many had, so Max settled in a deep armchair in a corner near the hearth and asked for Glühwein. He intended to pass the hour or so before ordering a meal attempting to thaw out mentally, as well as physically.

For the first twenty minutes he sat watching pictures in the fire, letting thoughts drift through his mind in dreamy fashion. Thoughts of childhood, of boyhood; remembering Scout camp fires, Guy Fawkes' night bonfires, helping his father rake up leaves for garden fires.

Gradually, these fond memories progressed to less restful ones. Buildings that became infernos at the hands of arsonists; men turned into living torches by the weapons of war. These he had seen, yet they led to one horror he had not. That hospital in Bosnia.

The stress he had sought to banish was back. Since forcing the confession from Peter Randolph, Max had tried to understand him and failed.

That stand-off in Bosnia had had to be resolved somehow. Bekov had done it in unpalatable fashion, but the entire situation out there had precluded normal, rational solutions. Worse things were being done daily. Inhuman, brutal things. Randolph had had no connection with the child Bekov handed to the Serbs. The boy had been a stranger. Randolph had later served in other savage trouble spots yet, seven years later, still felt so strongly about that single incident that seeing

Bekov again had brought the compulsion to retaliate. Why?

Why had the assured, smooth-talking descendant of distinguished generals done something that seemed so completely out of character; something that would shadow his bright future when it was made public during the trial?

Reaching in his pocket Max drew out the copy of the regiment's history he had borrowed from the library. Randolph's family had served with the colours through several generations, and he had so far been following that tradition with ease. Max hoped to find in the book some clue to what made the man tick. Was the bloodline wholly endowed with military perfection, or was there an errant streak that had appeared in some generations?

There was an impressive list of Randolphs in the index. The first of them had fought at Ciudad Rodrigo, where the regiment had gained another battle honour. From then on there had been a Randolph with the regiment throughout the cavalry years and on to the transition from horses to armoured vehicles. Reading of these blue-blooded heroes Max guessed there had been much disgust and angry twirling of moustaches from dyed-in-the-wool horsemen. Impossible to get a saddle over a tank!

RANDOLPH Francis Etienne (French blood entering the line?) won a VC at Colenso for bringing in a gun under heavy fire to prevent it falling into the hands of the enemy. The family had won medals galore, but his was the only VC. Was the Robert Redford lookalike hoping to remedy that? It made interesting reading and Max concluded the males knew they would be soldiers from the day of their birth. Or even in the womb! God help any future Randolph who yearned to be a gentlemen's outfitter. Or a pop star!

Scanning the section in the book covering what was defiantly referred to as 'The Great War – 1914–18', a name suddenly caught Max's eye. His nerve ends began to tingle as he read an account of an incident at Albert, when a decimated company led by a subaltern on his first operation was pinned down in a wood from first light until sunset, waiting for backup troops that never came because they had been wiped out. When darkness fell, the raw subaltern announced that he would go back to discover where the reinforcements were. His sergeant, a seasoned soldier who knew his way around the area, advised the nervous boy officer to stay with the men while he reconnoitred to gauge the situation.

The sergeant had not returned by dawn, whereupon the officer concluded that he had been captured or killed, so he decided to fall back to their original position. On leaving the wood, they were immediately exposed to unexpected enemy artillery. Only the subaltern and a corporal survived the barrage. Both were wounded. The corporal died the following night.

The sergeant came into the lines unharmed two days later, when the youthful officer charged him with desertion. A field court martial was convened. The sergeant said in his own defence that he had returned to tell his commander to move forward without delay, because the enemy had now brought up heavy guns on their flank, but the company had moved from where he had left them. He searched all night but failed to make contact.

When it grew light, he again searched the wood without success. He then attempted to reach British lines, lying low in a French farmhouse until it was safe to move. He hotly denied the charge of cowardice in the face of the enemy.

Despite his unblemished record he was found guilty. Witnesses testified to his anger over the appalling loss of life to gain just a few hundred yards of muddy desolation. He had been overheard to say the war would only end when no troops were left alive and France was layered a mile deep with corpses. He had also publicly declared he would like to line the generals up and machine-gun them all for what they were making their men endure.

The court judged his behaviour to be detrimental to good order and military discipline by preaching sedition. This charge was added to the other, and he was executed by firing squad.

With growing excitement Max read brief references to the family's long campaign to vindicate him, citing the MO's opinion that battle fatigue had caused the man to act out of character, like a vast number who had been in France longer than two years. The family claimed he should have been classified as shell-shocked and hospitalized, not branded a coward and shot. Only ten years after the war ended had they accepted defeat. *The sergeant's name was Ernest Harkness.*

Abandoning his Glühwein, Max grabbed his topcoat and headed for his office. Once there, he sat before his computer and logged on to WAMI. Tom had checked out James Harkness at the start of the investigation, but Max went through the list of Harknesses starting with an Alan. When he reached William John he stopped. Listed as the man's next of kin was – James Allyn (brother).

Max let out a long, long sigh. Captain W. J. Harkness had served in Kosovo in the same area at the same time as Leo Bekov.

Eighteen

As soon as it grew light a helicopter flew them out to where the NATO exercise was well under way. Max had to fight to requisition an aircraft; go through several channels. The simulated war being fought engaged a large proportion of those British resources presently in Germany. Only a small emergency reserve remained on site, so to beg transport to a highly restricted zone under such circumstances was certain to meet with resistance. One testy individual even went so far as to demand why the arrest could not wait until the exercise ended.

'After all, your suspect can't hoof it. Anyone caught where he shouldn't be is liable to be shot at. They're using live ammo.'

'Our suspect used live ammo on an unarmed man. Not an exercise, but for real. The victim is *dead*. Now put through my request for a chopper,' Max snapped.

Once authorization had been given, the pilot then had to go through his own channels of communication to gain permission to enter airspace currently controlled by NATO. Flyers generally being a more laid-back species, this one stretched the truth to claim the flight was in response to an emergency. He got clearance!

The journey took just over an hour across a winter wonderland. It was deceptive. Down there among the conifers heavily laden with snow, along white glistening aisles cutting through dark stands of trees, careless of red squirrels searching for food stocks, men in Arctic gear shouldering heavy packs and carrying rifles were moving stealthily. What should have been frozen silence over an area of natural beauty was instead a medley of rifle fire, rocket-launching, thundering rotors, rumbling tanks and sharp commands in many languages.

The helicopter landed amid a mini-snow-storm stirred up by its rotors in the clearing used by aircraft attached to 'Picasso Force'. Max and Tom jumped to the icy ground churned up by numerous heavy-duty boots and helicopter skids, then tramped across to a white tent concealed by trees. This was a control sub-centre manned by a squadron leader, a Rifles captain, a Signals corporal and two female privates who kept tabs on progress with coloured flags on a huge map of the battle areas.

Everything halted, however, and all eyes fixed on the two men who entered without ceremony. They had sensibly donned uniform, but it was the normal disruptive pattern which now looked alien against the padded white worn by these people. They could have been Martians from the suspicion with which they were confronted.

Max swiftly held up his identification. 'SIB. We came in on that chopper. It's waiting to take us back with a suspect we need to question,' he said to the five astonished people.

The Rifles officer found his voice. 'We're conducting a major NATO exercise, for God's sake!'

'And we're investigating the murder of a British major.' Max approached the hostile group, giving Harkness's name and regiment and asking where he could be found.

One of the young women broke the long silence. 'Major Harkness is acting as a marshal from Zone Two.' She indicated a cluster of yellow flags on the map. 'Here.'

'You can't pull him out at a moment's notice,' protested the squadron leader.

'Actually, we can,' said Max. 'If this war was for real he'd be instantly replaced in the event of death or injury. They'll have to do that now. We'd like a vehicle and driver to take us to him.'

The captain shook his head. 'No can do. It's too dangerous. They're using live ammo.'

'And some of 'em are very jumpy,' added the RAF man. 'Not as disciplined as us. Liable to take a pot shot at anything unexpected.'

'We'll go in under a white flag,' said Tom belligerently.

They ignored him. The captain said: 'This'll have to be authorized by the C-in-C. He's Norwegian and I doubt he'll be sympathetic to something like this.'

Max gave a thin smile. 'Our Provost Marshal got the go-ahead from the C-in-C before we flew up here. It's you lesser mortals who're kicking up a fuss. I suggest you contact Major Harkness and tell him to come in here ASAP. As a marshal he'll have clear identification to guarantee his safety through the battle areas. That should solve any remaining problems you might have, gentlemen.' He indicated a bench containing tea- and coffee-making facilities. 'While we wait for him we'll have a hot drink. We had a very early breakfast and it was a bloody cold flight.'

The hiatus ended; work was resumed as Max and Tom made themselves mugs of coffee. After several grateful sips, Tom said quietly, 'Think he'll make a run for it?'

Max shook his head. 'He risked discovery to tie the body up outside the mess; reckoned it was worth it to make his point. He won't run. It's not his style.'

'What if we'd nailed someone for it?'

'He has more faith in us than he let on. He knew we'd get to him sooner or later.'

'Wonder what Bekov did to his brother to warrant murder.'

'*Nothing* warranted his murder! Ernest Harkness at least had a trial before execution. Bekov was given no opportunity to defend himself. In my book that's unforgivable.'

Eighty minutes passed before a Land Rover pulled into the clearing and James Harkness entered the tent, a tall, erect figure in padded white. He ignored everyone save the SIB men. 'This is execrable timing, Rydal. Surely this could have waited until the exercise ended.'

Max walked across to him. 'We're dealing with the taking of a man's life, Major, not a minor military issue.'

'Point taken. I'll sort out somewhere we can have a private discussion.'

Max indicated the clearing outside and, with Tom on Harkness's other flank, walked him from the tent. Once outside, he turned to face the man. 'James Allyn Harkness, I'm arresting you on suspicion of the murder of Major Leo Bekov. You do not have to say anything, but it may harm your defence if you do not mention when questioned something which you later rely on in court. Anything you do say may be given in evidence.'

Harkness drew himself up even straighter; said quietly, 'You could have waited until this finished. I wouldn't have escaped your net, and this exercise is damned important.'

'To Leo Bekov his *life* was damned important. I intend to bring to justice those who took it from him, irrespective of what else may be happening around us. When we arrive at our headquarters you may telephone your solicitor or request the presence of a military lawyer during questioning. We have an aircraft waiting.'

On the point of climbing into the helicopter, the prisoner glanced back and said calmly, 'As we hoped, the freeze is holding. It makes things so much easier for us.'

Harkness declined the offer of a lawyer; he remained unruffled as they settled in the warm interview room at Section HQ. Max began the interrogation by establishing the blood link with Ernest Harkness and Captain William John.

'You were smart to pick up on that,' said James, divested of his combat whites and looking suddenly older in his usual garb of khaki woolly-pully and trousers.

'I read your regimental history,' said Max.

'Splendid account, isn't it? Eleven VCs, thirty-six DSOs, sixty-two—'

'And an experienced regular service sergeant charged with cowardice,' put in Tom smoothly. 'It appears to have been a controversial case.'

'He was the scapegoat to cover the criminal ineptitude of Second Lieutenant Boyce, who ordered a retreat which cost the lives of every man under his command. *He* was the coward, not my great-grandfather, who searched that wood high and low for them when he returned with a sitrep informing them of the guns that had been moved up to their rear. Boyce was sent home immediately for fear of morale being undermined, and the bastard survived to make a fortune in the family brewery.

'You'll have noticed he was the sole Boyce listed in the regimental history. A conscript!

Hadn't the pluck and guts to volunteer like the rest of his school chums. The court sentenced Ernest, a true and loyal soldier, to death on the word of a wimp whose beer-brewing parent happened to be able to afford to send him to public school. Family began as itinerants, you know. Travelled from town to town taking on labouring jobs. They were in Kent hop-picking when the owner's daughter was rolled in the hay by a licentious Boyce, who went to the altar at the end of a shotgun. The entire line is unprincipled, to say the least.'

'How do you know all this?' asked Max, aware that it was the build-up to why a man who had crossed the path of a Harkness descendant had had to die.

The Major leaned back in his chair. 'Ernest's brother, Jim, was a cripple unable to fight in the trenches, so he fought at home to clear Ernest's name. He spent almost every penny he owned on the campaign. It eventually killed him. My grandfather, and Jimson, continued the battle. They managed to get a newspaper editor interested in the case, which aroused a great deal of public sympathy. Their MP even raised the issue in the House.'

His expression grew more bitter. 'Of course, old man Boyce had friends in the right places, and young Alfred wore the right school tie, didn't he! The MP was silenced: the editor moved the story from the front page to a small piece inside, smothered by inconsequential tittle-tattle. It was ever thus.'

'And the army? Did your family get nowhere in that direction?' asked Tom.

'Closed ranks!'

Max said quietly. 'Which you now know all about.'

The blue eyes that had been alive with anger now grew blank. 'How about tea and biscuits? Lunch was a meagre affair taken some hours ago.'

Max was happy with that suggestion. It marked a convenient pause in the interrogation which was confirming what he had maintained from the start: the symbolic displaying of Bekov's body had been a compulsive act. Very clearly, that wartime execution in 1916 still blighted Harkness pride. It struck him that by waging such a determined campaign, the family had publicized their shame to the entire country. By leaving well alone it would have been known by a very few, and fairly soon forgotten in the post-war troubles that eventually led to a general strike.

However, Max knew it was not the events of 1916 which had prompted this murder. They had merely dictated the treatment of the body. He was beginning to get some inkling of what was to come. William John Harkness and Bekov must have been involved in a scenario in Kosovo similar to that one long ago. A scenario damaging enough to prompt a killing.

The recorder was switched off while they all enjoyed the welcome tea and talked about the regiment's long history. Max and Tom knew this enlivened their suspect and would ease the in-depth questioning ahead.

When they recommenced, Max immediately angled for a confession. 'Major Harkness, did you on the night of February the twelfth of this year shoot and kill Major Leo Bekov, afterwards tying his blindfolded body to a post outside the officers' mess?'

There was slight hesitation. 'I was prepared to spare him if he agreed to tell the truth.'

'The truth about what?' asked Tom.

'The bastard refused to discuss it. Simply walked away muttering something about retribution for lost souls. That's when I rang Frances to tell her it was on.'

Tom reacted. 'Your wife? *She* was your accomplice?'

Harkness gave him a blue-ice stare. 'A participant in meting out justice. It concerned her equally. Her sister married my brother. We had a double wedding. Full regimentals, arch of swords. Left the church in a horse-drawn carriage with outriders dressed in our old cavalry uniforms. Caused a stir, I tell you. Pictures in the glossies. Splendid publicity for the regiment.'

'Tell us about the events on the night of the regimental dinner,' invited Max, drawing him back to the vital subject. 'You decided to go ahead, so you contacted your wife. What happened then?'

'As you must be aware, I was dancing attendance on our VIP guests, so had no chance to keep Bekov under observation until that duty was done. Frances kept watch outside the mess after I left, dressed all in black and keeping to the shadows. She kept me updated on her mobile. Bekov looked set to make a night of it; bloody presumptuous considering the celebration concerned a regiment he had no affiliation with. I was free of top brass by the time Frances patched through to tell me our quarry was leaving with Judy.'

Max intervened at that point. 'Your plan was reliant on a great deal of luck, surely. Wasn't it more than likely Bekov would leave with Mark Ingham and return to his quarter?'

'Very *un*likely.' Harkness gave a smug smile. 'I was well aware that Mark was extremely loath to host Bekov. Heard rumours there was no love lost between them: something concerning the flighty Reena. So I turned the screws to oblige Mark to take him in. Much too good-natured, Mark. Soon as they entered the mess it was clear they'd already crossed swords. Then someone revealed that Reena had walked out to spend the night with Bobby Foyle's wife. They had played exactly the right game.'

'But Lieutenant King threw a spanner in the works?' suggested Tom.

'Stupid bitch! I joined Frances outside the gym and she told me Mark had followed them in. God knows why. Just then, a figure carrying a dog materialized and also entered. He soon exited and walked off, but it wasn't until shortly before 03:00 that Bekov came out alone and wandered in the vague direction of the quarters. We followed in the Land Rover, lights off, knowing he wouldn't get in because Mark was still in the gym with Judy. What a slut!'

'And Captain Ingham; what would you call him?' asked the father of three girls, who knew what the man had almost certainly done in the gym that night.

Harkness ignored the question. 'Bekov kicked up such a row he woke Ingham's neighbours. Luckily, none offered him a bed for what remained of the night and he wandered off again along the perimeter road. Perfect! We diverted through the quarters and parked up ahead of the copse, which was ideal for our plan.'

His eyes narrowed with recollection. 'We couldn't believe it when we saw Pete Randolph appear from the darkness and hood Bekov with a sack as he stopped for a pee. We followed as Pete marched him into the copse and watched him put a pistol to Bekov's head. It seemed he was going to do the job for us, and a minute or so later, it sounded as though he had.

'When Pete left, Bekov was lying face down on a picnic table. Dead, we thought. Then he moved, slowly pulled off the sack, and began retching. That's when we moved in.'

'You shot him while he was throwing up?' asked Max.

A grim smile. 'Oh, no! We wanted him well aware of why he was going to die. Ridding himself of the excesses of the evening after a hell of a fright at Pete's hands swiftly sobered him. When I pushed the Browning against his chest he was bloody sure this time it would be for real. I told him what I was going to do with him once he was dead, and why. He couldn't walk away from me again. He recognized that the time had come to pay for his treachery.'

'Did he say anything?' asked Tom.

'It was brief and incomprehensible. Could have been Russian. A prayer? The bastard stared straight in my eyes as he said it, so I guess it could have been a curse. He didn't flinch.'

'Then you pulled the trigger?'

'Yes, Rydal, *I* pulled the trigger. Frances merely cut off the buttons and badges of rank while I tied the blindfold. She then brought the Land Rover up to the copse for me to load the body. She of course helped me tie it up, but nothing more. She had no hand in the actual execution.'

Max did not argue that she had played a very big part in it. She would be charged with complicity in the murder Harkness chose to call an execution.

'It was our intention that the body would be seen by a great number when morning activity began around the base. Bekov's punishment witnessed by all and sundry! But that stupid bitch Judy came upon it far too soon, and it was immediately enclosed by canvas.' He gave a smile of satisfaction. 'But some greedy squaddie has given away the details, and headlines in newspapers have sent the bald facts further than we could have hoped.'

'Some *squaddie*, Major?'

He stared at Max. 'It wasn't me, Rydal. Sorry to disappoint you.'

Tom then asked the all-important question. 'What did Leo Bekov do in Kosovo that involved your brother and led you to take this drastic step?'

Harkness appeared about to contradict that statement, but he instead gave a thoughtful sigh and answered it. 'Bill's squadron was tasked to seek out and capture the Serb leader responsible for a massacre during the early days of the war. The able-bodied males of the village had taken up arms with the KLA, leaving their families vulnerable when it was eventually overrun. The small boys and old men were roped together and thrown in the turbulent river swollen by melting snow from the hills. Women and girls were raped without exception, then their throats were slit. No wastage of valuable ammunition that way,' Harkness added with contempt.

'I Corps interrogated a captured Serb, who revealed that the man who had instigated the mass murder was then hiding out in that same village. It had been deserted ever since the day of the atrocity. Bill was to lead a detail of three Warriors on the op. An hour before the off, Bekov turned up out of the blue and attempted to take command. There was no

373

need whatever for him to be there. Claimed he was to act as their interpreter. Guess he'd twisted a few arms to get a piece of the action for once.' Harknessmouth twisted. 'As any true fighting soldier knows, when faced with the barrel of an SA80 words of explanation in any language are unnecessary. Seems Bekov's hide was thicker than a rhino's. Refused to stay in the rear while our lads did the dirty work so I Corps could get their man.'

After a moment, Max asked quietly, 'And did they?'

Harkness leaned back in his chair and began to tell of the events that led him to commit murder.

Nineteen

It had taken Leo all day and late into the night to break the prisoner, but he had no doubts about the man's eventual betrayal of his former commander while disclaiming any involvement in the massacre. Colonel Byers acted immediately on Leo's assurance, but he was reluctant to comply with his urgent request to go on the search-and-capture operation. Leo's powers of persuasion had their usual effect, however.

After little more than two hours' sleep, a long cold shower, several bacon rolls and a gallon of black coffee, Leo was raring to go. Personal triumph had so elated him he hardly needed the input of caffeine, and he chatted brightly to the pilot who flew him the short distance to where troops were readying to set off well before first light.

On meeting their commander, Leo considered this was a man who definitely needed an injection of some kind of stimulus. Captain William Harkness was either so laid back he had forgotten how to emote, or he was still half asleep. He spoke in an affected drawl and went about preparing for action as if he found it a bore. This type of officer was hot on spit and polish but often led edgy, uninspired men. Leo had no time for 'by the book' soldiers and he was angry that one should be leading this bid to capture a wanted war criminal. It was vital that Ivanisovic should be taken alive, but in the coming tense action Harkness's men were liable to act impulsively and fire at anything that moved. Leo's task was to prevent that.

Under relentless interrogation the prisoner had claimed the Serb mass killer was holed up with no more than half a dozen of his loyal followers, trapped between British and American units in the village they had ethnically cleansed and torched many months earlier. Hunger would soon drive them to make a bid to reach safety, so it was essential to move in on them fast.

Within the partitioned canvas office, Leo attempted to apprise Harkness of the urgency of the operation, emphasizing the utmost importance of taking their targets alive.

'Under interrogation, I can get from them intelligence that'll lead to proof of further war crimes against Albanian civilians.'

He was treated to a hostile stare. 'I was informed less than an hour ago that some I Corps bod had got himself attached to this operation. I've already fully briefed my lads. We know very well what we have to do. You're just along for the ride, and I'll thank you to keep well clear of us until it's over.'

The antipathy Leo had felt on first meeting William Harkness grew stronger. 'These men have been hiding in deprived conditions for some days. They're liable to act unpredictably when cornered; desperate to avoid capture. They have nothing to lose. I aim to make contact with them at the outset. Talk them out of putting up any kind of resistance; give them the irrefutable bottom line. *We need them in our hands alive, Harkness.* We're not out after rabbits. I don't want anyone taking pot shots at them. Did you stress that in your briefing?'

The other man's plump face reddened with anger. Not so laid back, after all! *'I'm* in command of this op, Bekov, and I'm a real fighting soldier not some jumped-up prick who's only in uniform because he speaks the language of these barbaric peasants. If you imagine you're going to go ahead of us to offer them an amnesty, you're way off beam. My brief is to rout those bastards out. How I do it is up to me. *I'll* be making all the decisions. Is that clear?'

'What if they shout a request to hold your fire because they're willing to surrender? Are your lads going to mow them down because you are the prick who *doesn't* understand their language?'

Harkness looked daggers. 'Don't try acting the solo hero or I'll have your balls! I don't know whose arse you licked to get here, but you'll keep to the rear until we've mopped them up. That's an order!'

At that point, a sergeant entered the tent without ceremony. 'The lads are ready, sir. Engines running.'

Harkness let fly. 'Have you forgotten how to salute?'

The NCO stiffened and whipped his hand up to his protective helmet. Leo saw the flash of anger in the man's dark eyes and sympathized. They were in a war zone about to set out across hazardous terrain at night, not on a parade ground.

He smiled and introduced himself. 'I'm Leo Bekov. I'm coming along to mediate with our targets because I speak their lingo. It's my job to prevent possible bloodshed – on *either* side.'

'Right, sir.' He remained stiff as he turned back to Harkness for further instructions.

'My briefing is unchanged, Sergeant Flynn. Make sure the men understand that.' He checked his watch. 'Departure in five, at 04:15.'

'Sir!'

After the sergeant departed, Harkness picked up his helmet, rifle and map case, saying over his shoulder, 'You'll ride in the rear vehicle.'

'What's the date of your commission, Harkness?'

'What?' Blue eyes pure ice now.

'When were you commissioned?'

Leo gave a malicious smile on hearing the information. 'I have twelve months' seniority on you, so don't order me around, there's a good chap!' He walked from the tent donning his UN helmet, accepting that Serb war criminals would not be his only problem on arrival at the village.

The crew of the Warrior were a surly bunch, their young officer lacklustre. Harkness had a lot to answer for! Leo settled in the belly of the armoured vehicle with soldiers who took no notice of him, and soon closed his eyes feigning sleep. He hated being confined; did not envy men who fought by this method. His mind shied from thoughts of being roasted alive in a tin can on caterpillar tracks, a hang-up dating from the deaths of his parents in a blazing car. He still felt their loss acutely; still occasionally suffered the pain of Caroline's failure to be there when he desperately needed her support.

They jolted, plunged and reared along unmade roads for almost an hour, by which time Leo was feeling nauseous. He hoped to God Harkness had not lost his way in the darkness. He dearly wanted a successful result today. He was in line for promotion and it would tip the balance, but his main object was to seal the fate of a man who had ordered the massacre of innocents. The Balkan races were historically volatile and savage, but they were now fighting with modern weapons and international guidelines to govern the rules of engagement. Ivanisovic had transcended normal humanity to revert to barbarism. Leo burned to ensure the man paid the price of his actions; not with a swift, merciful bullet but with world condemnation and a life sentence behind bars. Death was too kind. Incarceration as the years dragged past bringing despair and old age would be a more fitting punishment for a man only now in his mid-thirties.

The Warrior jerked to a halt. The subaltern, who had been keeping watch through his hatch, said quietly, 'We're on the outskirts of the village, lads, at point zero two four nine. Sun should appear on the horizon fifteen from now. I'll get confirmation from the Boss that we're still going as per briefing. Stand ready!'

He climbed through the hatch and jumped to the ground. Leo opened the rear door and followed him. Harkness spoke only to his two subordinates, ignoring Leo. It did not matter. He merely wanted to be familiar with their plan. If it was to go in with all guns blazing, he would be forced to intervene; argue the case for a softly-softly approach.

In the pearly pre-dawn light the village lay as a grey shadow against a dark wall Leo knew to be thickly forested hills rising behind it. Those heights had been combed by US troops during their swift advance as a likely cover for Serb groups. The ruined village had not been considered as such. Ivanisovic had gone there, presumably reasoning that he was safe in a place peopled only by restive ghosts, only to be later sandwiched by UN forces.

Harkness illuminated his map with a pencil torch. 'Charles, you're to take up position here by the burnt-out church. Philip, park your Warrior across the track leading on to the bridge across the river. I shall be on your right flank at the site where the bodies were found in a mass grave. Everything clear?'

'We've already been over it twice,' murmured Charles, whom Leo had travelled with.

'It's vital to be *certain* where we all are and what each of us has been tasked to do,' Harkness said pettishly. 'I don't want anyone acting solo here. This is to be a coordinated op. Understood? Once in position, I'll give the signal to leave the vehicles and advance on foot. We'll fan out to encircle the ruins. Our targets are certain to be within that area. The outlying terrain was razed by fire after the massacre. Nowhere to hide there.' He glanced up at his support officers. 'No one is

380

to go rushing in. We take it slowly and respon-
sibly. No itchy trigger fingers! We're not after
rabbits.'

Leo gave a sour smile on hearing his words
repeated by this pedantic commander. He
thought it time for his own input. 'We want
these bastards taken alive. If you believe
you've located them, call me up. I'll then do
my best to talk them into accepting the overwhelming odds and surrendering.'

The subalterns regarded him in silence,
their faces no more than pale ovals. Then they
turned back to Harkness. 'As we check out
each house or building, we report in and
slowly close up,' said Philip, consolidating
their plan. 'That should leave them nowhere
to run.'

Charles grunted. 'If they're brainless
enough to attempt it, they'll find themselves
swallowing the barrel of an SA80 or two.'

'Or three,' finished Harkness grimly. 'Let's
take up positions. Sun'll be up in an instant.'

Leo was tempted to walk the rest of the way
to the village, but it was not yet light enough
to see the ground he would be covering. He
reluctantly re-entered the tin can on tracks
feeling apprehensive about the coming
action. Those subalterns might be steady and
sensible, but Harkness was undermining their
confidence with his constant reminders. He
was treating them like boys in a school's
Officer Corps.

Leo's own participation was being dismissed by Harkness and so, by example, also

by his two subordinates. This meant he would have to act independently to carry out his own CO's instructions to 'bring 'em back alive'. It would not be the first time he had operated alone and, doubtless, would not be the last. He secretly preferred it that way.

A fleeting memory of the Croatian boy he had handed over, and then shot to ensure he died painlessly, returned to remind Leo of one time when he wished he had not had to take control of a painful situation. That child had haunted his dreams for a while, until he had witnessed depravity here in Kosovo. Catching Ivanisovic today meant a great deal to him: raising a voice for all those deprived of the chance to condemn.

It is impossible for Warriors to arrive anywhere secretly. They took up their positions with the usual rattle and grind, kicking up dust from the summer-baked track to haze the pinkish dawn. Leo climbed out, followed by soldiers with rifles held ready. He, himself, carried his loaded Smith and Wesson only as a means of self-defence.

Burned and blackened partial walls were all that remained of the Albanians' houses. The church beside which Charles had stationed his vehicle was a shell doomed to collapse before long. What had been the main thoroughfare was still littered with charred wood, broken glass and the fire-damaged debris of everyday living.

Leo's spine began to tingle icily. It would be

sacrilege to enter this place inhabited by tormented souls. For several minutes he stood overwhelmed by disquietude. Then he mentally shook himself. He was allowing his passionate Russian blood to override his British aplomb. This silent, haunted place held only the men who had desecrated it. He must bring them to account.

Charles had silently signalled his squad to spread out and advance line abreast. The silence was strategically unnecessary because their arrival would have alerted their quarry. Even so, the grim aspect of the place discouraged speech. Leo saw the other two units also advancing with caution, using hand signals. They were all keyed up, swinging their heads from side to side watching for the slightest movement.

It came out of the dawn like an avenging force. A deafening roar, an ear-splitting whine, an earth-trembling explosion. The dazzle of the emergent sun was suddenly intensified by two fireballs. Leo's heart pounded with fear; he could not believe what he saw. The Warriors on the right flank and by the bridge had been blasted apart and were alight. Thick black smoke arose from them to darken the embryo morning. Through it, Leo could make out soldiers bending over others on the ground.

As he ran to them, his racing thoughts dismissed his initial stunned reasoning that the hidden Serbs possessed hand-held rocket-launchers. He had heard the lightning scream of jet engines split seconds after missiles hit the vehicles. The attack had come from the sky and, dear God, was probably a blue on blue. Friendly fire!

This swiftly organized operation could have left some UN units unaware of British presence in a halfway zone. He had been shot up by uninformed Yanks in Kuwait. It happened in war. But why bloody *now*, he thought single-mindedly as he reached the confused scene.

The drivers inside both Warriors were dead, as were two soldiers who had been closest to them. There were three men on the ground quite badly hurt; several others dazed and bleeding from minor cuts. It was bad but, five minutes earlier, they could all still have been in the vehicles.

Sergeant Flynn had summoned Casevac and was on to their HQ giving a sitrep. Charles and Philip were supervising first aid. Their calm authority was getting through to shaken men doing what they could for their comrades. Leo noted this with satisfaction as he offered quiet reassurance to a lad wandering aimlessly, temporarily stunned by blast, his eyes reddened by smoke.

From the dark haze, William Harkness swooped on Leo, yelling, *'You're* responsible for this! That prisoner had you suckered to bloody rights. You brought us here exactly to his plan. They were waiting for us. Waiting to shoot us to hell.' High on adrenalin he waved his arms to indicate the broken ranks around them. 'These are *my* men you've led into a death trap, you bastard! You speak their lingo, you've been *insisting* we hold fire against them, and you've a Russian name. Ivans are well known to support the Serbs,' he raged. 'You're nothing but a bloody *traitor*!'

At that moment, Leo spotted movement on the lower slopes behind the village, and his heartbeat accelerated. Ivanisovic and his henchmen had taken advantage of the air attack to make a break for it. He began to run, shouting over his shoulder that the targets were getting away. He went in the confidence that the troops would fulfill the task for which they had been briefed, in spite of the attack on them. They were trained to cope with the unexpected.

Just before the Serbs were swallowed up by the forest, Leo gauged that there were no more than fifteen of them. Quite enough to search for in a summer-thick forest ranging several miles wide across the hills. He grunted a hearty Russian oath as he reached the foot of the slope. He had hoped to corner them in the village. It would now be a cat-and-mouse business that could last all day; even longer. A swift backward glance showed him the reassuring sight of a large body of troops hot on his heels. Despite Harkness's wild accusation made in the aftermath of shock, the man had clearly regained sufficient self-control to organize his men.

It was dark beneath the forest canopy; enough of a contrast partially to blind Leo after the brightness outside. He slowed to a wary walking pace until his vision adjusted well enough to hasten progress between the trees. The scent of pines and damp under-growth registered only vaguely. His senses were wholly intent on the hunt: predator and prey, except that both were human and death was not the intended end game. He hoped to God Harkness would keep that in mind.

With his eyes now accustomed to the green dimness, Leo stood listening. It was not easy to walk silently across the forest floor, but there were also animals moving around to confuse the situation. The foliage was high, leaving a more open aspect at man level where shafts of quivering sunlight pierced the shadowed areas to create illusions of move-ment.

Leo cautiously advanced up the hill. He reasoned that the basic human instinct to climb away from danger, added to their quar-ries' reluctance to approach UN bases to west and east, would send them to the summit. He checked on the others. Whether from similar reasoning, or a decision to follow him, they appeared to be in line abreast a hundred yards to the rear, the nearest of them first visible then hidden by shadows. A line of beaters driving the prey inexorably forward!

Leo pushed on for an hour or so, a wry smile breaking through. He was leading this operation after all! Harkness would be livid, but the further in advance of the rest he could get the greater his chance of preventing a bloodbath. Ideally, he wanted to first confront Ivanisovic. He had seen photographs of him; would easily recognize him. If the fates were kind...

His heart suddenly thudded as a figure slipped from behind a tree, then melted into the dimness again no more than seventy-five yards ahead. He instinctively gave hand signals to any soldiers who might have him in sight. *Closing on enemy; adopt caution.*

Treading carefully now, Leo challenged the fugitive Serb to preserve his own life by walking out with hands in the air. His voice sounded unnaturally loud in the hushed surroundings. He repeated the instruction several times, his eyes straining for another glimpse of the man apparently unmoved by an offer of clemency given in his own language.

A shot rang out. Then another. Leo swore. Harkness's men were giving no leeway over to his left. They were set on killing these Serbs they believed had targeted the Warriors and their mates, because their commander had told them that was what had happened,

More shots. A mini-battle taking place! Bloody hell, they would wipe out the lot, including Ivanisovic! Hesitating momentarily, Leo then swung round, revolver at the ready, as a man emerged from the trees to his right. A man he immediately recognized. All the saints be praised! Ivanisovic did not have his hands up, but he held his rifle loosely and pointing at the ground. He halted when there was a gap of fifty feet between them. His ravaged features were dark with hatred. He spoke harshly.

'I do not approach you to preserve my own life, but those of my friends and comrades. You will stop this killing. Order your men to cease firing.'

Leo stood his ground, revolver lowered but ready to use. 'Not while you hold a weapon. Hand it over and I'll consider your request.'

'It is not a *request*.'

Leo contained his sense of loathing only because he knew he was to be instrumental in leading this man to lifelong punishment for his crimes.

'You can't see them, but my men are all around you among the trees. One false move and they'll shoot. We're not helpless old people; women and babies. We're the British army acting under UN authority. You're in no position to make demands of me.' He began slowly to move towards the Serb, revolver still lowered but with his finger on the trigger. 'The road ends here, Ivanisovic. Your only way forward is into eternal sleep.'

He halted with a mere ten feet separating them, his nerves as taut as bowstrings, primed for any sudden move from the other man. Ivanisovic stared long and hard at Leo, a look of damnation. The surrounding forest seemed to be holding its breath, so silent had it become. Three or four distant shots broke that tense hiatus, and Ivanisovic gave a slow nod.

With hand outstretched to take the rifle from him, Leo advanced two or three paces overwhelmed by a sense of immense fulfilment. Those haunted souls roaming the village below *would* be avenged.

Crack! Ivanisovic's hand became a bloody mess. His rifle fell to the ground. Leo spun on his heel, raising the Smith and Wesson. Harkness stood in a broad shaft of sunlight, his SA80 pointing at them.

'Hold your fire,' Leo cried.

Another bullet got Ivanisovic in the shoulder, and Leo realized he had called the instruction in the language he had been using. He repeated it in English, moving to stand in front of the Serb. Harkness fired again, and earth kicked up beside Leo's boots. Another inch and...

Unbridled fury sent him forward, gun raised. Harkness had gone crazy! 'Hold your bloody fire!' he roared 'We want him *alive*.'

A ring of armed soldiers emerged swiftly through the trees. *Crack, crack, crack!* The Serb fell lifeless beneath a hail of bullets. Through the nightmare quality of a quiet morning turned violent, Leo heard Harkness shout another order.

'Disarm and arrest this officer!'

Immobilized by disbelief as they closed on him, Leo yelled, 'If any of you attempt to lay hands on me, I'll fire. Back off! *That's an order!*'

As the soldiers stood irresolute, the subaltern named Charles approached Leo with his

389

rifle lowered, speaking quietly. 'The action is over, Captain Bekov. If you'll be good enough to accompany me to the village, we can all wind things up and return to our base.'

After long moments during which he fought his rage and a bitter sense of failure, Leo slowly holstered his revolver and prepared to go with a young man who had just proved his worth as a level-headed officer.

He pointed at Harkness. 'Keep that maniac well away from me, or I won't answer for the consequences. Ivanisovic constituted no threat. I was about to disarm him. Harkness shot him with deliberation quite unnecessarily. If you and your men hadn't come on the scene when you did, he'd have finished me off, too. He's just deprived those slaughtered innocents the right to retribution. I'll not forgive him for that!'

Twenty

'Four men killed outright; others lying around torn and bleeding. Two Warriors taken out!' Harkness continued his account with barely contained anger. 'They'd been led into an ambush. The bloody Serbs had been waiting for them. Everything then made sense to Bill. Bekov had interrogated the prisoner who'd pinpointed that village. Bekov had a Russian name; he spoke fluent Serbo-Croat. He was in league with the bastards!

'Bill charged him with treachery; of betraying them all. Bekov immediately took to his heels, hared off to join his Serb friends heading for the hills. My brother organized his men and set off in pusuit. The lads were determined to get the brutes who'd killed their comrades.'

'They intended to shoot on sight?' asked Max, to clarify the point.

Harkness gave him an icy stare. 'They were in no mood to *talk* after being attacked by hand-held rocket-launchers.'

'No need for a translator, then,' put in Tom. 'Where was Bekov?'

'In the depths of the forest with the enemy. One by one, our men cornered and took out

391

the Serbs before they could launch another attack. By a stroke of good fortune, Bill came upon Bekov parleying with Ivanisovic, clearly on good terms. When the bugger made to shake the Serb's hand, Bill fired a warning shot at them.' The blue eyes frosted over with fury. 'Bekov actually shielded that mass-murderer with his own body.'

'He stood in front of the Serb at risk to his own life?' asked Max incredulously. 'Did he return fire?'

'After Bill put a warning shot at his feet, Bekov ran at him with his gun raised. Charles Ancram's group came through the trees just then, swiftly assessed the situation and took out Ivanisovic. Bekov then went completely berserk; threatened to shoot anyone who approached him. However, he soon realized he was outnumbered and surrendered.'

Harkness drew in air and exhaled slowly, almost painfully. 'Bill nominated Ancram as Bekov's escort back to their base, where he accused the Russian of conspiring with the enemy.'

Max waited; kicked Tom's foot warningly as he made to break the silence. The most crucial piece of evidence was about to be given. Harkness was best left to offer it in his own time. The Major was in the grip of a fervour that had clearly ruled him from the time of that fatal Kosovan action. When he next spoke it was in an almost tracelike tone.

'There was a whitewash. It seemed the Warriors had been shot up by UN pilots who mistook them for Serb tanks. Bekov admitted to running away after being accused of treachery, but he claimed it was because he saw the Serbs escaping. Said he shouted words to that effect and called for backup. *He was believed*, although no one had heard him shout anything as he ran off. Bekov also claimed he had shielded Ivanisovic because the Serb was wanted to stand trial for war crimes, and *he was believed*. Unfortunately, no one but Bill had seen him shake hands with the Serb; no one else had witnessed Bekov threatening Bill with his revolver just before Ancram's men had burst through the trees. Bekov was the I Corps's golden boy. He could get away with anything, and did. But my brother knew what he saw; swears to it to this day.'

Another emotive silence. 'Bill was reprimanded for failing to take Ivanisovic and his men prisoner, although the Board allowed that, in the belief that the rocket attack had been launched by them, he had been entitled to take defensive action. The reprimand went on his service record, of course, but it was what was *not* officially recorded that has damaged him so badly. In his evidence Bekov stated that my brother lost control of the situation and would almost certainly have killed *him* in order to take out the Serb, in spite of his command to hold his fire.

'Bekov had a silver tongue. How else could he have survived in the Balkans without the authorities realizing where his true sympathies lay? How often had he betrayed our troops without being caught out? Like Boyce in 1916, he came from a line of nobodies and his lies destroyed a Harkness. A man of stirling worth!'

His cold gaze fastened on Max. 'My brother was sent home to command a TA squadron. Given some crap about imparting his experience and knowledge to men who might soon be called upon to serve in the Balkans. He's still there, having been passed over for promotion. Frances's sister is on the verge of a breakdown. They have three boys at public school and a large mortgage. Bill has the choice of leaving the army, or being shunted from one backwater job to another knowing the career that means so much to him – to us all – has hit the buffers. All because he had the courage to expose a fellow officer as a traitor. A fellow officer who was promoted just three months after that appalling affair, and is now the shining light on General Pomeroy's staff.'

'No, you put an end to that,' Max reminded him sharply.

'If he had had the courage to admit the truth, agree to vindicate Bill when I tackled him that night, I would have spared him to face the consequences. It was his arrogance in saying he had been unable to forgive a man who had robbed a hundred and twenty-three souls of the peace that comes with retribution that sealed his fate. Whatever the events of that night, I would have contrived to put him

394

to death the way any traitor deserves to die. With dishonour and the greatest military contempt. Justice has now been done!'

As Max studied the fanatical expression of righteousness on the killer's face he recalled all he had garnered about Leo Bekov during this case and sensed, without a shadow of doubt, that the gravest *in*justice had been perpetrated against a man others either loved or hated but would follow anywhere.

Mark Ingham recovered from his injuries and faced a board of inquiry. He was found guilty on charges of conduct unbecoming and attempting to pervert the course of justice. He resigned his commission and, after a period of adjustment, has become a director of a small company manufacturing model soldiers. He and Reena have divorced.

Judith King left the army and went back-packing in the Antipodes. She took a post as games mistress at an elite girls' school, but found the regime too similar to a military one and was soon on the move again. She still has not found that elusive free spirit she seeks.

Peter Randolph broke with family tradition and applied to transfer to the Intelligence Corps. He finds the work more varied and involving than riding around in Warriors. The Randolphs have not exactly cast him from their noble ranks, but he sees little of them now.

After a bitter battle between grandparents, Briony Fielding was made a ward of court and placed with Sergeant and Alice Foster with whom the child was familiar and happy. The Fieldings are launching an appeal.

Bill Harkness's military career collapsed completely beneath the weight of his brother's arrest for murder, and the subsequent media coverage. He is now struggling to run a small bar in Spain with the help of his wife, who finds the easy access to alcohol very beneficial!

During the trial of James and Frances Harkness, Max encountered Caroline Bekov again. He took her to dinner and glimpsed the possibility of happiness to come. But that is as far as it went. She is still in love with Leo. Probably always will be.

Charisma is a curious force.